Accidental
LOVE

By B.L. Miller

ACCIDENTAL LOVE

© 2005 B.L. MILLER.

ISBN 1-933113-11-1

THIS TRADE PAPERBACK ORIGINAL IS PUBLISHED BY INTAGLIO
PUBLICATIONS, GAINESVILLE, FL USA

CREDITS

EXECUTIVE EDITOR: TARA YOUNG
COVER DESIGN BY SHERI (GRAPHICARTIST2020@HOTMAIL.COM
COVER PHOTO BY GYPSY FOSTER

Chapter One

Rose Grayson zipped up the front of her dark blue sweat jacket and pulled the hood down over her head. The string that normally would have kept it in place had been removed long before she purchased it from the thrift store. She had no doubt that the first gust of the biting cold wind would push it off her head, but for the moment, it was the best she could do. She looked out into the brightly lit parking lot of Money Slasher, the large supermarket that she worked at part time. She had been hoping to be full time by now, but with the economy the way it was, full-time jobs were hard to come by. The crazy hours they assigned her made it impossible to get another part-time job to fill in the gaps, and Rose couldn't take the chance on quitting. It had taken weeks of applying to stores all over Albany just to get this job.

The small flakes that had been falling when she started her shift had turned into a full-blown blizzard. Rose looked down at her threadbare sneakers and groaned. This was the worst part about taking a job two miles from her apartment. The long walk home guaranteed that her feet would be frozen, not to mention the rest of her body. Sometimes she was lucky enough to get a ride from Kim, the store manager, but not tonight. Kim got off duty an hour ago, and there was no way Rose would ask her to wait. Taking a deep breath, she tucked her reddish blonde hair into the hood, bent forward, and stepped out into the unforgiving elements.

Veronica Cartwright glanced at her diamond-studded watch for the tenth time in an hour. Of all the miserable nights to have to make an appearance at Sam's, the oyster house that doubled as the social gathering place for Albany's rich and powerful. On any given night, one could go there and see the governor, state senators, and common folk who wanted to spend a hundred bucks on dinner. The maitre d' knew who was who and seated them accordingly. Never would someone like Veronica Cartwright, who headed up one of the largest family-owned corporations in the area, be seated near someone who didn't even own their own home. Ronnie, as she preferred to be called, never liked to go there, despite the world-renowned cuisine. Tonight, however, she had little choice. Mark Grace, the Zoning Board of Appeals commissioner, was fighting a zoning change request, and it was up to her to smooth his ruffled feathers and get that variance pushed through. Her cousins ran a small offshoot of the family corporation, Cartwright Car Washes. It was small in terms of the revenue it brought to the family but huge in the eyes of the public, especially with the thirty car washes scattered about the area and the numerous television ads. "Get your car washed right at Cartwrights" was a hugely successful slogan and made the longtime financial barons' family name a household word. John and Frank, the cousins in charge of the car washes, wanted to build a new one on the corner of Lake and State streets. It was a prime location in a predominantly residential area. They even went so far as to buy out the corner store that had previously been there and the adjacent houses in hopes of getting the variance. Now Commissioner Grace was questioning the destruction of three of Albany's "grand old buildings" to put up another "stupid car wash." Meetings and negotiations didn't work; offers of great civic donations didn't work; even outright bribes failed. When the brothers had exhausted all their ideas and still were unable to sway him, it was up to Ronnie to set things right. The commissioner jumped at the opportunity to meet with one of the city's most eligible women and insisted on dinner that evening.

As a result, she had to leave her fine home—in the middle of a blizzard—to wine and dine the commissioner into giving them the variance. It was a part of doing business, and Veronica was used to it. The only problem was that Grace wanted more than goodwill from the raven-haired beauty who ran Cartwright Corporation. Because of his insistence that they meet that evening, there had been no chance to make reservations. For almost anyone else, it would have meant not getting into the prestigious oyster house. But for Veronica, the maitre d' placed them in the bar while desperate attempts were made to find a place for the president of Cartwright Corporation and her guest. During the wait, the blue-eyed woman suffered having to listen to the whiny little snipe of a man tell her all about his degrees and how smart he was and how she should really consider spending more time with him. The only good point of the evening had been the waiter's constant refilling of her wine glass with the finest of vintages. At least she had been able to enjoy a good buzz while listening to him drone on.

Now an hour and a half later, they were seated at their table, dinner having been served just a few minutes before. "So, Veronica...you know that's such a pretty name. A pretty name for a pretty lady." Mark reached over with his fork to take a piece of baked lobster from her plate. "I don't understand why you feel that an area with such class and beauty needs a car wash. Can you imagine all the traffic that'll go through there? Interrupting people while they're sleeping, disturbing them with all the loud noises those machines make." His fork found another piece of lobster, the remainder of the tail. "Surely, you wouldn't want one of those right next door to you, now would you?"

Blue eyes glared at the best part of her lobster making its way into someone else's mouth. She had been polite and pleasant all evening, and now it was time to teach the little man a lesson. She dabbed her lips with the linen napkin. "The car wash is only open from eight in the morning until ten at night. I'm sure no one's sleep will be disturbed, and if you filch one more piece of food off my plate, I'm going to stab your hand with this fork. Do I make myself clear?" she said evenly while raising the wine glass to her lips. "Now you and I both know that those streets see plenty of traffic as it is, the residents like the idea of a car wash coming to their area, and it also means ten more jobs to the community. What do you think will happen in the next election if we support the Democrat and give him this little piece of information? What good would your appointment do if the new mayor decides to clean house?"

"Now you're just blowing smoke, Miss Cartwright," he said, sitting back and lighting up a cigarette. Smoking of course was prohibited in that section of the restaurant, but Mark believed his position put him above what he considered to be a silly law. "The Cartwrights have always supported the Republicans, everyone knows that." He took another drag of his cigarette, the smoke tickling Ronnie's nose.

"Really?" she drained her glass and set it down on the linen-covered table, suppressing a grin at the thought of the bomb she was about to drop on the hapless commissioner. "Let me tell you something, Mr. Grace. The Cartwrights have financed more than one Democrat over the years, and now that I'm in charge, there'll be plenty more as time goes on." Her blue eyes bore into his as she leaned forward and took the cigarette out of his hand, sinking it deep into his stuffed crab. "This variance means nothing to me except getting my cousins off my back. Your position means nothing to me.

I'd spend a hundred thousand on the next election if it meant getting you out of office and putting in someone who sees jobs as being more important than power plays, so you need to make a decision. You can be the good guy who brings ten jobs to the area or you can be the idiot who gets voted out of office, the decision is yours." Veronica had already made up her mind that there would soon be a new commissioner. "I do believe this meeting is over. I hope you enjoyed my dinner." At his startled look, she added, "What? Did you think you were going to get lucky tonight, Mr. Grace?" Her eyes gave him a quick once-over. "I'm sorry. I don't sleep with dogs. You never know when they might have fleas." She picked up her attaché and strode out, leaving the fuming but cornered commissioner with nothing but a hard-on and the check.

Rose crossed the street and entered Washington Park, a mammoth place of greenery in the middle of the city. The park was closed at dusk each night because of the crime and cruising that went on there. Normally, Rose would go around, but that meant an extra six blocks out of her way, and with the howling wind and bitter cold, the most direct route home was needed. In the five-block walk from the supermarket to the edge of the park, Rose's ears were beet red from the cold, and her nose had already started to run. She couldn't feel her toes, and the pockets of her sweat jacket did nothing to protect her fingers. Deciding from the lack of prints in the snow and the subzero temperature that it was safe, Rose trudged along past the huge statue of Moses that marked the entrance and the snow-covered sign that warned against being in the park at night. The fierce wind refused to let her keep her hood on, and her shoulder-length hair flapped loosely about her face. Her body shivered fiercely, and all she could think of was getting home and sinking into a nice hot bath. She was halfway through the park and within sight of Madison Avenue when she heard them approaching, their quick footfalls crunching the snow under their feet. "Well, well, well, what do we have here?" She turned her head to see four men rapidly approaching her, not quite running but certainly walking very fast.

"Come on, honey, we've got something for ya."

"Yeah, why don't you come party with us?"

The deep cold made her legs feel like lead, but the idea of being caught in the middle of the dark park by the four men put new life in her steps. She tried ignoring them and continued on her way, but the men followed her.

"Come on, bitch, let Danny have some fun," the closest one said, causing Rose's heart to pound painfully in her chest. She had to get out of there and get out of there now. She began running, more like stumbling, through the snow and toward the bright lights of Madison Avenue.

Ronnie breezed through the lights of the sleeping city, mindless of the way the Porsche slipped around in the snow. It wasn't like anyone else was around at the late hour. She passed Lark Street without meaning to and cursed loudly. Now she'd have to go all the way past the park to catch the next cross street. Seeing no cars in front of her, she punched the pedal of her Porsche 911 and threw it into second gear. She was going far too fast for the snow-covered street, especially since it didn't look like the plows had been through recently, but she didn't care. It wasn't like she had to stop any time soon, and she was still under the posted limit, although definitely faster than the road conditions dictated. The next cross street was at least a half-mile away. Suddenly, a flash of blue and gold appeared in front of her, a figure darting out from between parked cars. Veronica jammed both feet on the brakes and jerked the steering wheel hard to the left, but there was just no time. The snow gave her no traction, and an eerie silence filled the air as she watched the low front of the Porsche strike the pedestrian and throw the helpless person up onto the windshield. The red sports car finally came to a halt several car lengths later, and the broken body slumped off the hood onto the ground. For several seconds, Ronnie could do nothing but grip the steering wheel and stare at the spider web pattern that now made up her windshield while her heart pounded mercilessly. The reality of what had happened finally sank in, and with shaking hands, she opened the door. She looked around for anyone who could help, but at 12:30 on a Tuesday night, the street was deserted. She never saw the gang of thugs that had been chasing the victim turn around and slink back into the darkness of the park.

Blood was beginning to pool on the ground beneath the body, although the extreme cold made the flow far less than it would normally have been. Veronica knelt down beside the crumpled form and with her gloved hand, rolled the victim over. She gasped when she saw the battered face of a young woman. "Oh, my God." She glanced over at the cross street. New Scotland Avenue. She was only three blocks from the medical center. She quickly opened her trunk and pulled out the new quilt she had purchased that afternoon, glad that she had it to bundle around the injured woman. Next she pulled the lever that reclined the seat. Ronnie knew that the best thing was to try and immobilize the woman, but there wasn't any way she could do that at the moment, and the puddle of blood was steadily growing. The hospital was too close to think about calling for an ambulance and wasting precious minutes. The decision made, Veronica slipped her arms under the unconscious woman's shoulders and dragged her to the car. Less than a minute later, they were speeding toward the medical center.

As she pulled into the drive marked "Emergency," a thought occurred to the corporate magnate. Not only had she been speeding and hit this woman, but if a cop chose to do a Breathalyzer test, there was no way that she would pass, not after all the wine she had consumed at Sam's a short while earlier. She jerked the car to the right at the last moment and pulled into the one of the surgeon's parking slots. In the dark with only the back of the Porsche showing, no one would question it being parked there. She exited the car and walked toward the emergency entrance, trying desperately to think of what to do. The answer came to her when she spotted a gurney sitting just inside the glass doors. Ronnie grabbed it and wheeled it out to her car. Hours spent in her private gym made it easy for her to lift the unconscious woman onto the gurney. During the transfer, a small sports wallet fell out of the victim's back pocket and landed on the ground. Veronica picked it up, tucked it in the pocket of her coat, and ran as fast as she could while pushing the stretcher toward the emergency entrance. Blood was starting to seep through the thick quilt by the time she pushed the woman through the door.

"I need some help here! This woman's been hit by a car!" she yelled as soon as the inner doors slid open. The charge nurse and the night intern raced over to begin triage. "We've got multiple injuries, check the board and see who's on call for the OR." the blonde doctor said. A clerk immediately left to page the surgeon and to call for assistance while the nurse began taking the unconscious woman's vital signs. Standing back out of the way, Ronnie watched in horror as the doctor cut the young woman's jacket and clothes off her body. Everything seemed to be covered with blood, especially the pants. An older doctor arrived on the scene, his hair mussed from sleep.

"What do we have?"

"Hit and run. Compound breaks of both tibias and fibulas, Dr. Maise," the young doctor replied. "Probable internal injuries, as well. Whoever hit her was going fast."

"Have them prep OR 2. Type and cross-match six units of blood and page Gannon and Marks to assist." The rest of the conversation was lost on Veronica as she put her hands in her pockets and felt the cold wallet tucked inside. She opened the thin billfold, surprised at the lack of contents. There were no pictures, no credit cards, not even a driver's license. A blue library card identified the victim as Rose Grayson and gave her address as Morris Street. A Social Security card and a Money Slasher check-cashing card were the only other pieces of identification. She opened the Velcro compartment inside and found two bus tokens, one house key, and twelve cents. There was nothing else. Well, at least they'd have a name and address to go on, she thought as she walked over to the charge nurse's desk. As she approached, she heard the two women behind the desk talking.

"Looks like an indigent to me. Put her down as Jane Doe...let's see...." She shuffled papers around on the desktop. "...number seventy-seven. Once she's out of danger, they'll transport her over to Memorial anyway."

"Excuse me," Ronnie interrupted. "She's been hit by a car and badly injured. Why would they move her to another hospital?"

"Look, Miss," the charge nurse, whose badge simply read Mrs. Garrison, said. "This hospital is mandated by the state of New York to provide medical care to all who come here in urgent need. Once they're no longer in danger of dying from their injuries, we can transport them to another hospital that hasn't met its requirement for indigents."

"Requirement for indigents?"

"We are required to provide full care for a certain number of indigents at no cost each year. We've met that requirement. It's obvious she has no money and most likely no insurance. They're taking her into surgery now, surgery that she'll probably never pay for. This hospital doesn't operate on good intentions alone. If she has no ability to pay, she gets transported over to Memorial. They haven't met their obligation this year."

The dark-haired woman understood the implication...no insurance, no staying at the best medical center in the region. "But she has insurance," Ronnie blurted, her decision made. "I mean...I know her. She's an employee of mine."

"She has insurance?" Nurse Garrison asked incredulously. "Miss, it's twenty below out there with the wind chill. She's running around in a spring jacket that looks like it was taken from the garbage can. Insurance fraud is a crime in New York. Where's her insurance card?"

"No, I'm telling you she has insurance. Look," Ronnie reached inside her jacket and pulled out her small business card case. "I'm Veronica Cartwright, president and CEO of Cartwright Corporation." She quickly looked down at the library card in her hand. "Miss Grayson just started working for us. There hasn't been time for them to issue her card, but I swear she does have insurance through my company. Now is there a form or something that I have to sign to authorize this?"

Now realizing that she may have made a mistake, the charge nurse backpedaled. She reached over and grabbed one of several clipboards already set up with a non-removable pen and multi-part forms. "Fill out sections one through ten to the best of your ability. Do you know how to contact her next of kin?"

"Uh, no…I'm sure that information is at the office somewhere. I can call with it tomorrow."

"Fine." The nurse turned to address her coworker. "Change the chart for Jane Doe Seventy-seven. Her name is…." She turned back to the tall woman questioningly.

"Rose Grayson."

"Rose Grayson," Nurse Garrison repeated, as if the younger nurse didn't hear it the first time.

Ronnie walked away from the charge desk and slumped down in one of the orange vinyl chairs to fill out what little information she did know and settle in for the long wait.

By the third hour of surgery, Ronnie was becoming very worried. There had been no word on the young woman she had hit, and the lack of information set the executive's nerves on edge. What if she died? Ronnie shuddered at the thought. Then another thought came to mind. Daylight would arrive soon, and the obvious damage to the front of her car would be noticeable. Noticeable meant questions, questions she didn't want to answer. She pulled out her cell phone. The woman who always granted favors now needed one. Ronnie dialed the familiar number. On the third ring, a sleep-filled male voice answered. "You'd better have a fucking good reason for waking me up."

"Frank, it's Ronnie."

"Ronnie?" The tone changed immediately. "Hey, Cuz, what's up?"

"I need…" she swallowed. "I need a favor."

"Did you get that idiot to grant the variance?"

"It's in the bag. Listen, Frank, this is important." She heard the flicker of a lighter as her cousin lit a cigarette in an attempt to fully wake up. "I need you to come pick up my car and drop me off another one."

"Since when did I become your private tow truck service?"

"Since I had to spend an evening bailing your ass out with that jerk Grace," she growled. "It's in the emergency parking lot at Albany Med. Park the other car in the general lot and bring the keys to me in the emergency waiting room. Frank, you have to do this now. It can't wait until morning." She knew that the cost of asking the favor would far outweigh the actual favor, but sometimes that was just the way it was. At least she knew whom to turn to when she needed something done discreetly. Her favorite cousin was nothing if not careful.

"The emergency room? Ronnie, you okay?"

"Quiet down, Frank. You'll wake Agnes up. Yes, I'm fine, just a bit shaken." She looked at her watch. "I really need you to come down here and get the car."

"Is your car drivable or did you wrap it around a tree?"

"The windshield and front end are smashed up. You're better off driving it a couple of blocks, then putting it on a flatbed."

"Jeez, you don't ask for much, do you? You know I'll have to get John to help me. I can't drive a wrecker and a spare car."

"Put the spare on the wrecker, then you won't need another driver. Just do it now." She hung up the phone and picked up a four-month-old issue of People and had just begun flipping through it when Dr. Maise stepped into the room.

"Grayson. Anyone here for Grayson?" he asked loudly, although Ronnie was the only person in the room.

"Here." She rose to her feet quickly. "How is she?"

"As well as can be expected, I guess. She's resting now. Are you family?"

"Uh…no, I'm her employer."

"Oh…have you contacted her family yet?"

"Not yet. My secretary is working on it," she lied. "How is she?"

"Well, both legs were badly broken, and there was a hairline fracture to her skull. Other than abrasions and a gash on her face that required several stitches, there wasn't much else. No internal injuries anyway. She'll live, but it'll be quite a while before she's able to return to work, I'm sure." He took off his glasses and wiped them with the corner of his coat. "I'd say probably three months for the legs to heal, then maybe three to six months of physical therapy."

"Oh, God." Ronnie sat back down, unable to believe that in a split second she had ruined someone else's life for who knows how long.

"Did you see the accident?" he asked, pulling her back from her thoughts.

"Uh, no, I didn't," she said, praying that Frank hadn't fallen back to sleep and was on his way with the wrecker and a spare car.

"Well, whoever it was hit that poor girl hard. Probably some drunk who didn't even realize he hit her."

"Probably," she repeated.

"Well, if you'll excuse me, I need to go check on her." He left the waiting room. She watched him go, then sunk back onto the orange chair. The woman, Rose, would live. She breathed a sigh of relief at that, but the guilt still weighed heavily upon her. In one brief moment, she had destroyed the young woman's legs, possibly crippling Miss Grayson for life.

The sky was still dark when Ronnie closed her eyes, fatigue threatening to claim her. Minutes later, they opened again when her nose was assaulted by the scent of far too much cheap cologne.

"Cuz."

"Hi, Frank," she said wearily as he plopped down in the seat next to her. "Did you take care of it?"

"All done," he said proudly, holding out a set of keys. "Blue Mazda. Third level, dealer plates. Can't miss it."

"Thanks."

"No problem. Always happy to do a favor for my favorite cousin." He smiled, showing off teeth that were too white to be real. "So what'd ya do? Hit someone?"

"Shut up!" she hissed through clenched teeth, amazed at the amount of stupidity that her cousin seemed to possess.

"Sorry." He held up his hands in a placating gesture. "Jeez, is it your time of the month or something?"

"Thanks for taking care of that, Frank. Do me a favor and make sure the Porsche is taken to my place. Park it in the garage. I'll call Hans to take care of it"

"I don't understand why you go to him instead of having Michael work on it. You know he owns–"

"Michael owns a Toyota dealership. He works on Toyotas, not Porsches. Hans is the best. Just make sure it's put in the garage, out of sight. Move the Jeep if you need room."

"Fine," he sighed, knowing that he would never win the argument. He looked around for something to occupy his interest.

"Is that it?" she queried, looking at him, then at the door.

"You're not gonna tell me why you're here or why your car is all smashed up, are you?"

"Frank, what happened to my car or why I'm here, that's my business, just like where all the profits from the car wash go are your business. Got it?"

"Got it." He knew better than to piss off his cousin, knowing full well just how volatile she could be sometimes. He stood up. "You know my number if you ever need anything."

"Yup." She opened the People magazine and flipped through the pages, effectively dismissing him. She waited until he was out the door before heading to the nurse's station to inquire about the young woman's condition.

Ronnie stepped out into the dreary gray of another day. The snow had stopped, and now the streets were full of people trying to make their way to work through the frozen slush. She reached in her pocket and pulled out the library card. Morris Street. She tried to picture where the street was in relation to the hospital. Certain that it wasn't far and that she could find it without a map, Ronnie headed for the multi-level parking garage.

The small blue car was parked right where Frank had said it would be. The raven-haired woman tossed her attaché into the passenger seat and folded her long frame into the small space of the driver's seat, fumbling around until she found the lever that allowed her to push the seat back so her knees weren't kissing her chin. She had to turn the key several times before the 323 would sputter to life. Ronnie gunned the gas repeatedly until the old car seemed willing to continue on its own. "Frank, you son of a bitch," she swore as the beat-up excuse for a vehicle slowly putt-putted out of the parking spot and headed down the ramp.

Ronnie took a left out of the parking garage and drove up New Scotland Avenue, heading toward the park. She went two blocks before the street sign she was looking for appeared. As she thought, Morris Street was a one-way, of course in the direction opposite the way she wanted to go. A quick turn on Madison and another on Knox put her at the other end of the block, and finally, she was able to go up the narrow street.

Morris Street was once home to doctors and families of wealth but had long ago changed to a street known more for the occasional drive-bys and roaches than anything else. The homes were packed tightly together, usually with less than a foot between them. Ronnie pulled over at the only open space she found, ignoring the red fire hydrant prominently standing on the broken sidewalk. She grabbed her attaché off the seat next to her and stepped out of the car. She briefly thought about locking the battered heap but decided that it wasn't worth the effort. If a thief wanted to fight with the stupid thing to get it running, it was fine with her. She climbed over the snowbank and looked around for house numbers. Most buildings were missing one or more digits, but eventually, she found the place that Rose Grayson called home.

Ronnie climbed the rickety and slippery steps until she reached the outer doors that led to the first- and second-floor apartments. A look at the three wall-mounted mailboxes showed that Rose lived in the basement apartment. She pulled the small stack of mail from the box and stepped back out onto the landing. Cursing at the thought of negotiating the snow-covered stairs again, she placed her gloved hand on the shaky metal railing and slowly made her way back to street level. Under the stairs, she found a door missing most of its paint. A small card taped to the glass read simply, "Grayson." Ronnie knocked several times but received no answer. Perhaps the young woman lived alone. Reaching in her pocket, she pulled the key out of the worn sports wallet and wiggled it into the lock. It took a few tries, but finally, the lock turned, allowing her to enter the small dwelling.

To say that Rose lived in abject poverty would have been kind. The first room Ronnie entered was most likely the living room, although no one would have known from the furniture. A lawn chair missing several strips sat in the middle of the room, books marked "Albany Public Library" piled up next to it. That was the extent of the furnishings. Not a single picture or poster hung on the walls. Not that a dozen pictures would have made a difference. The old, crumbly plaster was missing in several places, showing the dried-out slats beneath. The ceiling was in a similar state of disrepair. Yellowed water stains formed jagged circles, and in several places, it sagged noticeably. Ronnie doubted it would be long before the ceiling began to cave in. The apartment was extremely cool and a quick check of the thermostat showed why. Dust had settled on the dial, indicating that the temperature hadn't been changed in quite some time. It was set at sixty degrees, but with the drafts coming from the old windows, the room felt more like fifty. She set her attaché down on the rickety lawn chair, then reached into her pocket and removed the two letters that she had taken from Rose's mailbox. The first was nothing more than junk mail announcing that if the winning number matched the one in the envelope, "Dose Graydon" would be the winner of eleven million dollars. The other letter was a yellow envelope from the power company. Although she knew she shouldn't, Ronnie slipped one well-manicured fingernail under the corner and opened it. As she had suspected, it was a disconnection notice. She tucked that one back in her pocket and headed for the bedroom, hoping to find an address book or something that would indicate whom she should notify that the young woman was in the hospital.

The bedroom was just as revealing as the living room. A small rollaway bed was pushed up against the wall, and a fold-up chair served as a makeshift dresser. Two pairs of jeans that had long ago seen better days and equally worn sweatshirts made up the small pile of clothes, along with a few pairs of socks looking more like Swiss cheese than footwear. A thorough search, not that it took much effort, failed to reveal any address books or other personal items. Not one letter from a friend, no pictures, nothing that indicated that Rose knew anyone...or that anyone knew Rose.

The bathroom was just another depressing stop on Ronnie's tour. The medicine cabinet contained one nearly empty stick of deodorant and a flattened tube of toothpaste, both sporting the Money Slasher brand name. Two tampons sat on the back of the toilet along with a half-empty roll of toilet paper. A worn towel was draped over the edge of the tub, and three pairs of tattered underwear hung over the shower rod. "How do you live like this?" she asked aloud as she turned to leave the small bathroom. As she did, she noticed the one item that she had previously missed before. Sandwiched between the sink and the wall was a small litter box. "Well at least you're not alone." As if on cue, an orange and white kitten no more than four months old came scampering into the bathroom, yowling loudly to announce its presence. "Hello there."

"Mrrow!" Ronnie leaned down to pet it, but the cat took off toward the kitchen. "Come here. I'm not going to hurt you."

"Mrrow!" The cat remained at the entrance to the kitchen, refusing to come any closer. "Fine, be that way, see if I give a shit."

She walked past the kitty and entered the kitchen, wishing quickly that she hadn't.

The stove was an old gas model that probably was quite efficient back in her grandmother's day. A small frying pan and pot sat on top, while a well-used cookie sheet rested inside the oven. She opened one drawer and took a step back as several roaches scampered about, trying to sneak back into the darkness. She shut the drawer quickly, but not before noticing the one mismatched set of silverware that it contained. The refrigerator held a plastic milk bottle that had been refilled with water, half a jar of mayonnaise, a stick of margarine, and an almost empty bottle of ketchup. When Ronnie reached for the cupboard door, her legs were encircled by the anxious cat.

"Meow, meow, mrrrow?" Sure enough, the cupboard held within it one half-empty box of Money Slasher cat food and a box of elbow macaroni. "Mrrow, meow?"

"Okay, okay, I get the hint," she said, pulling the box out. The orange and white cat scrambled over to her bowl, waiting none too patiently for the tall human to feed her. "How much do cats your size eat?"

"Mrrow?"

"Never mind." She poured the dry food into the bowl until it reached the brim. "There, that should keep you for a while." She looked at the water dish. "I suppose you'd like some fresh water, too, your majesty." The cat was too busy chowing down to answer. Ronnie took the bowl to the sink and dumped the remaining water before turning the tap on. A horrid clunking sound came from the pipes, and she quickly shut it off. "Looks like you get the water from the fridge." She set the bowl on the floor next to the food dish and was about to continue her search when she heard pounding on the door.

"Grayson, I know you're in there. I heard you turn the water on," the angry voice on the other side yelled. "It's the third already, and I want my fucking rent money now!" He pounded again. "Goddammit, I'm sick of your whining about your tiny paycheck. If you couldn't afford this place, then you never should have moved in here...goddamn piece of trash!"

The door flung open to reveal a portly man who reeked of alcohol despite the early morning hour. "Who the fuck are you? I told her that roommates cost extra."

"How much does she owe you?" Ronnie queried, trying hard to keep her temper in check.

"Four fifty. Six if I find out you're living here, too," he growled. "So who the fuck are you?"

Ronnie didn't answer, instead walking over to the lawn chair and rummaging through her attaché until she found her checkbook. "What's your name?"

"What's it matter to you?"

"If you want to be paid for the rent, I need a name to write on the check...or should I just fill in the word asshole?"

"I don't take fucking checks. They always bounce."

"I guarantee this one won't bounce. Give me a name."

"Cecil Romano, but I'm not taking any fucking check."

"Have you heard of the Cartwright Corporation?" she asked while filling in the various parts of the check.

"Of course, who hasn't?"

"Well, I'm Veronica Cartwright. This check is from my personal account. If you want your rent money, I suggest you take this." She handed over the check. Cecil looked at it carefully, certain that it was a trick.

"I'll need to see some ID."

"Fine." She reached into the attaché and pulled out her wallet. At that moment, the orange and white kitty decided to come out and see what all the fuss was about.

"What the fuck is that?"

"Looks like a cat to me. Tell me, are you capable of forming a complete sentence without the word fuck in it?"

"I told her no pets. No pets means no fucking pets. No pets, no roommates, no...whatever the fuck you are." He folded up the check and stuffed it in his pocket. "I've had it. She bitches about everything from a little noise in the pipes to wanting me to paint the walls and now this. When you see the little bitch, you tell her that I want her out of here by the end of the week. She and that flea-ridden thing can go live on the street for all I care."

"Fine. I'll see to it that her things are moved out of here immediately. I assume you own the hundred-year-old stove and fridge?"

"Goddamn right I own them. I own that bed she sleeps on, too. She was supposed to buy it from me for fifty bucks, but I haven't seen it yet."

"Well, now you won't. You can keep it." She tucked her wallet and checkbook back into her case. "Is there anything else, or do you feel the need to continue to assault me with your stinking breath?"

"I don't give a fuck who you are, you can't come in my house and talk to me that way. Just make sure the place is in the same condition as when she moved in or she doesn't get her security back."

"I doubt you'd give it back anyway," Ronnie countered. "After all, you are the epitome of a slumlord."

"You'd better take that damn cat with you when you leave, or I'll wring its fucking neck and throw it out in the trash." He flung the door open, letting the cold air mix with the cool air already inside the apartment. "And make sure she forwards her fucking mail," he growled as he slammed the door.

Ronnie turned and rubbed her forehead.

"Meow?"

"Well, I guess I have company for a few days, huh?" She sat down on the bare floor next to the cat. "Wish I knew your name. It'd be much easier than calling you 'cat' all the time."

"Mrrow," the kitty replied, climbing onto the raven-haired woman's lap. Ronnie allowed the purring feline to remain for a few minutes while she tried to think through what just happened. She had only meant to find out whom to contact to let someone know that Rose was hurt and ended up getting the young woman evicted. Not that it was much of a loss, considering the conditions she was living in. No matter, she decided. Her cousin Danielle ran Cartwright Properties, surely there was an affordable apartment available that they could put Rose into. "Something with real walls," she muttered, looking at a dinner plate-sized hole in the opposite wall. "Okay, cat, time to move." The kitty objected vocally but finally acquiesced when the tall human stood up. "Let's get your momma's things together and get you out of here and into someplace warmer."

Moving Rose's belongings was easy, especially when Ronnie decided that the only things that had to leave the decrepit apartment were the library books and the checkbook she found in the kitchen drawer. The worn-out clothes, the useless furniture…she decided that for four hundred fifty bucks, Cecil could clean them out himself. Tucking the checkbook into her attaché, the library books under her arm, and the cat inside her jacket, Ronnie left the apartment, not bothering to lock the door.

Chapter Two

Rose opened her eyes and looked around, groaning at both the pain and the realization of where she was. A young blonde nurse looked up and smiled. "Good morning, Miss Grayson. My name is Mary." She placed a protective sheath over the tip of the thermometer she was holding and put it in Rose's ear. "You've been in a very bad accident." She wrapped the blood pressure cuff around Rose's upper arm and pressed her stethoscope against the inside of the young woman's elbow.

"Excuse me...." Rose inhaled sharply as the nurse made a note on her chart. She felt dopey but scared at the same time. "Wha...what happened?"

"You were hit by a car last night. You're very lucky that your boss was driving by and saw you. She brought you to the hospital."

"My boss? Kim found me?"

"Oh, I don't know her name, deary. I wasn't here last night. I work the day shift." She carefully cleaned the skin around the neat row of stitches on Rose's cheek. "You were in surgery for quite a while, and you're in the recovery room right now. We just need to make sure you're stabilized, then you'll be taken to your room."

"My legs?" She tried to sit up, but that only served to increase the intense pain she was feeling in her lower extremities.

"Both your legs were broken. The surgeons worked for hours last night putting the bones back in place."

"It hurts." Rose lifted her head to see the stark white of full leg casts.

"I'll let the doctor know you're awake."

The instant the nurse left the room, Rose broke down in tears. Her face and ribs hurt, but it was nothing compared to the excruciating agony in her legs. She didn't even want to think about the hospital bill, which no doubt was increasing with every hour she spent here. She reached over to pour herself a cup of water from the plastic pitcher on the stand next to the bed, but the movement caused so much pain that she was unable to complete her task. Whatever they were giving her for the pain was also making her limbs feel extremely heavy, and it didn't take long for Rose to fall back into an uneasy sleep.

Ronnie pulled the Mazda into her driveway and parked it next to the garage. To her great annoyance, removing the key from the ignition did not shut the engine off. Instead the blue car continued to sputter and wheeze for a minute before finally dying. "Well, Cat. I think it's safe to say that the next place this piece of shit will go is to the junkyard."

"Mrrow?" The feline replied as it tried to climb onto her lap.

"No, no, no. This isn't petting time." She tucked the cat under her arm and opened the door. "Come on, let's see if Maria can find something in the kitchen for you to eat."

As she exited the car with the cat in tow, Ronnie glanced over at her three-car garage. The middle door was unlocked, and through the half-moon window, she saw her Porsche. She silently thanked her cousin Frank for helping her out. The cat squirmed in her grip. "Oh, no, you don't. I'm not running all over the neighborhood looking for you."

Ronnie opened the sliding glass door and entered into the kitchen. Once inside, she locked the orange and white kitty in the laundry room and rushed upstairs to change out of her blood-spattered outfit. It felt good to get out of the soiled clothes, and she bundled them up and shoved them in a canvas bag to dispose of later.

"Maria? Maria, are you here?"

"I'm here," a voice from the living room called.

"We've got company," Ronnie responded.

Maria was an older woman working on her thirtieth year with the Cartwright family and was near and dear to Ronnie's heart. Jet black hair had long ago given way to a salt and pepper, and her middle-age spread made her lap perfect for whenever the young children came over. Maria walked into the kitchen. "It's not good for you to be out all night, Ronnie," she chastised. "If your mother knew–"

"I wasn't out whoring around, Maria," she responded, pleased with the shocked reaction on the older woman's face. "Do we have anything here to feed…." She opened the laundry room door.

"Mrrow?"

"…a cat?" she finished.

Maria looked down at Ronnie's feet to see the orange and white feline rubbing against her. "Oh, my. You brought home a cat?"

"It's not a permanent arrangement. He's only going to be here for a few days while his owner is in the hospital."

The housekeeper bent down and picked up the now purring feline. "I hate to tell you, Ronnie, but he is a she. What's her name?"

"I don't know. Call it Cat for now."

"Hi, sweetie, what a pretty kitty you are," Maria cooed, holding the happy pet to her ample chest. "Would you like some tuna?" She carried the cat over to the pantry and pulled out a can. "Hmm, doesn't that sound nice?"

"I don't think he, I mean she, has ever had tuna before. I think she's only had dry food."

"Oh…well then." Maria put the can on the counter and set the cat gently on the floor. "It's not good to take her from dry right to canned. It'll be too rich for her. I can mix them together."

"I didn't bring any. I guess we'll have to get her some food."

"Well, I've already been shopping this week, but if you want, I'll run out now. I can start lunch when I get back." She wiped her hands on her apron and reached for the ties.

"No, that's fine. I'll go out and pick up some food for her. I guess we need a litter box, too."

"You took a cat without even getting a litter box? Ronnie, what am I going to do with you?"

"Well, her box was dirty, and I wasn't about to touch it," Ronnie protested. "Look, just make me a cup of coffee while I go take a shower and change. I'll run out and pick up the things the cat will need."

"I'll make you a list. Knowing you, you'll get the box and forget the litter."

"Funny" came the sarcastic reply, although in fact she hadn't thought about getting stuff to put in the litter box. "I'll be back down in a little bit. Try and keep the fuzz ball off the couch and away from the antiques, okay?"

The mall was busy for a Wednesday afternoon, and Ronnie ended up parking at the far end of a row. A quick press of the button on her keychain, and the bright blue Jeep Cherokee's doors locked, and a warning light on the dash indicated that the alarm system was armed.

It took her fifteen minutes to navigate her way around the mall until she located the pet store. Once inside, she found shelves of everything from fake mice and scratching posts to catnip and collars. Ronnie hated shopping, and when the teenage clerk offered to help her pick out things for her new pet, she readily agreed. The result was seventy-five dollars worth of litter, toys, food, catnip, and various other items that the young girl insisted were necessary for a happy and healthy cat.

After finishing her shopping, Ronnie went to the hospital to check on Rose. She wasn't at all prepared for what she saw. The sheet covering the young woman's legs outlined the full-length casts. A nasty-looking row of stitches surrounded by an equally nasty-looking bruise covered one cheek, and dried tear streaks prominently showed on her face. An IV with several bags hung from one side, giving the injured woman the fluids and pain medications she needed. A catheter disappeared under the blanket. Ronnie's heart ached for the pain that Rose was in, as well as the pain she would go through as she recovered, knowing deep inside that her recklessness behind the wheel was the reason the young woman was here. As if sensing her presence, the reddish-blonde head turned, and green eyes focused on her.

"Hello," she said politely, her voice a bit raspy.

"Hello, Rose. How are you feeling?"

"Lucky to be alive, I guess," she croaked, her eyes trailing toward the water pitcher. Ronnie immediately walked over and poured some into the yellow plastic cup.

"Here." She handed the cup over but quickly reclaimed her grip on it when she saw the young woman's hand shake. "Let me help." Together they got half the cup down Rose's throat before Ronnie returned it to the small stand. "Do you remember anything about the accident?"

"No, not really. I was running…some men were chasing me…I got out of the park and ran out into the street…that's all I remember before waking up here."

"You don't remember anything about the car that hit you?" Ronnie prodded. "The color, the type of car, the driver, anything?"

"No, nothing. I'm sorry. Are you with the police?"

"No." Inwardly, Ronnie breathed a sigh of relief. Rose couldn't remember what happened. With a little luck, she might just be able to pull this off.

"Then I suppose you're here to talk to me about the bill," Rose said, deciding that the beautiful, well-dressed woman had to be a hospital administrator.

"Actually, I do need to talk to you about that, but–"

"I have no money," she interrupted. "I don't have kids. I don't qualify for any programs." She gave a defeated sigh. "I'll give you whatever I can each week, but I'm afraid it won't be more than five dollars or so." She resigned herself to giving up her bus fare to help pay for the impossible bill.

"You don't need to do that," Ronnie said, amazed that someone with obviously little or no money was so quick to take financial responsibility for the hospital bill. "Perhaps you'd better let me explain."

Rose nodded.

"My name is Veronica Cartwright. I own Cartwright Corporation. I um...I found you after the accident and brought you here. When I realized that you didn't have insurance, I told them that you worked for me. Cartwright has an excellent benefits package including medical coverage. You won't have to pay a cent for your care, I promise."

"You? But they told me that my boss...." Realization set in. "You told them you were my boss?"

"Yes."

"Oh." Rose seemed to ponder the information. "So instead of owing the hospital, I'll owe you?"

"No, no, no. By the end of the day, your name will be added to the insurance rolls. I'll have it backdated to before the accident, and you'll be covered."

"But isn't that fraud?"

"Only if you didn't work for me." Damn, why did she have to be so difficult? Couldn't she just accept that the bill would be covered? Ronnie couldn't understand why someone who had nothing was questioning a good thing when it was being offered to her. "Tell me, where do you work now?"

"I...." Rose looked down, clearly embarrassed. "I work part time as a cashier at Money Slasher. I should say I *worked* part time. I'm sure they won't hold the job for me until I can walk again."

"Do you have any skills? I mean, can you type or take dictation or anything like that?" The crestfallen look on the young woman's face answered the question. "Well then, I guess you're a clerk. It's an entry-level job, but it's better than bagging groceries."

"But I can't work." She looked down at the casts covering her legs. "I can't even walk."

"The job will be there when you're ready. Until then, you just concentrate on recovering." It was so simple, why was she making it difficult? Ronnie didn't plan on this.

"Mrs. Cartwright?"

"It's Miss, but please call me Ronnie."

"Why are you doing this? I mean, you don't know me." After a lifetime of being handed the short end of the stick, an act of such great generosity was too much for her to believe. There had to be something more to it. Everything had a price attached.

"I guess I just wanted to help. I saw you lying there on the street, and I reacted. The only way to keep you here at the med center was to tell them you had insurance, and the only way to give you insurance was to make you an employee. I run a large corporation that operates several smaller ones. Adding you to the rolls isn't a big deal. I'm sorry I don't have a better explanation." The only other explanation would involve the truth, and Ronnie couldn't afford that. "Don't worry about why I'm helping. Just let me. Now is there someone I should contact to let him or her know you're in the hospital?"

"Um…I guess Kim should know so she can hire someone else for my slot," Rose said quietly, mourning the loss of the job she had worked so hard to get. It was too much for her to believe that she was being offered a job with a company as large as Cartwright Corporation. "She's the night manager at Money Slasher on Central. I have to turn in my smock to get my last paycheck."

"Would that be the gray thing you were wearing under your jacket?" Rose nodded. "I'm afraid the doctor in the emergency room cut that to pieces when they were treating you."

"Oh." Another crestfallen look. "They charge eight dollars for ruined smocks."

"Don't worry about it," Ronnie said, not fully understanding how important the small sum of money was to the young woman. To Rose, that was half her weekly allotment for groceries, part of which went to cat food. Through her drug-filled haze, a thought came to her.

"Tabitha!" She exclaimed. "Oh, my God, someone has to take care of Tabitha."

"Would that be your cat?"

"Yes, how did you know?"

"I found your key in your wallet and went to your apartment, hoping to find a name or number of someone to contact for you."

"Did you feed her?" Her concern that someone was in her run-down apartment was overshadowed by her worry over the one thing that brought some kind of joy to her life.

"Yes, I did," Ronnie replied as Rose turned away, letting a long silence form between them. A lone tear made its way down the young woman's cheek. "Hey, what's wrong? Are you in pain? Do you need me to call the nurse?" Ronnie's hand was already reaching for the call button.

"No," the young woman sniffed, wiping away the errant tear. "It's just that…" she sniffled again, "…if I'm not there to take care of Tabitha, they're going to take her away."

"No one's going to take Tabitha away from you. I promise. In fact, she's at my house right now. She can stay with me until you're all settled." Ronnie's heart lurched with the thought of how easily she had destroyed Rose's life. In one move, she had cost the young woman her job, her home, and far more pain than anyone deserved to have. Now she was sitting there, lying to her to protect herself. "I swear no one will take Tabitha away."

"I…I can write you a check for her food. She doesn't eat much. She's very friendly." The words rolled out of Rose's mouth, and there was no way the older woman could miss the desperation in her voice.

"Don't worry about it. Please, I want you to concentrate on getting better. Tabitha will be fine with me. I live alone, I'm sure I'll enjoy the company."

The dark-haired woman was about to say something else when a firm knock on the door caused them to turn. Ronnie's heart skipped a beat at the sight of the blue uniform and shiny badge. "Excuse me, ladies. I'm here to take a report on the hit and run last night." He stepped in and pulled a small notebook out of his shirt pocket. "You're Rose Grayson, right?" He continued on without waiting for an answer. "Now I understand this happened on Madison Ave. around midnight."

"I think it was more like twelve thirty," Rose said.

"Yes, twelve thirty," he repeated. "Now is there anything you can tell me, like the make and model of the car that hit you, the license number, the color?"

"No, I never saw it." She turned her head toward Ronnie. "Do you remember?"

"You were there, too?" The officer queried. No one had told him there were any witnesses.

"I got there after the accident. I didn't see anyone."

"That sure was a hell of a storm last night. What were you doing out so late, Miss…?"

"Cartwright, Veronica Cartwright. I had a business dinner with Commissioner Grace at Sam's and was heading home."

"Cartwright, as in the car wash Cartwrights?"

"Yes, among other holdings," she replied, annoyed that after all her hard work, the most well-known part of her company was the cousin's stupid car washes.

"Well then.…" He turned his attention back to the victim lying in bed. "I guess you're pretty lucky to have had her come up on you. Looks like he hit you pretty good. Probably a drunk driver. Hard to believe the bastard didn't have the guts to stick around and make sure you got help, but I guess all that matters is that you're alive."

"Yes, I was very lucky that Miss Cartwright came along when she did. Who knows how long I was lying there."

"Well, if I could just get your address and phone number for the report, we'll be all set. I have to tell you that there isn't much to go on, so don't get your hopes up. Unless this guy is stupid enough to be driving around with a lot of front-end damage and admits to being on Madison last night, there's not really much we can do."

"I understand," Rose said quietly. She didn't expect them to find the man who hit her. "I don't have a phone, but my address is 98 Morris St."

Ronnie's emotions alternated between relief at having such an uninterested cop investigating the accident and guilt at the fact that she was lying to protect her own skin at the expense of Rose's peace of mind.

"Well, I guess if there's anything I missed, we can find you here. From the looks of your legs, I don't think you'll be going anywhere for a while." Ronnie bristled at the comment, but Rose appeared unaffected.

"Thank you," the young woman said. The cop turned toward the door and noticed a friend of his walking down the hall.

"Hey, Don, wait up. Ladies, thank you. I'm sure I have all I need right now." He was gone before either could respond.

"They're not going to find him, you know," Rose said quietly. "I know life isn't like television. They don't even know what kind of car to look for." She shifted slightly, grimacing at the pain that was now her constant companion. "Doesn't matter anyway," she sighed. "The damage is done. Even if they did find him, it wouldn't make my legs heal any faster."

Ronnie didn't know what to say and was grateful when the television vendor walked in. "Good afternoon, Miss..." she looked down at her clipboard, "...Grayson. Would you like your TV turned on?"

"No, thank you," Rose said quickly.

"Why not?" Ronnie asked, although she was certain she knew the answer.

"I don't like television."

"Uh-huh." Ronnie turned toward the vendor. "Turn it on and leave it on for as long as Miss Grayson is here."

"It's three dollars a day, twenty dollars per week."

"Fine." Ronnie picked her attaché off the floor and pulled out her wallet. "Here." She handed the television woman two twenties.

"Very well." She made a notation on her clipboard, then reached behind the TV and unlocked the attached box. A few seconds later, the set hummed to life with Judge Judy yelling at the defendant on her courtroom show.

"There, now you'll have something to help you pass the time," Ronnie said after the vendor left.

"You didn't need to do that," Rose replied, feeling uncomfortable. "I would have been fine without it. You were in my apartment. You know I don't own a TV." She sighed. "Besides, whatever they're giving me for the pain makes me tired. I don't know how much I would watch. Certainly not twenty dollars worth."

"Let's make a deal here, okay? You need help, and I want to help. Now the television is paid for. You can either accept it and enjoy it or you can leave it off and stare at a blank screen all day."

The noise from the television interrupted their conversation. "...and if you think for one minute that I believe that some stranger broke into your apartment and stole everything that belonged to your roommate here and left all of your stuff behind, then you're a complete idiot. I wasn't born yesterday, Mr. Richards. Judgment for the plaintiff in the amount of $653.12. Case dismissed." Ronnie looked over to see Rose watching with complete interest.

"It's like being in court," the young woman said, her attention never leaving the set.

"It's a good show."

"Is it on every week?"

"Every day, Rose. You can watch it every day at noon." She smiled and whispered conspiratorially. "I'm too busy to watch it when it airs, but I tape it and catch up on the weekends."

"Thank you," the young woman said sincerely, her green eyes smiling at Ronnie. "It will make it easier to pass the time here."

"It's the least I could do." She leaned her arms on the railing of the bed. "So are you going to tell me who I can contact besides your job to tell them you're here? Surely someone will miss you."

The small smile that had been on Rose's face disappeared. "There's no one to contact."

"No one? Not even a friend?"

Rose gave a sad smile. "I haven't lived in Albany that long," she said, not wanting to reveal the truth, that she deliberately avoided making friends because friends liked to stop by and visit and she was too embarrassed at her meager living conditions. She shifted, and a shooting pain burned up her left leg, making her cry out. "Oh, God, that hurts," she hissed. Ronnie immediately reached over and pressed the call button repeatedly.

"What is it?" Mary asked as she entered the room.

"She's in pain. Can't you give her anything?"

"She's receiving an appropriate amount through her IV, but if she needs more, I can give her a shot." She looked at Rose, who was trying hard not to cry. "Miss Grayson?"

"Yes, she is. Can't you see she's suffering?" Ronnie answered testily.

"Miss Grayson?" The nurse repeated. Rose reluctantly nodded, the pain too much to bear any longer. To her surprise, a larger hand enfolded her own. Another twinge of pain shot through her, and she gripped Ronnie's hand tightly. The nurse left and returned a minute later with a needle. She unceremoniously pulled the sheet and hospital gown back to expose Rose's right hip and stuck the needle in. "This will sting for a minute." The young woman gripped Ronnie's hand even tighter as the medication was injected. "There, all done." The nurse looked up at the dark-haired woman. "She'll probably fall asleep in a few minutes."

"Fine, I won't be much longer." The nurse nodded and left, not bothering to pull the sheet back into place. Ronnie used her free hand to reach over and cover Rose's hip with the stark white linen. "Do you want me to stay for a while until you fall asleep?"

"No, that's...." She was unable to stifle a yawn. "...that's all right...I'm fine...." The powerful drug acted quickly, causing her head to loll to the side and her eyes to take on a glassy look. "Are you sure you're not an angel?" she asked sleepily as her eyelids sagged. "You look like an angel...you...." Another yawn. "...act like...." Her eyes closed, and the hand that had been holding Ronnie's fell limply to the side.

She waited several minutes until she was certain that Rose was asleep before standing up and tucking the blanket around the injured woman. "Sleep well, Rose," she whispered.

Chapter Three

Ronnie opened the door and dragged the litter box, scratching post, and bag of toys inside. "Tabitha, come on you little fuzz ball, I've got toys for you." She sat on the floor and pulled out the items. The orange and white cat came bouncing over to see what the tall human was up to. She sat back and watched as Ronnie opened the many packages and tossed fake mice, bagged catnip, and various toys into a pile. "There you go," Ronnie said, fully expecting the feline to dive into the pile and play. Tabitha did what any cat would do, walked past the pile of cat toys and started batting at the empty wrappers. "Hey, the toys are over here." She grabbed the little ball with the bell hidden inside and shook it to get the cat's attention. "See? Toys here, garbage there." Tabitha looked at it, looked at the wrappers, and went back to playing with the clear plastic.

"Fine, be that way, see if I care," the dejected woman said, stuffing the wrappers into the plastic bag. "I got you a litter box, too, think you'll use that?"

"Mrrow?"

"That's what I thought." She stood up, tucked the bag of litter under one arm, the cat box under the other, and headed to the kitchen. "Seventy-five bucks on toys and the stupid thing wants to play with the packages they came in." She set the bag and box on the table. A note held to the refrigerator with a magnet told her that Maria had left for the day, along with instructions on how long to microwave the dinner that she had prepared.

Exhaustion begged her to stop and rest, but there were just too many things that had to be done. She quickly set up the litter box and put it in the mud room, leaving the door ajar so Tabitha could come and go freely. That task done, Ronnie strode to the living room, picking up the cordless phone and dialing the familiar number on the way.

"Cartwright Insurance, how can I help you?" the crisp feminine voice on the other end of the phone asked.

"Susan Cartwright, please."

"She's busy right now, may I ask who's calling?"

"Veronica Cartwright. Interrupt her, this is important."

"One moment." She heard a click followed by the most boring hold music she had ever heard. Ronnie flopped down on her soft brown leather couch and kicked her shoes off, tucking her feet beneath her. Tabitha bounded out of the kitchen and climbed up next to her.

"Mrrow?"

"What do you want?" She reached out with her free hand to scratch the cat behind the ears. "Let's get something straight right from the start, okay? I bought a scratching post for you. The couch is off limits to your claws, got it?"

"Mrrow." The orange and white feline laid her upper body across Ronnie's thigh and began purring.

"Ronnie, how are you?"

"Fine, Sis. Listen, I need you to add an employee to the insurance rolls."

"Usually human resources sends over their paperwork once they've reached the appropriate service mark." Ronnie heard the clacking of the keyboard. "What's the person's Social?"

"She's not in the computer yet, Susan. I need you to add her and push the paperwork through."

"She has to be in the system. All employees are added once they've filled out their I-9s and W-4s."

"She hasn't filled them out yet. She's a new hire." Ronnie heard the clacking stop and the squeak of her sister's chair moving.

"What department does she work for?"

"Um…she's a clerk in the accounting office downtown."

"An entry level? Ronnie, don't you know they have to have six months of service before we give them benefits?"

"I didn't realize that." She rubbed her forehead, drawing a protest from the purring pile of fluff on her leg.

"What's that?"

"I'm watching a friend's cat for a few days. Look, I hired her personally and promised her full benefits. Can't you push it through?"

"It's so rare that my only sister asks me for a favor. Of course I can. Fax me her forms, and I'll add her to the rolls."

"Actually, Susan, I need you to fax me the forms for her to sign. I also need you to give her the best medical plan we have and backdate it to the first of the month. Can you do that?"

"It'll cost you," the younger sister said in a sing-song voice. "Dinner with Mom next Friday."

"Can't I just buy you a new car or something?" Ronnie groaned.

"Veronica Louise, you never spend any time with Mom. Jack and I are there every Friday night for dinner, and Tommy is there on Sundays. She always asks about you."

"She knows my phone number, Susan. I talk to her."

"I know. We heard for two weeks about how you called her on her birthday. Funny, that was a month ago."

"All right, all right. Fax me all the forms, and I'll get them back to you later tonight."

"So we'll see you next week at Mom's?"

"Fine. I'll be there, but don't expect me to stick around after dinner while she goes through the scrapbook and tries to relive our childhood."

"At least you'll be there. That'll make her happy."

"Whatever. Fax those forms over, will ya?"

"They'll be there in a few minutes. Wish you'd let me in on why you personally hired someone for an entry-level job."

"Sis, if I thought you needed to know, I'd tell you. Nice talking with you, too, bye." Ronnie pressed the off button on the cordless and set it on the coffee table. "Well, Tabitha, that's all set. How about you hop down and play with some of your toys while I take a nap, hmm?" She tried to nudge the feline, but the purring pile of fur refused to move. "Fine, be that way." She adjusted the end pillow and closed her eyes. At first, the rhythmic purring annoyed her, but within a few minutes, Ronnie was sound asleep, as was a contented Tabitha.

Rose was awake but very obviously in pain by the time Ronnie returned to the hospital. "Hi."

"Hi, Rose. How are you feeling?" She set the attaché on the floor and pulled the chair next to the bed.

"Everything hurts, but other than that, I'm fine."

"Doesn't the medicine they give you help?"

"It puts me to sleep, but yeah. It's the only thing that touches the pain," she replied, smoothing the blanket covering her.

"I brought some forms that I need you to sign. I filled them out as best I could, but I didn't know all the answers." She pulled a manila folder out of the case and set it on the bed. "I never realized how many forms it takes to hire someone." She held the pen out and was surprised to see Rose take it in her left hand. "You're a lefty?"

"Yeah."

"Me too," she smiled. "The first three just need your signature. The others have some blanks that you have to fill in."

"You know, I still can't believe you're just giving me a job, especially since I can't even work." Rose shook her head. "It just doesn't make any sense."

"I do a lot of things that don't make any sense, just ask my mother."

Rose signed the forms quietly before handing the pen back. "Are you close to your mother?"

"Not really. We have different opinions on how I should live." She hesitated for a moment before deciding to broach the subject that had tugged at her mind. "What about your family? Did you have a falling out with them or something? I mean, it seems strange that you wouldn't want them to know you're in the hospital."

Green eyes turned away to stare at the Venetian blinds that covered the window. "I was a baby when they died. Car accident. A drunk driver ran a stoplight and hit them. That's all I know."

"I'm sorry, I didn't realize." She felt bad for bringing the subject up.

"It's all right," the young woman said with a dismissive wave of her hand. "I don't remember them. I guess you can't miss what you never had." Rose tried to sound casual about it, but Ronnie suspected that it was an act put on for her benefit.

"Who raised you?"

"The state. Sometimes foster families, but mostly, I lived in state-run orphanages or homes. As soon as I graduated high school, I got a job working as a cashier. I've been on my own since then." Not wanting to continue the topic of her past, Rose changed the subject. "So how's Tabitha?"

"She's fine. She likes to purr a lot."

"Mmm, that means she's happy," Rose replied. "You must be good with animals."

"I wouldn't know. This is the first time I've ever had one."

"You never had pets while growing up?"

"No. My father was allergic to cats, and my mother was afraid that a dog would wreck the place. How'd you end up with Tabitha?"

"Oh." She reached for the water glass only to have Ronnie help her. She took a long swallow of the cool liquid before answering. "I found her, or rather she found me. I was walking home one night, and she appeared out of nowhere. Just skin and bones. Followed me home. She's been with me since." A fearful look came to her eyes. "The landlord didn't see her, did he? I'm not supposed to have any pets."

"Actually…he came downstairs while I was there."

"Oh, no." A worried look covered the young woman's face. "Was he nice?"

"Not in the least," Ronnie replied. "He seems to think the word *fuck* is an adjective and should be used every time he opens his foul little mouth."

"What did he say to you?" The trepidation was evident in her voice.

"Nothing you need to worry about right now."

"He kicked me out, didn't he?" While Ronnie would never consider it a great loss, the young woman was obviously upset by the news.

"Rose, don't worry about it, please. I promise everything will be all right." She looked at her watch. "Come on, I think *Jeopardy!* is coming up soon. We'll sit back and see who gets the most questions right, okay?"

"I like *Jeopardy!*" Rose said, pressing the button to raise the head of the bed slightly. "There's TV in the employee lounge at work, and sometimes my dinner break is at seven thirty so I can watch it. I'm pretty good, too, although I don't know if I'll be able to stay awake too long."

"Do you want me to leave so you can get some sleep?"

"No." She reached out for Ronnie's hand. "Please stay."

"Sure, just don't get upset if I get more answers right. No one will play Trivial Pursuit with me."

"Oh, do you have that? It's such a fun game. I played it once down at the community center."

"I'll make you a deal. I'll bring it in tomorrow for us to play, and I promise not to beat you too badly."

"We'll see who beats who," Rose countered with a smile. The *Jeopardy!* theme song drew their attention to the television. "Ooh, it's starting." She settled her head back into her pillow to watch the show, but before the first commercial break, she was sleeping. Ronnie tucked Rose's blanket in and shut the television off. She sat there for several minutes looking at the large casts and the stitches that formed a line on the young woman's cheekbone.

"I'm sorry," she whispered before leaving the room.

Tabitha was waiting none too patiently at the door when Ronnie returned home. "Mrrow!"

"What? You have food."

"Mrrow!"

"You have toys, and you have food. What more do you want?" Tabitha responded by rubbing against Ronnie's leg, leaving orange and white hairs all over her black slacks. She bent down and picked the feline up, apparently turning on the purr button at the same time. She held the happy cat with one arm and the attaché in the other. "Wanna see how the fax machine works? Come on."

Ronnie's office was on the first floor near the stairs. Five minutes later, the insurance forms were faxed, and the dark-haired woman ran upstairs to change into her comfortable clothes, namely an oversized sweatshirt and sweatpants. She glanced at her watch and groaned. She had a meeting first thing in the morning and had yet to review the monthly reports. "I think it's gonna be a long night, Tabitha." She plodded over to her desk and turned on her computer, dreading the idea of spending the next few hours poring over spreadsheets and reports. Of course the heads of each division would go over the same things with her tomorrow, but Ronnie prided herself on knowing exactly how good or bad each department was doing before hearing the glossed-over version from her relatives. A push of the power button and the computer hummed to life, the Cartwright corporate logo covering the twenty-inch screen. She typed her password, and the logo disappeared, revealing the main screen.

"Mrrow?"

"No. This is human stuff, nothing up here for you to see." She said to the anxious cat standing on hind legs in anticipation of being picked up. Tabitha extended her front claws into the light gray of Ronnie's sweatpants. "Don't even think about it."

"Mrrow?"

"No. Go play with your toys." She turned her attention to the first report, Cartwright Real Estate. Ronnie's younger brother, Tommy, was in charge of that division. Several tracts of land had been purchased throughout the region in anticipation of building housing developments, but they were seriously behind in their growth projections. The timetable had called for one hundred homes to be built and sold, yet as of the end of last month, only twenty had actually been completed, and barely half of those had bids in on them much less sold. "What am I gonna do with him?" She leaned back in her comfortable leather chair and rubbed her eyes. The movement seemed to be an open invitation to Tabitha, who quickly jumped onto her lap. "Come on, I can't get any work done if you're here." She gently scooped the purring animal in her arms and set it down on the floor. "Go play."

The clock in the lower right corner of the computer read 2:53 a.m. by the time Ronnie gave up and shut the computer down for the night. She went to the main room to set the security alarm when she spotted the dark blue vinyl checkbook sitting on the entry table next to the library books. Common sense told her not to look, that Rose's financial business was her own, but curiosity got the best of her, and she found herself sitting on the soft brown leather sofa with the checkbook in hand.

There weren't that many entries. The register only went back four months, but it gave a wealth of insight into the life of the woman lying in the hospital. Small, neat writing detailed every deposit, every check. No deposit was over one hundred fifty dollars. Four withdrawals were listed as being for rent, each time wiping out money that had taken most of the previous month to build up. Two entries existed for the power company, and several were written to Money Slasher. Every week, deposits of various meager amounts were recorded, followed by checks to the supermarket for groceries. The highest check was for slightly over ten dollars, and the lowest was for just over five. What Ronnie found most interesting were the remaining checks, all written to someone named Delores Bickering. Those checks ranged in amounts from five to twenty-five dollars, each one taking what little remained in the young woman's account after paying for her weekly expenses. Those entries appeared just as often as the checks to Money Slasher. The current balance showed $112 and change in the young woman's account, far less than the rent that had been due. Ronnie's eyes went back to the entry for the November rent. It was that week that Rose had purchased the five dollars and change worth of groceries, the register showing a negative amount of two dollars and fifteen cents after that. It was the only time that Rose had overdrawn her account, and Ronnie couldn't even imagine what the young woman had purchased to try and survive that week.

She closed the checkbook and set it on the coffee table. Why was Rose, who didn't have two dimes to rub together, constantly writing checks to someone else? Did she have an old debt she was trying to pay off? What other explanation could there be? The young woman said there was no one to contact, so this Bickering person couldn't be a relative. The late hour and the heavy thinking took its toll as exhaustion finally won out, and the couch once again became the wealthy woman's bed for the night. Tabitha curled up against her.

Somewhere in the distance, a phone was ringing. Ronnie rolled over, disturbing the sleeping cat. The ringing became louder and louder, penetrating her dream world and pulling her out of her sound sleep. Her arm shot out and clumsily fumbled about the coffee table for the annoying telephone. "Mmm…Cartwright."

"Ronnie?"

"Yeah?" came the sleep-muddled reply.

"Ronnie, do you have any idea what time it is?" The sound of her sister's voice helped to clear the cobwebs in her mind as she slowly rolled into a sitting position. "It's quarter to ten."

"Oh, shit!" Blue eyes shot open as she realized the purpose of the call. "Damn it, I fell asleep on the couch. I'll be there as soon as I can." She was already heading for the stairs, cordless phone in hand. "Susan, not a word. I had a flat tire, got it?"

"I can't believe you overslept," the younger sister chuckled. "I thought you had a built-in alarm clock. Wait until Mom hears this."

"Susan…" she growled, reaching the top of the stairs and racing into her bedroom. "I'll be there, stall them or something." She hit the off button on the phone and tossed it on the bed as she headed for her bathroom. Ten minutes later, she was in her Jeep Cherokee and heading for Albany, speed limits be damned.

At ten thirty, the double oak doors opened wide as Ronnie raced into the meeting room. "Sorry, flat tire," she said while taking her seat at the far end of the long rectangular table. "Shall we get started?" The silence she received caused her to take a look around. Apparently, she wasn't the only one to have trouble getting to the meeting on time. "Where's Tommy?"

"I don't know. I've been calling him, but there's no answer at any of his numbers," Susan replied. Seated just to the right of her older sister, the head of Cartwright Insurance could never be mistaken for Ronnie. Susan had, thanks to hours with a stylist, flaming red hair that had been permed into large curls that swarmed about her head and down to her shoulders. Though married for thirteen years to a successful lawyer, she refused to give up her family name, deciding that the stature it provided was far better than the common name of Smith. Unlike Ronnie, who could only rarely be coerced into wearing the slightest amount of makeup, Susan believed wholeheartedly that it enhanced her features and thus spent two hours each morning applying everything from base to blush to mascara.

"Did you try his beeper?" It was a stupid question, but Ronnie still had to ask. Over the last few months, her youngest sibling had become increasingly difficult to get hold of and his attentiveness at meetings left plenty to be desired. "Fine, we're running late enough, let's just get started." She opened her portfolio and pulled out the first report. One by one, they went around the room as ten different Cartwrights or relations of Cartwrights explained how his or her particular division was doing and what the plans were for the next month. Most of the words sailed past Ronnie, who nodded occasionally but rarely paid any attention. Her mind was several miles away, wondering what Rose was doing, how she was feeling, and how Delores Bickering fit into the young woman's life.

It was quarter past twelve when the doors opened to reveal a sandy-haired man, hair disheveled, suit rumpled. "Sorry," he mumbled, slinking over to his chair. "Power outage, alarm didn't go off."

"I suppose you didn't have a clean suit either," Ronnie said disapprovingly. The various cousins and relatives surrounding the table looked from the raven-haired woman to Tommy and back again, fully expecting a battle. The young man, however, pretended not to notice his oldest sister's comment.

"Did I miss anything important?"

"No, of course not," her tone barely betrayed her annoyance at him. "I was just getting ready to go over the figures for your latest project."

"I'd say we're in pretty good shape, all things considered," he replied. Ten pairs of eyes flew back to Ronnie.

"And just what things would you like me to consider in light of the figures I'm looking at?" She pulled out the computer-generated report and flipped through the pages until she found what she was looking for. "Sales are off almost thirty percent over last year, and expenses are through the roof."

"I can't help it if the contractors raised their prices. Inflation, you know," he shot back angrily. Ronnie didn't miss the bloodshot eyes or the way Tommy kept looking at his watch.

"Inflation has nothing to do with this. According to these figures, over fifty housing units should be completed. As of last week, only twenty were finished. What the hell is going on, Tommy?"

"I'm on top of it, all right?" he yelled, his fist striking the tabletop with enough force to shake the water glass in front of him. Silence filled the room as everyone waited for Ronnie to react. Instead she turned her attention to Frank.

"I hear you got the variance you wanted. When's the groundbreaking?" For the rest of the meeting, Ronnie refused to look at her angry brother and vice versa. Tommy left the instant the meeting was over, only adding to the speculations and comments by the relatives.

Susan pulled the executive aside, concern clearly written on her face. "Ronnie, what's going on with him? He's been so strange lately, so angry.

"I don't know what I think, Sis, I just know that something is wrong." She glanced at her watch. "I need to be somewhere."

"Yeah, what's going on with you? What's with this Grayson person?" Susan's natural curiosity for gossip, particularly whenever it concerned anyone in the family, was showing through.

"Nothing, just someone I met and decided to hire. Did you take care of that insurance?" As she was talking, Ronnie was heading toward the door.

"Of course. It's on my list of things to do today." Susan replied casually.

"No. It has to be done right away. And don't forget to backdate it to the beginning of the month. It's very important." She gripped her younger sister's upper arm to stress her point.

"I'll do it the instant I get back to my office. Really, Ronnie, you'd think it was a life-or-death situation."

"Just make sure it's done today, Susan. Fax the confirmations to me at home." Ronnie walked out to the elegant hallway and pressed the down button for the elevator. She stepped in only to have her younger sister stick her arm out to keep the doors from shutting.

"Hey, I almost forgot to ask. What'd you get Mom for Christmas?"

"I've got to go, Susan." She pressed the button and waited expectantly.

"You mean you haven't gotten her anything yet? Christmas is only twenty days away."

"That's twenty days that I have to pick something out. Don't worry about it. Mom will have an appropriate gift from me. Come on, Susan. I need to get going here." She pushed her sister's arm out of the way of the doors.

"Just don't forget to be at Mom's next Friday for dinner. You promised."

The Jeep wound its way up Madison Avenue just as a light snow began to fall. Ronnie remembered her promise to bring a Trivial Pursuit game with her, but the darkening clouds and the late hour made her decide to forgo a trip to the mall to pick one up in favor of getting to the hospital before it got too much later.

She walked through the open door to Rose's room only to find the bed empty, an orderly changing the sheets. "Where's Miss Grayson?"

"X-ray. They'll be bringing her back in a few minutes," the burly man replied, tucking the last corner in. Ronnie went to the chair in the nearby corner and sat down to wait for the young woman's return.

Fifteen minutes went by before Rose was wheeled back into her room. The first thing Ronnie noticed were the fresh tears that streamed down the sides of Rose's face. The two orderlies were as careful as they could be with their patient, but Rose still cried out in pain when they switched her from the gurney back to her bed.

"Hey, how ya feeling?" Ronnie asked softly, pulling the stiff plastic chair closer to the bed.

Rose forced a smile to her face at the sight of the raven-haired woman. After a long night of being in agony and an even more grueling morning of having doctors and residents coming in to poke and prod her, the sight of the woman who made her recovery possible was quite welcome. "They took new x-rays of my legs to make sure everything is still lined up right." Her face betrayed her pain as she shifted, and she rubbed her hip. "They're giving me Hepa-something to thin my blood. Dr. Barnes is worried about clotting."

"Did he say anything about how you're doing? I mean, he doesn't foresee any long-term problems, does he?" Ronnie reached over and helped adjust one of the pillows behind Rose's head.

"*She* said we won't know that for weeks."

"What did you think of her? Did she seem competent? If you don't like her, Rose, you just let me know. I'll get you another doctor." The words came out in a rush, and Ronnie was just as surprised as the injured woman. "I mean, if you aren't happy with the way she's treating you, you have the right to ask for another doctor." She hoped her explanation didn't sound as lame to Rose as it did to her.

"No, she's fine, really. I mean, she can't help it if I'm in pain. She said I'm getting the most pain medicine she feels comfortable giving me."

"If you need more—"

"No. Any more makes me so groggy I can't even get a drink of water without spilling it all over myself. It just hurts so much all the time. Even when I'm sleeping, I'll move and the pain is just so strong it wakes me up." She looked down dejectedly at her smashed legs and ankle. "It feels like the pain will never end."

"Rose, it may not seem like it now, but you will get better. It's just going to take time." Ronnie tried to keep her voice as reassuring as possible. "Tabitha is quite the character," she said, hoping that the change in subject would help take Rose's mind off her injuries.

"She's the best thing that ever happened to me," the young woman said honestly. "Whenever I need her, she's right there. All she ever asks for is food and attention."

"And I'm sure you gave her plenty of both."

"Well, the love and attention I can always give her." The green eyes took on a sad look. "Food isn't always as easy." She looked up at the sculptured features of her generous benefactor. "I'm sure she's very happy with you."

"Rose, I haven't taken Tabitha away from you, believe me. I'm only watching her while you're here. Once you're back on your feet, I'll bring her right back to you, I promise."

"I don't know what I'm going to do," she said softly, tears from both the constant pain and the fear of losing her beloved pet clouding her eyes and threatening to spill over. "I can't even take care of myself anymore much less her. I don't even have a place to live."

"That place wasn't fit for a rat to live in. When you get out of here—"

"When I get out of here, I won't be able to walk, I'll have no money, and I won't even have a place to live," Rose snapped. "You should have left me there on the street."

"NO!" Ronnie stood up and leaned over until she was only inches from Rose's face. "Listen to me. You will walk again, and you don't have to worry about finding a place to live. I'm not going to give up on you, so don't you go giving up on yourself. You're a survivor, I know that. Don't let this take that away."

"What am I supposed to do when they release me? It's the fourth already. Cecil would certainly have changed the locks by now. He warned me to never be late with the rent again or he'd lock me out."

"That overgrown bully wouldn't bother changing the locks."

"He did kick me out, didn't he?"

"Yes," Ronnie admitted. "But I wouldn't have let you continue to live there anyway. It's not fit for a human to live in and certainly not you. When they release you from here, they'll probably send you to a rehabilitation center until you can walk again. After that, I'll make sure you get a decent place to live." She returned to her chair and took a deep breath before continuing. "Rose, we both know that you need help and that I want to help. I know you've been taking care of yourself for a long time, but right now you need someone else to look out for you. Please let me be that someone."

The room was quiet for a minute while Rose looked down at her lap, chewing her lower lip. "I haven't had to rely on anyone to take care of me for a long time. I guess I don't have much choice now." Her face betrayed her feeling of failure and the hopelessness of her situation. "This is hard for me. I'd rather go without than take charity."

Ronnie found it hard to believe that it was so difficult for Rose to accept the help being offered when the alternatives were so clear, but when she paused to consider the story that the checkbook told, it made perfect sense. There was a depth to the young woman's character that she wouldn't have believed still existed in the modern age when so many people seemed more than ready to accept anything the state or government offered, whether they deserved it or not. "Don't think of it as charity. I don't."

"What do you think of it as?" she asked curiously. Rose shifted slightly, and another blast of intense pain shot through her legs. "Oh, God, it hurts," she hissed. "It hurts so much." Tears streamed down her face. "Make it stop, please make it stop hurting."

Unable to take the pain away, Ronnie did the only thing she could think of. She sat on the edge of the bed and pulled Rose into a tight embrace, unmindful of the tears that soaked her silk blouse. It didn't matter, nothing mattered except trying to help the incredibly brave young woman get through this. "It's okay, Rose. I've got you," she murmured into the golden hair while her hand gently rubbed up and down the bare back exposed by the hospital gown.

"It hurts…it won't stop hurting…oh, God, please make it stop, make it stop hurting so much," Rose sobbed, her grip around Ronnie's neck tightening. The strong arms wrapped around her offered comfort, something that had almost never been offered to the young woman before, and Rose accepted it gratefully.

"I'm sorry, Rose, I'm so sorry," Ronnie whispered over and over, feeling her own emotions threatening to come forth in empathy for the young woman's pain, pain caused by her actions on that fateful night. "It's gonna be all right. Shh…okay now, it's all right." She continued to make shushing noises and hold Rose as the sobbing continued. Mercifully, the nurse arrived a few minutes later and gave the injured woman enough medication to bring on an uneasy sleep. Ronnie remained for quite a while after, watching Rose sleep and wishing there was something—anything—that she could do to remove the damage she had done.

Chapter Four

Rose awoke several hours later to find herself alone. She pressed the call button for the nurse.

"What do you need, deary?" The dark-skinned woman asked as she entered.

"Nothing really, "Rose replied, embarrassed about having pressed the button just to see another face. It had been four days since she was brought in, and the only people she ever saw were hospital personnel and Ronnie.

"Well, I'm glad you're awake," the nurse replied. "It's time to check your vitals."

"Do you know what time Miss Cartwright left?"

"Would that be your friend who was here earlier?" Rose nodded. "She left shortly after I went on duty, so I'd say about an hour or so ago. She left you a note."

It was only then that Rose saw the cream-colored paper folded in half sitting on her bed tray. She reached for it, but her arms weren't long enough. The nurse handed it to her before wrapping the black blood pressure cuff around her upper arm. Rose let the note lay on her chest until the nurse was done, preferring to read it in private. She grimaced as the cuff constricted more and more around her small arm. When she thought it couldn't possibly get any tighter, she heard the hiss of the air being released. "Fine. Your pressure is good, and your temperature is normal. At this rate, you'll be out of here in no time." The nurse removed the Velcro-fastened cuff and made a notation on the chart. "Your dinner will be here shortly, and I'll be back later to check on you."

"Thank you." Rose smiled, she had been put back on solid food the day before, and her appetite had returned stronger than ever.

Once the nurse was gone, Rose picked up the note and unfolded it. There on Cartwright letterhead was a note from Ronnie.

Rose,

*I had to return to the office to take care of a few things.
I'll be back to see you later. Try to rest, and don't be afraid
to ask for more painkillers if you need them. Leave some
room after dinner. I hope you like Chinese food.*

Ronnie

The young woman's fingers slid over the textured paper. Where
her own handwriting was small and neat, Ronnie's was full of
flourish and style. She grinned at the comment about leaving room
after dinner. When it came to Chinese food, Rose knew she could
always eat everything in front of her and then some. She pressed the
remote for the television, once again silently grateful to her
benefactor, then took the plastic comb off the table and ran it through
her thick golden hair, trying to make herself look more presentable to
her new friend. "My friend," she said aloud, smiling at the thought.
She thought about the way she had cried so hard earlier and how
good it felt to be held by Ronnie. In her arms, she felt safe, cared for,
comforted. Strangely, Rose found herself wishing for that feeling
again, to be held in those strong arms, to smell the light scent of
perfume on the tall woman's tanned neck, to feel the compassion and
tenderness within her touch and voice. Rose still didn't understand
why Ronnie chose to befriend her, but she was grateful that she did.

Wheel of Fortune was halfway over when Rose was treated to the
sight of Ronnie entering the room, a small bag full of delightfully
smelling food in one hand, the ever present attaché in the other. "Hi
there."

"Hi," the young woman replied, happily sniffing the air as
Ronnie set the bag on the bed tray and took her usual seat next to the
bed, her leather bomber jacket tossed haphazardly across the back of
the chair. "Smells wonderful."

"Did you save room? I've got shrimp chow mein and boneless
barbecued spare ribs," she said while pulling the white boxes out of
the bag along with two sets of plastic utensils.

"When it comes to Chinese, I always have room," Rose replied,
taking the fork offered to her. Her legs were throbbing, but somehow
the pain seemed to be diminished by the presence of her new friend.
The cost of eating out was not in her meager budget, and she had
been happily anticipating this treat ever since reading Ronnie's note
that afternoon.

"I didn't get any bowls or plates, so we'll just have to share," Ronnie said as she opened the boxes to reveal steaming hot food. "I didn't know what you liked, but I figured I couldn't go wrong with the ribs."

"I've never had shrimp chow mein, but yeah, the ribs won't last long." Her fork was already headed for the box.

"Oh, you'll have to try it. It's really good." She pulled out a forkful of the chow mein and put it into her mouth, drawing air in at the same time to try and counteract the burning hot temperature of the food.

Rose was busily pushing the small pieces of meat into her mouth, humming with delight.

"Oh, this is sooo good," she mumbled around the mouthful of pork. "Thank you."

"You're welcome. We've even got fortune cookies for dessert. I knew I wouldn't have time to stop anywhere for dinner, so I figured I'd pick some up and have it here."

"I'm glad you did." Rose pulled the box of chow mein close to her mouth and pulled out a forkful of vegetables and shrimp. "This is delicious."

"Told you." Ronnie smiled, pleased that her choices were so well received. "Did you rest well? I'm sorry I had to leave, but I had some matters to take care of at the office."

"Is everything all right? Helping me isn't causing any problems, is it?" Rose asked with concern, not wanting to do anything to add stress to her new friend.

"No, Rose, my problems are with one of the divisions." She set her fork down and gave a polite burp. "Oh, that was good. I've forgotten how tasty Chinese food is." The theme music for *Jeopardy!* began on the television, followed by the host introducing the contestants. "You didn't answer me. Did you have a good rest?"

"Yes, I slept very well, thanks." She turned to catch the deep blue eyes of the older woman. "Thanks for staying until I fell asleep."

Their picnic was interrupted by the nurse returning. She took one look at the two empty boxes and the guilty looks on the women's faces and frowned. "You really shouldn't be bringing food into the hospital," she chastised. "Miss Grayson, you're not on any special diets, are you?"

"No. I'm sorry, I asked her to bring it," Rose said, trying to take the blame.

"In the future, you really should stick to the food we serve. Our nutritionists work hard to design a meal–"

"Who is Abraham Lincoln?" Rose blurted, her attention on the show and not on the lecture she was receiving.

"Nah, it was Johnson."

"No. He didn't take office in February, he took it in April." The host verified that Rose's reply was correct, complete with the dates that the presidential succession took place. The nurse looked at the two women focused on the television and gave up her attempt to explain why the Chinese food wasn't as good for a patient as hospital food. She left the room knowing full well where she was going to go on her dinner break.

Just as the theme music was ending, the announcement came over the loudspeakers that visiting hours were over. "I guess that's my cue to leave," Ronnie said reluctantly. "I'll see you tomorrow." She stood and picked up her jacket. "Oh, I almost forgot." She reached into the pocket and pulled out a business card and pen. "Let me leave you my number in case you want to call or if you want me to bring you anything." She scribbled her home and cell phone numbers down on the back of the card and set it on the bed tray before picking up the empty food boxes and bag. "Really, if you want or need anything, just give me a call. I'm usually up until eleven." She smoothed an imaginary wrinkle on the blanket before donning her bomber jacket. "Rest well, Rose. I'll see you tomorrow."

"I don't want to keep you from your work."

"Trust me, I'd much rather be here than there. I'll be by sometime after breakfast. Remember what I said. Call me whenever you want to, even if it's just to talk." Just to be sure, Ronnie pushed the phone a bit closer on the side table.

"Thanks. Good night, Ronnie. Drive carefully."

Rose didn't notice the look that flashed across Ronnie's face before being covered up with a fake smile.

"Good night, Rose."

Ronnie was curled up in bed, Tabitha lying next to her, when the phone rang. A quick glance at the clock told her that it was almost eleven. "Hello?"

"Um...hi, it's Rose. I hope I'm not calling too late."

"No, no, it's not too late at all." She sat up, much to Tabitha's displeasure. "You okay?"

"Yeah, I um…I guess I just wanted to…see how Tabitha was" came the lame excuse. Ronnie smiled, propping a pillow behind her back and leaning against the oak headboard.

"The purr machine is fine. You want to say hi to her? She seems to think that wherever I am is a good place for her to be." Without waiting for an answer, she put the phone near the cat. "Say hi to Mommy, Tabitha." She held it there for a few seconds before putting the receiver back to her ear. "Did you hear her purring?"

"Yeah."

Ronnie could feel the smile through the phone and in turn smiled herself. "Is there anything you want me to bring tomorrow? I'll probably be there around ten or so."

"If it wouldn't be too much trouble, do you think you could check my mail for me?"

"Damn, I completely forgot about that. I'll have to stop at the post office and put a forwarding address in for you before that jerk Cecil starts going through your mail."

"Oh…I don't know where you could have it forwarded to."

"I'll take care of it, don't worry. But yeah, I'll swing by there tomorrow and see if you've gotten anything."

"I'd really appreciate it." There was a momentary silence before Rose continued. "Ronnie?"

"Yeah?"

"Um…sleep well, okay?" Ronnie smiled again.

"You too, Rose. I'll see you in the morning."

"Good night."

"Night." She waited a few seconds before pushing the off button on the phone and putting it back in the charger on her nightstand. Tabitha crawled onto her chest and tried to imprint her paw marks on Ronnie's internal organs. "Oof, I don't think so, missy," she said, gently pushing the cat back onto the bed and receiving a dejected meow in response. "Come on, I've got a lot of things to take care of tomorrow. It's a huge bed. There's plenty of room without you having to be right on top of me." She fell asleep with the purring feline curled up against her.

The alarm went off at six as usual, announcing the start to Ronnie's day. "Mrrow?"

"In a minute," she replied sleepily, throwing the blankets off and sticking her feet into the soft blue slippers waiting next to the bed. With eyes half closed, she trudged into her bathroom. Returning a few minutes later, teeth brushed and bladder emptied, she donned her light gray spandex workout suit with matching shorts that hung down to mid-thigh and headed for the basement.

Ronnie's private gym would be the envy of any fitness junkie. With the exception of the room that held the furnace and water heater, the rest of the basement was devoted to her myriad benches, machines, and mats. Growing up in the house that was now hers and hers alone, Ronnie had often dreamed of renovating the once musty basement into a place where she could just be herself, pumping iron and working up a healthy sweat. Her goal was accomplished with the private gym. The room was brightly lit from the overhead fluorescents, enhanced by the walls of mirrors. She grabbed a fresh towel from the shelf, turned on the stereo, and headed for the stair climber to get warmed up.

Duran Duran blared through the speakers placed throughout the large room while Ronnie pushed her calves and thighs to the limits on the stair climber. In her own private haven, no one could hear her singing to the music, see the sweat forming on her brow, neck and chest, or notice the way she pushed herself. She prided herself on her fit body and strength, but both required constant maintenance. Twenty minutes climbing stairs that never went anywhere and she moved on to the next piece of equipment, taking the time to tie her hair up to keep it off her face and the back of her neck. She checked the amount of weights on the bar before lying down on the bench, pulling the bar off its rest and bringing it down to her chest. She wiggled her fingers to make certain her hands were in the proper position and began her grueling repetition, pushing the barbell up to maximum height before lowering it back down to her chest. Then it was off to the leg press, the crunch machine for her abdominals, the forearm grips, then the skiing machine for a good all-over workout. By the time the CD was finished, Ronnie was a mass of well-earned sweat and muscles that begged for a break. She threw the soaked towel into the hamper near the door and made her way back to her bedroom where she peeled the sweat-covered spandex from her body and entered her bathroom. Her showerhead sent pulses of hot water against her body, massaging while cleaning. Ten minutes with the hair dryer and Ronnie was refreshed and ready to face whatever the day had to offer.

The bright blue Cherokee made its way up the narrow Albany streets, fighting the rest of the Friday morning traffic. Ronnie found a parking space on Morris Street and carefully made her way up the stairs to retrieve Rose's mail. She picked through it, planning on leaving the junk mail for Cecil to deal with when one small envelope caught her attention. She tucked it into the inside pocket of her bomber jacket and returned to the warmth of her car. Only then did she pull it out and examine the return address. D. Bickering, RR 3 Box 4120, Cobleskill. Cobleskill was a small village over an hour away from Albany, known more for its agricultural college than anything else. It was thought of as being mostly farmland, although there were a fair number of residents in the area. The overwhelming majority of people there were either farmers or those who were willing to travel forty minutes or more to get to work each day. Ronnie shoved the letter back into her pocket and put the Jeep into gear, determined to get to the hospital and hand the letter to Rose before the urge to go home and steam the envelope open got the best of her. She desperately wanted to know how the mysterious Delores Bickering fit into Rose's life and why the young woman with no money was writing checks to this person.

Ronnie arrived to find the nurse at Rose's bedside. As expected, the young woman's face showed the pain that the drugs couldn't completely erase. "Hey, you," she said softly, drawing Rose's attention from the nurse to her.

"Hi, looks like it's snowing again."

"Just a little," Ronnie replied, brushing the melting flakes off her dark hair and the shoulders of her soft brown jacket. "Should I come back in a little while?"

"I'm almost done," the nurse said without looking up from her task. She stood and made several notations on Rose's chart. "There. All finished for now." She peeled off the latex gloves and threw them into the red waste container. "Dr. Barnes will be in to see you in a little while," she said before leaving the two women alone.

Curiosity won out the instant they were alone. Ronnie pulled the envelope out of her pocket and handed it to Rose. "Here's your mail."

The smile that had been on the young woman's face melted at the sight of the writing on the envelope. She opened it and read the words written on spiral bound notebook paper while Ronnie hung her coat over the back of the chair, set her attaché down on the floor, and took her usual seat next to the bed. Rose was quiet as she finished reading the letter and put it back into the envelope. "Could you do me a favor and bring me my checkbook tomorrow?"

"Is something wrong? Anything I can help with?"

"No, it's just something I have to take care of." She couldn't bring herself to meet the piercing blue eyes looking at her. "I hate to ask, but could you spare an envelope and a stamp, too?"

"Of course, Rose," Ronnie replied, still dying with curiosity about the contents of the letter. "Look…if you have a debt that you need help paying…." She regretted the words instantly, thinking that her new friend would be offended.

"No, it's not that. It's from someone I used to live with." Rose's head never lifted up, and her whole mannerism changed, withdrawing into herself.

"A boyfriend?"

"A foster mother. I lived with her for about two years. She took care of me when no one else would." Rose's shoulders slumped, and she let out a defeated sigh. "She's had a hard time since the state took all the kids she was caring for away. You don't want to hear about this," she said, giving Ronnie a way out if she wanted it.

"Sure I do." Ronnie reached over to clasp the smaller hand. "That letter seemed to really bother you. Care to share?" She expected Rose to elaborate a little about Delores but was surprised to find the letter pushed into her hand.

"I think that pretty much will explain everything."

Ronnie looked at Rose before opening the envelope and reading the letter.

Rose,

I haven't heard from you for a while. Things are really hard here. I can barely keep a roof over my head much less anything else. The idiots at social services don't understand anything I tell them. I know you're busy with your life and don't have time for an old lady like me, but you have to remember that I took care of you when no one else would. I opened my home to you, put food in your stomach, and made sure you got to go to school. I hate to ask, but I really need more than what you've been sending. You know it costs a lot to feed someone else's kid. Without me, you would have starved. I was there when you needed someone to take care of you. I'll be looking forward to whatever pit…pittnce…whatever little amount you can send me.

Your Auntie Delores

Ronnie folded the note back up and shoved it into the envelope, trying hard to keep her temper in check. She set the envelope down on the tray and gripped the side rails of the bed with both hands so tightly that her knuckles turned white. She took several breaths to try and calm down before feeling the green eyes looking at her expectantly. "You don't owe her, Rose," she said through gritted teeth, unable to bring her head up to meet the gaze.

"I feel like I do," the young woman said sadly. "When I was living with her, there were four of us. She always made it clear that the state didn't give her enough to take care of us."

"Bullshit." The executive flew out of her seat and stormed over to the window, looking out at the falling snow. "I have no right to tell you what to do with your money, but she's just using you, playing on your sympathy. As long as you keep giving her money, money that you can't afford to spare, she'll just keep coming back for more." She turned to look at Rose.

"She didn't even thank you for the money you've sent so far, she just said that you needed to send more. She's guilting you into giving her money. Whatever debt you think you owe her, it's been paid long ago. Now she's just sucking you dry." She returned to her seat and lowered her voice, not wanting to upset Rose any more than she was. "She didn't ask how you were doing, not even one kind word. That letter was nothing more than 'send me money.' You don't deserve to have your kindness taken advantage of like that. You're too good a person to be treated like that."

"She's the closest thing I have to family," the young woman protested, albeit weakly. She had never shared this problem with anyone else before and was surprised to see her friend's reaction. Rose had heard for so long about how she owed Delores for taking care of her that she believed it to be a debt that she'd never be able to repay, regardless of her own personal feelings about it. To have someone voice the feelings that had been buried deep inside her was something she didn't expect.

"You don't need family like that. You deserve better," Ronnie said. She gave a resigned sigh. "I told you I would bring you your checkbook, and I will. I'll also bring you the stamp and envelope, but I really wish you'd think about this before you send her any more money." She reached out and took Rose's hand in her own. "Promise me that you'll give this some thought first, okay?"

"I will," Rose said, drawing a smile from Ronnie. "Let's talk about something else instead, okay?"

"Sure, name it."

"Why don't you tell me about your family? I'd love to hear about them."

"It's not as interesting as you might think." Ronnie was going to try and worm her way out of it, but the expectant look on Rose's face changed her mind. "All right, but I'll warn you, it's pretty boring." She shifted in her seat, wishing she was in jeans instead of her dress slacks. "I'm the oldest of three. There's me, Susan, and Tommy. Susan is the complete opposite of me. She runs Cartwright Insurance. She's married to Jack; he's a lawyer downtown." She grinned as if sharing some big secret. "Susan wears more makeup than Tammy Faye Bakker, and she thinks she's a knockout. But she can add numbers in her head faster than a calculator and brought the insurance division up from average earnings to being one of our leading revenue producers. I have to warn you, though, don't ever let her catch you alone at a party. My sister is the biggest gatherer of gossip and information in the state. Once she gets hold of you, she won't let go until she knows everything down to your blood type."

"What about your brother?" Rose asked, watching as the smile left Ronnie's face.

"Tommy's a lost soul. He's twenty-five, but he still acts like a teenager. It took him six years and three colleges to get his bachelor's degree because he wouldn't apply himself. The family insisted when he finally got his degree that I put him in charge of something, so I gave him the real estate division." She sighed. "I figured it was doing so well that he couldn't do anything to mess it up. Now we're posting the worst growth since the recession, and he acts like it doesn't matter. That's why I had to go back to the office yesterday. I hate irresponsibility."

Their conversation was interrupted by the arrival of Dr. Barnes. "How are you today, Miss Grayson?" she asked.

"Same as yesterday, I guess," Rose replied. "Oh, Dr. Barnes, this is my friend Ronnie. Ronnie, this is Dr. Barnes." She didn't see the smile form on Ronnie's face at the title bestowed on her.

"Hello," the shorter woman said. She looked at Rose's chart for a moment and made a notation. "Well, Miss Grayson, it looks like everything is healing up just fine." She set the chart down and moved to the head of the bed to check the stitches on Rose's cheek. "The bones are properly set, and I see no reason why you can't go home."

"Home? But...." She looked fearfully to Ronnie for help.

"How can you send her home? She can't even walk yet," Ronnie said, falling into the role of protector easily. It seemed a natural thing to do when it came to Rose.

"Look, Miss–"

"Cartwright, Veronica Cartwright."

"Miss Cartwright," the doctor said, unimpressed with the tall woman's name. "There's nothing more that we can do for her right now. Her body is reacting well to the treatment. There's nothing more to do except wait for the bones to heal."

"But she can't walk yet," Ronnie protested.

"She won't be able to walk for a very long time," the doctor replied. "There's no sign of infection, the thinning agents have kept any clots from forming, and the swelling has gone down to an acceptable level. At this point, there's nothing else the hospital can do except give her a bed. I'll write her a prescription for the pain, and she should come back next Friday to have the stitches on her face removed. At that time, I'll look at her legs and ankle, then we'll see where we go from there."

Rose's breathing increased, and she looked ready to cry. Ronnie quickly leaned over the bed, blocking the young woman's view of the bearer of bad news. "Rose," she whispered, "let me take care of this. I promise everything will be okay."

"I can't...I don't–"

"Shh, let me handle this. Trust me." She spoke softly, as if calming a small child. "Do you trust me?" She received a shaky nod. "I promise everything will be fine."

"But–"

"Trust me, Rose." She maintained her gaze, letting deep blue search out and calm green, silently trying to convey that everything would be all right.

Finally, the younger woman let out a heavy breath and nodded, placing her life in the hands of the woman who seemed so willing to help her. As scary as the prospect seemed, there was a comfort in knowing that Ronnie was there for her.

"What do I need to know about caring for her?" Ronnie asked, turning her attention to the doctor.

"I'll have the nurse show you how to properly bathe her to prevent infections. I suggest you get a home health aide or a private nurse if you can afford it." That comment earned a raised eyebrow from the woman who donated six figures to the hospital last year. The doctor made another notation on the chart. "I'll have an instruction sheet prepared to explain exactly what needs to be done each day."

"Fine," Ronnie said, her mind already figuring out which room would be turned into a recovery room. It was an unexpected turn of events but one that she would handle. She dimly noted that it wasn't guilt that was making her open up her sanctuary to Rose, it was something stronger—concern and caring. Somewhere in the course of trying to make up for her mistake, she had begun to care. "Whatever it takes to make her better."

"I'll have the nurse give you all the details. I'll sign the discharge papers before I start the rest of my rounds." She turned to look at her patient. "I'm sorry, Miss Grayson, I've heard you've become rather fond of our food." Her attempt at humor wasn't received as well as she hoped, earning only a weak smile. "Well, if there was a way I could justify keeping you here, I would."

"I know," Rose replied. "Thank you."

"Don't forget to make an appointment with our outpatient clinic to have those stitches removed next Friday. Make certain they schedule the appointment with me and not with one of the physician's assistants. I want to take a look at those legs, too."

"I will."

"I'll take care of it," Ronnie said firmly, leaving no doubt in the young doctor's mind that her patient would be well taken care of.

Chapter Five

After the nurse gave her the necessary info, Ronnie pulled out her phone and started making arrangements for taking Rose home. She called a surgical supply company to purchase a hospital bed, wheelchair, and various other things that the nurse insisted were necessary for Rose to recuperate properly. But no matter how hard she tried, Ronnie was unable to get them to deliver the bed that day. In frustration, she told them to just deliver the other items and called several furniture stores until she found one that sold adjustable beds. Even that one took some work to convince them to send a truck out with it that day. Then she had to call Maria to let her know what was going on. She explained to her trusted housekeeper which room they were to go in and what items needed to be moved to make room for the new furniture. The next call had been to a private ambulance service to arrange for transportation from the hospital to her house for Rose. The remaining calls had been to the various agencies in an attempt to get a private nurse to come in on a long-term, full-time basis, then back to Maria again to fill her in on the latest developments.

"Ronnie?" Rose called gently, drawing the tall woman's attention.

"I've got to go, Maria. Call me if there are any problems." She hung the phone up and sat on the edge of the bed. "I guess everything's ready. Now we're just waiting for the ambulance to arrive." She took her usual seat next to the bed.

"I don't know how to thank you," Rose whispered, her voice cracking with emotion.

"Shh...you don't need to be worrying about things like that."

"But no one's ever...I mean, it's so much...." Her eyes welled up with the heartfelt feeling.

"Hey, it's no problem, remember? I promised that I'd take care of you." Ronnie reached out and caught a tear before it fell down the cherubic face. "Hey, none of that. Tabitha misses you, and this is the perfect way to make sure that she has someone else to get her attention from so I can get some work done." She received the barest of smiles, but it was better than more tears. "Besides, I've been alone for a long time. It'll be nice to have the company."

As much as Ronnie wanted to ride in the ambulance with Rose to provide her comfort, there was the Jeep to consider, and the idea of leaving it in Albany overnight was an unpleasant one. She hadn't gone near the Porsche since the accident, although she did notice that Hans had been over the day before to start the repairs. That left her with either the vehicle that did well in the snow or her prized 1967 Mustang to get around with, and the Mustang would never see the salted winter roads of Albany if she could help it. Reluctantly, she chose to let Rose ride alone in the ambulance while she followed behind in the Jeep.

The ride to her home was the most agonizing drive of Ronnie's life. The roads were typical of early December; slush and ice chunks made the ride bumpy enough, but with the added factor of potholes, the ambulance found itself bouncing around far more than usual. Knowing that every bump meant pain for Rose, Ronnie yelped when the ambulance hit a particularly large pothole just as they were leaving Albany and crossing over into Loudonville where her home was located. The green and white ambulance bounced and shook over the uneven road, turning Ronnie into a nervous wreck before they finally hit the smooth streets of her hometown and turned onto Cartwright Drive.

Maria opened the door and stepped out just as the ambulance pulled up the driveway, followed close behind by the bright blue Jeep. Normally, Ronnie would use her remote to open the appropriate garage door and put her vehicle away, but she had something more important to do and therefore parked in the large area in front of the garages and waited for the back doors of the ambulance to open. She did her best to stay out of the way as they brought Rose out, noting that beyond a few tear streaks, she seemed to be no worse for the wear. "And I thought the hospital was cold," the young woman commented, the threadbare blanket and sheet doing nothing to stop the biting wind that had picked up.

"Don't worry, you'll be inside and toasty warm soon enough," Ronnie replied, noticing out of the corner of her eye that Maria had the double doors open to give them maximum room to get through with the stretcher and its precious cargo.

Flat on her back, the first thing Rose noticed when they entered the large structure was the high ceiling, dark beams against a cream-colored background. She turned her head, and her eyes widened at the sights. The living room was huge, easily larger than her whole apartment had been. When she felt the change in height, she realized that part of the living room was sunken, something she had seen in magazines at the library but never believed truly existed in someone's home. The wall-to-wall carpeting was the same cream color as the ceiling, thick and plush without a single sign of matting or wear. Large dark wood cabinets lined one wall; Rose guessed them to be either cherry or mahogany. A set of stairs took up another wall. They reminded her of the stairs from the television show *The Brady Bunch* except that instead of having a lower landing, these stairs curved around at the bottom. The railing was also the same deep color as the cabinets and ceiling beams. Maria stepped into her line of vision, and Rose got her first real glimpse of the housekeeper. "Hello."

"Well, hello there, you poor thing," the salt and pepper-haired woman replied.

"My name is Rose." She held her out her hand.

"I'm Maria, child," the housekeeper replied, taking the offered hand and shaking it. "Once you're settled in, I'll make you something good to eat. I'm sure you're sick of that awful hospital food."

"That's very kind of you, but I don't want you to go to any trouble."

"Oh, it's no trouble at all."

"Maria is an outstanding cook," Ronnie said. "You'll think you've died and gone to heaven."

"Ronnie, can you do me a favor?" Rose asked.

"Sure, what is it?"

"Can you cover my feet? They're freezing." A second later, Rose felt large warm hands clasp around her ice cold toes, the only part of her lower extremities not encased in a plaster cast.

"Why didn't you say something?" Ronnie looked up and glared at the ambulance attendants while adjusting the sheet and blanket to cover the exposed feet. "We'll get you in bed, then I'll run upstairs and get you a pair of nice warm socks."

It only took a quick look around for Rose to realize that the room she was being put into was Ronnie's office. Two tall file cabinets were pressed up against the wall, apparently to make room for the queen-sized bed sitting in the middle of the room. A computer desk with the largest monitor she had ever seen was against a near wall, and an immense television took up the remaining wall where she could see it comfortably. "Okay, Mike, you ready?" the one attendant asked, gathering the sheet beneath Rose in his hands.

"On three," Mike replied. "One…two…three." They easily lifted her up, but in the process of putting her back down, one corner slipped out of his hands, causing the heavily casted right leg to flop down onto the bed. The jolt sent a rush of pain through Rose, and the subsequent yelp brought Ronnie to her side. "Sorry, Miss," Mike said. "We need to roll you onto your side now so we can get the sheet out from under you."

"No," Ronnie said. "I'll get it." There clearly was anger in her tone, as well as concern that Rose not be injured any worse. With infinite care, she worked the sheet out from under the young woman until it finally came free. She tossed it to Mike's partner. "Is there something I need to sign?"

"No, ma'am. You'll receive a bill from us in a few days."

"Fine. Is there anything else?" Without waiting for an answer, she nodded at Maria, who was standing in the doorway. "Maria will see you to the door."

"It was an accident," Rose said once the attendants were gone. Ronnie was busily reviewing the instructions on how to operate the new bed.

"It was a stupid accident. He should have been more careful. What if you weren't over the bed?" She reached down and wrapped her hand over Rose's cold toes. "Let me get some socks for you. I'll be right back. Do you want anything from the kitchen?"

"No, thank you. I can wait until dinner."

"Uh-huh. Well, I know I could use a cup of coffee. Do you want something warm or cold to drink?"

"Um…." The look in the deep blue eyes told her that she'd better pick one or the other. "Warm, please."

"Here's the controller for the bed." She handed the white plastic device to Rose along with the instruction booklet. "It comes with heat and massage. Just press these buttons if you want to turn them on. These control the foot and the head of the bed." She watched as Rose experimented, raising the head up until she was at a forty-five-degree angle. "I'll let you get used to it, and I'll be right back with those socks."

Ronnie returned a few minutes later with a pair of thick white tube socks and a purring pile of orange and white fluff. "Look who I found hiding in the mud room," she said, setting Tabitha down on the bed and smiling when she saw Rose's arms wrap around her precious kitty.

"Hi, honey...I missed you," the young woman cooed to her contented cat. "You've gained weight."

"Mrrow?"

"Did you miss me?" She hugged Tabitha again, unmindful of the tears that spilled from her eyes. "Thank you," she whispered to Ronnie. "Thank you so much for taking care of her for me. I can't tell you how much...." Her voice broke off, and she gave up trying to speak.

"I know," Ronnie said softly. "And you're welcome." A week ago, she wouldn't have believed that it could mean so much to anyone to have their pet taken care of, but now Ronnie understood just how important the four-legged feline was to Rose. "Hey, let's get these socks on you." She moved down to the end of the bed, still watching the tearful reunion between Rose and Tabitha. "These were the warmest I could find," she said, untucking the blanket. She gathered the cotton material in her fingers and carefully slid it over the small toes of Rose's feet and the cast-covered foot and ankle. With the heel in place, the toe portion of the socks flopped over, clearly showing the difference in the sizes of the two women's feet. "Sorry about that. I'll get you some socks that fit you tomorrow."

"You don't have to do that, Ronnie. These will be fine. That is, if you don't mind me wearing your socks. Besides, they have to be big, or they won't fit over the cast." The heat emanating from the bed took more than just the chill out of Rose, it eased the pain in her legs and relaxed her to the point where her eyelids felt heavy and she was unable to stifle a yawn. "Would you mind if I rested for a little while?"

"Of course not. Rose, if you're tired, you just tell me." Ronnie looked over at the computer, groaning inside at the thought of the work that had been piling up all week waiting for her. "Will the keyboard bother you if I go and do some work?"

"Oh, no, go right ahead. It won't bother me at all." Rose didn't know if it would or not, but she wasn't about to tell Ronnie that she couldn't do her work in her own office in her own home.

Sleep didn't come easily for Rose, however. The clickity-clack of the keyboard drew her attention to the raven-haired woman working hard only a few feet away. There were computers at the public library, and she knew how to use them to look up the location of books but little else. Even from this distance, she could see that Ronnie was looking over some kind of spreadsheet. Though the sculptured face was away from her, Rose had no doubt that the head of Cartwright Corporation was frowning. A pencil with the end well chewed found its way into Ronnie's mouth again and again. When it wasn't being gnawed at, it was being bounced up and down on the desk, an apparent nervous habit. Every so often, an expletive would spew forth from the well-cultured woman's mouth, and the screen on the computer would change from one spreadsheet to another. Ronnie stood up and walked over to the file cabinets, pulling out wads of computer-generated reports. "What the hell are you doing, Tommy?" she asked the air before returning to her seat and comparing the information on the paper to what the screen was telling her. Through half-closed eyelids, Rose continued to watch her new friend struggle to make sense of what she was looking at. Several times, Ronnie leaned back in her leather chair and let out a frustrated sigh. It was those times that Rose could see her face, brow furrowed with thought, lips pursed, jaw clenched. The young woman finally fell asleep wishing that she could do something to ease Ronnie's problems the way the gentle woman had eased hers.

Ronnie shut the monitor off and turned in her seat to find that Rose had finally fallen asleep, Tabitha by her side. The orange and white feline was busily cleaning her paws and didn't even bother to look up when she left the room.

"How is the poor dear?" Maria asked when Ronnie entered the kitchen.

"She's sleeping right now. I'll wake her up when dinner's ready." She reached into the cupboard and retrieved a glass before taking a beer out of the fridge. "I really appreciate you staying late today to do that."

"Oh, it's no problem at all, Ronnie, you know that," the older woman said. "What happened to her?"

"She was hit by a car. She has no family and no one else to take care of her. She's going to stay here until she's completely healed, and I don't need my mother and sister to know about this," Ronnie warned, wanting to avoid any family discussions.

"I take it she's Tabitha's mother."

"Yeah." She took a sip of beer and sniffed at the oven. "Smells good."

"Uh-huh, and it *will* be good once it's done. Don't even think about sneaking in there and taking any." Maria remembered far too many times when forkfuls of dinner were missing by the time she removed it from the oven. "You didn't tell me what she liked so I made a pot roast."

"Oooh. Sounds wonderful." Ronnie's eyes lit up. "Hope you made plenty." She took another sip of beer and looked around at the rows of cabinets. "Do you know where that tray is that we used when Mom was sick?"

"Of course I do. Unlike you, I know my way around the kitchen."

"Hey, I know where things are. I found the beer with no problem." Ronnie grinned.

"Always the smart ass, aren't you, Veronica Louise?"

"Only with you, Maria," Ronnie replied, leaning over and giving her beloved housekeeper a peck on the cheek. "I'll take dinner in the office with Rose. If you need help, just give me a yell."

"Considering that I served your entire family when everyone lived here, I think taking two dinners into the office won't be a problem." She opened the oven door and poked at the roast and potatoes with a large fork. "Now you go see to your guest. Dinner will be at least another half hour."

Once alone again in the kitchen, the smile left Maria's face. She walked over to the sliding glass doors and peered out into the night. The large sodium lamp illuminated the garage...and the battered Porsche sitting inside it. "Oh, Ronnie..." she whispered. "What have you done?"

"That was delicious," Rose said for the umpteenth time, putting her fork down on the empty plate. "I never cared much for carrots, but those were terrific."

"I think Maria puts some sugar on them while they're cooking," Ronnie replied, removing the tray and setting it on the desk. "You ready for dessert?"

"Dessert?" Green eyes lit up.

"Dessert. I know there are fresh brownies out there, and if I look real hard, there might be some ice cream to go with them." The look of utter delight on Rose's face brought a smile to her own. "You keep that up and Maria will make you as big as a house. Nothing pleases her more than seeing people enjoying her cooking." She glanced at the young woman still in her blue and white hospital gown. "Of course you look like you could use a little meat on your bones, so that might not be such a bad thing. While I'm at it, I'll get you something a little more comfortable to wear than that thing."

"I guess it is a little drafty," Rose replied, tugging the material up over her shoulder.

"I don't have any pants that are big enough to go over those legs, but I'm sure I have a nightshirt somewhere. I'll be right back." She picked up the tray and left the room.

"Meat on my bones?" Rose queried Tabitha once Ronnie left. "I feel like I've gained ten pounds from all the food I've eaten the last few days."

"Mrrow?"

"Yeah, you look like you've been enjoying some of Maria's cooking, too." She grunted when the orange and white cat climbed over her thigh to rest on her lap. "I don't understand it." She scratched absently behind Tabitha's ears while voicing her thoughts. "She finds me on the street, takes me to the hospital, and that should have been it. Instead she takes care of both of us like we were the most important things in the world to her."

"Mrrow?"

"Oh, heaven forbid I stop scratching you, your majesty." She resumed her gentle scratching. "You, I can understand." She lifted Tabitha up to her chest and nuzzled the soft fur. "You're so adorable. Anyone who sees you falls in love with you." She listened to the soft purring for a minute, taking comfort in holding her precious kitty. "Nope, I don't understand it at all. I'm grateful, but I don't understand it."

"Here we go," Ronnie said as she entered the room. Each hand held a dessert plate with a large brownie and a scoop of vanilla ice cream pierced by a spoon, and a pale maroon nightshirt was slung over her shoulder. She set the plates down on the desk and handed the nightshirt to Rose.

"Dartmouth?" the young woman asked, holding the shirt up in front of her.

"I got my bachelor's from there and my master's from Stanford," Ronnie said as she handed one plate to Rose. "It's old and faded, but I still love it."

"What are your degrees in?"

"Mmm, good brownie. Let's see…I have a bachelor's in business administration with a minor in marketing, and my master's is in finance."

"No wonder you're the president of your company."

"Well, that and I'm the oldest," Ronnie grinned. "When it comes to Cartwright Corp., nepotism will get you everywhere."

"I'm sure it took more than that to get you where you are," Rose replied, spooning the tasty dessert into her mouth.

"It did, but if I were with any other company, I'd just be middle management. My father died less than three years after I graduated, and I took over the reins then."

"Were you close to your father?"

"Mmm." She shoved the last piece of brownie into her mouth. "I was the oldest and for a long time, the apple of his eye. You know, it's funny, no matter how busy he was, he always found the time to attend every parent-teacher conference, every play, even made it to all my Little League games. Not many men in his position would do that."

"Sounds like he loved you very much."

"He did. I was a hell-raiser, and he was always trying to keep me out of trouble." Ronnie set her plate down and leaned back in her leather chair. "I remember more than one time when one of Mother's antique vases would get broken with my roughhousing and he would take the blame." She smiled at the memory. "Only once did I get hurt, and he couldn't cover for me. I was sliding down that banister out there and fell off. Broke my arm good. Mother grounded me for the whole summer."

"If you grew up here, why doesn't your mother still live here?"

"Well, after Dad died, she did live here for a while. Eventually, she started spending more and more time with her canasta friends. They all live in a retirement community nearby. She figured that if she was spending all her time there, why not just live there, so we bought her a condo, and I took over the family home."

"Your sister and brother didn't want the house?"

"They didn't have a choice. I'm the oldest. That's how it works in our family. You done with that?"

"Oh, yes, thank you." Rose handed over the now empty plate.

"Besides," Ronnie continued, "Susan and Jack have a nice house a few miles from here, and Tommy seems to prefer apartments. If I hadn't taken it, Mom probably would have put the place up for sale." She stacked the two plates and swiveled around in her chair to face the large-screen television. "So it's almost ten. You tired, or do you want to see what's on?"

"No, I'm awake. That nap earlier helped." Rose shifted and inhaled sharply. "I do think it's time for another pain pill, though."

"I'll get it. You find something for us to watch."

Tabitha was contentedly sleeping next to Rose, who continued to stare up at the ceiling. Ronnie had gone to bed a half hour before, leaving the young woman alone with her thoughts. It surprised Rose to realize just how disappointed she was when her friend announced that she was going to bed. She had truly enjoyed the evening and the constant attention. It also seemed that when Ronnie was around, her legs and ankles didn't ache as much, didn't drive her to tears quite as often. She thought back to what had happened just after they started watching the late news. One wrong move had sent agonizing pain through her, and immediately, Ronnie was there. Ronnie, who held her tight, who whispered comforting words, who gently rocked her. Rose didn't want that embrace to ever end. She wanted to continue to feel the warm skin against hers, to breathe in the scent of Ronnie's perfume, to feel the rise and fall of the strong woman's chest against her cheek. When she did finally let go, it was with great reluctance and with a sense of loss. She adjusted the pillow behind her head and forced her eyes to close, but it did nothing to erase the vision of the beautiful woman.

Upstairs, Ronnie was staring at her own ceiling. She didn't want to leave Rose, but it wouldn't have looked right for her to keep the still recovering woman up too late. She listened to the sounds of the night, the occasional truck going down the main road, the owls hooting in the distance. None of that interested her. What she was listening for was the soft, melodic sound of Rose's voice calling out to her. "Damn, I should have gotten an intercom system," she muttered into the darkness. What if Rose needed help with the bedpan? What if she woke up and needed more Vicodin? Was it safe to leave Tabitha with her? What if she walked across Rose's legs? What if she was in pain again and needed to be held? Those and a dozen more questions passed through her mind, all convincing her that being upstairs wasn't the right place to be. With a sigh, she sat up, grabbed her pillow and blanket, and headed for the downstairs couch. With the office door open to let Tabitha in and out in case she needed to use the litter box, there was no way that she would miss hearing Rose. Yes, that was why she had to be closer to her...just in case she needed anything.

Ronnie was up and about by six o'clock. She returned her bedding to her room and changed into her spandex workout clothes before popping into the office to check on Rose. The young woman was still sleeping soundly, so she felt safe in heading downstairs to get her workout in. However, what normally meant wall-shaking decibels of eighties music was changed to absolute silence lest she miss hearing Rose call out for her. What was normally twenty repetitions with each machine turned into ten, and the skiing machine was ignored altogether. She ran back upstairs and checked on the sleeping woman one more time before going to take a much-needed shower. It was Saturday, which meant there would be no sign of Maria since she had the weekends off. It was up to Ronnie to figure out what to make for herself and Rose for breakfast.

As the steaming water rinsed the shampoo from her hair and the sweat from her body, Ronnie's eyes closed, and her mind drifted back to the fair-haired woman sleeping downstairs. There had been an almost guilty pleasure in holding her the previous night, knowing that she was the one responsible for the pain yet also the one to provide comfort from that pain. Oh, and how she enjoyed holding Rose, burying her nose in the spun gold hair, wrapping her arms around the soft body, feeling the warm breath against her neck....

Ronnie's eyes flew open, and she looked down to discover her soapy hand fondling her left breast. She quickly rinsed off, mentally chastising herself for fantasizing when she had much more important things to do.

Rose awoke to the sound of Ronnie entering the room, two platesful of pancakes and bacon in hand. "I'm not as good a cook as Maria, but at least I didn't burn anything."

"I'm sure it'll be wonderful."

"Do you want coffee or tea?"

"Oh, coffee would be great."

"There's a fresh pot made. Cream and sugar?"

"Just cream please."

"One coffee, cream, no sugar coming right up." She set her plate on the desk and Rose's plate on the tray before placing the tray on the young woman's lap. "We'll have breakfast, then I'll help you get cleaned up. The nurse won't start until Monday, but I think I can help you."

"You know, I really hate feeling helpless like this," Rose said. "I mean, I can't even lean forward without it hurting my legs. If I don't think and wiggle my toes, that's even worse, not to mention the whole bedpan thing." Her cheeks flushed slightly with embarrassment.

Ronnie didn't know what to say to that comment, knowing that if the roles were reversed, she probably wouldn't be as good about the whole situation. "I'll be right back with the coffee, and after breakfast, I'll see if I can find that Trivial Pursuit game." She headed for the door only to be joined by Tabitha.

"Mrrow?"

"And I suppose you want your breakfast, too." She received her reply in the form of the feline rubbing against the leg of her sweatpants. "Come on, if you're eating, that means you won't be bugging your mother for some of hers."

Chapter Six

Although Ronnie had helped Rose the night before with the bedpan, the young woman was still highly self-conscious of having the rich and powerful woman helping her. Not a word was spoken as the pan was slipped under her; she did her duty, and Ronnie took it into the adjoining bathroom. *Well, at least I don't have my period*, Rose thought to herself, dreading the fact that it was only a week or so away. She had no idea how she was going to handle that when it came up.

"All right, I suppose we should get you cleaned up. Do you want a Vicodin now or after?" Ronnie asked when she returned from the bathroom with a basinful of warm soapy water and a cloth.

"After. They put me to sleep too easily. I know I need them for the pain, but I hate feeling so dopey all the time."

Ronnie set the container of warm water on the nightstand. "If I get your back, can you get the rest of it?"

"Yeah." Rose leaned forward and pulled the Dartmouth nightshirt up and off her body, using it to cover her breasts. Firm fingers under the soapy washcloth worked their way across her back, drawing an unexpected groan from her lips.

"Did I hurt you?"

"No, sorry. I guess my back hurts from lying on it so long."

"I used to get the worst cricks in my back after studying all night during finals. My roommate was great at backrubs." Ronnie's mind briefly thought back to some of the other things Christine was good at. "Anyway," she said, pushing the image from her mind, "she showed me what to do. Can you lean forward a little bit more?" The young woman complied, and Ronnie put the washcloth aside. She shifted slightly to get a better position and began kneading the tight muscles with her long fingers.

"Oh, that feels good," Rose murmured sleepily, leaning back into the gentle massage. It seemed that every ache, every stiffness in her back melted away under Ronnie's touch. The soapy water made the strong fingers slide even easier across her skin. "You're in the wrong line of work, Ronnie. You should have been a masseuse."

"Is that so?"

"Oh, yes. You're gonna put me back to sleep if you keep that up."

"Well, we wouldn't want that, now would we?" She picked up the washcloth, wrung it out, and cleaned off the rest of Rose's back. "Okay, I'll leave you to finish up while I look for Trivial Pursuit."

Once Ronnie was out of the room, Rose let the shirt fall to her lap and washed the rest of her upper body and personal areas. She had just finished and started to pull the shirt over her head when her friend returned.

"I found...oh, sorry." Ronnie shut the door quickly. "Let me know when you're ready," she called through the closed door, the sight of Rose's firm breasts teasing her mind. That was one thing she did miss since putting in her own private gym. When she had been going to the local health club, there were lots of good-looking women running around the locker room in various stages of undress. It was easy for her to covertly eye their bodies and enjoy the sights without being noticed. Ronnie let out a sigh of disappointment at what she could not have, could never have again. Her experience at Stanford had seen to that.

"Okay," Rose's voice called out. "You found it?"

"Yeah, sorry about barging in without knocking. I wasn't thinking."

"It's okay. I'm sure you've seen half-naked women before."

"Well, I still should have knocked." Ronnie looked at the small tray. "Hmm...that's not going to be big enough to play on."

"You know, if you put the legs up on that wheelchair, I'm sure I could play at a table with you."

"You think you're ready for that?"

"Well, they put me in one to change the sheets on my bed at the hospital. I'm sure if we're careful, we could do it."

"I don't know, Rose. I don't want to hurt you."

"I'm in pain most of the time anyway. I don't think it'll make much difference." She looked up and smiled. "I really do want to play with you."

"Are you sure about this?"

"I'm sure. Besides, that way you can give me a tour."

Ronnie hesitated for a moment, weighing the dangers of moving Rose and trusting that the young woman knew her limits. "All right, but if you feel tired or want to lie back down, you tell me immediately, okay?"

"Okay."

It required bringing the chair against the bed and pulling Rose into it, but they were able to move her with a minimum amount of discomfort. Fortunately, the renovations Ronnie had done when she took over the house included nice wide doorways. With the exception of the sunken part of the living room, there wasn't anyplace that Rose wouldn't be able to go to on the first floor. "Are you ready for your tour?" Ronnie asked after double checking to make certain that the afghan tucked under the fragile legs wouldn't interfere with the wheels.

"Absolutely," Rose replied, reaching for the wheels only to find that she was already being guided out of the room by Ronnie's hands on the handles. The office was off the living room, and now upright, Rose saw even more of the magnificent area. Classic oil paintings hung on the walls. An antique coatrack stood near the door along with an umbrella stand that looked far too elegant to hold an umbrella, and every piece of furniture matched, from the trim on the leather sofa to the end tables to the cabinets that lined the wall. "It's beautiful," Rose whispered in awe.

"It's pompous," Ronnie replied. "I only leave it this way because I don't want to listen to my family if I changed it. Sometimes we have to have functions here, and I'm sure that the Monet goes over far better than a Witherspoon would." She noted the lack of response from the fair-haired woman. "Witherspoon is an abstract artist. I have some of her works hanging in the game room."

"You have a room just for games?"

"It's a throwback to my father's time. He used to entertain some of his more bawdy friends there. It's got a pool table and a bar, dart board, that kind of stuff. It's over here. I'll show you."

Between the office and kitchen was a door hidden under the stairs. "This is it. I haven't been in here in quite some time, except today when I went looking for the Trivial Pursuit game." Ronnie stopped pushing the chair, stepped in front, and opened the door.

Rose heard a click, and the room lit up with a series of hanging lights, all proclaiming one brand or another of beer as being the best. On the far left wall stood a fully stocked bar. The center of the room sported a claw-footed pool table, and the right end of the room had a few small tables complete with ashtrays. "It's just like a bar."

"Pretty much. Dad used to retreat in here with his friends when he needed a break from the stuffy business world. I learned to play pool right on this table." She ran her fingers across the felt in memory. "During Prohibition, my great-grandfather ran a makeshift speakeasy out of here, just for important clients, of course." She walked to the far wall and pointed at a small buzzer. "This was the warning bell. Grandpa also used it to warn when my grandmother was coming, and years later, my father did the same thing."

"Wow," Rose said, truly amazed at the history of the room. She reached over and ran her fingertips along the smooth wooden side of the pool table. "I'm surprised you don't spend time in here. It seems like a wonderful room."

"It is, but I'm really too busy most of the time to have friends over." Ronnie gripped the handles again. "Ready to see the rest?"

"Sure."

They left the game room and ventured around some more, Ronnie pointing out the mud room that led to the back driveway, the foyer, and the second bathroom on the first floor. They passed into an elegant dining room with a table longer than any Rose had seen before. "You could sit twenty people here," the young woman said.

"Actually, it seats eighteen with the leaf in, but it does look rather large, doesn't it?"

"It's beautiful." The table matched the china closets custom built into each corner, as well as the serving tray, a wooden table with wheels and fold-down side flaps.

"I suppose it is. I never use it except for family get-togethers. I usually eat in the kitchen or in front of the computer. Come on, you haven't seen anything yet."

Their next stop was the kitchen. Ronnie wheeled Rose into the center of the room so she could see everything in one glance. "When I took the house over, this was nothing more than two counters and a few cabinets. Maria and I worked with one of the best kitchen designers in the area to make this."

"It's beautiful. It's just like those kitchens you see in magazines," Rose said. The colossal refrigerator sported light oak panels on the front, matching the rest of the kitchen's decor. A state-of-the-art cook's island sat just off the middle of the room and was complete with a stovetop and sink, as well as a garbage hole and built-in cutting board. Above their heads was a wrought iron rack holding the brilliantly finished copper pots and pans. The opposite end of the room had large sliding glass doors that looked out at the driveway and the garages beyond. The entire kitchen was finished with oak, copper, and steel with lots of light, giving an airy feeling to the area. "What's that door?"

"That leads to the laundry room. It's nothing exciting, I never go in there."

"A room just for laundry? Can I see it? I mean, if it's not too much trouble."

"It's no trouble at all, Rose," Ronnie said, smiling at the obvious approval in the young woman's gaze and voice. She guided them to the medium-sized room. Calling it a laundry room was a bit of an understatement. Beyond the requisite washer and dryer, it also held the ironing board, several shelves to store off-season clothing, a cabinet with everything from fabric softener and detergent to spot removers and dryer sheets, and a counter to sort clothes on.

"This house is amazing. If I lived here, I'd never want to leave." Her eyes widened at the possible ways her statement could be taken. "I mean, it's a really nice place, not that I'd–"

"Relax, Rose, I knew what you meant. I don't like to leave here much myself. That's why everything is designed for my comfort and Maria's, of course." She reached over and shut the light off. "Well, that's it," she said as she wheeled Rose back into the kitchen. "The rest of the place is either upstairs or downstairs, and we're not going to venture there today."

"It's really a beautiful home, Ronnie."

"Thank you. I'm glad you like it," she replied, taking Rose's approval of her home far more seriously than she had taken anyone else's before. "So you up for that game of Trivial Pursuit or what?"

The rest of the morning was spent in the game room where they completed four games of Trivial Pursuit, ending with a tie of two wins apiece.

Shortly after lunch, Ronnie helped Rose back into bed and gave her a pain pill. The morning activities had taken their toll, and she was exhausted.

When Ronnie heard soft, gentle snores, she knelt down next to the bed and watched the steady rise and fall of Rose's chest for a few minutes before tucking the blanket in around her and leaving the room, making certain the door was left ajar.

Rose shook her head groggily and opened her eyes. It was dark out, but with the short days of winter, she couldn't tell if it was five o'clock or eight o'clock. A glance at the red numbers on the alarm told her that it was quarter to six. Her bladder told her that it was time for something else altogether. She sighed at the thought of having to ask Ronnie yet again to help her with the task. Her eyes fell on the bedpan, sitting on the small table next to the bed. It was within arm's reach...perhaps....

Ronnie grabbed another mushroom and began to chop when she heard a bloodcurdling scream. The knife hit the floor as she raced from the kitchen to the office as the screams continued.

"Oh, God...ahhh...." Rose was crying out in agonizing pain when Ronnie stormed in. The young woman had managed to roll onto her side in an attempt to get the bedpan underneath herself, but the heavy cast caused her left leg to drop over the right one and twist, sending intense waves of pain through her ankle. "Oh, God, it hurts!"

Ronnie wasted no time, grabbing the left foot and lifting the leg away from the right one trapped underneath it. She quickly got Rose positioned onto her back again. "What happened?"

"I...I just wanted...." Her words broke off into sobs as she cried helplessly.

"Okay now, okay." Ronnie scrambled up onto the bed and pulled Rose against her with one arm while reaching for the bottle of Vicodin with the other. "I've got you, Rose...it's okay now." The cap to the bottle went flying under the force of her thumb. "Here, take this."

Rose took the pill, followed by a few sips of water to get it down. Her sobs eased up slightly, but her arms remained wrapped firmly around Ronnie's neck.

"What happened?"

"I...I had to go...and...and...."

"Why didn't you ask me? I left the door open so I could hear you." Whatever Rose tried to give for an answer was lost in her sobs, the only words Ronnie could make out were "sorry" and "bother."

"It's okay," she cooed. "I've got you, it's all right."

It was a good ten minutes before she got the young woman calmed down. She worked the bedpan under Rose's hips. "I think we'd better take you back to the hospital so they can make sure that the bones are still lined up."

"I didn't hit it that hard."

"You don't know that, Rose. Even the slightest bit off and you'll have problems walking again, you know that."

"I don't want to go back," she said fearfully. "I'm sorry, please don't make me go back."

"Shh…I'm not making you go back. I just want to make sure you didn't do any damage, that's all." She pulled Rose close again. "I promise we'll only go to get your legs x-rayed, then we'll come back home."

It was almost midnight by the time they returned from the emergency room. Ronnie was annoyed enough at the length of time it took for the ambulance to arrive to take Rose there but was even more pissed off at the hour-and-a-half wait to get a return trip. The thought of purchasing a van just so she wouldn't have to depend on others to help her get the young woman around passed through her mind more than once. Fortunately, nothing was moved out of place, much to both women's relief. Dinner ended up not being the elegant feast that she had planned but leftovers warmed up in the microwave due to the late hour.

Ronnie got Rose settled back into bed and gave her a stern warning about trying a stunt like that again before tucking her in. "I'll be right here on the couch if you need me," she said before shutting off the light and heading for the door.

"Ronnie?"

"Yeah?"

"I'm sorry."

"I know you are, hon, and I know it's gotta be hard for you, but please, just ask for help next time, okay?"

"Okay." There was a pause. "Ronnie?"

"Yeah?"

"It's time."

Ronnie drained the last of her cup of coffee and looked out the window at the morning sun bouncing off the freshly fallen snow. Behind her, Rose continued to sleep soundly, not at all disturbed by the executive's early morning activities on the computer. Ronnie set the empty cup down on the desk and sighed. Three hours of poring over statements and spreadsheets still failed to turn up anything amiss with Cartwright Real Estate. Contractors were paid, receipts were posted, everything looked like business as usual. So why did she feel so strongly that something was terribly wrong? She slumped back into her chair and picked up the report again. The answer had to be there. But instead of returning to the world of ledgers and entries,

Ronnie's eyes drifted over to the bed, where the bright sun cast a glow around the sleeping form. "Just like sunshine," she whispered to herself.

Time ticked by as she continued to silently study Rose. Blue eyes started at the top. They noted the soft honey-colored hair that framed the cherubic face. Reddish-brown eyebrows framed closed lids with naturally curly lashes. A petite, upturned nose rested just above the softest-looking lips. Ronnie's gaze continued downward, past the oversized nightshirt and down to where the curves stopped. Her eyes remained riveted on the broken bones hidden by casts, reminding her just why the beautiful young woman was there. With a mix of guilt and regret, Ronnie turned her chair back to face the desk and buried herself in her work.

The rustling of the bedcovers accompanied by a painful groan announced that Rose was waking up. "Morning," she mumbled, trying to bring green eyes into focus.

"Almost afternoon, actually," Ronnie replied, putting down her work for a moment and turning to face the young woman. "I don't have much to offer in the way of brunch, but if you want, I'll run out and see if I can get some Chinese food."

"Ooh, that sounds wonderful." Rose's eyes lit up as if she were receiving the biggest Christmas present in the world. "I meant to thank you again for bringing that to the hospital."

"It doesn't take much to make you happy, does it?"

The young woman cocked her head from side to side in thought before answering. "No, not really. I never had much money, so extras like takeout food were out of the question."

"How long have you been on your own, Rose?"

"Oh," she blushed. "You don't want to hear about me."

"Sure I do." Ronnie moved her chair closer and propped her stockinged feet on the edge of the bed. "Come on, it'll be like a slumber party."

"I don't know...."

"Come on, Sunshine," she cajoled, realizing that she used a pet name only after she had said it. She shifted and glanced at the window. "It's cold outside. I'll call for delivery, and you can tell me all about Rose Grayson."

"There really isn't that much to tell. Certainly nothing that interesting."

"Let me decide that," Ronnie urged, her eyes pleading with the young woman to open up.

Rose looked down at the blanket for a moment, weighing her options and fears. She felt so safe, so cared for here. What if something she said made her new friend think differently of her? But…there was nothing in Ronnie's eyes to suggest that she would judge anything that was said. Maybe if she skimmed over the details….

"Well, like I said, there really isn't that much to tell. I was almost two years old when my parents died in a car accident. After that, I lived with my grandmother until she got too sick to take care of me anymore." She shrugged her shoulders. "Then I lived in different places until I was old enough to be on my own. That's about it."

"How old were you when your grandmother got sick?"

"Ten."

"She was your only relative?"

"Yeah."

"You know this feels more like an interview than a conversation," Ronnie said, drawing a shy smile from the young woman. "Tell me a story about you. Tell me about something nice that happened to you when you were a child."

"Something nice that happened to me, eh?" Rose pondered the thought for a moment before coming up with a suitable tale. "All right, but first you call for that food you promised."

Ronnie smiled. "Deal."

A few minutes later, the food had been ordered, and it was time for Rose to tell her story. "Okay, it was when I was six or seven. My grandmother came to me early one morning and told me that we were going someplace special. She packed us lunches, and we took the bus for what seemed like hours. We had to switch buses a couple of times before we got there." Rose's eyes gleamed at the memory, and her gaze was many years away from the office in Ronnie's house. "She took me to the zoo. Not the little petting zoos that would come to the bazaars from time to time but a real zoo. There were so many animals…tigers, bears, seals…it was incredible. We spent the whole day there and ate lunch near the cages with the bear cubs." She placed her hand on Ronnie's ankle and leaned in. "My grandmother told me not to feed them, but when she wasn't looking, I threw the rest of my sandwich into their pit."

"Sounds like a really nice day," Ronnie said.

"Oh, it was. It was one of those perfect days when it wasn't too hot or too windy or anything. Grandma even had a roll of dimes to put in the machines to get those pellets to feed the goats." Rose leaned back against her pillow and smiled at the ceiling. "I fell asleep on the way back, so I don't remember much of that, but I do remember how happy I was to be walking home with her from the bus stop."

"Sounds like she loved you very much."

"She did," the young woman replied. "Grandma always found ways to make our time together nice. After the chores were done, we'd always play Monopoly or cards or something like that." Rose's eyes misted, and she blinked back the pain that came with the memory.

"My grandmothers were always scrapping with each other," Ronnie said, hoping that a tale of her own would help keep her friend from thinking of the sad times growing up. "They were both the typical mother-in-law. Grandma Cartwright never thought my mother was good enough, and Grandmother Mitchell thought the same of my dad. You should have seen them at holidays."

"Did you always have a lot of people around on the holidays?"

"Yup, and always here, too, well, until I took over. Now they're held at Susan's house or at one of the cousin's places. But back then, we usually had thirty or forty people here for family get-togethers."

"Wow, it must have been chaos." Rose pressed the remote button for the heating unit built into the bed, hoping it would help ease the steadily growing ache in her legs.

"Chaos is a nice way of putting it. Tradition is a big thing in both families, and of course what was a Cartwright tradition wasn't a Mitchell one. On some holidays, there'd be fights ten minutes after everyone arrived."

"Fights?"

"Oh, not physical ones...usually," Ronnie grinned. "At Christmastime mostly, it would start with what we were having for dinner, then work its way up to how the tree was decorated."

"You're kidding."

"Nope, swear to God." She held her hand up in solemn oath. "Mother's family always waited until Christmas Eve to put the star on the top, but Dad's side would put it up long before that."

"That seems like a silly thing for people to get upset about, especially at a time when they should just be happy to see one another," Rose said, realizing that perhaps Ronnie's family wasn't as perfect as she thought they were.

"Well, maybe because my family saw way too much of each other. They all worked for Cartwright Corp. in one form or another."

"You'd think that would make them closer."

"Sometimes there's too close," Ronnie replied. "It's like a soap opera sometimes. We all know what's going on in one another's lives all the time. There's no real privacy."

"I never thought it could be so difficult. I guess not having a family, I didn't see the downside to having so many people around," Rose admitted.

"I never thought about how lonely it could be being an only child." The two women looked at each other thoughtfully as old ideas blended with newfound truths.

"When I was at Dartmouth," Ronnie began, "I loved the freedom that being away from home gave me. No curfew, no disapproving looks. It felt so good to not have to answer to anyone or worry about my image."

"I bet you were one of those who ended up spending all your time studying and getting the good grades," the young woman ventured.

"Actually, I graduated summa cum laude and was a member of the Honor Society, but I was also a regular at all the good parties. More for appearances and contacts than anything else, but still, if there was something fun going on, I was there. That's not to say that I didn't get into my fair share of trouble. For my sorority's senior prank, we bought a car that had been stripped by car thieves from a junkyard and sneaked over to the dean's house in the middle of the night and switched it for his car. We parked his down the block a little ways, but the look on his face when he came out that morning to get his paper and saw that hunk of junk sitting in his driveway was priceless."

"Oh, God, I bet he was ready to kill you when he found out," Rose said, trying hard not to laugh at the image of the dean looking at what he thought to be his car stripped down to bare metal.

"I have a video of it somewhere, wanna see?"

"Oh, I bet that would be funny."

"I'll get it." Ronnie stood up and headed to the door. "You know, I've got quite a DVD collection. Do you like comedies?"

"Love them."

"I've got a bunch. I'll bring some out, and you can choose what you want to see."

"Sounds great."

Ronnie left the room and returned with a stack of movies for Rose to look through. "I'll go get us something to drink while you decide what we'll watch."

The credits were just beginning when they heard a car coming up the driveway. "Food's here," they said at the same time, drawing mutual chuckles and smiles that would continue long into their lazy Sunday afternoon.

Chapter Seven

Monday came as it always does, forcing attentions to be turned to things of importance besides each other. This particular day also brought with it temperatures in the teens and blowing snow.

Maria was already bustling around the kitchen putting away the groceries she had picked up on the way over when Ronnie came down from her morning shower.

"Looks pretty nasty out there," Ronnie said as she entered the kitchen. "Think maybe I'll take the day off and stay home."

"Did you have a good weekend? I see you certainly left enough dishes for me."

"Actually, I did have a good weekend," Ronnie replied as she crossed the room looking for a fresh cup of coffee. "The roads are pretty nasty, right?"

"Well, they're not the best, but they're drivable."

"But it could get worse." It was more a question than a statement.

"I suppose it could, Ronnie. I didn't really get to see what the weather report said this morning."

"So it could get worse out there." The executive seemed pleased with her reasoning. "I'd better work from home today. Wouldn't want to take the chance."

"Of course not, after all you're what…eight miles from work or so?" Maria opened the refrigerator to survey the damage from the weekend. "Omelets?"

"Sounds good. I'll go check on Rose while you're doing that."

"What would you like in them?"

"I think mushrooms and green peppers…oh, and cheese, of course." Ronnie picked up her coffee cup and headed toward the office, leaving Maria to her tasks and Tabitha to follow around after the housekeeper in hopes of a treat.

Rose was still sleeping when Ronnie entered the office and sent email to her secretary and to Susan announcing that she was going to work from home that day. Rose slept through the sound of the television being turned on and the constant flicking from one station to another. The only thing that brought her out of her dream world was the smell of fresh omelets and muffins when Maria brought breakfast in to them. "Knew something had to wake you."

"Mmm? Oh, morning, Ronnie," she said, wiping the sleep from her eyes. "Morning, Maria, how was your weekend?"

"It was fine, Rose. How was yours?"

"Good." She sniffed the air. "That smells wonderful."

"Maria's cooking is always wonderful. That's why I keep her around," Ronnie teased.

"I knew there had to be some reason," the housekeeper joked back. She turned her attention back to the injured woman. "How are your legs feeling?"

"They ache a lot, but the heat seems to help."

"Good. You just do what the doctor says, and I'm sure you'll be up and about in no time."

"Yeah, as long as she doesn't try to do everything for herself," Ronnie chimed in. "We had to make a trip to the ER this weekend."

"You did? Oh, my!" Maria looked from one to the other. "What happened?"

Ronnie filled the housekeeper in on the incident while Rose savored her meal and added details between forkfuls. The head of the house was just finishing up her breakfast when the doorbell rang. "That must be your nurse," she said to the young woman.

"I'll see to her coat, then bring her in here," Maria said.

A few minutes later, the sandy-haired nurse entered the room. "Good morning. My name is Karen Brown, and I'll be your nurse," she said to Rose.

"Hi, I'm Rose Grayson, and this is Ronnie Cartwright. Pleased to meet you." She held her hand out to the nurse, but Ronnie merely nodded from her chair.

"Well, I suppose the first thing I should do is wash up and take a look at those stitches on your cheek. Are you still on bedpan or are you ambulatory yet?"

"I'm afraid that I'm still on bedpan."

"Well, that's fine." Karen looked up at Ronnie. "How long has she been home?"

Ronnie chose not to correct the nurse about Rose's residence status. "They released her Friday afternoon."

"Have you done any passive therapy?"

"No, but she's been up in the wheelchair a little bit."

"That's not passive therapy," Nurse Brown corrected. "Well then, I suppose we'll clean the wounds, then we can get started." She glanced at Rose's cheek and the stitches that ran across it. "There's no sign of infection there. When are you supposed to go back and have your stitches removed?"

"Friday. With any luck, I'll be up and walking again soon."

Karen pushed her glasses up on her nose. "I wouldn't get your hopes up, Rose. Your legs have been through a tremendous trauma. It's going to take a great deal of time and effort before you'll be able to get around on your own. Let's not worry about walking yet and just concentrate on getting you healed."

Ronnie stood up and grabbed her empty cup. "I'm getting some more coffee. Do you want some, Rose?"

"Yes, please, thank you." She held out her cup.

"What about you, Miss Brown?"

"Oh no thanks. I don't drink caffeine."

"Fine, I'll be back in a minute." She headed for the door but was stopped by the melodic voice.

"Ronnie?"

"Yeah?"

"Could you give me a few minutes?" Rose gave an embarrassed smile. "I have a couple of things that I need to take care of." She looked pointedly at the bedpan sitting on the small stand.

"Oh, okay. I'll be in the living room if you need me."

But Ronnie didn't go in the living room. Instead she haunted Maria while the older woman tried to get her daily chores done. "So you saw her, what do you think of her?"

"She's not my nurse. You should be asking Rose about her."

"But do you think she's all right? I mean, the agency said she was a registered nurse. Should I have gotten more information about her? I can call Susan and have her run a check with the state board."

"If you think you should, Ronnie," Maria replied, the duster in her hand flying over the antiques. "Has she said or done anything that you don't approve of?"

"Well…no, not really."

"Then what's the problem?"

"No problem. I just wondered if I should or not, that's all," Ronnie replied, her tone slightly miffed. She stood there silently for a minute, the tension building within her. "I have a lot of work to do, and my computer is in there."

"You have another one upstairs in your room that you could use if you had to."

"But the data I need are on this one," she lied, knowing full well that both computers connected to the network housed at the corporate offices.

"Ronnie, if you need to get in there, I'm sure Rose would understand."

The tone in Maria's voice made her realize just how she sounded. "No, I'll use the one upstairs. Let me know when lunch is ready." She turned and raced up the stairs.

Once inside her room, Ronnie flipped the switch on her computer and sulked over to her bed. She looked around the room, realizing as if for the first time how quiet and empty it was. The thick carpets and solid wood floors kept the sounds from below from filtering up to her. "This is stupid," she scowled, returning to her computer desk and sitting down. "I have work to do."

But the folder she clicked on wasn't a work folder, it was her solitaire game. That was followed by reviewing her appointment book and noting that Christmas was only seventeen days away. Well, it wouldn't hurt anything if she looked around the Internet for a while. The Macy's site gave her no ideas for a gift to get for her mother, although she saw several items that she thought Rose would like. By quarter of twelve, Ronnie still had no presents for the members of her family. "The gift that always fits," she decided, clicking on the gift certificate form. That problem solved, she shut the computer off and trotted downstairs to have lunch with Rose and watch *Judge Judy* together.

When Ronnie entered Rose's room, she was pleased to see that Karen was finishing up. "I'll be back tomorrow. Don't forget to do those exercises I showed you. You have to keep those muscles active as much as possible or it will only slow your recovery."

"I will, thank you," the young woman replied.

"Fine." The nurse turned her attention to Ronnie, correctly assuming that she was the one in charge. "I'll be back tomorrow around nine."

Lunch was a simple fare of soup and sandwiches, eaten while listening to the feisty judge reprimand someone for thinking that she would believe they had repaid a loan but just couldn't find their receipt. By the time the credits rolled, both women were looking at empty plates. "Maria can make anything taste good."

"Oh, she's a wonderful cook," Rose agreed. "Has she always worked for you and your family?"

"As long as I can remember. Her mother worked for us, too, but she retired shortly after I was born. Maria's been everything from housekeeper to baby-sitter to referee ever since." The high-pitched chirp of the phone interrupted her. "Probably another telemarketer," she grumbled.

"Aren't you going to answer it?"

"No. Maria screens my calls for me." As if on cue, Maria knocked on the door. "Okay," Ronnie called while reaching for the phone. "This is Veronica Cartwright."

"Miss Cartwright, this is Jonathan Barker from First Albany Savings and Trust. How are you today?" Recognizing the name of the bank's vice president, Ronnie's posture stiffened, and she pushed her chair over to the desk.

"Fine, Mr. Barker. What can I do for you today?"

"Well...I don't mean to bother you at home, but I felt this matter required your immediate attention." She didn't miss the touch of nervousness in his voice. "Mr. Cartwright hasn't returned any of my calls, and I'm afraid at this point I have to seek recourse somewhere else."

Ronnie rolled her eyes and picked up her pencil, lightly tapping it on the desk. "What's this about?"

"Well...as you know, when a loan is defaulted, we are obligated to go to the guarantor to recover our losses, and since you are the cosigner on Thomas' personal loan–"

"I cosigned a loan?" The pencil stopped moving. "When was this?"

"Oh, I um...." She heard papers shuffling about on Barker's desk. "Yes, here it is. I have your signature dated April fifth as a cosigner for Thomas' personal loan." A touch of nervousness crept into his voice. "You did cosign a personal loan for him, didn't you, Miss Cartwright?"

The pencil began tapping rapidly. "I guess I must have forgotten about that, Mr. Barker."

"Well, I'm sure it was just a simple oversight on Mr. Cartwright's part, but I'm afraid that we haven't received payment in over five months. I really can't let this go on much longer."

"No, of course not." The pencil moved with more force. "You can transfer the overdue amount from my personal savings account."

"Well, I appreciate that, Miss Cartwright, but I'm afraid at this point the loan is considered to be in default, and we have to ask for full repayment."

"Fine. You can take whatever is owed from my account." She nestled the phone between her ear and shoulder, freeing up her hand to grab a piece of paper. "Can you please tell me the exact repayment amount so I can mark my records?"

The pencil dropped to the desk and clattered onto the floor. "What?"

"I said the total with interest and late fees comes to $17,642.12. I'll have that withdrawn from your account immediately."

"Mr. Barker?"

"Yes?"

"Make certain in the future that you check with me personally before approving any more loans for any member of my family."

"Certainly, Miss Cartwright."

There was a pause before Ronnie realized that he had said something else. "Excuse me, I'm afraid I didn't hear you."

"I asked if there was anything the bank could do for you today."

"No, I think you've done enough, thank you."

"Have a good day, Miss Cartwright," he said, but she had already hung up.

From her seat only a few feet away, Rose heard every word of the executive's side of the conversation. It wasn't hard to piece together what happened. "Ronnie?" All she got was a view of the back of the brown leather chair and the furious clacking of the keyboard. "Ronnie?"

"Do you need something, Rose?" Her tone was much harsher than she intended. The typing stopped. "You know, there are times when I wish I wasn't the oldest," she sighed, turning her chair around to face the young woman.

"Do you want to talk about it?"

Ronnie's first reaction was to say no, that family problems are always settled privately, but then she looked up into soft green eyes and realized that she did want to talk about it, she did want to share her frustrations and feelings with Rose. "Tommy took out a personal loan and forged my name on it as cosigner."

"That's terrible," the young woman gasped. "But why did you pay it?"

"Because that's what I'm expected to do," she sighed. "If I hadn't, Susan or Mother would have."

"But you're only making it easier for him to do it again."

"I know, but I didn't have a choice." She pushed her chair closer to the bed. "Even though I'm considered the head of the family now, there are still some things that I have to do whether I like them or not."

"It's a lot of pressure sometimes, isn't it?" Rose reached out and placed a gentle hand on Ronnie's forearm. "It must be very stressful to have to keep everything inside."

Ronnie looked up in surprise. "Yeah." It was the first time that anyone had ever expressed any understanding of her feelings when it came to being the family caretaker. "Tommy just soaked me for almost eighteen grand."

"Oh, my God! Eighteen thousand dollars?"

"It's not even the money that bothers me," Ronnie continued, deliberately not focusing on the fact that the amount meant completely different things to each of them. To her, it was a fraction of her savings and wouldn't really be missed. To Rose, well…she didn't even want to think what it meant to the young woman who spent less than twenty bucks a week on groceries.

"It's the fact that he used you."

"He forged my signature on a bank loan. I can't imagine why he would need a cosigner for that small amount anyway, but I don't manage his finances. I just can't believe he had the balls to do that, then to not bother to repay it." As she spoke, Ronnie's voice betrayed more of her anger and outrage. "He knew that I'd take care of it. He knew the bank would never question my signature on a loan for him."

"He used you."

"He used me." She looked at her desk and the still unsolved problems that waited for her there. The enormity of the issue made her take a deep breath. "I'm going to have to call for an audit of the real estate division."

"Do you think he's embezzling?"

"If you asked me that yesterday, I would have said that I wasn't sure." She leaned over and picked up the manila folder. "Today? Now I know he's embezzling, I just can't prove it." She let the folder fall back on the desk with a thwap. Her body was a bundle of nervous energy, and she needed to release it. "Rose, I need to go downstairs and work out for a while. Do you think you'll be okay?"

"I'll be fine," the young woman assured her. "I know you have things to do. You don't have to keep me company all the time."

Ah, but, Rose, she thought to herself. *I like keeping you company.* She stood up and pushed her chair back over to the desk. "I'll be back in about a half hour or so. If you're up to it, we can watch some more movies."

"That'd be nice."

Yes, it would, Ronnie thought.

A grueling workout did nothing to improve Ronnie's mood, and it only seemed to worsen the longer she thought about her brother and what he had done. The punching bag suffered an onslaught of blows, accented by a string of curses that would make even the most raucous sailor blush. Only when she was thoroughly exhausted did she remove the boxing gloves and head for the small refrigerator to get something to drink. As she removed the last bottle of Gatorade, Ronnie noticed the clock on the wall. It was after three, well past the half hour that she had planned on being. "Damn it."

The door opened to the office fifteen minutes later with a freshly showered Ronnie holding a DVD. "Sorry, guess I got caught up in what I was doing. We still on for a movie?"

"Oh, yes, of course," Rose smiled. She had heard the muffled sounds of Ronnie working out—or raging—depending on how one looked at it, and seriously doubted that the executive would be up to spending time with her.

"You've got to be tired of staring at the walls of this room," Ronnie said. "How about we watch the movie in the living room?"

"But how will you get me down those steps?"

"You let me worry about that. Now let's get you into your chair." Ronnie was becoming more adept at maneuvering Rose from the bed to her chair, and before long, she was pushing Rose down the hall toward the sunken living room.

"I don't know about this," Rose said as she eyed the steps. Before she could protest further, Ronnie grabbed the wheels of the chair and lifted both it and her off the carpet. Ronnie gently set the wheelchair down on the lower level. "Let me get the pillows for your head, then I'll help you on the couch. That way, you can still lie down and enjoy the show."

"But where will you sit?"

Ronnie just grinned. "Go take a good look at that couch."

Rose guided the wheelchair around to face the front of the couch. "Looks like a very nice couch, but–"

Ronnie came around the other side and sat down, reaching between the cushion and side to grab the hidden lever.

"Wow," Rose said, "it's one of those reclining ones."

"Yup...look at this." Ronnie snaked her hand between a fold of soft leather and pulled, revealing a hidden snack tray nestled within the center cushions.

"Oh, that is cool!"

"What can I say? I like creature comforts. Here, let's get you settled. You'll love how soft this is."

"Oooh, this is nice," the young woman drawled after sinking into the wonderful couch.

"I couldn't tell you how many times I've fallen asleep on it," Ronnie said as she walked over to the cabinets and faced the center one. The double doors opened to reveal the large-screen television and racks above it filled with Bose stereo equipment and a top-of-the-line CD player. She slid the doors into their recessed spaces before turning to face the sight of Rose comfortably relaxing on her couch. "I thought a romantic comedy would be nice...unless you prefer something else."

"No, I'm sure whatever you've picked will be fine," the young woman replied enthusiastically. And it was the truth. Rose would have been happy to watch a test pattern if that was what Ronnie wanted. The initial awkwardness was quickly fading, replaced with a sense of friendship and caring for the woman who had befriended her. She was surprised when Ronnie sat down on the middle cushion, only scant inches away from her. "Don't you want your footrest?"

"Nah, I feel like sitting up for a while," Ronnie replied, tucking her feet underneath her Indian-style. "You comfortable?"

"Very."

"Good." She pressed the play button on the remote. "Here we go."

The opening scene was almost over when Rose's nose picked up a most delicious scent. "Popcorn?" As if on cue, Maria appeared from the kitchen with a large bowl of the treat in hand, as well as several napkins.

"If you don't need anything else, I do need to be going," Maria said as she handed the bowl to Ronnie. "Dinners are in the refrigerator, microwave on medium for three minutes to heat them up."

"I think we're all set, Maria. Drive carefully."

"I'm only going home, Ronnie. You'd think I lived ten miles away," the older woman said. "I could walk if it weren't so darn cold outside."

"I know, but I'm still allowed to worry about you. After all, who'd do all the cooking and cleaning if you weren't around?" The twinkling in her blue eyes was the only sign that the she was joking.

"Ronnie!" Rose yelped.

Maria chuckled. "Keep it up, Veronica Louise, and you'll find out." She turned to Rose. "You keep an eye on her."

"I will," the young woman promised with a smile.

Once Maria left, Ronnie started the DVD again, and the two women settled in to watch Richard Dreyfuss try to win Marsha Mason's heart. The popcorn bowl rested between them, and both women were busily stuffing the buttered snack into their mouths. As it was bound to happen, the large and small hands reached in at the same time, and the greased fingers intertwined. "Oops" came the simultaneous apology as their digits were disengaged from one another.

"Good popcorn," Rose said as she reached back in, this time making sure to stay on her own side of the bowl.

"Yeah, really good."

As the movie wore on and the popcorn supply dwindled, their hands continued to brush against each other in pursuit of the tasty kernels. After the fourth or fifth time, both gave up on apologizing and just let it happen without comment. Rose still did her best to avoid touching Ronnie's hand, but it seemed to always be on her side of the bowl. When only the tiniest pieces were left along with unpopped kernels, the older woman moved the bowl over to the unoccupied cushion. "You want something to drink?"

"Sure, thanks."

"What do you want?"

"Anything would be fine. Water is good."

"Uh-huh." Ronnie rose gracefully from the couch and wandered out to the kitchen, returning a minute later with soda for each of them.

"Thanks," Rose said, taking the glass. "Do you want to back it up so you can see what you missed?"

"Nah, I've seen this one several times." She sat back down and tucked her legs underneath herself. "I'm a sucker for a good romance story."

Tabitha wandered out to see what was going on. "Mrrow?"

"No, we're up here right now. You go play," Ronnie said. Apparently, the orange and white cat thought she said "come on up" because she did exactly that, crossing over the executive's lap and settling down between the two women.

"Do you want her down?" Rose put her hand under the feline's stomach, ready to shoo her.

Ronnie looked at the purring cat. Two weeks ago, she never would have let an animal take control of her house. "I guess she's not hurting anything." The truth was that it made her smile inside to see Rose happy, and being around Tabitha did that. She reached out and let her long fingers join the smaller ones in petting the happy feline.

Tuesday brought with it the realization that the matters at Cartwright Corporation couldn't be ignored any longer. Ronnie bid goodbye to the still sleeping Rose and headed for her car. She guided the bright blue Jeep through the never-ending series of traffic lights and one-way streets until she reached the Hudson Avenue parking garage. She took a few minutes to put her head in work mode after being in caretaker mode for so many days. Feeling herself ready to face whatever awaited her, Veronica Cartwright stepped out of her vehicle and headed for the elevator.

"Morning, Laura. Anything important I need to know about?" Ronnie asked as she approached her secretary's desk.

"The reports are on your desk." The petite woman glanced over the schedule book. "You have a meeting at ten with the investors from Houston, and your sister has left word for you to call her as soon as you arrive." She took her boss's coat and crossed the room to hang it up in the closet. "She says it's important."

"It's always important to Susan." She opened her office door, then paused. "Call my house and get Maria on the phone for me."

Once inside the privacy of her corner office, Ronnie set her pumps under the desk and padded around in her stockinged feet, fetching a fresh cup of coffee from the private pot kept in her office. A few minutes later, she was sitting at her desk, the computer humming to life. A polite buzz and the flashing light on her phone told her that Laura's task was accomplished. She picked up the black receiver and pressed the button for line two. "Maria."

"Is something wrong?" the housekeeper asked. It was rare for Ronnie to call home.

"I just wanted to see how things were going with our guest."

"Rose is still sleeping. Do you want me to wake her up?"

"No." She tried to keep the disappointment from her voice. "Listen, when she wakes up, give her my office number and have her give me a call, okay?" The sound of the door to her office opening brought Ronnie's head up. Susan stood there, her body language indicating that something was life or death. "I've got to go. Have her call me." She set the receiver down. "What?"

"You know that 'new hire' of yours? Rose Grayson?"

"Yeah? What about her?"

"She's never shown up for work. The termination papers just hit my desk."

"Termination papers? Who authorized that?"

"Grace did. Accounting is her department. She said she had never heard of this woman and that she never showed up for work."

Ronnie punched the button for the intercom. "Laura, get Grace on the phone." She turned her attention back to her sister. "Anything involving Rose Grayson comes to my desk immediately. You are to do nothing involving her without my consent."

"Ronnie, what's going on? You hire someone for entry level, give her full benefits immediately, and she never even shows up to work."

"Don't worry about it, Susan. I'll handle it."

"Grace on line three," Laura's voice cracked through the intercom. Ronnie picked up the receiver.

"Grace, there's a problem with a new hire, Rose Grayson?"

"Yeah, like she never showed up for work," the cousin replied.

"Don't worry about it. She's on extended medical leave. Just process her paperwork every week. Under no circumstances are you to terminate her."

"What? Ronnie, she never showed up. I've never even met this Grayson woman. All I have is a few forms faxed over from Susan last week."

"I know all about it." There was a pause, and she thought her cousin was going to argue with her some more. "Grace, there's no discussion on this."

"Fine. You're the boss." There was a click followed by the dial tone. Ronnie hung up and glanced at the computer screen. "Is there anything else, Sis?"

"Of course there is." Susan replied, moving around the desk until she was standing next to her older sister. "Come on, Ronnie, what's going on?"

"Nothing you need to worry about. I'm sure you have more important things to do than worry about one little employee."

"One little employee that you mysteriously hired." The redhead leaned casually against the mahogany desk. "Ronnie, you have never directly hired anyone for a position, except Laura." A thought occurred to her. "This isn't like when you were at Stanford, is it?"

The mention of her great personal failure brought the executive's attention away from the computer. "Susan, can't you let anything die? That was ten years ago!" There was no mistaking her angry tone.

"Hey, you should have known better than to trust some poor white trash."

"Christine wasn't poor white trash. She was there on an academic scholarship."

"And what subject were you two studying at night in your room?" Susan jibed. "You weren't there when Dad answered the phone the night she called. You didn't hear the things she told him. The way she threatened to make it public knowledge."

"Drop it, Susan," she warned with a low growl. "I could have handled it."

"How? Would you have preferred that everyone knew that the heir apparent to Cartwright Corporation was queer?" She flinched at the blazing look in Ronnie's eyes. "Look, you're my sister, and I love you. I can understand that you made a mistake. You were young, you didn't know better. I just don't want you to have to suffer through that again."

"That's not what's going on." Ronnie picked up a pencil and began tapping it on the desk.

"You promised Dad that it wouldn't happen again."

"And it hasn't!" The pencil was tossed angrily, causing it to bounce off the desk and onto the floor. Ronnie stood up and looked out the window at the Albany skyline, seething inside at the reminder of her great humiliation. The vision of the blue-eyed blonde that once filled her with happiness only to turn into a blood-sucking blackmailer flashed before her eyes. "I've never...I mean...since...." She gave up and continued to stare out the window.

"Ronnie...." Susan stood next to her taller sibling and put her hand on her forearm. "I felt so bad for you when Mom and Dad went to pick you up at the airport that night." The call from Christine demanding money in exchange for keeping quiet about her affair came less than two hours before Ronnie arrived at the Albany County Airport to spend the Christmas break at home with the family. "That was the worst holiday I can remember. All the yelling and screaming."

It had been a subject that the two sisters never spoke of, not even at the time. Ronnie had never known Susan's true feelings on the matter of either her sexuality or the whole blackmail incident. Without turning around, the older sister spoke. "I had been looking forward to coming home. I missed Thanksgiving, and after Chris and I broke up...." She shook her head. "Was what I did so horribly wrong?"

"Trusting her or having sex with a woman?" Susan queried, turning and leaning her rear against the ledge of the window.

Ronnie shrugged. "Either...both...ah, never mind." She turned from the window and sat in her chair. "We both have work to do."

"No, it's okay," the redhead said, pulling a chair around to sit on the same side of the desk as her sister. "Look, what I said earlier about being queer, I didn't mean–"

"Forget it."

"No. It's your life. I have no right to judge you. Lord knows I've done things that I'm ashamed of."

"No judgment in that statement, is there?" Ronnie said sarcastically, turning her chair slightly and pulling out the keyboard tray. "I guess it's okay to have an affair with your personal trainer but not with someone of the same sex, right?"

"I didn't think you knew about André," Susan said hesitantly, wondering just how much her older sister knew.

"Not much escapes me." She tapped her password in, changing the screen from the corporate logo to her personal desktop. "Look, I've learned my lesson, okay? I don't hang out in the gay bars, cruise the softball fields, or have a parade of women going in and out of my bed."

"You're also thirty-three and not married. Ronnie, this is a business. We have to maintain a certain image."

"And I do!" She rose and began pacing. "I always attend all the charitable functions with the appropriate male escort. I've done nothing to upset the family's precious image."

"What is it about a woman?" Susan stood to face her sister. "What is it? Really, help me understand this, Sis. We grew up together. What happened?"

"Susan, we're at work. Let's drop this, okay?"

"Fine. The mysterious Rose Grayson stays on the payroll and insurance because you say so." The redhead was obviously miffed at the brusque tone. "Are there any other problems you're interested in, or is she it?"

"I'm the president, aren't I?" Ronnie scowled. "The whole Grayson thing isn't a big deal, Susan. You don't have to worry about seeing me leading the next gay pride parade either. Now can we talk about something else?" She stalked over to her desk and sat down. "Did you cosign any loans for Tommy?"

"Why would Tommy need a cosigner? He's got plenty of money. He doesn't even own a home except for that cabin in the Adirondacks."

"He defaulted on a loan that had my name forged on it as a cosigner."

"It must be some kind of mistake."

"No mistake. I'm going to have copies of the application sent over to me so I can compare it to my signature."

"Maybe someone forged Tommy's name, too."

"Yeah, maybe. I'll find out after I get the papers. In the meantime, I suggest you take a look at your bank records." She reached for the mouse and clicked open her link to the bank. "Oh, one more thing. I'm ordering an audit of real estate."

"What? You're auditing Tommy's books?" Susan all but shrieked. "Do you know how that will look to him?"

"Like I don't trust him. I don't." A quick typing of her account number and password and Ronnie was glancing at her recent transactions. The debit card that looked just like a Visa Platinum card was handy. All purchases were posted to her checking account within two days, making it easy for her to verify that her card wasn't compromised. She looked over the list, noting the familiar items like Tabitha's toys and Rose's bed. "You said yourself that you think something's wrong. Do you want me to find out what it is now, or do you want to wait until it blows up in the press? I thought you were worried about our image."

Susan bristled at the comment but reluctantly conceded that her sister was right. Trust was a big deal with the public image. They remembered names, and if they didn't, the nightly news would be more than happy to remind them. It was how scandals lasted so long in Albany. Thus far, the Cartwrights had been lucky enough not to be involved publicly in any, no matter what it cost them privately. "All right," the younger sibling sighed. "I can't see where it would hurt anything if he's innocent." She headed for the door. "Ronnie?"

"What?"

"If he is, you had better give him an apology. And you'd better make sure Mother doesn't find out about it." The intercom buzzed, followed quickly by Laura's voice.

"Rose on line one for you."

Ronnie looked up to see her sister's eyes light up at the name. "Is this the mysterious Rose Grayson?"

"Goodbye, Susan." She picked up the receiver and pressed the button. "Hi...." There was no mistaking the change in Ronnie's voice. It became softer...gentler. There was a tenderness in it that was in direct contrast to her earlier tone. "Can you hang on for a minute?"

"I'm going, I'm going. But this isn't the end of this conversation."

"Susan!" She looked pointedly at the door. The redhead left, determined more than ever to solve the puzzle of her sister and Rose Grayson.

"Hi, sorry about that. Did you sleep well?" Ronnie said, settling down in her chair and resting her stockinged calves on the desk.

"Very well. Maria said you wanted me to call."

"I just wanted to tell you that if you needed anything to let Maria know. She's going to stay there until I get home. She'll make you anything you want for breakfast, just ask her. Oh, and if there's anything you want her to pick up at the supermarket, just let her know that, too."

"I'm fine, but thanks. How's work going?"

"Oh, just a typical day," Ronnie replied sarcastically. "It's a wonder I don't have an ulcer sometimes."

"I wish there was something I could do to make it better for you," Rose said sincerely.

You already do, Ronnie thought to herself. "I'm fine. Tell you what. You up for seafood tonight?"

"Sounds great."

"Good. I'll have Maria whip us up something nice." The light on line two began flashing. "I think I'd better get back to work, I just wanted to check up on you."

"Okay, I'm glad you did."

"Um...you know, if you want to, you can call later."

"Oh. Okay, well maybe after lunch. I don't want to bother you."

"Sure. After lunch would be fine. I don't think I'm going to stay all day anyway."

"All right...well...I guess I'll talk to you later then."

"Okay, Rose. You relax and do what the nurse tells you."

"Bye."

"Bye." Ronnie listened to the click, then the dial tone for a few seconds before pressing line two. "This is Veronica Cartwright." Her voice was once again pure business.

Chapter Eight

It was well past six when Ronnie finally shut the computer off and left her office. There had been no sign of Tommy all day, and he refused to answer his beeper. Left with no choice, the head of Cartwright Corporation ordered a full audit of the real estate division to begin immediately. By the end of the day, all the hard copies of records and disk backups of the computer records were boxed and shipped to the independent auditor.

Ronnie was surprised to see the kitchen light on when she returned home until she remembered that she had asked Maria to stay until she got there. She and Rose had spoken briefly in the early afternoon, but a meeting had cut that phone call short. Now finally home, she was looking forward to spending the rest of the evening relaxing with Rose. She hung her coat up in the closet and kicked her shoes off before walking into the office.

"Hi!" Rose greeted enthusiastically, a huge smile coming over her face.

"Hi, yourself." She turned her attention to Maria, who was picking up the cards that she and the young woman had been playing. "Thanks for staying so late."

"I didn't mind a bit. She's better at rummy than you are," the housekeeper remarked, drawing a smile from Rose. "I can stay late tomorrow, too, if you need it."

Ronnie's first response was to say that it wouldn't be necessary, but upon reflection of what had transpired today at the office and what was going to happen once Tommy found out about the audit, she reconsidered her answer. "Actually, I think I may have to take you up on that. Perhaps you could come in later so you don't have to work so long. I can make my own breakfast."

"Make your own breakfast and dirty every piece of cookware in my kitchen," Maria snorted. "I'll be here at seven like I always am. The only night I can't stay late is Thursday. Carrie and Monica will worry if they don't see me there by six thirty."

"Bingo night," Ronnie explained to her houseguest. "Why don't you stay and join us for dinner tonight? I'm sure you made more than enough."

The older woman chuckled. "You know your mother would have a fit if she found out."

"Why? Doesn't her mother like you?" Rose asked, her curious expression turning to a self-conscious frown when Maria gave a short laugh and shook her head.

"Mrs. Cartwright likes me just fine, child. But it's considered bad form to share a meal with the hired help."

"Oh," the young woman murmured, embarrassment tinting her face. She wondered if her friend's mother would disapprove of her, as well.

"But my mother doesn't decide who I dine with," Ronnie said firmly. "Now do you think you'd like to eat in the dining room or in here?"

"Um…wherever you want is fine."

"I'll set some places at the table. It will take only a few minutes to heat everything up," Maria said, excusing herself from the room.

"Thanks," Ronnie said as the older woman brushed past her. Now alone with Rose, the persona that she had kept in place all day faded. Her shoulders slumped, and the headache that she had been fighting made its presence known with full force. She crossed the room and all but flopped into her leather chair. "What a day." She lifted her left leg up, bracing it over her right knee, and began rubbing her aching foot.

"Did you confront Tommy?"

"No, he never showed up," Ronnie sighed. "I ordered an audit."

"Oh."

"Yeah, it's not going to be a pretty sight when he finds out." She rubbed her foot with more force, using both hands to knead the sore muscles. "On top of that, I had a mountain of paperwork to get through. Laura took off halfway through the day."

"Laura?"

"My secretary," she clarified.

"Oh, she must have been the one who answered the phone when I called."

"Yeah, that's her." Ronnie reversed the position of her legs and began massaging her right foot. "Oh, great," she scowled, looking at the rapidly growing run moving up her stocking. "You know, someone should be able to figure out a way to make pantyhose so they don't run the instant you put them on." She stood up, smoothing the dark gray skirt. "I'm going to run up and change. By then, I'm sure dinner will be ready." Her eyes fell on the stringy strands of hair surrounding Rose's face. "After dinner, I think we'll wash your hair."

"How are we going to do that? I can't take a shower."

"I've got an idea."

After changing into her sweats and sneakers, Ronnie grabbed a set of keys and headed across the snow-covered driveway to the garage. The original garage had been torn down three years ago to make room for her idea of what a true one should be. Capable of holding four cars comfortably, the garage sported multiple rows of fluorescent lights and a separate alarm system, and the back half served as a storage place. Entering through the door on the side, Ronnie quickly walked over to the control panel and deactivated the alarm. A flip of the switch and the four bays were bathed in a sea of white light. The first bay housed a car hidden by a canvas cover. Distracted for a moment, Ronnie walked to the back of the car and pulled back the cover. The white vanity plate sported the Statue of Liberty on the left side and blue letters announcing the car as "Rons Toy." She pulled the cover back more to reveal the gas cap with the familiar Mustang logo. "Soon," she promised herself. Her prized muscle car had been painstakingly restored, and the harsh salt of Albany winters meant that it had to stay in hibernation until the flowers started to bloom again. Her fingers trailed over the deep blue metallic paint, and her mind drifted back to when she had first bought the car.

It was her senior year at Dartmouth. While she liked the Audi that her father had given her for her twenty-first birthday, she found herself always looking at the weathered Mustang that a sorority sister's boyfriend owned. The paint had been chipped away and surface rust was the dominant color, but when the pedal was put to the floor, the car could blow the doors off anything put up against it. When Ronnie had asked her father for permission to withdraw enough money to buy it, Richard Cartwright adamantly refused, citing that she had a perfectly good car and that a Ford was far too dangerous a vehicle. Ronnie was undaunted, however, and saved her allowance for the entire semester until she could afford to buy it on her own. She drove it home on spring break, much to the dismay of her parents. Her father called it a pile of junk, and her mother insisted that she would only get herself killed in that "death trap." They tried offers of a new Mustang, threats of financial cutoff, even the old "ladies of proper upbringing don't drive muscle cars," but none of it worked. By the end of the week, all they had accomplished was to make Ronnie even more determined to keep and restore her blue speed demon. Although it was no longer her primary car, she still took it out for a spin occasionally, and the metallic blue beauty was still her favorite.

A slight chill went through her, pulling Ronnie from memory lane and back to the present. She replaced the cover over her Mustang and walked into the next bay. The fire-engine red Porsche sat there. It was the first time she had seen it since the accident. The fourth bay was where she kept the Jeep, and thus far, she had made it a point not to go near the 911. Now she slowly walked around the car, blue eyes taking in all the repairs. Green tape surrounded the edges of the new windshield, no doubt to allow the new rubber sealant to set in. The hood, grill, bumper, and front right quarter panel were all gone, the dull gray metal chassis standing out in stark contrast to the rest of the vehicle. A rolling toolbox sat against the wall, further evidence of Hans's visits. Ronnie turned away from the car and leaned her hands against the toolbox while she fought to keep her stomach in check. She knew then that she would never be able to drive the Porsche again. She bit down the resurgence of guilt and took deliberate steps toward the storage room door, all the while telling herself that everything would work out, that Rose would completely recover, that the damage she had caused could be repaired.

She found what she was looking for immediately. In the corner, under a pile of drop cloths was a five-gallon bucket that once held quick-dry concrete. She took it to the work sink nearby and cleaned it out until the milky white water ran clear. Her task accomplished, Ronnie returned to the house.

"So what did you think of that last question?"

"It was too easy," Rose replied. "Everyone knows that even-numbered interstates run east-west and the odd ones run north-south."

"If everyone knows that, then why do so many people get lost when they travel?" Ronnie leaned back in her chair and set her bare feet up on the edge of the bed near Rose's left hip. Since the winter months were upon them and she had no reason to wear open-toed shoes, she didn't bother to get pedicures as often as she usually did.

In the process of wiggling her toes, a nail scratched against the one next to it. "Well, no wonder I'm ripping up all the pantyhose. I guess it's time to call for a pedicure." She saw a faraway look take over the young woman's face. "What?" she asked softly. "Share with me."

"You were talking about a pedicure, and I was remembering when I was thirteen." Seeing the expectant look on the chiseled face of her companion, Rose continued. "The state found a foster family for me for a few weeks, and they had a girl right around my age. Stacey loved having me around because I was a willing guinea pig for her to practice cosmetology on. She loved to play with nail polish. She had rows and rows of bottles on her dresser in every color you can imagine." Rose absently reached down and put her fingers on Ronnie's toes. "Well, one night we got in a mood. We painted every nail a different color. I can remember that on my toes, it went from plum to avocado to this hideous purple to...." As she spoke, her forefinger brushed across each nail of the bare foot. "We went to school the next day, and when we went to take a shower after gym class, everyone saw our toes." She chuckled. "It really was funny. I mean, between the two of us, there were twenty different colors on our feet. After that, Stacey deliberately wore different shades of polish on her fingers. That was the last time I polished my toenails."

Ronnie looked at her quizzically, then rose and went to the foot of the bed. Within seconds, the oversized socks were removed to reveal Rose's toes. "When was the last time someone gave you a pedicure?"

"That was it, if you could call that a pedicure. Ow, easy."

"Oh, sorry," Ronnie apologized, letting go of the little toe she had moved to get a better look at the one next to it. Can you feel that in your ankle?"

"Yeah, that's why I don't wiggle them. My legs hurt enough as it is."

"When was the last time you took a pain pill?"

"It's not that bad right now. I'd rather wait until I really need it."

"Are you ready to get your hair washed?"

"You figured out a way?" Rose sat up, prepared to get back into the wheelchair.

"No, you stay here. I've got it all worked out so you don't have to get out of bed." Ronnie looked at the adjustable bed, currently up in a comfortable angle. "You're gonna have to lie the bed flat, though."

A few minutes later, Rose was on her back across the bed, her head hanging off the side. A towel braced behind her shoulders dangled down to protect the mattress from any soapy water. Ronnie was sitting on a stool taken from the kitchen, the white five-gallon bucket nestled between her knees. A large towel lay on the floor below to catch any spills. "You ready?" she asked.

"Yeah."

Ronnie poured the water slowly over the honey locks, using her other hand to help distribute the liquid over all the hair. She poured shampoo on her hand and worked it into a generous lather. "How's that feel?"

"Nice," Rose murmured, green eyes half-closed. "You have strong fingers."

"Am I pressing too hard?"

"Oh, no, it's very nice."

"Good." Ronnie continued to work her digits into the soft hair. "Time to rinse. Keep your eyes closed." Using her left hand to hold Rose's head up, she gently rinsed the shampoo out. Once the majority was gone, she put another dollop of the strawberry-scented liquid into her hand. "Round two."

"You're going to wash it again?" Rose asked with surprise.

"Of course. You know the directions. Lather, rinse, repeat." She worked the shampoo into the golden hair before the young woman could tell her not to. "I take it you only wash it once."

"Yeah, it uses less shampoo that way. My hair always looks clean. Lots of people only wash it once." Nevertheless, Rose leaned into the gentle but firm pressure of Ronnie's fingers. She was treated to not only a second washing, but having conditioner combed through her hair.

Ronnie put down the blow dryer and handed Rose a mirror. "Looks great," she said, noting the smile that came to the cherubic face looking at herself in the handheld mirror. "Doesn't she, Tabitha?"

"Mrrow?" Two seconds later, the orange and white purring machine was perched across Rose's belly.

"Oof, you're definitely gaining weight."

"I think Maria's giving her scraps, but I can't prove it," Ronnie said with a smile. "I just know that every time she's cooking, that fur ball comes out of the kitchen licking her lips."

Ding dong, ding dong. The deep tones of the doorbell rang throughout the house. "Who could that be at this hour?" Ronnie asked, looking at the clock on the stand. "It's almost ten." The doorbell rang again, this time accompanied by furious pounding against the solid oak door.

"Ronnie! Ronnie, open the fucking door!"

"I'll be right back." She slipped her sneakers on and tucked the excess lace into the sides. Tabitha jumped off the bed, sensing that something more interesting was about to happen in the other room. "Oh, no, you don't. You stay here with your mother." Ronnie picked up the protesting feline and set her back on the bed, this time within reach of Rose's hand.

"Ronnie! I know you're in there, now open this fucking–" The words died in his throat when he saw the outside light come on and heard the lock being turned. "Well, it's about time."

"What are you doing here at this hour?" she scowled, having no doubt that her younger brother was quite drunk.

"What the hell are you trying to do to me?" Tommy pushed his way past her and through the foyer into the living room. "I don't show up to work one day and you order a fucking audit!"

"This isn't the time to talk about this, Tommy. Go home and sleep it off." Ronnie moved between him and the office, trying to guide him back to the door. She put her hand on his arm only to have it shoved off.

"Fuck you, Ronnie!" He paced to the other side of the room and punched the wooden front of the entertainment center cabinet. He turned to face her, and she could see several days of growth on his face, as well as the unkempt hair and clothes. Tommy had obviously been on a bender and only now heard the news. "What do you think I'm doing? Stealing from my own company?"

"I don't know what you're doing, but I'm not going to let it continue," she shouted back, her own short temper showing. "What is it, Tom? Drugs? Gambling?"

"Go to hell, Miss High and Mighty Goddess of Everything!" His fist slammed into the cabinet with enough force to knock a tiny vase off the top. Only the thick plush carpet kept the antique from breaking.

"Get out of my house, Tommy."

"Your house," he scoffed. "I grew up in this fucking house. What gives you the right to tell me to get out?"

"I bought the house from Mother, and you know it." Her eyes narrowed at the wild, almost inhuman look in her brother's eyes. Tommy was strong enough on his own, but if he was on drugs....

Ronnie's suspicions were confirmed a few seconds later when he lifted the end of the heavy coffee table and upended it. "You act like you're an angel, but you're not, Ronnie." For the moment, he was standing still, so she kept her distance. Her heart pounded as the adrenaline pumped through her. "You sit in that office day after day. You have no idea what it's like to work for a living. I can't just snap my fingers and make your wallet bigger."

"No, but you can forge my signature on a loan," she retorted.

"What?"

"You defaulted on a loan, and they had my name on there as a cosigner. Why would you need a cosigner, Tommy?"

The sandy haired man blinked a few times as the information sank in. "Shit. That's all you're ever worried about, isn't it? The fucking money?"

"Someone has to worry about it. You certainly don't. Now get out of my house!"

"This isn't over! I don't care what your damn audit turns up, you can't kick me out of the company." A thought occurred to him. "You may own the most stock, but you don't have controlling interest. You think anyone is going to vote with you to get rid of me?" He gave a short laugh, his energy fading as the high he had been riding began to wear off. "Face it, Ronnie. You can't do a thing about me. You think Mom is going to vote with you to toss me out? Frank? Susan? You can't win this battle." He made his way toward the door. "Any fool can see that. Leave me alone, Sis, or you'll regret it." Tommy slammed the door behind him, leaving a bundle of nervous energy in one room and a terrified woman with an equally upset cat in the other.

"You okay?" Ronnie asked when she entered the room. She noticed the pallor of fear on Rose's face. "Hey, it's okay."

"He was pretty angry. What went crashing?" Rose's demeanor was calmer now that her protector was there with her. She patted the empty place on the bed next to her.

"Nah, thanks," the tall woman continued to stand, although the soft pillow was beckoning her. "He flipped the coffee table and knocked something off the top of the cabinet. Nothing broken." She looked at the TV, still on but with the sound muted. "Hey, there's one of those news magazine shows."

"Yeah, they're supposed to have a thing on those rental trucks and how unsafe they are." She patted the bed again. "Come on, I've got the heat and the massager on. This has got to be more comfortable than that chair." She turned on the small lamp on the table next to her just before Ronnie shut off the overhead light. The softer glow was preferred by both of them for television watching.

"You'd be surprised how comfortable that chair is," Ronnie replied, kicking off her sneakers and reluctantly accepting the offer. She sank into the vibrating warmth and closed her eyes with hedonistic delight. "Oh, that's nice. I've got to get one of these for my room." She adjusted the pillow behind her head, slipped her feet under the covers, and opened her eyes. Rose pressed the button, and they began watching the show. With Ronnie right next to her, she felt a sense of safety, and her rapidly beating heart returned to a more normal level.

"Wasn't that interesting?" the young woman queried when the show was over. Receiving no answer, she turned her head to see her companion's eyes closed. "Ronnie?" No response, just the rhythmic rise and fall of the sweatshirt-covered chest. Rose shut the television and lamp off and lowered the bed, but still Ronnie did not stir. The bed was plenty big enough, and Rose decided that there was no reason for her to wake Ronnie up just to send her to her own bed. "Sweet dreams," she whispered, closing her eyes and letting the even breathing of the woman next to her lull her into a sound sleep.

Blue eyes fluttered open shortly after six and looked around, trying to get her bearings. "What the...oh," she mumbled, realizing that she had fallen asleep on Rose's bed. Taking a moment to wipe the sleep from her eyes, Ronnie propped herself up on one elbow and looked down at her sleeping companion. The morning rays highlighted the upturned nose, the rust eyebrows, the full lips parted slightly in sleep. The seconds ticked by as she watched the slumbering woman. It amazed her how easily she had fallen asleep next to Rose. With the exception of Christine, Ronnie had never slept with anyone, and even then, it was done only because it was expected by her lover. Truthfully, she never did feel comfortable sharing the bed and often would slip away and sleep in the unused bed in their dorm room. Yet obviously, she had no problem curling up and sleeping next to Rose. It was a curious mystery that Ronnie knew wasn't safe to ponder. She felt the slight hum of the massager beneath her. That's it. It had to have been the massager. It relaxed her enough to put her to sleep regardless of the presence of someone else in the bed. She smiled to herself with the logic of her thought, yet chose to ignore the fact that she was still lying there next to Rose. She contemplated playing hooky, but the voice of responsibility won out. With a disappointed sigh, she quietly slipped out of bed, careful not to disturb her companion, and padded off to the bathroom.

A vigorous workout and a refreshing shower prepared Ronnie for the day. She inhaled the cup of coffee that Maria made for her, then grabbed her floor-length wool coat. The temperature had dropped significantly overnight, putting the temperature outside down to single digits. She was headed for the door when the phone rang.

"Cartwright residence," Maria answered. "Just a moment. Ronnie, it's Susan. She sounds upset."

She took the cream-colored phone and nodded at her housekeeper. "Susan."

"Ronnie, we have a problem."

"I'm sure we have more than one. What has you so bugged that you couldn't wait until I got to the office?"

"Both Ricky and Timmy came down with chicken pox."

"So? Susan, your kids being sick isn't the end of the world. It's only chicken pox."

"Ronnie, the family Christmas party is tonight."

"So?" She unbuttoned her coat, deciding that it wasn't going to be a quick and easy phone call after all. "I'm too busy to go. Why'd you plan the party for a Wednesday night anyway?"

"It was the best date that we could come up with. People always have parties to go to on the weekends. Putting it on a Wednesday guaranteed that everyone would show up. But that's not the point. The point is, we can't have the party here."

"So rent a hall somewhere." A thought dawned on her. "Oh, no you don't. Susan, I'm not having the party here."

"Ronnie, it's too late to rent a hall and get directions to everyone."

"You're not having it at my house. No, no, no." The coat now found itself draped across a nearby stool. "Sis, I can't have the party here. Do you have any idea how much work that would take?"

"It's perfect. Everyone knows where you live, and they'd love the idea of a good old-fashioned party at the Cartwright house."

"I've told you before. This is my house now, and I don't want every relative in the world trampling through here." She watched Maria preparing eggs for Rose's breakfast. "Sis, I've got company staying with me. It's really not convenient to have people here." The call waiting tone beeped. "Hang on, Susan, I've got another call." She pressed the flash button. "This is Veronica."

"Ronnie, it's your mother."

"Hello, Mother." She rolled her eyes, drawing an amused look from her housekeeper.

"I'll be there after I go to the airport to help with the caterers and to make sure you don't put up any of those gaudy decorations."

"What, did Susan call you first? I have her holding on the other line."

"Yes, she did, and we decided that the house would be the perfect solution."

Perfect solution for everyone but me, Ronnie thought to herself. "Mother, I can't have the party here. Couldn't we just reschedule it or get a hall somewhere?"

"No, we can't," Beatrice Cartwright replied. "Now, Veronica, we don't have time for all this selfish nonsense. I have to pick your Aunt Elaine up at the airport by three. Send a car for me at two, and make sure I don't get that incompetent boob like last time. It took him over an hour to get there."

"Mother, it was a snowstorm, and the traffic was backed up for miles. It wasn't his fault."

"He should have taken an alternate route. He couldn't even get in front of the terminal. You just make sure I get someone else this time."

"But–"

"No buts from you, young lady. Now I have things to do. You talk to your sister, and don't forget to call for my car."

"Mo–"

"Goodbye, dear. Nice talking with you." *Click.* Ronnie took the phone from her ear and stared at the receiver for a moment before hitting the flash button.

"Susan? You still there?"

"I'm here. I assume that was Mother on the other line."

"You assume correctly. Nothing like bringing in the heavy artillery."

"I'm sorry about that." Ronnie doubted her sister's sincerity. "I'll bring some ornaments that the boys made. Ooh, they're so cute. Ronnie, you'll love them. Ricky made this one with green glitter–"

"Sis, I need to get going here." She gave a defeated sigh. "I guess I have a party to get ready for."

"Oh, sure. Jack and I will be by around six. I'll let the family know."

"I'm sure Mother's already called them," Ronnie said in a dry tone. "You deal with getting the decorator and caterers over here. Oh, and, Susan?"

"Yes?"

"This makes us even."

Rose was surprised to see Ronnie walk in and turn on the computer. "Good morning."

"Morning, Rose," she replied, setting her coffee cup down and typing in her password. "Maria will be bringing your breakfast in a few minutes." She clicked on her mail file and quickly scanned the unread ones.

"Is something wrong?"

"Wrong? What could possibly be wrong? My mother and sister have decided that the family Christmas party is going to be held at my house tonight, but nothing's wrong."

"Oh." A momentary pause, then, "What are you going to do?"

"What can I do? I guess I'm going to get this place ready for them." She began tapping the pencil in her left hand on the desk. "At least a third of them smoke. I put those carpets in three years ago, and they're still perfect. You think they'll stay that way? Ha, I bet you there's gonna be at least a half-dozen burn holes in it before the night is over." Ronnie stopped ranting long enough to take a swallow of coffee. "I have to rearrange all the furniture, have Maria clean the game room, and set up the bar in there, have the liquor store make a delivery...." The tapping increased. "And on top of all that, I have to go get both of us something to wear."

"Us?" Rose swallowed hard at the implication.

"Well, yes, of course." Ronnie looked at her quizzically. "You don't want to greet everyone wearing my Dartmouth shirt, do you?"

"Uh...." The shock hadn't worn off yet, and Rose was at a loss for words. "I...well...."

"Rose, I'm not trying to punish you by making you meet my family, but I'm not going to lock you up in a room all alone for the evening while there's a party going on." The pencil found its way to perfect white teeth, which began gnawing at the eraser. "Actually," she mumbled around the yellow writing implement while looking around the room. "Think we can both hide in here all night?"

They chuckled for a few seconds before the seriousness of the situation took over. Ronnie set the pencil on the desk and moved her chair closer to the bed. "As much as I'd like to let you stay hidden away, everyone knows that there's a bathroom in here." They were interrupted by Maria bouncing into the room with the tray of food and a decanter of coffee.

"Where are you going to want the tree?" the housekeeper asked.

"In someone else's house," Ronnie wisecracked, drawing a snort from her companion. "I don't care. Rose and I are going to hide out in here all night."

"Don't even think about it, Veronica Louise." Maria set the tray over Rose's lap and began pouring coffee into the ceramic mug. Ronnie held her own cup out expectantly. "There isn't enough time to get the carpets cleaned."

"Vacuuming will be fine. Thanks." Ronnie pulled the cup to her lips and took a grateful sip. "Do you want me to call somewhere and get extra help to get the place ready?"

A look akin to hurt flashed through the brown eyes of the housekeeper. "Just because you don't run around like your mother checking for dust doesn't mean that I've let this house go unattended. I polish the silver regularly, even if you don't use it. Except for a quick run of the vacuum and moving the furniture, we're all set for company. Of course I can't put that coffee table back the way it should be."

"I'm sorry, Maria, I didn't mean to suggest that you did anything less than a perfect job. I'll take care of the coffee table and everything else." She drained her cup. "Right now, I need to run out and get a few things." Ronnie stood up and gave Rose a smile. "Your nurse should be here in a little while, and I'll be back in a couple of hours. What's your favorite color?"

"Really, I don't–"

"Color?"

Rose looked into deep azure depths, and the answer came without thought. "Blue."

"Easy to find something nice in that color. What shade? Do you prefer light tones like turquoise or dark ones like cobalt?"

"Um…a bright blue, I guess. Something deep and rich." Rose shifted nervously and looked down at her toast. "I guess any shade is fine."

"I'll make sure to pick something nice out." Ronnie smiled inwardly at the thought of being able to pick a dress for her to wear.

"If it's too much trouble, I can go in another room. I could take a book into the laundry room. No one will go in there," Rose offered, feeling very much in the way.

"No," Ronnie answered quickly. "I'm not going to hide you. You're a guest in my home, and they're just going to have to accept it." She flashed a look to Maria, who nodded in agreement. "I'll be back before lunch."

Chapter Nine

It was easy enough for Ronnie to walk into the exclusive boutique and pick out a dress for herself. It was quite another thing to pick out something for Rose to wear. For the better part of an hour, she sat there watching the model try on different combinations of blouses and skirts, pantsuits, and dresses. Nothing seemed right.

"Perhaps if you told me what exactly you were looking for, Miss Cartwright," the manager said.

"I'm not really certain how to explain it, but none of these will work." Ronnie waved a hand at the rack of clothes. The matronly woman looked at her particular customer and frowned.

"What is wrong with them? Perhaps we can figure out what you're looking for that way."

"There's nothing *wrong* with them so much as they're just not right." She pinched the bridge of her nose. "Maybe I should just look around and see if there's something I like."

"By all means." The boutique manager waved her arm. "Joyce will be happy to model anything you wish."

Ronnie walked through the racks of expensive garments, barely giving any of them more than a passing glance. Then she saw it. Tucked into the corner, she almost missed it and in fact, wasn't even sure what made her look in that direction. She reached over and pulled the dress out to look at it. Just a shade below a bright blue, the silk shimmered with beauty and softness. The material gathered at the elastic waistband before flaring out again. Ronnie guessed that it would reach down to Rose's ankles, easily covering the casts. "This one," she announced, drawing the manager's attention.

"Would you like Monica to model it?"

"That won't be necessary. This is the one I want." She glanced at the size tag. "Yes, this will be perfect."

The Jeep worked its way through the holiday traffic. A glance at the clock on the radio told Ronnie that it was almost eleven. So far, she had been to the boutique and the jeweler. Now it was off to the mall to fight with other shoppers for the little things that were needed...like gifts. She was within a mile of the mall when a corner lot full of trees caught her eye. She pulled the Cherokee over and walked through the aisles of pine and balsam propped up against wooden rails. Seeing a sale, the stocky merchant dashed over to her side.

"What can I help you with today?"

"I need a tree with nice full boughs and a sturdy top." Ronnie gave disapproving looks at the group in front of her.

"We have very nice ones toward the back," he said, gesturing toward the taller pines leaned against the chain link fence that ran along the back of the lot. "How tall are you looking for?"

Ronnie's brow furrowed as she tried to imagine just how tall the trees in her home usually were. "Tall. Over eight feet."

"Oh, well then." His eyes lit up even more, and his pace quickened. "We have some beautiful nine- and ten-footers."

Ronnie settled on a ten-foot tree that seemed to want to burst forth from the ropes holding it. The man called his son over to help, and the three of them lifted it to the top of the Jeep. It hung over the front, the white rope running from the tree to the front bumper. A pair of ropes did the same to the back. Once fully secured, Ronnie resumed her journey to the mall.

Holiday ditties were piped through the speakers, adding to the general din of the crowd. Everyone had bags in his or her hands and was in a hurry to finish shopping. Ronnie gripped her purse closer to her body and headed for Macy's. A few gift certificates and her shopping would be done. As she moved through the bustling crowd, she saw the Christmas shop, a generic store opened just for the holidays to sell everything from tinsel to lights to ornaments of every possible design. Ronnie picked up a shopping basket and began filling it with the usual decorations. Soon the basket was full, but she wasn't finished. After nailing down a clerk to help her, Ronnie spent the better part of an hour picking both tasteful and fun things to convert her dour residence into a festive home. Just as she handed the clerk her credit card, she noticed one item that had been overlooked. "Oh, wait. I'll need that, too." She pointed an elegant finger at the item in question. As the sprig of mistletoe was added to her purchases, Ronnie's mind entertained the possible benefit of catching Rose beneath it. "Add a few more, will you, please?"

"What's going on?"

Rose looked up and saw Ronnie's concerned face as she entered the room. "I-it's okay," she croaked, embarrassed at the drops that continued to run down her cheeks. "I have to stretch, and it hurts."

"Let's try again," Karen said gently, putting her hands in position.

"No, wait, please. Can't we try again later?" she implored, desperate to take her Vicodin and ease the pain.

"Let me try," Ronnie said, replacing Karen's hands with her own. The young woman watched as the nurse explained how to properly stretch. Blue eyes looked down at her. "You think you're ready?"

Rose stared back, her eyes conveying her fear of the pain. "Be gentle." She was still hesitant, but there was something reassuring about the warmth of Ronnie's hands on her foot.

"I swear." The softly spoken words bathed her with a sense of reassurance. She closed her eyes and concentrated on the feeling of the strong fingers on her skin. Slowly, she raised her leg to the point where she felt the pull up the back of her thighs.

"Come on, Rose...that's it, just a little more now."

Rose felt her limb being raised higher and resisted the urge to fight against it. "That's good, you're doing great. You think we can go a little higher? Just a little bit?"

Ever so slowly, Rose lifted her leg until she couldn't take the pain anymore. Dimly, she realized that it was higher than she had been able to go before, but that was immaterial at the moment. "Please...."

"Okay, relax now. We're going to go back down." Rose's eyes were closed tightly, and she clung to Ronnie's words and soothing tone fervently. "There you go, almost done now." Soon the cool sheet greeted her heel, and she let out a deep breath.

"How do you feel?"

Rose opened her eyes with surprise at the proximity of the voice and found herself staring into the endless blue depths. "It hurts."

"Shh, it's over now." Ronnie looked up at Karen. "I think we're done for the day. I have a party here tonight that we have to get ready for. Is there anything else that has to be done?"

"Just bathing Miss Grayson."

"Oh." Rose looked from one woman to the other. "I can wash myself mostly if someone can get the water and washcloth for me."

She tried to tell her benefactor with her eyes that this was what she preferred to do.

"Okay. I guess we can handle everything else, Karen. We'll see you tomorrow."

Rose relaxed with Ronnie's words, until she remembered the rest of them...*a party here tonight that we have to get ready for.* "Oh, God, the party."

"Don't worry about it," Ronnie replied, walking into the bathroom. "I'll get the things together that you'll need to wash up, then we'll get you dressed." The sound of water running into the basin mixed with the words. "I've got to get everything from the car and find the stand for the tree." She returned with the washbowl, soap, and cloth. "I think it's in the attic. Do you need anything else before I go?"

"No, this is great." Rose maintained her smile until the older woman left the room. That's when the panic set in. A party. A party full of strangers. A party full of high-class strangers. A party full of high-class strangers related to Ronnie. The Dartmouth shirt found its way off her body and onto the bed. Rose felt the pressure building from within not to do anything to embarrass her friend. The soapy cloth moved over her arms and shoulders as she thought about the possible disasters that could befall the evening. Her legs could get bumped accidentally, she could spill a drink down her front, say the wrong thing—all those thoughts and a dozen others passed through her mind while she continued to clean herself.

She was just finishing up when Ronnie knocked on the door. "May I come in?" Rose covered her chest with the fluffy towel before answering. She gasped when her friend walked in with a bag in one hand and the most gorgeous dress she had ever seen in the other.

"It's beautiful," she whispered in awe.

"Glad you like it. I've got all the things you'll need to wear with it, so it's just as good a time as any to get you dressed." Ronnie walked over to the bed and set the bag down. "Then you can help me with the other things that need to be done." She reached into the bag and pulled out a lacy brassiere, snapping off the price tags effortlessly. "I got one that closed in the front." Rose noted that the older woman wouldn't look directly at her. "I thought that would be easier for you."

"Yes, it would be, thank you." She wasn't sure how to take what appeared to be shyness mixed with enthusiasm from her friend. Ronnie seemed almost nervous to her. She took the bra and ran her fingertips over the lacy trim. They were low-cut cups, designed to be worn with something that showed cleavage and had no padding, not that she needed any help in that department. Rose was quite comfortable with her 36C bust that had only recently began to droop as all breasts are required to do after age twenty-five. She looked at the size tag. 36B. Well, it would still fit, she decided, just make her appear more busty. She let the towel drop and slipped her arms through the straps before hooking it. "It fits nicely, thanks," she said, drawing Ronnie's attention away from the sales receipt that she had been studying intently.

"I wasn't sure what size to get. Do the straps need adjusting?"

"Actually, yeah, they do." Rose sat up as best she could while Ronnie sat down next to her on the bed and slipped her fingers under the thin strap.

"Let me know when it feels right," she said. Rose nodded and tried to focus on the task at hand.

"A little higher...no, a little less than that...yeah, that's good." She placed her hand on the side of her right breast and checked the fit. Yes, it felt just right. Ronnie walked around to the other side and repeated the process. The end result was exactly what Rose thought it would be. Her breasts pushed up from the confines of the lacy bra, appearing to her to be larger than usual.

"Um...do you like it? I can still run out and get a different one if you don't like it."

"No, it's fine, really," she assured. "Truthfully, I don't think I've ever owned such a pretty bra." She looked up to see a smile on Ronnie's face. "It's very nice of you, thanks."

"Oh, there's more." She returned to the bag and pulled out a silky lace half-slip and equally delicate panties. "I had to guess at the size for these, too, but they should be close."

With Ronnie's help, Rose pulled the half-slip over her head and into position. She flushed with embarrassment as Ronnie helped her get the panties on, unable to take over the job herself until they were within inches of being pulled all the way up. "How are we going to get the dress on?"

"Easy. We have to put you in the chair first, though."

Sitting in nothing but undergarments in the wheelchair, Rose patiently waited while Ronnie gathered the layers of blue material. "Put your arms up." She did as told, and soon the dress was in position. It hurt her hamstrings to lean forward while it was zipped and tucked around her waist, but it was over quickly. A new pair of large tube socks covered her feet and ankles. "That's the best I can do. I don't think slippers or anything like that would fit over the cast."

Ronnie stepped back to admire her handiwork. She had good reason to be proud. Rose was a vision, even with the stitches still prominently displayed on her right cheek. Her golden hair hung loosely over her shoulders, creating an aura that captivated the older woman. The rich blue of the dress highlighted alabaster skin, and the low front accented another set of lovely features. As she gazed at the vision before her, Ronnie could no longer deny that she was feeling an attraction to the young woman. "You look beautiful," she said, sadly knowing inside that she could never act on that feeling. The truth of the accident ruined any chance of that.

"Thank you," Rose replied. She ran her hand down the shimmering fabric. It was so delicate, so beautiful. A lump formed in her throat, and she found herself blinking rapidly. It was obvious that Ronnie had taken great care in picking out the clothes. She didn't even want to think about how much everything cost her wealthy friend. A tear started down her cheek. "Everything is perfect...it's all...."

"Hey, if it really is too much for you, I'll figure something else out," Ronnie cooed, kneeling next to the chair.

"No, I can do this. I..." Rose sniffled and lifted her head, convinced that she had her emotions under control. "I told you about my life. I've never been to fancy parties or worn beautiful clothes like this. I've given up on trying to figure out why you're helping me, but it's still a bit overwhelming sometimes." She clasped the larger hand resting on her own. "I know I thank you all the time and I seem to cry at the drop of a hat, but I can't remember when anyone has been so good to me." She lowered her eyes, the gentle green partially obscured by naturally long lashes. "You're a very special woman, Veronica Cartwright."

"So are you," Ronnie countered, squeezing the hand beneath hers. The grandfather clock in the living room bonged with the arrival of the top of the hour. "I'd better finish getting everything inside and get changed. The decorators and caterers will be arriving soon." She stood up, reluctantly removing her hand from between Rose's. "Do you want to hang out in the living room or stay in here for a while longer?"

"I think I'd like to go out there if I won't be in the way. It'd be nice to watch everything get set up."

"Fine." Ronnie smiled and grabbed the handles of the wheelchair. "I'll put you to work then. You can direct traffic and make sure the decorations are evenly spaced on the tree."

"Tree? You bought a tree?" Rose's eyes lit up with excitement.

"Hey, I may not want to throw this party, but if I'm going to do it, I'm going to do it right. Besides, wouldn't you like a tree for Christmas?"

"I uh...yeah, that would be very nice." She didn't believe that Ronnie would decorate at all based on their earlier conversations, but now.... "A tree would be very nice."

Ronnie decided that the smile she received was worth all the trees in the world. "Great. Let's go get this place ready."

Maria expertly controlled the traffic of caterers and decorators. Calls for surge protectors and extra outlets were met with ease by the experienced housekeeper. Whether it was tacks to hang up the streamers or the mini steamer to clean up a spill on the carpet, she was one step ahead of them. Even the issue of Tabitha had been settled. Feline, food, litter box, and a bag of catnip were now relaxing in the laundry room. With her chair in the far corner of the living room, Rose stayed out of the way but was still able to keep an eye on the symmetry of the tree decorations. With Maria busy and Ronnie nowhere in sight, the decorators turned to her time and again for instructions on where to place this ornament or that string of lights. Rose tried to think about how her friend would like it to look. She decided that tasteful yet appealing to the eye would be nice with just a touch of flair thrown in.

Ronnie stopped halfway down the stairs and just gaped at what she saw. A colorful array of blue, yellow, and red ornaments accented the branches of the tree, no one area screaming for more attention than the other. Tinsel was draped in light strips throughout, also with the same sense of symmetry. Multi-colored strings of lights twinkled and glowed with the exception of one set. Blue and red chaser lights formed a double-helix design from the base up to the top, drawing attention to the traditional star resting there. The tree was absolutely perfect to her.

Slowly, her head turned to take in the rest of the effect. The decorations were scattered about the room, transforming it into an open and welcoming space. Twisted streamers of red and green rimmed the room, old family ornaments hanging off them like tassels.

Ronnie smiled as the sense of nostalgia flooded through her, and images of childhood parties superimposed themselves over the modern scene.

The hostess wasn't the only one stunned into silence. Rose looked up and found she couldn't tear her eyes away. The velvet dress stopped just above the knees and was the same shade as Ronnie's hair. A gold herringbone necklace and matching belt accented the diamond-studded earrings and bracelet, giving color to the outfit. A touch of blush enhanced the natural highlights of her cheekbones, and a shade called coincidentally enough, *Always Rose*, emphasized her lips and nails. The soft velvet scooped down respectably in the front, perfect for family occasions, and the three-quarter sleeves highlighted every movement of her long arms. Veronica Cartwright was, in a word...stunning.

Ronnie worked her way down the stairs, still enchanted by the miracle performed on her living room. "It's perfect," she said when she reached the young woman's side.

"I saw the box of old ornaments and thought it might be nice to put them out where everyone could see and remember them. I hope that was all right. It gave color to the entire room instead of just the corner with the tree."

"It was a wonderful idea, and I love it." She gave a smile reserved for Rose alone. The grandfather clock chimed. "Mother's going to be here any minute." Ronnie knelt down next to the chair. "Sometimes my mother can be a bit...harsh. I'll try to keep her away from you. Don't forget what I said about Susan being a gossip. I have to walk around and speak with everyone, but I'll try to spend as much time near you as I can." The sound of a limousine pulling up in the driveway filtered through to them. "That's probably her and Aunt Elaine."

As expected, Beatrice Cartwright arrived with her younger sister Elaine. Beatrice took her role as matriarch seriously, feeling that it outranked everything else, including the president of Cartwright Corporation. She was no sooner in the door than she was ordering the decorators around and scrutinizing the caterer's work. While Ronnie was busy listening to her mother's demands about the party, Elaine wandered into the living room and spotted Rose.

"Hello there."

"Hello."

"Elaine McCarthy, Ronnie's aunt." She held out her well-manicured hand.

"Rose Grayson. I'm...a friend of Ronnie." She returned the gesture. Elaine removed her red scarf to reveal dyed brown hair.

"Well..." the older woman said, looking around, "Seems like Ronnie did a halfway decent job." She reached into her overstuffed pocketbook and pulled out a silver cigarette case. "I'm surprised the party is here this year. She's managed to worm her way out of the last two family get-togethers." A press of the button on the silver lighter and the cigarette glowed to life. "You know where the ashtrays are?"

"Um, no, I don't," Rose replied, hoping that the woman would take her foul-smelling vice somewhere else.

"Well, I don't need it right this instant. So tell me, what happened?"

"I was hit by a car." She shifted in her chair, uncomfortable with the memory.

"That's a shame. But that's what insurance is for, I guess. I hope you have a good lawyer." Elaine exhaled, sending a stream of smoke into Rose's face. "My plane was over twenty minutes late getting into Albany. I can drive through snow with no problem. I don't understand why pilots whine so much about the snow. It's not like they have to come to any sudden stops or anything." The smoke hung in the air, forcing Rose to blink rapidly to keep from tearing up. "I guess people always have *something* to complain about."

Rose thought briefly about pointing out the fallacy in the wealthy woman's thinking but decided against it. "I guess so," she said, craning her head around to look for Ronnie.

"Exactly!" Elaine said enthusiastically, her movements causing ashes to fall on the carpet.

"Oh, let me go find you an ashtray." Rose gripped the wheels of her chair and prepared to make her exit.

"Now why bother doing that?" Elaine caught the attention of a passing waiter. "Excuse me, I don't see any ashtrays around here." Her condescending tone wasn't missed by either the young man or Rose.

"I'll get you one right away, Miss," he replied.

"And I don't think it would hurt anything for someone to start tending bar." She turned her attention back to Rose. "Really, you'd think we paid them to stand around." Another ash fell onto the carpet. "When my husband, Richard, was alive, the workers never even thought about striking. They knew where their paychecks came from.

Then the damn unions came along..." Elaine paused long enough to pull a chair over, effectively cutting off any thought Rose had of escape.

Ronnie wasn't faring much better in the kitchen. "Mother—"

"Now there's nothing wrong with saying the truth, Veronica." She cast a disdainful look around the room. "The refrigerator should be opposite the stove, not next to it. That's why we had it on the other side of the room."

"It's easier for Maria to work with it over here." Ronnie had forgotten that her mother hadn't been over since the remodeling last summer.

Beatrice stepped away from her daughter. "Heaven forbid Maria walk a few steps to get the butter. It didn't bother her mother when she worked for us." She shook her head dismissively. "Coddling, Veronica. I've warned you about coddling."

"I don't think moving the fridge ten feet constitutes coddling, Mother."

"Of course you wouldn't, dear." The hairs on Ronnie's neck bristled at the tone. "And what did you get for rearranging the kitchen? Did Maria still ask for her annual raise? Of course she did. I'm sure most of this..." she pointed at the cook's island and the dishwasher, "...was her idea."

"Why don't we go see the tree? They did a very nice job decorating it."

"We'll see." Ronnie reluctantly followed her mother out of the kitchen.

Rose watched the two of them enter the living room. "See how the ornaments from when we were kids are out? Isn't that nice?"

"Very nice." For the first time since she entered the house, Beatrice actually smiled. "I remember how every year you gave me an ornament. I guess some family traditions are destined to fall by the wayside." She turned and noticed her sister and the woman in a wheelchair. "Ah, there you are, Elaine. And who do we have here?"

"Mother, this is Rose Grayson. Rose, Beatrice Cartwright." Ronnie's voice remained pleasant, but her eyes narrowed at the wisps of smoke rising from the crystal plate being used as an ashtray.

"Pleased to meet you, Mrs. Cartwright," the young woman said.

"Grayson...Grayson...." The wrinkled brow furrowed with thought. "I don't recall any Graysons. What happened to your face? And the rest of you?"

"I was in an accident."

"Oh," she tsked. "You poor thing. Such a pretty face ruined like that." Beatrice moved to get a better look at Rose's right cheek. "Well, don't give up hope, dear. It's amazing what they can do with plastic surgery these days."

Rose looked down at her lap, wishing she was keeping Tabitha company at the moment instead of being subjected to this torture. She didn't see the empathetic gaze being cast on her by Ronnie. "I'm just happy to be alive."

"Of course," the matriarch said before turning to face her daughter. "So what brings her to our *family* Christmas party?"

Rose wasn't sure which bothered her more, the fact that Beatrice was speaking as if she wasn't there or that with just a few short words, the older woman made her feel more like an outsider than ever. Suddenly, a warm hand rested on her shoulder. "Rose is staying with me while she recovers."

"Couldn't her own people take care of her?"

"She's a friend and a guest in my home, Mother." The hand on her shoulder gave a quick squeeze before withdrawing, a reassuring gesture Rose greatly appreciated.

Beatrice looked at her daughter and nodded. "Of course, Veronica. We had no way of knowing that you had company. I'm sure the caterers can come up with an extra plate."

"I'm sure they can." On the surface, Ronnie appeared calm, but the rhythmic clenching of her jaw didn't go unnoticed by Rose.

"Well...." Beatrice looked at her sister. "Elaine, I think there's too much red on the lower branches. Come help me show these people how to properly decorate a tree."

Elaine made only the barest of attempts to put her cigarette out. "The problem isn't the balls, it's the lights." She set her purse down next to Rose's chair. "Be a dear and keep an eye on this for me. I don't want to have to drag it around." She walked away without waiting for an answer.

"You okay?" Ronnie asked once the older women were out of earshot. She could only imagine what Elaine had said to Rose before she and her mother had entered the room. The young woman took a deep breath before answering.

"They're quite a pair, aren't they?"

"I tried to warn you."

"You weren't exaggerating." She looked up into deep blue eyes. "Ronnie, if it's going to be a problem, I can go into the laundry room. I don't mind, really."

"I should have let you take that escape when you could," she said apologetically. "Unfortunately, they've seen you. You're stuck just like me until the last guest is gone." She leaned down and whispered conspiratorially, "Welcome to the world of the rich and snobbish." The doorbell announced the first in a stream of arrivals. "I guess it's time to meet the rest of the family."

In groups of twos and threes, the relatives arrived. Limousines and luxury cars lined the long driveway and filled the parking area while taxis dropped off even more attendees. The electronic age allowed word to travel quickly, and word was that the place to be that evening was the old Cartwright Mansion.

Susan and Jack arrived almost an hour later than expected. The redhead joined her mother and sister while her husband headed for the bar. "What a crowd," she said joyously as she approached.

"Yes, it does appear to be shaping up to be a success," Beatrice replied. "Your brother isn't here yet, though."

"What a shame," Ronnie muttered before taking a sip from her long-stemmed champagne flute.

"What was that, dear?"

"Nothing, Mother." She scanned the room. "Excuse me, I have to go tend to my guests. Susan, you can help greet the new arrivals." Long legs carried her away before they could respond.

The corner opposite the tree seemed to be a good place for Rose to hide out. People stopped by, inquired about what happened to her, gave sympathetic looks, and moved on. She had been eavesdropping on a nearby conversation about the history of a particular ornament when she saw Ronnie moving through the crowd. Blue eyes smiled warmly at her, and the tall hostess headed in her direction. "How are you?"

"Fine. Is that your sister?" She pointed at the redhead standing next to Beatrice.

"Mmm." Ronnie took a sip, letting the tiny bubbles tickle her nose. "Everyone seems to be having a good time. I've heard more than one compliment on the decorations. Putting the old ornaments out along the streamers really was a good idea."

"Thank you." Rose smiled shyly and looked around the room. "Quite the crowd."

"Yeah, and some of them were actually invited. Susan said there'd be close to forty, and we're well past that figure now." She tasted the champagne again. "Where's yours?"

Rose lowered her voice and looked around, not wanting to be overheard. "I didn't think I should...you know, with the Vicodin and all." She felt alone enough being in a roomful of strangers, but without being able to even join them in a simple toast made her feel even more isolated.

"Oh...I didn't think of that." Ronnie looked around and waved a serving person over, taking a step away from her in the process. The din of the crowd and the holiday music made it impossible for Rose to hear what was said. A few whispers later, the elegant hostess returned to her side.

"Is everything okay?"

"Fine. I just had to take care of something." Ronnie retrieved her glass. "Have you met everyone?"

"I think so. It seems like I've been saying 'hit by a car' all night long." The injured woman gave a short laugh. "There's a little boy running around."

"Tyler."

"Yeah, he's a cutie. Anyway, he was over here earlier. Stepped up on the coffee table before I could stop him and asked me if my stitches hurt."

"Stepped...." Ronnie looked past her to see if there were any scuff marks. "He walked on my table?"

Rose smiled at her friend. "Don't worry, I made him get down, but before I did, he leaned over and kissed my cheek."

"He what?"

"He kissed my cheek. Said his mother did that to his boo-boos."

"Tyler did that?"

"Yeah, the little boy." She watched as Ronnie's expression changed from one of annoyance to one of pleasure at the kind act.

The serving person arrived with a long-stemmed glass filled with amber liquid. "Here's your drink, Miss."

"I didn't–" Rose stopped when she saw the look on Ronnie's face. "I mean, thanks." She took the glass, thinking that perhaps her benefactor had wanted another drink without anyone knowing about it. The waitress smiled and walked away to take care of the other guests.

"It's ginger ale. I thought you'd like something to drink that looked like the champagne," the older woman said, taking a sip from her own.

"Yes, this is perfect," Rose replied, bringing the glass to her lips. The tiny bubbles from the soda tickled her nose much like she supposed the champagne would. The color match was almost perfect. The ginger ale was so light in color that no one would suspect that it was anything different than what they were drinking.

A blonde woman in a blue dress stopped by to talk with the hostess, giving Rose the opportunity to watch her friend. Ronnie's body language spoke of friendliness, but her eyes told a different story. Obviously, there was something about this particular person that the wealthy woman didn't like. The blue eyes darted about as if looking for an escape, yet the words continued to flow freely from her lips. Rose decided that she liked the way that particular shade of lipstick looked on Ronnie. The discreet slit in the black velvet revealed that the tall woman chose to wear a garter and stockings that evening instead of hose. The fair-haired woman had never seen anyone wear such an item before, being far more familiar with the kind that came from a plastic egg than expensive boutiques. Rose watched expertly manicured nails tap the champagne glass in a nameless rhythm as the conversation between Ronnie and the woman in blue dragged on. Again the young woman's mind went back to the puzzle of why she was there. Surely, someone like Veronica Cartwright didn't lack for company. So why did someone like that want her around?

The woman in blue finally found someone else to talk to, and Ronnie was once again standing by Rose's side. "That's Agnes, Frank's wife."

"And Frank is...?" Rose tried, but there were just too many Cartwrights to remember.

"Cousin, car wash."

"Oh, right. Is he the one who cheated on his taxes?"

"They probably all do that, but he has it down to an art form. How'd you know that?"

Rose smiled at the quizzical look. "The man with the toupee and one with the cigar were talking, and I heard one of them comment on it." She gave a sheepish grin. "I was just sitting here, and they were right there. I couldn't miss it."

"So you're the one to go to when I want information, huh?"

"I guess it depends on the information."

Ronnie put her hands on the arm of the wheelchair and knelt down so that only Rose could hear her. "So what are they saying about the party? I know what they've said to me, but what are they saying to each other?"

"Everyone is raving about how nice it is. That it reminds them of parties from years ago. You're getting lots of compliments." She didn't miss the look of pride that crossed Ronnie's face.

"So they're really having a good time?"

"Yes, a fabulous time, actually. I heard more than one say that they wished you'd do it every year."

Ronnie looked around. "You know, it is nice to see the whole family here again. It's like when Dad was alive."

Rose put her hand on her friend's shoulder. "You really miss him, don't you?" Blue eyes regarded her seriously before she received an almost imperceptible nod.

"He enjoyed these parties." Ronnie pivoted and looked at the tree. "Christmas was his favorite time. He'd get such a kick out of seeing the kids opening their presents or reminiscing with everyone." Her face took on a faraway look. "He used to drag out the projector and screen and show the old home movies." There was a long pause. "Yeah, I miss him." Ronnie stood up, withdrawing her hand from under the smaller one. "He would have liked this." A commotion near the door drew their attention. "Damn."

Rose watched the transformation before her. Lips pressed tight, eyes narrowed to intimidating slits, jaw muscles clenching...everything about Ronnie's appearance spoke of being ready for trouble. The gold and black outfit only moments before had made her appear soft. Now it helped to make her seem downright dangerous. Rose turned her head to see what had captured her friend's attention. "Is that Tommy?" At Ronnie's nod, she studied the man who dared to return after the fiasco the evening before. Good looks ran in the family, she decided, taking in his sandy hair, piercing blue eyes, and athletic body. It was hard for her to reconcile the image before her with the screaming maniac of a man who had flipped over the mahogany coffee table. "I can't believe he showed up," she finally said after a minute.

"It's an act, you know. Him smiling and being all nice-nice like that. He's just charming Mother and Susan...and anyone else who's foolish enough to fall for it."

"What are you going to do?" Rose couldn't imagine Ronnie confronting him in front of the whole family at the Christmas party, but she also couldn't see her putting up with his presence all night long.

"I guess I'd better get over there and say hello to my brother." She held her glass out. "Keep an eye on this for me. I'll be back in a few minutes."

"Ronnie…" she said, taking the crystal. "You okay?"

"Part of being in my position is having to be nice to people I can't stand. If I don't get over there, Mother will think that I'm snubbing him."

Rose watched her walk away, thinking to herself how hard it had to be for Ronnie to be pleasant to her brother after the previous night's antics. She said a silent prayer for the evening to go well.

As Ronnie headed toward her siblings, she felt a tugging on her dress. She turned and looked down to see a round face smiling up at her.

"Hi, Cousin Ronnie."

"Hi, Tyler," she replied, kneeling down to his level. "How are you? Are you having a good time?"

"Yeah." He held out a little cookie covered with red sprinkles. "There's lots of stuff to eat."

"So you like the cookies, huh?" She reached out and wrapped one long arm around him. "That was very nice of you to give Rose a kiss." Tyler smiled shyly and put the holiday treat in his mouth.

"If you kith the boo-boos, they get better," he mumbled, spewing cookie crumbs with each syllable.

Ronnie pulled him close and gave him a hug. "I hope so." She stood up and tousled his hair. "You're a good boy, Tyler." She turned to go, but he tugged on the velvet again. "What is it?"

"Do you know where the baffroom is?" He grabbed himself to stress his urgency.

"Yup, come on, you." She picked him up and quickly moved across the room, not stopping until she was in the office. "In that room." She pointed at the other door.

While she was waiting to take him back out, she noticed the Vicodin sitting on the table next to the bed. *Oh, I don't think that's a good idea,* she said to herself, snatching the brown plastic bottle. Once Tyler was finished, she sent him back out into the living room and put the prescription on the top shelf of the medicine cabinet, certain that up there it would be well out of reach of any curious little hands. That task finished, she stepped into the living room and steeled herself to greet her brother.

"Oh, here comes Ronnie," Susan said.

"Good. I don't know where she's been all this time," the matriarch said in a disapproving tone.

"Sorry, I had to help Tyler find the bathroom," Ronnie said, giving a smile full of teeth. "Hello, Tommy."

"Hi, Sis, how are you?" He leaned over and kissed her cheek. "Bitch!" he hissed before stepping back. "That dress looks wonderful on you, doesn't it, Mother?"

"It's very nice but too dark." She reached out and tugged on the velvet sleeve. "You should wear lighter colors, Veronica."

"Well, I think she looks lovely," he said, sounding totally supportive of his oldest sister. "Ronnie looks good no matter what she wears."

That's right, lay it on thick, you son of a bitch, she thought to herself. "You look nice tonight, too, Tommy. New suit?"

"Actually, it is. I didn't think anything I had was good enough for tonight."

"I'm sure of that." Blue eyes shot daggers at the sandy-haired man.

"After all, I do believe this is the first time that you've allowed the family in here since you took it over." He gave her a sinister grin, daring her to push it.

"I think it looks very nice here tonight," Susan chirped. "I like the way you hung all the ornaments around. Everyone's stopping to look at them. I want to see the one I made in the third grade. Ronnie, can you help me find it?"

Ronnie gratefully took the escape offered her. "Yeah, I think it's over here."

They walked through the crowd until a flash of golden hair caught Susan's eye. Immediately, the redhead's direction changed. "Where are you going?" Ronnie asked.

"To meet the infamous Rose Grayson," she replied. "Aunt Elaine said she was in a car accident."

"Susan...."

"Now what kind of hostess would I be if I didn't stop by and meet everyone?" Her eyes twinkled with mischief.

"I thought I was the one hosting the party. It is my home."

"Whatever." The redhead replied, obviously not interested in silly technical details like that. "Either way, I really should meet her." She felt a firm hand grab her upper arm.

"Don't you dare put her through one of your famous inquisitions." Ronnie lessened her grip but only slightly. "I mean, she's kinda shy."

"How am I supposed to learn anything about a person if I don't ask them questions?" Susan teased, but the serious look on her sister's face made her reconsider. "I just want to say hello. I'm not going to ask her for every personal detail of her life."

"Promise?"

"I promise."

Rose was finishing her ginger ale when she saw the sisters approach. "Rose, I'd like to introduce you to my sister, Susan Cartwright."

"Younger sister," the redhead corrected. She held her hand out. "I've heard a lot about you, Rose. It's nice to finally meet you." Truth be told, Susan had grilled both her mother and aunt in search of information about the mysterious woman. She looked at the row of stitches and tsked. "What a shame to mar such a pretty face."

"Susan, I think Alexandra is around here somewhere. You haven't seen her in a while."

Ronnie's attempt to get her sister away failed. "No, you go ahead, Sis. I'll stay here and chat with Rose." Susan crossed in front of the chair-bound woman and sat demurely on the coffee table, a much more comfortable position in which to interrogate her unknowing victim. "So tell me, Rose, how do you know Ronnie?"

"I um...." Green eyes looked up to blue, pleading for help.

"She was a sorority sister at Pi Epsilon Gamma," Ronnie blurted.

"Really?" Susan looked from Rose to her sister and back again. "But you look so much younger than Ronnie."

"Um...I skipped a couple of grades in school."

"Oh, that's nice. Still, you must have been a freshman when Ronnie was in her senior year."

"I was," Rose replied, still exchanging looks of desperation with her friend. She wasn't sure the exact reason for the lie but understood that there was no way to go back now.

"So where are you from?"

"Oh, well...I grew up in and around Albany." She was afraid of lying and mentioning a city that the worldly redhead would be familiar with.

"Really? Well, Ronnie and I went to Saint Sebastian's Academy."

"Home of the Tigers," Rose offered, drawing a smile from Susan. She was now grateful for the hours spent at the library reading the local newspaper.

"Yes. I was the head cheerleader the year we went to the state championships."

"Which sport?"

"Well, basketball of course," the redhead said, her eyebrows rising slightly. "I'm surprised you didn't know that. Ronnie played...." She looked at her sister quizzically.

"I played guard," Ronnie said, silently wishing someone, anyone would come by to distract Susan.

"Yeah, that's right. You were all-conference that year, weren't you?"

"All-state."

"All-state," the redhead repeated, not particularly worried about that detail. "Anyway, enough about Ronnie. So what happened to you? I heard you were in a car accident."

"Actually, I was hit by a car."

"You mean you were walking and got hit?"

"Yeah."

"That's terrible. So are you paralyzed or something?"

"Susan," Ronnie admonished. "Her left ankle and both her legs are broken."

"That must hurt quite a bit, huh?"

"Well...yeah." Rose couldn't figure out why anyone would ask such a silly question. "My legs were broken very badly."

"That's a real shame. Well, at least you're lucky enough to have Ronnie taking care of you."

"Very lucky," Rose agreed. "I don't know what I would have done without her." She gave a smile to her friend, an action not unnoticed by Susan. The redhead stood up and smoothed her skirt. "Well, if you two would excuse me, I have to mingle. It was nice meeting you, Rose. I'm sure we'll see each other again soon."

"Nice to meet you, too."

"Ronnie, can you help me in the kitchen for a moment?" Susan asked in a sing-song voice, the kind that always grated on her older sister's nerves.

"Actually–"

"It'll only take a minute." She grabbed the velvet-covered elbow and tugged Ronnie away from Rose and into the kitchen, leaving the younger woman alone to her thoughts.

The caterers and Maria were occupying the kitchen, affording them no privacy. Susan spotted the laundry room door. "In here."

"You don't want to go in there," Ronnie warned, but it was too late. Her younger sister opened the door to reveal an annoyed pile of orange and white fluff.

"Mrrow!"

"You have a cat?"

"Well, don't just stand there. She'll get out." Ronnie gave her younger sister a shove and shut the door behind them.

"Does Mother know you have a cat?"

"She will about twenty seconds after you leave this room," Ronnie said knowingly. "So what did you want to talk about, as if I didn't already know?"

"She wasn't a sorority sister. I'd bet my Bentley that she never even went to Dartmouth." Susan leaned against the closed door, a Cheshire cat smile crossing her lips. "You know what I think, Ronnie?" She continued on without waiting for an answer. "I think this is a repeat of what happened at Stanford."

"You don't know what you're talking about. Rose is just a friend who I'm helping out, that's all."

"Is it? You give her a job, insurance…is she living with you?"

"She's staying with me while she heals."

"Oh, so this is a temporary arrangement?" Susan looked down at the cat, who was desperately trying to get Ronnie's attention. "So is it hers or yours? Or does it belong to both of you?"

"Stop it, Susan. Tabitha is Rose's cat, there's nothing going on between us, and this discussion is over." She reached past her sister and grabbed the door handle.

"Ronnie," Susan placed her hand on her older sister's shoulder. "Say what you want, but there's more to this than just helping out a 'friend.'" She stressed the last word, making it clear that she didn't believe that was the appropriate title for the honey-haired woman.

"Think what you want, but right now there's a roomful of people I need to attend to. And, Susan?"

"Yeah?"

"I don't think that Jack would be too happy to hear about André, do you?" Ronnie said, playing the only trump card she had on her sister. There was silence in the laundry room for a moment before Susan nodded, accepting the unspoken threat.

"This better not blow up in your face, Ronnie. You can't afford another incident like Christine."

"I know," Ronnie said solemnly.

Chapter Ten

Ronnie checked all the doors and set the alarm system once everyone was gone. "I'm glad that's over." She shut the lights to the Christmas tree off and turned to face Rose. "So that's my family. What do you think?"

"There's a lot of them," Rose replied. "Tyler's nice."

"He's too young to be a snob." Ronnie looked at her carpet. "Look at that. I knew someone would burn it." She scanned the rest of the room looking for damage, then realized that it was far too quiet. "Rose?" She didn't expect to see the sad face looking back at her. "Hey." Long legs crossed the room quickly. "What's wrong?"

"Nothing. I guess I'm just tired, that's all."

"No, there's more to it than that." Ronnie sat down on the coffee table, her knee touching the right wheel of the chair. "What's going on? Did someone say or do anything to upset you?"

There was silence for a moment before she received an answer. "Are you embarrassed by me?"

"Why would you say that?"

Rose shrugged. "I don't know, never mind."

"No." Ronnie reached out and placed her hand on the smaller one. "Is this because I lied to Susan?" The quick look away gave her the answer. "Rose, I'm not embarrassed or ashamed of you."

"Then why did you make up that story about me being a sorority sister?" Green eyes looked at her, revealing the confusion and hurt.

"I don't know," Ronnie sighed. "I'm not ashamed or embarrassed by you. If anything, I'm embarrassed by my family." She pulled her hand back and ran her long fingers through her dark hair. "Susan didn't believe me anyway." Realizing that she still owed an explanation, she continued. "I guess I just figured it was easier."

"Than telling them the truth? That I'm just a poor bum with nowhere else to stay?" Rose turned her head away, blinking rapidly to keep the tears in check.

"No, that's not it at all." Ronnie reached out and captured the young woman's chin with her fingers. "You're here because I want you to be here, not because there's nowhere else for you to stay," she said emphatically. "My family wouldn't understand that. I'm sorry if my attempt to protect you made you feel that I was embarrassed by you." She released Rose's chin and looked down. *Fucked up again,* she thought to herself. "You know how everyone acted toward you because you were in a wheelchair?"

"Yeah."

"If they knew that you didn't come from money, it would have been much worse. You would have been the topic of conversation instead of the hors d'oeuvres."

"So instead of being the cripple, I would have been the poor cripple living off you," the young woman clarified.

Ronnie chewed her lower lip, trying to think of a way to deny the truth in Rose's words. Finally, she gave a defeated nod. "That's how they would have seen it, yes, but that's not how I see it, and that's all that matters." She patted Rose's hand and stood up. "Right now I think we'd better let Tabitha out before she decides to claw her way through the door."

The clock on the stand next to the bed read 12:15 by the time Rose was changed out of the blue dress and back into the Dartmouth nightshirt. Tabitha paced back and forth across the bed, loudly protesting her time in confinement and demanding extra attention. Ronnie helped the young woman into bed and adjusted the pillows. "All set?"

"Yeah, I guess so." Rose looked around. "Do you know where my Vicodin is? I thought it was on the stand, but I don't see it."

"Sure do." Ronnie headed into the bathroom. "I put it up so Tyler wouldn't find it," she called out. Rose heard the medicine cabinet open and poured herself a cup of water in preparation. The sound of items being shoved back and forth on the shelves caused her to turn her head in the direction of the bathroom.

"Is something wrong?" She was answered with the continued moving about of items followed by the slamming of the medicine cabinet. "Ronnie?"

Ronnie exited the bathroom, her face an unreadable mask. "Someone took it."

"The Vicodin is gone?" The throbbing in Rose's legs that had begun earlier seemed to intensify at the news. Ronnie began pacing back and forth between the bed and the desk, her anger rising with each step.

"Tommy. I'll bet you anything it was him. I can't fucking believe he did that." Her hands balled into fists, and her jaw was visibly clenched. "Bastard comes into my home and does this to you. He had to know those were for you, your name was on the bottle. What kind of asshole takes medicine away from someone who so obviously needs it?"

"You don't know for sure that it was him."

"Oh, yes, I do. I can feel it." Her leather chair got in the way of her pacing, and she gave it a hard shove. "Unfuckingbelievable."

"Hey..." Rose said softly, reaching out and putting her hand on Ronnie's forearm, feeling the muscles bunched up beneath the skin. She let her thumb slip to the soft underside of the angry woman's arm and began gently rubbing. "There's nothing you can do about it now."

Ronnie's fury was close to the breaking point when she felt the soft touch. For reasons she couldn't explain, the anger seemed to dissipate, the tensed muscles relaxing under the soothing motion of Rose's thumb. She nodded in agreement and tried to think of a solution to their immediate problem. "I'll call the doctor. Maybe she can give you a new prescription." She headed to her desk and grabbed the thick phone book. "I'm sure there's a twenty-four-hour pharmacy somewhere." Ronnie flipped through the yellow pages, tearing several of them in the process with her desperation. "Doctors, see Physicians. Damn it, why can't they make it easy to find?"

"Ronnie...."

"Barnes...Barnes...there's no Barnes listed. I'll try the hospital." More pages flipped, more torn.

"Ronnie...."

"It'll be all right, Rose. We'll get a new prescription and you'll be all set in no time."

"Ronnie!"

"What?" She finally looked up from her frantic searching.

"Stop."

"But–"

"It's too late now to do anything. I'll have to wait until morning."

"Rose, you can't wait until morning." She looked back down at the yellow pages. "Look, there's an all-night pharmacy less than five miles from here."

"You can't go out now."

"Sure I can. I can be there and back within a half hour." She reached for the phone.

"Ronnie, no." She shifted, well aware of the pain in her legs. "It's starting to snow out there."

"So? I've driven in snow before." Her hand rested on the phone but didn't pick it up. "Rose, you need the Vicodin, you know that. How are you going to make it through the night without it?"

"I'll have to manage. Ronnie, I don't want you to drive tonight. It's snowing, and you've been drinking."

"I haven't had that much. I'm fine to drive." She rose to her feet, fully intending to change into more suitable clothes to go out in instead of her velvet dress.

"I'm sure the person who hit me felt the same way," Rose said quietly, causing Ronnie to stop and look at her, the words hitting home harder than Rose realized. "I don't ever want you to have to go through that."

Even though Ronnie knew she was unable to argue the point, she hesitated before lowering her head. "Are you sure that's what you want? I could take a cab," she offered.

"No. It's too late. Please, I can make it through one night." Even as she said the words, Rose wasn't all that sure. The pain had been steadily increasing, and she really wished she had a pill at that moment. "Do you have some Tylenol or Advil?"

"You know that won't touch the pain."

"It's better than nothing."

Ronnie left and returned a minute later with several bottles of over-the-counter painkillers from her medicine cabinet. While upstairs collecting them, she also grabbed her sweats and a T-shirt to sleep in, knowing that the couch would be her bed tonight. She went into the bathroom and changed while Rose sifted through the various products promising to relieve pain and took three pills. "You need anything else?" Ronnie asked when she returned.

"No, I think I'm all set." She reached for the covers, but her benefactor was faster.

"I got it. Move, Tabitha." The feline protested but moved out of the way. Ronnie tucked the blanket around Rose's body. "There you go."

"Thanks." The orange and white cat jumped back up and resumed her position on the bed.

"If you need anything, I'll be out on the couch."

"Oh, Ronnie, you don't have to do that. I'm sure your bed is much more comfortable."

"No, really, the couch is fine. I'll leave the door open in case the fuzz ball needs to get out." She reached over and petted the purring feline. "Do you need anything else?"

"No, I think I'm all set."

"Okay then, I guess it's time to say good night."

"Good night, Ronnie."

"Good night, Rose." She smoothed an imaginary wrinkle in the blanket before heading to the door. "Remember, if you need anything, just call out. I'm a light sleeper."

"I will," the young woman promised as the light was shut off and Ronnie left the room.

Swirling memories of Christmases past danced in the wealthy woman's dreamscape. Presents wished for and received, laughter and merriment, wrapping paper ripped apart in anticipation of the treasures hidden within. The sound of someone crying slowly broke through the fog, pulling Ronnie away from her childhood and back to the present. Her eyes opened to the darkness of night, and it took her a moment to realize where she was and what she was hearing. "Rose," she whispered to herself, shaking off the weight of sleep and getting up.

"Rose?" she called from the doorway.

"Did I wake you? I'm sorry," the young woman choked, grateful that the darkness kept her tears hidden from her friend's gaze.

"I knew the stuff I had wouldn't do any good," Ronnie said as she entered the room and sat on the bed. "You want me to run out now? I'm completely sober."

Rose shook her head. "No, please don't leave." The pain was practically unbearable, but the thought of suffering through it without Ronnie was even worse. "Please." She reached out and gripped the larger hand with her own. "Can you...can you stay here with me?" There was a shift in weight as the taller woman slipped under the covers.

"I'm right here." Ronnie moved as close as she dared, telling herself that it was for Rose's comfort and not her own. She was surprised when she felt the soft cheek press against her shoulder.

"Is this all right?" Rose whispered. Ronnie felt the tears soak through her cotton tee and realized that Rose must have been crying for quite a while before she had been awakened.

"It's fine," she answered, moving a bit closer.

"It hurts," Rose admitted, lifting her head to allow Ronnie's arm to slip underneath. They shifted their bodies into more comfortable positions, as comfortable as they could considering Rose's injuries. Ronnie managed to bury her face into the soft golden hair, breathing in the gentle scent. Rose found herself snuggled into the crook of the older woman's shoulder, a place far more comfortable to her than the softest pillow could ever be. In Ronnie's arms, she felt safe, protected, cared for. The throbbing pain was still there, yet somehow it seemed bearable now.

Rose awoke to the sound of Ronnie clacking away on the computer. "Good morning."

"Morning. Your pills are there on the stand." Ronnie stopped typing and turned around to face her. It was then that Rose noticed that Ronnie was dressed for work, a tailored gray skirt and blazer combination accented by a cream-colored blouse.

"You went out already?" The young woman sat up, clearly surprised.

"I called the hospital as soon as I woke up and explained the situation to them. They phoned a prescription in for you right away." Ronnie took a sip of her coffee. "Then it was just a matter of running out and picking it up." She turned and pressed a few more keys. "I've got to get going. Do you need anything before I go?"

"No, I'm sure Karen will be here soon. Is Maria here?"

"Yeah, she got here about a half hour ago. I'll let her know you're awake." Ronnie stood up and shut the computer off. "Are you sure I can't get you anything?"

"No, really, I'm all set. You have a good day at work. Do you think Tommy will be there?"

"I doubt it. He said something last night about not being in the office today." A flash of anger over the previous night's events clouded her features. "He'd better not show up either." She reached over and gave Tabitha a quick pet. "My office number is two on the speed dial if you want to give me a call."

"Oh, I wouldn't want to bother you or anything." Rose silently wished that Ronnie would give her a hug goodbye but couldn't bring herself to ask for one.

"If you feel like calling, you do it. Don't worry about bothering me because you won't." She hesitated for a moment. "It's kinda nice to hear a friendly voice in the middle of the day."

"Okay then. I'll call you later." The words made Ronnie smile, which in turn made Rose smile.

It was late afternoon when the door to Ronnie's office opened and Susan entered, carrying a manila folder. "I was right," the redhead said triumphantly as she tossed the folder onto the desk.

"You were right about what?" Ronnie asked uninterestedly, not bothering to turn away from her computer.

"Your guest." She picked up the folder and opened it, reviewing the information she had acquired. "Rose Grayson graduated from Albany High School. There's no record of her ever attending college anywhere, owning a credit card, she doesn't even have a driver's license."

Ronnie stood up quickly, sending her chair rolling back as she grabbed the folder out of Susan's hands. "You investigated her?"

"I had to," the younger sister protested. "You obviously believe everything she says."

"And what does it matter to you?"

"Ronnie, she obviously has nothing and saw a good meal ticket."

"You have no idea what you're talking about." She slammed the folder down on her desk. "Rose isn't using me."

"No? Do you know where she was employed before you gave her a job?"

"Money Slasher. She was a cashier there."

"A part-time cashier," Susan corrected, "making minimum wage. From what I can tell, before that, she bussed tables at a diner."

"What's your point?"

"My point is, why are you doing this? Why are you letting some poor white trash live off you?"

"Don't...you...ever call her that again!" Ronnie roared. "You have no idea what you're talking about, and as far as 'white trash' goes, have you taken a good look at Tommy lately?"

"You're trying to change the subject."

"Am I? You're judging her because she doesn't have the money that you and I do. How fair is that?" She walked over to the window and looked out at the dreary gray sky. "Did you take the time to talk to her? To find out what kind of person she is? No. Not everyone who doesn't have money is scum, and not everyone who is rich is a good person."

"I'm not saying that."

"You're not? You find out that she wasn't born to privilege, and right away you assume she's a gold digger."

"Then what is she, Ronnie? Help me understand because right now I don't. Try looking at it from the family's point of view. A woman we've never heard of suddenly moves into your home, complete with a cat and obvious medical problems, and you expect us to just sit back and not be concerned."

"Yes. It's my life, Susan. Who stays in my home is my concern, not yours. I didn't run an investigation on Jack when you announced that you were going to marry him."

"Are you planning on marrying her?"

"You still won't accept that she's just a friend, will you?" She crossed the room and flopped down on the black leather couch. "Why does it bother you so much?"

"I just don't want to see you hurt...again."

"This isn't like Christine, I told you that before."

"You may not think so, but from what I see–"

"Then you'd better look again. Rose doesn't want anything from me. She's just a friend. Stop trying to make this into something more than it is." She kicked her shoes off and tucked her feet up under her legs. "You don't know her, Susan. You don't know what she's like. Last night, her bottle of Vicodin was stolen. I offered to go get more, but she didn't want me to. Does that sound like someone who's only interested in my money? She hasn't once asked me to buy her a damn thing. Everything I do, I do because I want to, not because she asks me to." She waved her hand dismissively. "You don't understand, forget it."

"Look, you're an adult. You have to make your own decisions. I ran every check I could on her today. All the info is in that file. Do with it what you want." Susan headed for the door. "Ronnie, don't forget dinner tomorrow at Mother's."

"Oh, I'm looking forward to it," she said sarcastically. "Did you fax her a copy of your precious report? Or did you just take an ad out in the *Times Useless*?"

"That wasn't necessary, Ronnie. I'm just looking out for you."

"Last time I looked, I was taking care of myself just fine. I don't recall asking you to baby-sit me."

"Fine. Do what you want, you will anyway." Susan left, not bothering to close the door. Laura, who had been listening to the raised voices, discreetly closed it and returned to her desk, knowing that the intercom would buzz in a few seconds.

"Laura, hold my calls." A second later, line two lit up, and the young administrative assistant would have bet her entire paycheck that she knew who her boss was calling.

"Cartwright residence," Maria answered.
"Hi, Maria, can I speak with Rose please?"
"Hello?"
"Hi there." At the sound of Rose's voice, Ronnie smiled, the stress of her conversation with Susan melting away. "How was *Judge Judy* today?"
"Oh, you wouldn't believe the cases she had."
"Tell me about them," she urged, settling back into a comfortable position. Ronnie couldn't explain it, but the sound of Rose's voice had a soothing effect on her, and at the moment, she needed that comfort.

"Almost finished," Dr. Barnes said, removing the last of the stitches on Rose's cheek. She stepped back and threw the rubber gloves in the red waste receptacle. "Looks good. Remember to keep it out of the sun until it's fully healed. Not that that's a problem this time of year." She made a notation on Rose's chart. "You're recovering splendidly. At the rate you're going, I see no reason why you won't be on crutches by late spring."
"Late spring?"
"Late spring," the doctor repeated. "Your body suffered a severe trauma. Your ankle alone was broken in seven places. It's going to take time to heal. Understand this, Miss Grayson, we're talking months of therapy, not weeks." The young woman's heart sank at the words. She knew it would take time, just not that long. How would Ronnie react? Surely, that would be too long to stay at the place she was quickly thinking of as home.
Despite Rose's fears, Ronnie took the news well, seeming more concerned about the progress of the recovery than the time frame.
"You know I could stay home tonight," Ronnie said as they turned onto Cartwright Drive.
"No, your mother and sister are expecting you. I'll be fine."
"But what if you need to use the bedpan or something? What if you need a drink?" She pulled the Jeep into the driveway and turned off the ignition.
"I'll go before you leave. If you fill that pitcher on the stand, I'm sure I'll be fine."

Ronnie was late arriving at her mother's condo. She blamed it on the Friday rush-hour traffic, but the truth was that she found it difficult to leave Rose alone. She left a full pitcher of water, cans of soda cooling in the ice bucket, and various snacks within easy reach of the injured woman.

The small round dining table had just enough room for everyone. Ronnie found herself seated between Elaine and Susan. It was bad enough to be a lefty stuck next to a right-handed person, but the pungent smell of her aunt's perfume threatened to take away Ronnie's appetite. "Smells wonderful," Susan said as the platter of meat was placed on the table.

"Thank you, dear," Beatrice replied as if she were the one who had spent hours preparing the food instead of her part-time helper. "You know your sister always enjoys a good pork roast."

"Yes, I do," Ronnie readily agreed, reaching for the platter.

"Hey, leave some for the rest of us."

"Now, Susan, don't you worry about it," her mother chastised. "There's plenty for everyone." She turned to her eldest daughter. "You just take as much as you want, dear. I'm sure you must be tired of those reheated dinners that Maria makes for you."

Ronnie poured the steaming gravy over her pork. "Maria's a great cook, Mother, you know that."

"I know that when I ran the house, she worked until eight o'clock each night. I never had to worry about dirty dishes piling up until morning."

"I have a dishwasher."

"Humph, another appliance purchased so she could work less, no doubt." Beatrice ladled some gravy onto her plate. "You know you spoil her."

"I know," Ronnie grinned, drawing a smirk from her sister and an annoyed frown from her mother.

"First it was every weekend off, then it was shorter hours. At the rate she's going, you're going to pay her to stay home just like those welfare people."

"Mother, she puts in a full workweek just like anyone else."

"I'm sure she's busier than ever with your friend there," Susan chimed in.

"Yes, how is that poor dear?" Elaine asked. "She seemed like such a nice girl. What was her name? Rachel, Ruth...?"

"Rose," Ronnie corrected.

"Ah, yes," the visiting relative replied, not at all interested in the correct name. "Well anyway, she seemed like a nice girl. Pass the corn, please. Bea, did you see in the paper where they're rabble-rousing about health care again?"

"You'd think the president would have better things to worry about," the matriarch replied. "Jack, do you know anyone without insurance?"

"Of course not, Mother," he replied, learning long ago exactly what answers his mother-in-law wanted to hear.

"See, that's my point exactly. They need to worry about more important things like reforming the tax code or bringing prayer back to school." Beatrice took a sip of wine. "I'm telling you, that's where the country went wrong. There was a time when children respected their elders. Now I can't get the paperboy to leave the paper between the doors when it's raining. And he wonders why I don't tip him. Tips should be earned, but nowadays they seem to think that they deserve it just for doing their jobs."

Throughout the rest of dinner and into the after-dinner drinks, Ronnie tried to pay attention to the conversation but found her mind slipping back to thoughts of the woman waiting for her at home. She wondered if she would sleep on the couch or if Rose would let her share the bed again. She hoped the latter. Ronnie's mind was so far away that she never heard her mother address her, and it was only Susan kicking her under the table that brought her back to the present. "I'm sorry, what?"

Beatrice gave an annoyed huff. "I asked you if you planned on coming here for Christmas. Honestly, Veronica."

"Sorry, I was just thinking about something."

"Or someone," Susan said so quietly that only her sister could hear.

"Actually, I thought I'd spend Christmas at home this year," Ronnie replied, shooting a glare at her younger sister.

"Oh, good. Elaine asked me to join her on a cruise, but I didn't want you to have nowhere to go."

"What about Tommy?" Susan asked.

"He said he had other plans this year. Something about going up to the mountains with some friends of his. You and Jack have the boys, so the only one I was worried about was your sister."

"I'll be fine, Mother." Ronnie looked at her watch. "I didn't realize the time. I need to swing by the office and pick up some files before it gets too late." She stood up and tossed her napkin on the now empty plate. "Dinner was wonderful, as always."

"That's my daughter, always working," Beatrice said. "Perhaps someday you'll find the time to settle down and make me some grandchildren."

Ronnie ignored the jibe and donned her jacket. "I really need to get going." She glanced out the window. "It's beginning to come down really hard out there."

"Of course, of course. You go work on making money. I guess I'll have to depend on Jack and Susan to give me a granddaughter."

"I guess so," Ronnie said as she reached for the door handle. "Jack, you'd better be careful on the way home, looks like sleet. Good night everyone."

"Hey, you're still up," Ronnie said when she walked into Rose's room.

"Yeah, it's only ten."

"Anything good on?"

"Not really." Rose used the remote to mute the television before patting the space on the bed next to her. "So how did your dinner go?"

"Draining." Ronnie took the offered seat on the adjustable bed and leaned back into a comfortable position. "Now I remember why I hate family dinners so much."

"Why's that?"

"Everyone talks about nothing. They went on and on about things they have no control over like taxes and tipping. Not to mention Mother started in again about my not giving her grandchildren."

"That's too bad. Does she do that a lot?"

"Every opportunity she can," Ronnie shrugged. "Come on, let's see what's on TV."

They settled back and watched a crime drama, both guessing who the murderer was long before the cops figured it out. When it was over, Rose found herself unable to stifle a yawn. "Sorry, must be more tired than I thought."

"That's okay. It is getting late. I guess I'd better get going and let you sleep." She made a move to get off the bed only to be stopped by Rose's hand on her arm.

"Are you going upstairs?"

"No, I'll probably crash on the couch, why?"

"You know, it is a big bed, and I'm sure it's more comfortable than the couch is. You could stay here." Rose bit her lower lip. "I mean, if you want to, I don't mind."

Ronnie hesitated for only a second. "Well, I wouldn't want to crowd you or anything."

"You haven't yet."

"It is more comfortable than the couch...but only if you're sure." Truth be told, she could fall asleep in either place, but one definitely was preferred over the other.

"I'm sure." Rose pulled one of the two pillows out from behind her head. "Here, I'll even share."

"Let me change and get the light."

A few minutes later, Ronnie was in her sweats and a cotton T-shirt. She shut the light off and scooted under the blanket, consciously keeping her body from moving over and pressing against Rose no matter how much it wanted to. Her resolve lasted only until the moment sleep overtook her. Then her body did what it so desperately wanted when she was awake.

Half asleep, Rose woke up completely when she felt the arm rest across her stomach. Ronnie gave a soft sigh of contentment in her sleep and snuggled closer, her warm breath caressing the smaller woman's shoulder. Rose smiled in the dark and brought her left hand down to rest atop the larger one. It should have seemed strange to sleep next to someone after spending the first twenty-six years of her life sleeping alone, but it didn't. Lying next to Ronnie felt natural, comfortable, right. She believed that Ronnie truly cared for her, something Rose had never really felt before. It filled her with a sense of...well, whatever it was, she couldn't quite name, but it was a wonderful feeling just the same. Another sigh and the other woman moved even closer, her chin resting just above Rose's shoulder and her face buried in the reddish-blonde hair. Time ticked by while the young woman enjoyed the sensations, the warmth of Ronnie's hand through the cotton nightshirt, the gentle breaths tickling her ear, the feeling of safety and security that covered her like no blanket ever could. Rose had friends growing up, playmates, girls to share secrets with, but she never felt toward them what she felt toward Ronnie. Her feelings ran deeper than anything she had known before, and although it should have scared her, it didn't. She turned her head to the side and placed a gentle kiss on Ronnie's forehead. "Sweet dreams," she whispered before closing her eyes and letting sleep overtake her.

Chapter Eleven

The rusted-out station wagon chugged its way up Morris Street. Delores Bickering spotted the address she was looking for and parked in front of it. She had planned on visiting her sister but decided that since she was in the area anyway, it wouldn't hurt to stop in and see Rose, especially since she hadn't received a reply—or a check—from the young woman yet. She rolled down the window and reached for the outside handle, the only way to open the car door, and stepped out. She walked down the steps leading to the basement apartment, frowning when she saw a Hispanic couple milling about inside. She knocked on the door. "Does Rose Grayson live here?"

"No, we just moved in. You might want to check with Cecil. He lives upstairs."

"What the fuck you want?" Cecil asked when he opened the door.

"I'm looking for Rose Grayson. I thought she lived here."

"Moved out," he grunted. "Damn bitch didn't give me no notice either."

"Do you know where she moved to?"

"Who the fuck are you?" He looked at Delores suspiciously.

"I'm her mother," she lied.

"I don't know, and I don't give a shit. If you want to know, you should ask the bitch who was here. Hang on, I got her name here somewhere. I wrote it down in case the check she gave me bounced." He went back into the apartment, leaving her standing outside. He returned a minute later with a Post-It note with scribbling on it. "Here, that's the name and address of the bitch who moved her stuff out."

Delores took the paper and looked at it. V. Cartwright, One Cartwright Drive, Loudonville. "Did you get a phone number?"

"Do I look like the fucking information booth?" he snarled. "That's all I know. Now unless you're interested in renting the third floor, you're wasting my fucking time." He shut the door without waiting for an answer. Delores walked back to her car, puzzled. Anyone who lived on a street with the same name as theirs was no doubt rich, and the fact that it was in Loudonville, where no one on welfare could afford to live, was even more intriguing. She decided that she needed to find out more. She adjusted the pillow on the front seat, the only thing keeping the worn springs from pressing into her ass, and turned the key several times before the twenty-year-old station wagon sputtered to life.

She stopped at the nearest convenience store to gas up the car, not bothering to pull up to the farthest pump. Let them wait, she thought to herself while putting the nozzle into the tank. She put exactly five dollars worth of gas in before entering the store. Once inside, she picked up a street map of Albany County and headed for the back where the soda coolers were lined up. While opening the case with one hand, Delores used her other to stuff the street map into her pocketbook. She approached the pimply faced clerk with a bottle of Pepsi in her hand. "Seventy-five cents for the soda and five for the gas," the clerk said. Delores pulled a worn bill out of her jacket pocket along with a one-dollar food stamp. The clerk nodded and returned her a quarter, completely unaware of the shoplifting. As she always did, Delores couldn't resist smirking as she exited the store, having once again gotten away with getting something for nothing.

The station wagon sputtered and worked its way through the congested traffic of Albany into the quieter suburb of Loudonville. In the village where the average income was well into six digits, the rusted-out Ford with fake wooden panels stood out amongst the newer vehicles in Ronnie's neighborhood. Deciding that the large mansion at the beginning of the street had to be number one, she pulled the car into the long driveway, stopping it just behind the bright blue Jeep Cherokee. She removed the key from the ignition and waited for a moment while the car continued to run before it finally gave a dying gasp and went silent. Drips of oil stained the driveway as she rolled down the window to reach the door handle. Yup, no doubt about it, this had to be One Cartwright Drive. If Rose knew the person who owned this place, that certainly was worth investigating, Delores reasoned. She spotted the shoveled flagstone walkway that circled the lawn and led to the large double-door entrance and followed it.

Ronnie was working on her computer when she heard the rattling sound of a car pulling into her driveway. A quick look at the bed confirmed that Rose was still sound asleep. She stood up and walked to the window, blue eyes widening at the sight of the brown, white, and rust-colored station wagon sitting in her driveway. "What the hell...?" The window rolled down, and an arm reached out for the handle. She watched as a rotund woman, poorly dressed, stepped out of the car and looked at the house. Ronnie's first thought was that it was either a lost traveler or one of those annoying door-to-door salespeople. She took another look at the peacefully sleeping woman and decided to intercept the unexpected arrival before the doorbell could wake Rose.

Ronnie opened the door and realized that this was no door-to-door saleswoman. A black knit cap with a pom-pom at the tip covered the head of a woman who appeared to be in her mid-forties while a dirty yellow jacket littered with various stains covered the upper body. She held an oversized purse in hands that bore no gloves, and her feet were covered with a pair of sneakers that long ago stopped being considered white. Ronnie looked down at the shorter woman and frowned. "May I help you?"

"Um, yes," Delores said, looking up with surprise. "How did you know—"

"I heard your...car park in my driveway. What do you want?"

"I'm looking for someone, and I was told that you would know where she is. Her name is Rose Grayson."

"Who told you that I know where she is?" Ronnie now knew who the woman standing before her was, and she wasn't the least bit happy with the revelation. She had promised to bring Rose's checkbook to the hospital, but with the unexpected release and everything that had happened since, there hadn't been any more mention of the subject. As far as Ronnie knew, Rose hadn't mailed out anything since coming to her home. So how did this leech find her?

"I stopped at her old apartment, and the landlord told me you paid her rent." Delores shivered and looked pointedly at the door. "Can I come in? It's pretty cold out here, you know."

Ronnie mentally cursed whomever it was who created manners and stepped back, holding the door open. "Come in, Miss...?"

"Bickering, Delores Bickering," the rotund woman said, walking past her and pulling her knit cap off to reveal straight brown hair that looked in need of a good washing. "So you're V. Cartwright?"

"Yes," Ronnie said without bothering to elaborate further. Now she was faced with a moral dilemma. She could pretend that Rose wasn't here and send Delores packing, but that risked upsetting the young woman. Then again, she wasn't sure she wanted to let the vulture walking into her living room near her companion. Reluctantly, she accepted that the decision wasn't really hers to make. "Wait here."

Ronnie crossed the room and entered the office, making sure to close the door behind her. She knelt onto the bed and placed her hand on the sleeping woman's shoulder. "Rose...Rose, honey, wake up."

"Hmm?" Green eyes opened and blinked wearily.

"We have company, you have to get up."

"Company?" Rose gave a healthy yawn and rubbed her eyes. "Who?"

"Delores." Ronnie did her best not to let her annoyance show through.

"Delores? Bickering? Here?"

"Delores. Bickering. Here." She watched as the words sank in, and Rose's demeanor changed. "Hey, if you don't want to see her...."

"No, if she went to all this trouble to find me, then I should at least see her."

"Rose...." She took the younger woman's chin in her hand. "You don't owe her a thing. Whatever she did for you in the past, you've already paid back and then some, I'm sure." She gentled her tone, realizing that it wasn't helping. "I'm sorry, I know you feel you owe her, and I shouldn't be telling you how to think or feel." She withdrew her hand and sat back. "I just don't like to see you being used, and I'm afraid that's exactly why Delores is here." She picked up the brush and began to straighten out Rose's sleep-mussed hair.

"Ronnie?"

"Mmm?"

"Would it be too much to ask if I could borrow the shirt you wore yesterday? I can cover the rest of my body with a blanket."

"It'll be a little big on you, but it's fine with me." She leaned back and used her long arm to pluck the gray button-down shirt from its position across the back of the chair. Rose pulled off the nightshirt at the same time, and when Ronnie straightened, she was greeted by the sight of what she considered to be the most perfect pair of breasts. She reluctantly tried to keep herself from staring by concentrating on helping Rose get her arms through the sleeves. "I'll let you button it up while I get the chair ready," she said, abruptly leaving the bed and retrieving the wheelchair from the corner. A few minutes later, Rose was comfortably settled in her chair, the afghan tucked neatly around her legs and hips. "You ready?" Ronnie asked.

"Yeah" came the halfhearted reply. The last person she wanted to see was Delores. She didn't reply to the last letter and had no doubt in her mind that the former foster mother would bring up the subject of money, especially after finding out where she was living. "Ronnie?"

"Yes?"

"Could you...I mean, if you don't mind, would you...stay with me?" She hoped Ronnie's presence would keep Delores from asking about money, but more than that, she wanted the emotional support that she knew her friend would give. She smiled when she felt the warm hand squeeze her shoulder.

"I'll be right there, don't you worry."

Delores turned from her inspection of the various ornaments still dangling from the streamers and gasped when she saw Rose in a wheelchair. "What happened to you?"

"I was hit by a car," the young woman replied. "How did you know where I was?"

"Your landlord told me," she said smugly. "So did you sue the guy who hit you?"

"The police don't know who it was. He took off after the accident."

"They couldn't find him? That's a shame. If they found him, you could have sued. I know a good lawyer who'll help you if you need him. He represented me when I slipped in some water in the supermarket. Got me almost four thousand dollars." Delores stepped into the sunken part of the living room and flopped down on the leather couch, drawing a disapproving look from Ronnie. "So come tell me what you've been doing. I haven't heard from you in almost two months now." She reached into her oversized pocketbook and pulled out a worn vinyl cigarette case and lighter, lighting one up without a thought.

"I don't allow smoking in my home," Ronnie said.

"Oh, don't worry, I have my own ashtray," Delores replied as she pulled a small brown one out of her purse.

"I don't allow smoking in my home," Ronnie repeated, not caring a bit about the glare she received from the large visitor but caring a great deal that Rose didn't make a sound of objection.

"Oh, that's fine." Delores took one long drag before butting out the cigarette. "So, Rose...." She exhaled, filling the air around her with the translucent smoke. "How long are you staying with Miss Cartwright, or do you live here now?"

Rose blinked in surprise and realized that she wasn't certain of the answer. She looked to her benefactor, asking the same question with her eyes. Ronnie swallowed, uncertain of how to answer, of what Rose really wanted. There was no doubt in her own mind that she wanted the fair-haired woman in her life—and in her home. Did leaving the decision up to her mean that Rose wanted to continue living here, too? Ronnie inhaled deeply and took a chance, letting her heart guide her answer. "She lives here."

Rose opened her mouth, then closed it, shock taking away her ability to speak for a moment. "Y-yes, that's right." Her voice cracked, and she fought to keep a smile from her face. "So what brings you up to this area? Visiting Isabel again?" she asked, referring to Delores's sister. The rotund woman nodded.

"The Tupperware came in. You know she'll never get around to delivering it to me. If I don't come down and get it, she'll end up using it herself or selling it to someone else for the money just like the cookie episode. You remember that, don't you, Rose?"

"Isabel collected all the money for the Girl Scout cookies but didn't have it when it came time to pay for them," Rose explained to Ronnie.

"Sounds like quite a family," the executive said dryly.

"Not to mention that her kids got into them before they were delivered," Delores added, always ready for a chance to run the rest of her family down, even if she were guilty of the same things. "Anyway...." She turned her attention to her former foster daughter. "So what do the doctors say? I hope you went to a real hospital and not just down to the clinic. You know they don't know anything down there. I fought with them for five years over Jimmy, and they never did find anything wrong with him," Delores said. Rose nodded politely, thinking to herself that the reason they never found anything wrong with her foster brother was that there never was anything wrong with him. Jimmy was the picture of health during the time Rose stayed with them, yet Delores dragged him from doctor to doctor, insisting that some dreadful rare ailment affected her son. "You know he's in college now."

"Really?" Rose didn't think he'd make it through high school. "What's he majoring in?"

"Acting. Someday he'll get his own series just like Seinfeld. He even got an offer to play downtown," she boasted, as if downtown Cobleskill was anything to brag about. "Yup, they're doing *Joseph and the Amazing Technicolor Dreamcoat*. Andy Gibb played the lead on Broadway, you know."

Delores continued to ramble on and fill the young woman in on all the trivial events that had happened in her family recently. Eventually, as Ronnie suspected it would, the conversation turned to money.

"You know the state stopped paying for Jimmy when he turned eighteen. It didn't occur to them that I needed that extra money each month for the other kids. One in college and four other kids still in school."

"Doesn't Jimmy help out?" Rose queried.

"He only works weekends at Fred's gas station. He needs that money for gas to get back and forth to school."

"Sounds like Jimmy needs to get another job and help out," Ronnie quipped.

Delores shifted, focusing her attention on Rose and wishing that the dark-haired woman would go away. To her delight, it was at that moment that Ronnie's bladder demanded attention, and she excused herself for a moment. The scheming woman leaned forward in her seat.

"The state doesn't care. The idiot social worker doesn't care either." She paused, sighing for effect. "It's so hard when you're alone. You understand that, don't you, Rose?"

"Yes," she replied. Delores smiled inwardly.

"You know how hard it was when you were there, all the sacrifices I had to make just to keep you and the others out of the state orphanages and group homes." She watched Rose nod. The hook was set, now to reel her in, the dumpy woman thought. "You must be getting some kind of disability money, aren't you?"

"Actually, no. I didn't get any benefits at Money Slasher, and I haven't applied for anything." Rose's head drooped, a visible expression of her knowledge of where the conversation was going and her inability to speak up and stop it.

"But you're living here. You can't tell me that someone like her lets you live here rent free. You must be paying her something."

"I think that's a matter between Rose and me," Ronnie said as she re-entered the room, her tone effectively ending the subject. She didn't miss the quick look of relief passed her way from Rose. She also didn't miss the way the young woman's shoulders were slumped.

"Well, I don't see what the big deal is. I just asked a simple question." Delores tried to appear hurt, but no one was buying it.

"And it was answered," Ronnie replied firmly as she took her seat. She crossed her arms, making it clear that she wasn't leaving the room again. She had no doubt that if she hadn't returned that the leech would have guilted Rose into giving her money. Ronnie would be damned if she was going to let that happen.

"I think Rose is old enough to speak for herself, don't you?" Delores made no attempt to hide her anger. Her quickly laid plans were beginning to dissolve before her eyes. She had only one shot left. "Rose, I think you should come stay with me until you recover. I always took such good care of you when you were a child."

There it was, the threat was on the table. Delores was making Rose choose between her and Ronnie, and the overweight woman was confident that the quiet child she once knew and controlled would come forth and pick her.

"I...I...." Rose felt the pressure closing in around her. It had been so automatic to do whatever Delores bid for so long. Now she actually had a choice, an option to make up her own mind. Submit to the long-standing status quo or plunge forward into the unknown with Ronnie. She lifted her head and gazed into soft blue depths, seeing only warmth and concern. "I...I don't want to leave." She said it to Ronnie just as much as Delores. She watched the executive release a breath and give a small smile. On the other hand, the former foster mother looked furious.

"Rose, I want to talk to you privately, or does she make all your decisions for you now?" Delores glared at Ronnie.

"Rose is her own woman," Ronnie said. "I don't control her or manipulate her," she accused. Her own temper was rising rapidly, and her thoughts centered on throwing the fat woman out on her ear and hopefully out of Rose's life.

"Then why don't you let her tell me that for herself?" Delores snarled, visibly upset that her plans were crumbling around her. "You don't know how hard I worked to keep a roof over her head when no one else would."

"You took her in to get money from the state. That's all there is to it." Ronnie stood up and began pacing. "Have you once asked her if there's anything you could do to help her? No, you asked what happened, then went into your own little world of problems, half of which would be solved if you'd get off your lazy ass and get a job instead of living off everyone else." She deliberately avoided looking at Rose, certain she would see disapproval in her eyes. She knew she should stop, let her friend fight her own battles, but she'd be damned if she was going to let Delores Bickering bully Rose into giving her one more cent.

"I don't have to listen to this," the large woman said angrily, rising to her feet and retrieving her pocketbook. "Rose, you're letting this bitch control you. You're going to turn your back on me? On the only family you have?" She stepped up onto the main level and headed for the door. "After everything I've done for you?"

Rose let a lone tear slip down her cheek. "Wait." She looked up at Ronnie. "Please?"

"Rose, you don't have to do this."

"Please, just a few minutes. I'll be all right." She winced inwardly at the hurt look on Ronnie's face but knew she needed to do this.

It went completely against her better judgment, but finally, Ronnie nodded. "I'll be downstairs." She shot a murderous look at Delores before leaving the room.

"Humph," Delores grunted as she returned to her seat. "I don't know, Rose. These rich people, they think they can control everyone just because they have money."

"Ronnie's not like that," the young woman protested.

"She won't let you speak for yourself. You're a grown woman. What you do with your money is your business, not hers." She reached into her bag and pulled out her cigarette case. "You'd think you were a child the way she treats you."

"Delores, please don't." Rose pointed at the cigarette case.

"Obviously, she doesn't know how to treat guests either," the large woman grumbled, shoving the case back into her purse. "Well, I can't stay long. I have to pick up the Tupperware and hope I have enough gas to get home."

"Delores, you understand I'm not working. I don't have any money."

"Rose, you live here. You can't tell me that if you needed something that she wouldn't help you out," the large woman pointed out the obvious. "You're not going to starve...or run out of gas on some lonely stretch of highway on the way home..." Delores paused for effect. "I remember the time it was snowing and I had to take you to the doctor's for...what was it again?"

"Strep throat," Rose replied sullenly, knowing full well that the older woman remembered.

"That's right. I had to get prescriptions for both you and Jimmy because he hadn't had it yet. I couldn't afford to go to bingo that week because of that, you know."

"I know."

"You know the coverall is worth two hundred fifty dollars, and I had just as much chance to win it as anyone else in that room."

"I know," Rose repeated, sinking farther and farther into the role she knew so well.

"You know how scared little Jessica will get if I don't come home?"

Whatever strength and reserve Rose had crumbled with the last implied threat. Jessica was nine and very much attached to her mother. "How much do you need?"

Delores relaxed against the couch, triumphant. "At least thirty dollars."

"I don't have that much," the young woman lied.

"Well, how much do you have?"

Rose thought quickly. "The most I can spare is fifteen dollars."

"Well, if that's all you can do, then I guess that'll have to do."

"I'll get my checkbook." Hanging her head in defeat, she turned her chair and wheeled her way into the office, returning a few minutes later with the check on her lap. Delores already had her coat on.

"Thank you, Rose. I hope to hear from you on Christmas." Delores reached for the check only to have the young woman jerk it out of reach.

"Wait...." She summoned her courage and took a deep breath. "I...I really can't afford to give you any more money after this."

"Fine, I'll remember that if I end up with no food or anything that I shouldn't call you for help." She leaned forward and snatched the check out of Rose's hand. Now having what she came for, Delores was ready to leave, but not without doing her best to reinforce her hold over the young woman. "You just remember that while you're sitting here in all this," she spread her arms out to encompass the room, "that I struggled and suffered to take care of you for so long."

Delores opened the door, letting in the cold air. "I hope you get back on your feet soon. Perhaps someday you'll stop being so selfish and realize just how much it took for me to keep a roof over your head." The door shut, and soon Rose heard the sound of an engine straining to turn over. After a few false starts and a backfire accompanied by a cloud of black smoke from the rusted-out tailpipe, the station wagon backed out of the driveway and headed down the street.

The door to the basement opened, and Ronnie appeared, looking about for her unwelcome guest.

"She's gone," Rose said in response to the raised eyebrow. Worried that her benefactor would be upset about the check, she hid the checkbook beneath the cover of the afghan. "Ronnie, I'm sorry about—"

"No, don't worry about it," Ronnie said, cutting off the apology. "You had no way of knowing she'd show up here." She walked over to stand behind the wheelchair. "You hungry?" she asked while hoisting the chair and passenger onto the main level. "Never mind, silly question."

"What can I say? Maria's a great cook," Rose replied. Her beaming smile earned a quick hair tousle from her companion.

"Okay, you head on in and find something on the tube while I see what goodies Maria left for us."

Nothing more was said about Delores Bickering as the day progressed, both women far more interested in sitting side by side on the bed and watching television together. It was only after night had fallen and both were settling down to sleep that Rose broached the subject.

"Ronnie?"

"Mmm?"

"Would you be mad at me if I told you that I ended up giving Delores money?"

"I don't think I could ever be mad at you," Ronnie admitted, rolling onto her side and propping her head up with her hand.

"Disappointed?"

"No," she sighed. "Rose, if I seemed short or aggravated or—"

"Hostile?" the younger woman offered. Ronnie looked at the shadowed form in the dim moonlight and arched an eyebrow.

"I don't think I was hostile, Rose. Personally, I think I did a great job of being civil to the witch, especially considering what I really wanted to do was throw her out into the snowbank."

Rose reached out in the darkness and ran her knuckles up and down the forearm that Ronnie was propped up on. "I know you did...and I appreciate it."

"I don't like to see anyone use you," she whispered. "You deserve better than that." Ronnie hesitated for a moment before continuing. "So how much did she take?"

"Fifteen bucks" came the reply. "But I told her this was the last time," Rose added quickly.

"Have you ever told her that before?"

"No."

"Well then, that's a start anyway." She reached over with her free hand and softly cupped Rose's cheek. "Hey, I understand, I really do. It's hard to say no after saying yes for so long. Look at me and my family."

"So you're really not upset with me?"

Ronnie leaned over and gave her young friend a hug. "I could never be upset with you," she whispered into Rose's ear. She didn't expect to feel arms wrap around her neck and pull her close.

"I don't know what I ever did to deserve a best friend as good as you," the young woman choked as her grip tightened. Ronnie returned the embrace, smiling at first with the feeling of holding Rose. Then memories came unbidden to her mind...a flash of blue flying over the hood and into the windshield, blood pooling on the ground, and a series of lies designed to cover up the truth. The smile faded, replaced with a look of sadness.

"I'm the one who doesn't deserve you," Ronnie whispered. She held on for a moment longer before rolling back to her side of the bed. "It's time for us to get some sleep."

When sleep claimed her, Ronnie's body betrayed her as it did every night. Just as Rose was drifting off, she felt the warm weight of the older woman's arm flop across her stomach and warm breath caressing her shoulder. She smiled and fell asleep. Deep in the land of dreams, they let the warmth of each other's bodies fight off the night chill the century-old home couldn't keep at bay.

Chapter Twelve

"Ronnie, got a sec?" Susan asked as she stepped into the office. "There's a claim here that doesn't make any sense."

"Since when do you come to me about something like that?" She didn't bother to look up from the computer screen.

"Since it involves lost materials and equipment totaling over a hundred thousand dollars."

"What?" Ronnie motioned for her sister to take a seat in the chair on the other side of the desk.

"Orbison Contractors filed a claim for lost equipment and materials from that mini-mall remodeling site. They say that everything from lumber and tools to a brand new work truck were stolen." She handed Ronnie a copy of the multi-page claim form. "Since they had full protection with us, they also are filing for lost wages due to lack of equipment."

"Are you sure this is legit? Maybe they're just trying to put one over for the insurance money." Ronnie flipped through the pages, frowning at each figure. "Did they file a report with the police?"

"Sure did. They found the truck, stripped to the metal out in Arbor Hill."

Ronnie read the report carefully, looking for any clue that it was a fraud. "Does Tommy know about this?"

"No, can't reach him. I've left messages everywhere for him."

"He's probably still drugged up from all the Vicodin he stole from my house during the Christmas party."

"What?"

"Nothing, never mind." Ronnie's teeth sank into the soft wood of her pencil while she continued to pore over the report. No sign of forced entry, not that much was needed to get past a simple chain link fence surrounding the work site. The truck was a total loss, and there was no sign of inflated figures for the missing tools and materials. "I can't see anything out of the ordinary here, Sis. Other than the cost, what is it that's bothering you?"

"I ran a check against the reports we have on file, and from what I can see, that project should have been finished or almost close to it. But according to the loss report, they had barely started. I gave Mike Orbison a call, and he said they were at least three weeks away from completion."

"If they were so far away from being finished...." Ronnie looked at the paper again. "Then why was so much stuff there? Look at this...all the large panes of glass, paint, sheet rock, even carpeting. I thought those were the last things to be delivered."

"That's what I thought. Maybe they expected to be finished before this."

"No...Mike's been in business long enough to know exactly what he needs and when he needs it. I can't imagine him ordering stuff to be brought on site without it being used right away. He knows how easily things are stolen from construction sites." Ronnie's brow furrowed as she tried to make sense of the puzzle. "And you're sure that these things were on the site?"

"I can't imagine him lying to us after all this time. His family's worked for us since the sixties, and this is only the fifth time they've ever filed a claim."

"I'm sure it's the first time that it was in the six figures." Ronnie picked up the phone. "Laura, get hold of Mike Orbison for me." A minute later, the buzzer announced that the task was accomplished. "Mike? Veronica Cartwright...fine and yourself? Good. Mike, I wanted to talk to you about this claim you filed with Cartwright Insurance. Sure, I understand that...yes, that seemed strange to me, too, that's why I wanted to call you...no, there's no problem with that....yes...absolutely...uh-huh...yes...no, I didn't know that....uh-huh...when was this?"

"What's going on?" Susan queried, drawing a frown from her sister.

"Yes, Mike, I'm still here, go on....uh-huh....when did you talk to him last?...I see. Mike, let me ask you something, other than your people, who else had keys to the building?...what?...well, when did this happen?...did you ask him about it?...when?...and that's the last time you talked to him?...Okay, Mike...no, I understand perfectly....of course...you too...yes, say hi to Sarah for me....okay, Mike, goodbye." Ronnie hung up the phone and sighed.

"So what did he say?"

"He said everything was ordered weeks in advance per the projected production schedule, but Tommy kept pushing the dates back. That's why everything was on site when the robbery happened. Did the police report say whether the truck was hot-wired or not?"

"I don't think so. I didn't pay that much attention to it, why?"

"Mike said Tommy stopped by there last week, and after he left, a set of keys turned up missing."

"Keys for what?"

"The building, the truck, the equipment boxes, everything. Mike said it was on his desk when Tommy stopped by, but he couldn't find it later that day."

"Ronnie, you don't think—"

"That's exactly what I think." Ronnie rose and went to the window, the bright sun reflecting off the snow below. "Susan, I want you to contact all the other contractors and tell them to deal with me directly from now on instead of Tommy. If he shows up anywhere, I want to know about it."

"Why would he steal? It's not like he needs money."

"He stole from me!" Ronnie growled angrily. "Why are you defending him? The truth is right in front of your face." The phone buzzer interrupted her tirade. "What?"

"John Means from Means Auditing on line one," Laura replied.

"Terrific." She slumped down in her chair and picked up the receiver. "This had better be good news," she said before pressing the button. "This is Veronica Cartwright."

Ten minutes later, a fully pissed off Ronnie and a shocked Susan stared at each other. "Now do you believe me?"

"I can't believe he would steal from his own family," the redhead replied quietly.

"Well, he did. A few more weeks of that, and he would have crippled the real estate division, not to mention what it would have done to the company as a whole. We'll be lucky to post a profit this quarter."

"What could he possibly need with that much money?"

"What do you think, Susan? You're the one who mentioned drugs last week."

"I know I said it, but I didn't really believe it."

"Well, you should have." Ronnie picked up the phone and buzzed her secretary. "Laura, I want you to call the security company and the locksmith. I want all the locks changed and Tommy's key codes blocked before the end of the day. Call downstairs and make sure no one lets him in. Then call all the heads in for a meeting. I don't care what time, just make sure everyone is there."

"I just can't believe it," the younger sister repeated.

"Believe it. Our baby brother is a thief and a liar, and I'll be damned if he's going to get away with it."

By the end of the day, all the locks had been changed and the news broken to the rest of the family. Ronnie shut down every construction project until further notice and announced that Frank's brother John would run the real estate division until a suitable replacement could be found. As an added precaution, she called the bank and reported Tommy's corporate credit card stolen only to find that large cash advances had been taken on the card during the last two weeks and it had reached its limit. Yet another piece of information to add to Ronnie's already pounding headache of problems.

"What about a nice scarf?"

"She'll hate it."

"Hmm...what about a bottle of her favorite perfume?"

"Ugh, I hate her perfume."

"Well, what does she like?" Rose flipped through the glossy pages of the Macy's catalog. "They've got some pretty jewelry in here." They had spent the last two hours flipping through the various catalogs and fliers to no avail. Everything suggested was dismissed just as quickly, and Rose was running out of ideas to help her friend.

"No, Mother's got more jewelry than she knows what to do with." Ronnie tossed the Bloomingdale's catalog on the desk, picked up another, and sighed. "I hate Christmas."

"Oh, don't be a grump now, I promise to help you find something for her." Rose gave her a smile. "It can't be that hard to find a present for your mother."

"Beatrice Phoebe Cartwright is without a doubt the hardest woman to buy a present for." Ronnie took a sip of wine and placed the long-stemmed glass on the desk. "Maybe I should just send her on a cruise." Blue eyes twinkled with mischievous thought. "Maybe a nice, long cruise."

"Would she like that?"

"I would," the executive replied with a devilish grin. "Maybe one of those around-the-world tours. You know, maybe six, eight...months."

"Oh, you stop," Rose playfully chastised, reaching out to lightly swat Ronnie's forearm. "Your mother's not that bad, she's just a little...a little...." She put her finger to her lips, trying to figure out one or two words that could accurately describe her friend's mother. "Stuffy."

"My mother is a snob, hon." Ronnie took another sip of the rosé wine. "She doesn't take no for an answer, expects perfection all the time, and worries more about the family image than how we feel." Another sip. "Maybe I should just get her a gift certificate and let her pick out what she wants."

"Are you sure?" Rose flipped a page in the catalog and held it out for Ronnie to see. "Here. There's a toll-free number you can call to order one if that's what you really want to do," she said, her tone making it clear that she didn't believe that to be the case. Despite having only known her for three weeks, Rose was beginning to understand some of the facial expressions and mannerisms that betrayed Ronnie's true feelings. Pencil gnawing meant frustration, fingernail tapping equated boredom, and the firm yet gentle embrace that held her each night spoke of something neither of them would dare put words to.

Blue eyes looked up from the liquid for a moment, then back down again. "No," Ronnie grudgingly admitted. "I just hate feeling so much pressure. I feel like I have to get the perfect gift."

Rose opened her mouth to protest, then closed it, realizing that in her friend's family, it wasn't far from being the truth. The Christmas party proved that. Not only was the entire thing thrust upon Ronnie's shoulders, but there had been no sense of appreciation from Susan and Beatrice for all the effort. Rose decided to take a different approach. "Okay, then what's the perfect gift?"

Ronnie's eyebrows lifted, not expecting this reaction from the fair-haired woman. "Um...I don't know, something...something...." She motioned with her hands, causing the wine to slosh about inside the glass. "I guess I never really thought about it."

"Well then, let's think about it. Come over here." Rose patted the space next to her, booting Tabitha off in the process. "Come on, if the only thing you can get her is a perfect gift than let's find one." She turned the pages. "Maybe the trick is to get the perfect gifts, you know, a collection of things that she likes instead of one big gift. Bring a pen, and I'll mark anything we find."

Ronnie reached for something to write with, but all her pencils were gnawed, and there wasn't a pen in sight. She lifted a small pile of papers on her cluttered desk, but no pen appeared. Opening the drawer showed paper clips, spare staples, even a pile of Post-It notes, but nothing to write with. "President of a multi-million-dollar corporation, and I can't find a pen when I need it."

That's it! Rose thought excitedly. There before her eyes were pen and pencil sets in a multitude of price ranges and designs. The Mont Blanc sets were exquisite but completely beyond her meager spending level. She turned the page and saw it. There in the center of the page was a nice set, a marble design in a shade of blue that reminded Rose of the brilliance of her friend's eyes. Hesitantly, she focused on the price written in smaller print below and gulped. It would take most of her remaining funds. She looked up to see Ronnie still hunting for the elusive pen, then back down at the catalog. The problem of finding a present for Beatrice hadn't been solved, but another problem had. Rose discreetly bent the bottom corner of the page, then flipped back to the jewelry just as Ronnie found the missing pen and came over to the bed. Rose took the offered ballpoint and moved the catalog so her friend could see. "Now let's figure this thing out. What's your mother's favorite place to visit?"

"Europe. She's taken two of those country-by-country tours and raved about both of them." Ronnie smiled, the tension and worry of the last few days draining from her face. "That's it! She'd love it. A tour of Europe. I can't believe I didn't think of it before." She took the catalog from Rose and began flipping through the pages.

"Wow...that...that's a wonderful gift." She tried hard not to seem too awestruck, but it showed in her expression nonetheless.

"You think that's enough?" Ronnie asked as she looked at the glossy pictures, unaware that Rose, used to thinking in terms of pennies, was now trying to fathom the thousands of dollars a trip like that would cost. "I was thinking maybe a new wardrobe or...." She looked up and was struck by the beauty that gazed back at her. They studied each other for several seconds before Rose gave a shy smile and looked away.

"So um...." She picked at a non-existent piece of lint on the blanket as a slow flush crept up her cheeks. "You said something about clothes?"

"Um...yeah, clothes." Ronnie closed the catalog, no longer having any interest in picking out presents. What she wanted to do was shut off the lights and curl up against the younger woman. "You know, it's getting late."

"Yeah, I guess it is." Out in the living room, the grandfather clock announced the ten o'clock hour, but both women chose to pretend not to hear it. Rose reclined the bed into a sleeping position while Ronnie ran around shutting off lights and checking the locks on the doors. Within minutes, the house was dark, and they were lying in bed together. Usually, Rose fell asleep quickly, but with the early hour, she found herself still awake.

Staring up at the blackness, the young woman thought about what had happened earlier. For that brief moment, there had been something...special between them. Rose heard the sound of a fist punching a pillow and wished that Ronnie would just wrap those strong arms around her and hold her tight. Usually, that didn't happen until she was almost asleep.

Ronnie tossed and turned enough for the both of them. One particular toss jarred the injured legs, and the young woman hissed at the sudden pain. "I'm sorry, Rose. I just can't seem to get comfortable tonight."

"It's all right. It just hurt for a second, that's all." She was glad it was dark as a tear slipped out.

"I'll go out on the couch." Ronnie moved to get up but was stopped by the feel of the young woman's hand on her shoulder.

"Why don't you just put your arm around me like you usually do? You seem to go to sleep just fine after that." She gave a gentle tug on Ronnie's top. Slowly, reluctantly, the weight next to her shifted, and she felt the familiar warmth of Ronnie's body against hers. A second later, her wish came true as an arm draped itself over her belly. Rose let out a contented sigh and closed her eyes. By the time Tabitha decided they were done moving about and jumped back on the bed, both women were sound asleep.

"So what did you get Maria?"

Ronnie hit the mute button on the remote and turned her head to look at her companion. "A present." The corner of her mouth curled up in a teasing smile.

"Come on, tell me, please?" Rose gave her best puppy eyes. "I won't tell, I promise."

"I told you...a present." She tossed a piece of popcorn into the air and caught it in her mouth. "Now I thought you wanted to watch this show."

"I do, but I want to know what you got her, too. One clue?"

Ronnie pretended to consider the request for a moment before smirking with a devilish glint in her eyes. "It's not something that Maria would go out and buy herself. How's that?"

"That's a rotten clue," Rose groused, reaching for her cup.

"Ah, empty. You want more?" Ronnie took the cup off the snack tray and stood up.

"No, I've had enough hot chocolate for tonight. Any more and I'll be up half the night." She held her hand out. "Come on, sit down and relax. You're missing the show."

"Do you want the snack tray up or down?"

"Up. We won't need it anymore," Rose answered. Ronnie complied instantly, knowing that the snack tray going up was a prelude to something far more enjoyable than watching a television show. She set the empty mug on the coffee table and returned to her cushion, this time with her feet up and resting between them. As expected, within minutes, they were in Rose's lap, the younger woman's knowledgeable fingers rubbing out the aches of the day. Ronnie had no choice but to moan with pleasure.

"You do that sooo well...."

"It's easy with you. I know just where to push and rub." Rose demonstrated her skill by pressing her thumb firmly across the arch of Ronnie's left foot.

"Mmm, you can stop that in about...oh, seven or eight hours."

"Or maybe I'll stop if you don't tell me what present you got Maria." Her fingers stilled as if to carry out her threat.

"You drive a hard bargain," Ronnie admitted. "It's not much, just a plane ticket."

"A plane ticket? To where?"

"Arizona."

"That's where her son is," Rose remembered.

"She hasn't seen him in over a year. I thought she might like to take a trip out there." She raised an eyebrow. "So are you going to continue?" She stressed her point by wiggling her toes.

Rose laughed and continued the massage. It had become an unspoken ritual between them. Ronnie would groan about her feet, and Rose would immediately offer to rub them. They would spend hours on the couch like that, Rose sitting in the reclined position with her legs straight out and Ronnie lying across the length of the couch with her feet being pampered. The younger woman only paid a passing glance at the television, her attention focused on the soft flesh beneath her fingers.

Rose took special pleasure in rubbing Ronnie's feet. With the exception of cuddling at night, it was the only other physical contact they generally shared. She couldn't explain why, but it made her smile to hear the hedonistic groans coming from her friend's lips in reaction to her fingers. With all the stress about the audit and Tommy not speaking to anyone but his mother, the massages were one of the few things that brought a smile to Ronnie's face. And that smile was something that Rose tried to see at every opportunity. She looked down and studied the elegant foot before her. Baby smooth skin gave way to the slightest callous at the widest part of the heel. She let her fingertips glide over the softness from toe to ankle before moving her thumbs back down below to knead out the tightness. Rose pressed with a little more force than usual and was rewarded with a moan that teetered on the edge of sensual. She repeated the motion but only received a lesser version of the desired sound. Undaunted, she released Ronnie's foot and pulled the other one in her grasp. "You know, when I get out of these casts, I'll give you a backrub you won't forget."

"Mmm...." A slow, sexy smile crossed Ronnie's lips. "You're too good to be wasted in an office job. I think I'll change your position to chief masseuse."

"Uh-huh...do I get a raise with that new title?"

"You keep touching me like that and I'll pay you whatever you want." Ronnie's eyes closed as Rose's fingers pressed in all the right places.

"I'll remember that," the younger woman replied, her mind traveling to thoughts of having Ronnie's strong back beneath her fingers in the future. *Hmm, some oil, a nice summer day....you roll onto your stomach and unlace your bikini....* Her fingers stopped moving, and she shook her head to clear the odd thought. Yes, she enjoyed touching Ronnie, but that? She gave a short laugh and concentrated on what she was doing.

"What's so funny?" Ronnie asked, opening one eye and looking down at her friend.

"Oh, nothing...just something on *Home Improvement*. He really is a menace around tools, isn't he?"

"Hmm?" *Oh, is that what we're watching?* "Uh, yeah." She sensed that there was more to it than what Rose let on. She thought briefly about saying something, but the rubbing started again, and Ronnie closed her eyes, turning herself over to the gentle touch. They stayed in that position for the next hour, both silently enjoying what used to be a massage but was now a light caresses. The blissful and peaceful scene was shattered a moment later when the phone rang.

"Damn." Ronnie reluctantly sat up and pulled her slippers on. "If it's one of those MCI people again, I'm going to kill him." Her toes felt cold where only seconds before they had been held in Rose's soft hands. The phone was nowhere to be seen, and she padded to the kitchen and found it sitting on the table. "Cartwright residence." She began walking back into the living room, phone in hand, when she stopped. "When did that happen? Well, did they catch anyone?" She stepped into Rose's view. "Is that the one on Central? Yeah, I'll meet you there in a half hour. Okay, bye, Susan." She hung up the phone and shook her head.

"Ronnie?"

"Unbelievable." She sank onto the couch and let out a long breath. "Someone broke into the office tonight."

"Oh, no. I hope no one was hurt."

"Susan didn't say." Ronnie had to smile inwardly. *First thing out of your mouth is worry for others. My first concern was if anything was taken.* It was yet another example of the little things about Rose that she found so endearing. "I have to meet Susan at the police station. They caught one of the robbers." She reluctantly stood up. "I'd better get going." She looked down at the eyes almost emerald in color thanks to the soft lights of the living room and had an irrepressible urge to hug her. *Ah, the hell with it.* Ronnie leaned in quickly and wrapped her long arms around Rose's shoulders. "I'll call you if I'm going to be late." She smiled when she felt a return squeeze.

"Be careful. It's been snowing," the young woman said once they separated.

"I will."

Chapter Thirteen

Ronnie made it to the police station first and spoke with the night sergeant who directed her to one of the detectives. She returned to the lobby several minutes later, seething with anger at the information the officer had given her.

Susan and Jack came down the hallway, both shaking snow off their coats. "I went down to the office. You wouldn't believe it. They've got that yellow tape up, and your office looks like a bulldozer went through it," the redhead said as she hung her coat up on the nearby rack. "It looks like they were trying to get into the safe."

"He was," Ronnie replied coolly. "I guess it's a good thing I changed the combination last week, huh?" To her sister's confused look, she nodded and continued. "That's right, Susan. Go ahead and guess who broke into the offices and tried to steal from us, from our family!" Her raised voice drew the attention of several nearby officers, forcing Ronnie to speak through clenched teeth in an attempt to keep her anger in check. "The prodigal son is down in the lockup now. Probably being fingerprinted and introduced to his new girlfriend for the next five or ten years." She made no attempt to hide the anger in her tone.

"You mean Tommy...?" Susan shook her head. "No, that's impossible."

"You're right, Susan. The strung-out junkie down in lockup just looks like Tommy and carries his wallet around with him," she replied sarcastically, clenching her fists in disbelief.

"But...maybe he just went back to get something. You changed all the locks, maybe he set the alarm off accidentally." She looked to her husband for support but saw only the truth reflected back.

"Sweetheart, I think your sister is right this time. You were there, you saw the office." He gave Ronnie an apologetic look. "I've heard that drugs can make people do all sorts of things, even steal from their own relatives."

"Well, that's real enlightening, Jack. Are you just now realizing that Tommy has a drug problem?"

"Ronnie, just because you're upset doesn't mean you can take it out on Jack. After all, it's not his fault."

"No, Susan, it's not Jack's fault Tommy's in jail, it's Tommy's. I think we should leave his ass there until he straightens up."

"What?" The redhead stood between her sister and husband. "You can't honestly be thinking about leaving him here...in jail."

"Why the hell not? He broke into the office, tried to break into the safe. Susan, if we keep coddling him—"

"I'm not coddling him. I'm just saying you can't leave him in jail overnight."

"Oh, well, thanks for explaining the difference," Ronnie scoffed, turning away and rubbing her face in exasperation. "Susan...." She kept her back to her younger sister. "Tommy has a drug problem. First it was stealing money from the real estate projects, then it was forging loans. Now he's committing robbery to try and get money for his habit. I think it's time for some tough love." She turned to see streaks in her sister's makeup from the tears that were starting to fall. "Look, maybe this is the best thing for him. A few days to get those drugs out of his system will do him a world of good."

Susan shook her head adamantly. "No. It's two days before Christmas. I can't let my younger brother—my only brother—spend Christmas in jail, I just can't." She looked up at her husband. "Can't you do something?"

"I'm a tax attorney, honey. If he was being arrested for cheating on his taxes, then yes, I could help him. I'm not that versed on criminal law."

The redhead tapped her finger to her chin, unwilling to give up. "I've got it!" Her eyes grew wide. "We'll refuse to press charges. No crime, no jail."

"That'd be fine except for one little detail." Ronnie held her forefinger and thumb slightly apart. "It seems that Hercules in there decided that he didn't want to go willingly with the cops. He bit one of them." She wiggled her fingers together as if wiping away her sister's idea.

"What about bail? We can get him out on bail, can't we?"

"Susan, it's better to leave him in there, don't you understand? He needs help, help that he won't get if he's allowed to roam the streets."

"Ronnie, I know you two haven't always gotten along, and I know he's jealous of you, but how can you be so petty that you'd let your own brother spend Christmas in jail?"

At that moment, a bald man came walking into the station, his briefcase in one hand and cellular phone in the other. "I came as soon as I got the call." It was Richard Jenkins, the family lawyer who did little more than fix their parking tickets in exchange for his huge annual retainer. "I've been on the phone with the ADA for the last half hour."

"Who called you?" Ronnie asked.

"Why, your mother did, of course. Tommy couldn't remember my number."

"You mean Tommy called her?" Ronnie turned away from them and cursed silently. Of course he would call her, who else would continue to rescue him from scrape after scrape? There was one last hope. "What about biting the cop?"

"All taken care of." Jenkins smiled proudly. "He only tore through the guy's shirt and didn't touch his skin, so we were able to bargain it down to restitution and community service to be served after the new year." He opened his briefcase and put the phone away. "If you ladies will excuse me, I'll be back in a few minutes with your brother." He nodded at Jack. "Good to see you again."

"Likewise, Richard."

Ronnie had enough. She fished her coat off the rack and roughly tossed it on.

"Where are you going?" Susan asked.

"I don't feel like sticking around to celebrate." She looked down to see that in her haste she had misbuttoned her coat. "I'm telling you, Susan, letting him out like this is a big mistake." She gave up on the buttons and angrily tugged the belt around her waist. "What he needs is rehab, not a get-out-of-jail-free card."

"Maybe what he needs is to know that his family loves him and supports him," Susan snapped back. "How do you think he felt to find out that his own sister had him locked out of the family business?"

"How did you feel when you heard the result of the audit? You enjoy watching your annual dividends go into Tommy's pocket?" Susan opened her mouth to protest, then closed it, realizing that her sister was right.

"Maybe it'll work out, Ronnie. Maybe this is what he needed to get himself back on track."

"Don't get your hopes up. I have a feeling this is only the beginning."

Too angry to go straight home, Ronnie drove around the streets of Albany for over an hour. She returned to a dark house. Trying to be as quiet as possible, she slipped into the room and began to undress in the dark. "I'm awake," Rose said as she switched on the lamp.

"I was trying to be quiet."

"I was waiting up for you. How did it go?"

"Not well." She turned her back and removed her shirt. "It seems our burglar is none other than my baby brother."

"Tommy?"

"Nice way to treat his family, don't you think?" She pulled the T-shirt over her head and slipped under the covers. "I didn't bother going down to see the damage firsthand. I have enough of a headache." She brought her fingers to her temples.

"Let me," Rose whispered. She replaced Ronnie's fingers with her own and gently rubbed the tender area. "How's that?"

"Mmm...a little harder...hmm, right there...."

There wasn't an ounce of relaxation anywhere in Ronnie's upper body, the young woman soon discovered. Every muscle was bunched, tight, and tensed as if ready for battle. She moved her hands down to the broad shoulders, pressing gently at first, then with more effort as the muscles finally surrendered to her manipulations. "That's right, just relax," she cooed. "Close your eyes."

"They are closed."

"Think about the day after tomorrow. Think about all the lights on the tree...the presents...."

"Are you trying to hypnotize me, Rose?"

"Of course not, silly." Rose moved her thumbs to the base of Ronnie's skull and kneaded the area gently. "I just want you to relax and think about how much fun Christmas is going to be.

"Mmm."

"That's right...." Rose's touch became lighter as she felt Ronnie relax. "Does that feel better?"

"Much."

"Good." A self-satisfied smile came to the young woman's lips. "How about we get some sleep and leave all the bad stuff for morning, okay?" She nudged Ronnie back onto her own pillow. "Good night."

"Good night, Rose." It was silent for a moment before Ronnie added, "Thank you." The burden off her shoulders for at least one night, she quickly fell into a peaceful sleep.

Ronnie took a sip of coffee and looked out at the picture perfect Christmas morning. A light dusting of snow had fallen overnight, covering her backyard and the trees that surrounded it with a light blanket of white. The sun was just coming up, the whole scene reminding her of a Currier and Ives print. Tightening the sash on her terrycloth robe, she opened the sliding glass door and stepped onto the deck, the thin layer of snow crunching under her blue slippers. She set her mug on the table, the heat causing a small ring of snow to melt and reveal the green-painted metal beneath. Ronnie took a deep breath and smiled. It was cold enough to keep the snow from melting, but the lack of wind kept it from being bitterly so. She stood there and drank her coffee, enjoying a family of rabbits scampering across the field. Their gray coats were a sharp contrast to the crisp white snow. *Perfect. I'm going to make this the best Christmas you've ever had, Rose. At least I'm going to try my damnedest.* She thought of the presents under the tree. As much as she hated malls and shopping in general, Ronnie took great pleasure in personally choosing each and every gift for Rose. Finally, the cold registered through her robe, and she retreated inside.

The kitchen clock showed that it was just past seven. *Damn, too early.* Setting the empty cup in the sink, she headed into the living room. Hundreds of tiny lights twinkled and flashed over the tree, their multitude of colors reflecting off the shiny paper covering the gifts piled on the floor. Ronnie smiled. Everything was perfect, now it was just a matter of waiting for Rose to wake up. She looked at the grandfather clock, hoping that she wouldn't have to wait much longer. *I haven't been this excited about Christmas in years.* "Come on, Rose," she muttered to herself, noting that the time seemed to be passing by slower than usual. She rearranged the presents and had another cup of coffee. The clock now read seven thirty. Tabitha rubbed against her legs. "What do you want?"

"Mrrow?"

"Breakfast for you isn't for another half hour."

"Mrrow?" The orange and white cat walked over to the cabinet where the cat food was stored and cried again. When crying didn't work, the frisky cat rolled onto her back and turned her head at a ridiculous angle. Ronnie chuckled and shook her head.

"Well, since it's Christmas." She knelt down next to Tabitha and opened the cabinet. "Okay now, let's see what we've got here." She pulled out a can and held it in front of the now purring feline. "You want turkey for Christmas?"

"Mrrow." Tabitha batted at the can with her paw.

"Fine, turkey it is then."

Feeding Tabitha didn't use up as much time as Ronnie would have liked. When the grandfather clock chimed the eight o'clock hour, the anticipation was killing her. "I think that's late enough, don't you, Tabitha?" She reached down and scooped the cat up in her arms. "Let's go wake Mommy so she can see all the pretty presents, hmm?"

Ronnie set Tabitha down at the foot of the bed and crawled in next to the sleeping woman. "Rose? Rose, time to wake up." A gentle nudge to the shoulder. "Rose? It's Christmas morning. Don't you want to get up and open presents?"

"Hrmmphf."

"Come on, it's time to get up. You don't want to waste the whole morning in bed, do you?" Eyelids lifted slightly, revealing sleepy green.

"What time is it?"

"Eight." The eyes snapped shut, and the young woman let out a groan. She pulled the blanket up over her face only to have a stronger hand pull it back down.

"But it's Christmas. You can't sleep in on Christmas." Ronnie hopped off the bed and pushed the portable commode over. "Come on, up and at 'em."

Rose gave one more groan but slowly opened her eyes, deciding that Ronnie was entirely too chipper in the mornings...until Ronnie's words sank in. "Oh, God, it's Christmas!"

"Merry Christmas," Ronnie chuckled, pulling the blanket out of the way and lying on her side, using her elbow to prop her head up. "It's a beautiful morning, and it would be a crime to let you sleep through it."

"How long have you been up?"

"About an hour and a half."

"I'm surprised you waited this long." Ronnie was about to defend herself when she saw the twinkle in Rose's eyes. She pounced playfully on the smaller woman, the two engaging in a brief tickle fight. "You are ruthless," Rose said when they finally broke apart.

"Well, I guess you're awake now, aren't you? I'll just leave you to take care of business."

"Uh, okay. I'll just be a couple of minutes."

"Sure, just give a shout when you're ready. I'll take your coffee into the living room. You can drink and open presents at the same time."

Rose listened carefully until she was certain Ronnie wasn't coming right back, then retrieved the small present hidden in the drawer of the nightstand. An unexpected fear passed through her. Suddenly, the pen and pencil set she had Karen pick up for her didn't seem like such a great gift after all. If Ronnie wanted one, she would have had it by now. Maybe she didn't like mechanical pencils because she couldn't bite them. "Stupid, stupid, stupid," she grumbled to herself before setting the gift down on the stand and pushing herself over to the commode.

Fifteen minutes later, she was dressed, wearing a light beige shirt that Ronnie insisted on giving her. Rose didn't believe for a minute that it was too small for her benefactor. It hung a good eight to ten inches past her own hips, and the cuffs had to be folded over several times before she could see her fingertips. Still, it was something given to her by Ronnie, and like the Dartmouth nightshirt, it was something that Maria was hard-pressed to get away from the young woman long enough to wash.

A final run of the brush through her hair and Rose was ready. She set the present on her lap, then covered it with the quilt before calling out. A few seconds later, Ronnie appeared.

The large pile of presents spilling out from under the tree captivated Rose's attention as Ronnie helped her into the sunken level of the living room. Even when she stayed with a family of five one Christmas, she had never seen so many presents stuffed under the tree. She recognized the large flowing style of Ronnie's handwriting on all the gift tags. "Is your family coming over today?"

"No."

Why put all their presents under the tree if they aren't stopping over? Her expression became even more puzzled. "Well, aren't those their presents?" Ronnie gave a short laugh and squeezed her arm.

"Those aren't their presents. They're yours."

Rose's eyes grew as wide as saucers, and for a few seconds, she forgot how to breathe. *Mine?* "Y-you mean...?" Giving up on speech, she merely pointed at the presents.

"Yup, they're all for you." Ronnie's brow crinkled. "Is something wrong?"

"N-no...I...." She looked up at the most important person in her life as tears slid down her face. Rose had to fight to keep her lip from quivering. "I never...all those...for me...." She reached out and was met halfway to be enfolded in strong, comforting arms. "Oh, Ronnie."

"Shh, I've got you." Ronnie left one arm around Rose's back and used the other to stroke her hair. "I'm sorry. I wasn't thinking about how many there were. I just kept seeing things I thought you'd like and bought them."

"B-but I only got you one."

Ronnie put her fingers to Rose's lips "Shh, it's the thought that counts, not anything else." Wiping away a tear streak with her thumb, Ronnie spoke again. "One gift from you is worth a thousand from anyone else, got that?"

The reddish-blonde head moved with a shaky nod. "Can I give you my gift first?"

"You know what...." Ronnie wiped away the other streak from Rose's cheek. "I'd rather wait until after you open your presents. Would that be okay?"

"Are you sure?"

"Yeah." She stood up and reached for the handles of the wheelchair. Come on, we'll sit back and drink our coffee, then open presents."

Rose was just settling on the couch when they heard a crash from behind the tree. "What the...?" Ronnie exclaimed. She got her answer a second later when Tabitha came tearing out from under the tree and raced into the kitchen. Before either could speak, the orange and white blur returned and dove back into the mountain of gifts.

"What's wrong with her?" Rose asked, her voice full of concern. "I've never seen her move so fast before."

"I think...." Ronnie crossed the room, knelt down, and began moving presents out of the way. "Yup...Tabitha, you greedy little girl." She moved back to let the younger woman see. The cat was lying on her back, batting at an ornament ball dangling above her. "Your little baby there got into her Christmas present." Ronnie reached in to retrieve the package only to have her wrist caught between Tabitha's front legs. "Don't you even think about clawing me," she warned while slowly trying to pull her hand back. Soft paws revealed their weapons, the claws pressing against her skin until she stopped moving. Tabitha looked up at her for a second, then began purring and licking Ronnie's wrist. "Miss Grayson, I do believe your cat is stoned out of her mind." She pulled out the bag of catnip. It was still wrapped in festive green paper, except for the prominent piece missing where it had been chewed into.

"You put catnip under the tree?"

"Yeah, but it was in a plastic bag and wrapped in paper."

"Ronnie, they can smell catnip a mile away. Tabitha? Come here, honey."

The cat moved three steps before falling into a lump on the carpet and cleaning herself.

"I don't think she's going anywhere, Rose." *Enough of this. I want you to open your presents.* She reached over and picked up a shirt box wrapped in silver paper. "Since I'm over here anyway, let's start with your first gift." She returned to the couch and handed it over, trying hard to control her enthusiasm and excitement.

Small fingers ran over the fancy paper and red bow. "It's almost too pretty to open."

"It's just wrapping paper. Open it," Ronnie urged. *Come on, open it up and see what I got you.* A smile akin to a child's grew on Ronnie's face.

Rose looked around. "There's no place to throw the paper away."

"Toss it on the floor. I'll pick it up later. Open it." Ronnie scooted over until she was on the cushion next to the younger woman.

"I can't toss it on the floor." Her fingertip traced the bold writing on the gift tag.

"But...." Ronnie looked around, frowning when she didn't find anything suitable in sight. "I'll be right back." She hopped off the couch and went into the kitchen. Rose listened to the sound of cupboards opening and shutting, followed by drawers.

There was a muttered curse followed by, "There it is." A few seconds later, Ronnie returned, shaking the garbage bag open. She handed it to Rose and returned to the adjoining cushion, tucking her bare feet underneath her thighs. "Okay, now open it."

The young woman looked from the present to Ronnie. "Thank you."

"You don't even know what it is yet." *Hurry up and open it.*

Rose slipped her fingernail under the tag and carefully separated it from the package, setting it on the side table. Another pass and one corner flap opened.

"Just tear it," Ronnie growled playfully. "Or we'll be here until next Christmas."

Rose looked at the beautiful package, her friend's overly excited face, then at the present again. Small fingers curled beneath the open flap and with a quick tug, tore a large strip of paper away. A few more rips and the box was opened to reveal a rust-colored shirt. She picked it up by the shoulders and held it out to look at it. "It's very nice."

"Do you like it?"

"Oh, yes, absolutely." Rose looked at the length of the sleeves, noting that they were a perfect match to her shorter arms. "I won't have to fold over the cuffs."

"Of course not. I made sure to get the right size." Ronnie smiled. "Do you like the color?"

"Very much so."

"It matches your eyebrows. I bet you'll look great in it."

Rose turned the shirt this way and that, nodding with agreement. It was, quite simply, terrific, and she couldn't wait to wear it. She folded it up and handed it to Ronnie, who set it on the empty cushion at the end of the couch. The trash was moved out of the way and another present retrieved from under the tree.

Rose forced the last piece of wrapping paper into the already overstuffed trash bag and wiped another happy tear from her cheek. "You really are amazing, you know that?"

"I'm glad you think so," Ronnie replied with a warm smile. It had been a morning full of tears and smiles from Rose, and Ronnie couldn't have been happier. "Those are the only things I wasn't sure about." She gestured with her hand at the pair of blue and white sneakers on Rose's lap. "I can take them back if they're too big."

"No, they're perfect."

"Great." Ronnie reached over and picked them up, then looked around for an empty place to put them. The cushion was piled high with clothes, and the coffee table was littered with software programs and various other items. She went to set them on the carpet, but Tabitha came running over. "Oh, no, you don't." In the end, the sneakers were placed on top of the pile of sweaters.

Rose gave a short sniff and blinked several times before moving her hand beneath the afghan. "I guess it's time for your gift now. I'm sor–"

"No, wait." Ronnie jumped off the couch. "There's one more. Don't go away, I'll be right back."

The young woman fingered the thin bow on the gift in her lap, her gaze settling on the pile of clothes. A fresh tear rolled down her face, causing a frown to cross the blue-eyed woman's face upon her return. "You know, it wasn't my intention to make you cry." She resumed her position on the couch only inches from Rose. "I probably should invest in Kleenex."

That earned a chuckle. "I'm just a bit overwhelmed, I guess," Rose replied, haphazardly wiping the salty drops off her cheeks. "I've never gotten so many things at Christmas ever." She looked around, still amazed at the multitude of presents piled about. "I just can't...." Rose looked down at her lap and shook her head. "Listen to me, I make it sound like my life was straight out of *Oliver Twist*." She took the offered linen handkerchief.

"Of course you don't," Ronnie said softly. "Come on, let me give you your last present, then you can give me mine." She set the jewelry box in Rose's hands.

"Oh, my." The young woman's hand began shaking only to be steadied by a much larger one wrapping around hers.

"Open it" came the whisper near her ear. "It's okay, it won't bite." After a few seconds, long fingers pried the box open to reveal its contents.

Rose stared in amazement at the pendant attached to a thin rope chain. Only an inch and a half long, the white gold had been carefully molded into an exquisite representation of a rose. Tiny emerald and ruby chips made up the petals and leaves while a diamond solitaire rested at the base of the stem. Her lower lip quivered as she touched the pendant reverently with one fingertip. "It's beautiful."

"A rose for a Rose," Ronnie said, repeating the slogan that had drawn her to the jewelry in the first place. She took the necklace out of the box and opened the catch. Rose stayed very still as the cool metal touched her skin and Ronnie fastened the chain. "Looks perfect on you."

"It-it's too much, Ronnie, I ca–" She was stopped by a pair of fingers pressing against her lips.

"Rose...." Ronnie wiped another tear with her thumb. "Listen to me. I wanted you to have this."

"But...." Rose looked around. "All these clothes, the programs, the shoes and sneakers, and–" Long fingers silenced her again.

"You deserve nice clothes. You deserve things that fit and look good on you." Ronnie took the young woman's chin in her hand and forced her to meet her gaze. "And you deserve to wear something pretty. Now...give me a hug, tell me how much you like it, and give me my present." She said the last part with a playful smile, forcing Rose to smile along with her.

"It's more than pretty, it's wonderful. I love it." The young woman wrapped her arms around Ronnie's neck and pulled her in for a hug. "It's so beautiful," she whispered. "I love it so much, thank you."

"I'm glad."

"You really are my guardian angel, aren't you?" She pulled back and looked at Ronnie, green eyes sparkling with moisture. "You're the best friend anyone could ever have." She reached under the afghan and pulled out the present. "I just wish I had something more to show you just how much you mean to me. Merry Christmas, Ronnie." Rose nervously handed over the present, a million thoughts flying through her mind. Her anxiety grew as Ronnie slowly removed the gift tag and slipped it in her pocket. "Well, open it."

Ronnie laughed and tugged on the thin red ribbon. "You're as bad as I am...oh." She opened the long velvet box. "Rose, they're beautiful."

"Do you like them?"

"Yes, very much." The executive pulled the pen out and held it up to the light, the smile never leaving her face. "That's a very pretty design. All those blues and greens swirling around. I like that gold band there, too."

"You really like it? You're not just saying that to make me feel good, are you?"

"No, hon, I'm not just saying that. I really do like it." She leaned over and gave Rose a hug. "It really is a thoughtful gift," she said, leaning back.

"You said you could never find a pen around here."

"I never can," Ronnie agreed. "I guarantee I won't lose this one."

"I didn't know if you liked mechanical pencils. Probably not since you can't bite them, huh?"

"Rose, mechanical pencils are fine. Really. I only use the wooden ones because that's what we have in the supply office at work. I never had any reason to go buy a pencil like this." She turned the metal at the tip, watching the lead grow from the end. "I'll promise you this, I won't chew the end of this one."

"You'd better not," Rose playfully teased, her fears eased by the smile on Ronnie's face. Her tone grew serious. "I'm really happy you like it. I've never bought anyone something like that before."

"You know I would have been happy no matter what you got, even if it was just a card." She looked down at the set and smiled. "These really are beautiful." She reached over for another hug, much to Rose's joy.

"This is the best Christmas I've ever had," the young woman whispered into Ronnie's ear. "Thank you so much."

Ronnie smiled and hugged even harder. "You're welcome. Thank you for making my Christmas so special." She reluctantly ended the embrace, her hand still gripping the pen case. She looked over at the clock. "Wow, I didn't realize it was so late. It took that long just to open presents?"

"There were a lot of presents to open," Rose replied with a smile. "I have no idea what to do with all those programs." She gestured at the pile on the table.

"You're going to learn from them." Ronnie set the pen case down and picked up one of the software boxes. "This one teaches you how to type. It's self-paced and shows you how to format business letters and memos." She set the box on Rose's lap and picked up another one. "This teaches the fundamentals of bookkeeping and accounting. There are programs to do all the actual calculations, but if you're going to be in the business world, you really should know these basics." She put the programs back on the table. "I'll install them for you tomorrow and show you how to bring them up so you can work on them. Once you're comfortable, I'll show you how to log into the corporate network, and you can go onto the Internet."

"That sounds like fun. I've been on the Internet before. They had it at the library. I found a great site once that had all sorts of information about how to take care of cats."

"Anything you're interested in is out there on the Internet. When I first got used to being on a computer all the time, I spent hours surfing the Net looking at different things. My bookmark file must have been a mile long."

"Bookmark file?" Rose shook her head. "I don't know if I can get all this computer stuff."

Ronnie laughed. "Oh, Rose. Trust me. A few weeks and you and the computer will be best friends. I'll have to drag you away from it."

"I don't know about that."

"I do. It's very addictive."

"Ronnie? I understand how the typing and the other programs are supposed to help me, but what is the *Rescuer of the Maiden* supposed to teach me?" Rose pointed at the brightly colored box with knights battling on the cover.

"Uh...well...." Ronnie gave a sheepish smile. "That one teaches you how to be the great knight who rescues the fair maiden from the evil king's dungeon. I thought you might like a game to relax and take a break with."

"A knight rescuing a maiden, hmm?" Rose glanced at the cover again, noting that the maiden was fair-haired, like she was. She looked over at her own personal knight in shining armor. "I'm sure I'll enjoy it."

Ronnie smiled back and stood up. "Right now I think we'd better hit the kitchen and eat. I'm starving."

Rose watched as the wheelchair was brought over. She allowed herself to be lifted into the chair, but before Ronnie could pull back, she wrapped her arms around her neck and squeezed, burying her face into the dark tresses. "Thank you. You're the best friend I ever had, and today is one of the happiest days I've ever known."

Ronnie returned the embrace, smiling into the golden hair. "You're welcome."

As they reached the threshold of the kitchen, Rose looked up. "Hey, look at that."

"What?"

"The mistletoe. You've left it up there all this time and I didn't notice."

"Hmm, guess I have." Ronnie's heart began beating faster. They were directly below the green leaves. "Um, would it be okay if...."

"Well, we're both under the mistletoe, and it is Christmas." Rose swallowed, nervousness creeping in although she wasn't sure why. *After all, it's just Ronnie.* "Yes." She turned her face up to meet the dark head coming down. Their lips touched once...twice before Ronnie pulled back.

"I um...I guess we'd better get the food started." She guided them into the kitchen, knowing full well why her heart was pounding like a rocker's drum. Rose's lips were soft, so very soft that she almost lost herself in them, stopping herself just before her tongue could work its way out of her mouth. Ronnie knew she couldn't afford another kiss like that. She made a mental note to let Rose wheel herself out of the kitchen.

Rose turned her head forward, hoping that the blush she felt rising to her cheeks wasn't noticeable to Ronnie. No one had kissed her in a long time and certainly not with as much gentleness and tenderness. She felt warm inside, as if swallowing a strong drink. She dimly realized that Ronnie was speaking to her. "I'm sorry, what?"

"I asked if you wanted to make some sugar cookies."

"Oh. Do you like sugar cookies?"

"Well, they're okay, and they are the traditional holiday cookie." Ronnie opened the refrigerator and smiled. "Of course we do have a roll of chocolate chip cookies here, too." Her tone made it clear which type she preferred.

"Sounds good to me." Rose wheeled her way over to the lower cabinet and retrieved a cookie sheet. The counters were really too high for the young woman to easily help with the preparations, but she wanted to do what she could. Ronnie turned on the radio in the corner and soon festive music filled the air, making the perfect setting to bake holiday cookies. Neither knew the other was thinking about the mistletoe and what had happened. Rose felt confusion. She enjoyed the kiss more than she thought she should have. She tried to equate what she felt now with kisses friends exchange but couldn't. It didn't feel like that. What it did feel like, she wasn't sure, but she knew it was different.

Ronnie had her own internal dilemma with the kiss. She knew exactly what it felt like, and she wanted more. Her mind and body screamed for her to taste the softness one more time, to show Rose just how much she meant to her, to take her into her arms and never let go. It was torture, plain and simple, and the cool air when she stepped outside to clear her head did nothing to lower the temperature of her fevered soul.

Chapter Fourteen

Rose had just folded up the last pair of panties and put them in the lower drawer of the dresser when Ronnie returned from the other room after having a long phone conversation with her mother. She and Susan had planned the conference call to say a quick Merry Christmas to their vacationing mother. It was expected, and Ronnie had hoped that with her mother busy on the cruise, it would be just that, a quick call. She was wrong. She flopped down on the bed, her long arms folded behind her head.

"It didn't go well?" Rose queried, noting the somber expression. She wheeled herself over to the side of the bed and put her hand on Ronnie's forearm.

"No, everything was fine, it's just that...." Ronnie turned her gaze away from Rose and glanced at the ceiling. "Sometimes I wish I wasn't the oldest. It's too much responsibility."

"What happened?"

Ronnie gave a sigh and looked back at her companion. "Mother's not happy with the way I handled the whole thing about Tommy embezzling from the company."

"How does she know about that? I thought you weren't going to tell her."

"There are no secrets in this family, Rose," she said sadly. "The thing is, she isn't questioning whether or not he did it but how I handled it. She said I should have kept a lid on it until I was completely sure, then should have talked to him before removing him from his office."

Rose's hand began moving up and down Ronnie's arm in a comforting motion. "Did Susan at least stick up for you?"

"She didn't say a word. Not a peep. You know, sometimes I wonder why I don't just say screw them all and quit. I could move to Chicago or Boston and start my own company."

"Then why don't you?"

There was a long silence before Ronnie answered. When she did, it was with quiet resignation. "Because they need me." She reached for the remote. "Come on, all those Christmas shows will be starting soon. HBO is rerunning that Rich Little version of *A Christmas Carol*."

"I've never seen it."

"It's pretty funny. He does all the characters as impersonations of famous celebrities. I saw it when I was a kid. Come on...." Ronnie found the right station and set the remote aside before rising and helping Rose get into bed. Midnight would find them as it always did, the longer one curled up against the side of the smaller one, both sleeping contentedly.

Rose stared at the screen, concentration causing her brow to furrow. She pressed the mouse button and moved the red seven under the black eight. She was taking a short break from the typing program, having worked on it steadily for almost three hours. She was pleased with her progress after only three weeks of practice. Her speed was improving rapidly while the number of mistakes declined. A flat board resting across the arms of the wheelchair served as a makeshift desktop, the full leg casts making it impossible for Rose to get under the desk far enough to use the keyboard tray.

Maria entered the room with a sandwich and cup of coffee. "You need to take a break." She waited for Rose to put the mouse and keyboard back on the desk, then handed her the sandwich, setting the cup on the nightstand within easy reach. "I swear you're as bad as Ronnie is sometimes. I've left some evenings with her on that thing and come back in the morning to find her still sitting in front of it." The middle-aged woman shook her head. "When she was in high school, she was the same way."

"What was she like? When she was younger?" Rose gripped the wheels and turned her chair, silently asking Maria to sit and join her. The housekeeper relaxed into the soft leather of Ronnie's chair and laced her fingers together.

"So you want to know what she was like?" A friendly smile worked its way across her face. "Ronnie's her own person, always has been. She's always known what she wanted to be and where she was going."

"No, that's not what I meant." Rose shook her head, trying to think of how to phrase her request. "Tell me about her. Something she did, something that happened to her, something about her."

"I'm not sure I should. You know it's the cardinal rule of housekeepers to keep what they see and hear private."

"You don't have to tell me her deep dark secrets, Maria," Rose chided. "Ronnie told me herself that she was a hell-raiser. I'm sure you must have a tale or two that you remember. I'm sure she wasn't the example of a perfect child."

"Perfect? Hah!" The older woman laughed, her eyes crinkling at the corners in a motherly way. "Ronnie was many things growing up, but perfect wasn't one of them. That child had me running around more than her brother and sister put together."

"Oh, really? Do tell." Rose's eyes widened with expectation as she took a bite of her sandwich.

"Wait, let me get something to drink." Maria left and returned a minute later with a tall glass of soda and a coaster. She settled back into the chair and took a sip before continuing. "I remember a time when she was thirteen and her parents were out of town. Some friends of hers wanted her to go to the mall with them. Now normally, it would have been fine, but she had skipped school a few days before, and her father grounded her while they were gone."

"What did she do?"

"What any kid her age would do, she sneaked out. She went into her room and climbed out the window. I knew where she went, but there was no way I could go after her with Susan and Tommy in tow. He wasn't more than four or five at the time and a handful all by himself."

"So what happened?" Rose was listening intently, imagining a thirteen-year-old Ronnie slipping out to spend time with friends at the mall.

"She and a couple of friends of hers decided they wanted to try cigarettes. Well, of course no store in the mall was going to sell three teenage girls a pack of cigarettes. Ronnie was tall for her age, but still.... Anyway, they decided that if they couldn't buy them that they'd try to shoplift them."

"Did they get caught?"

"Not in the store. The fools were walking down Consaul Road smoking and wearing their school jackets. A policeman saw them and picked them up."

"I bet you were furious."

"At first I was, but then I found out that she took all the blame, even though the cigarettes were found in one of the other girls' pockets."

"You mean she took the blame for someone else?"

Maria nodded and took another sip of her soda. "I didn't tell her father, figured that being dragged down to the police station was enough to put a scare into her."

Rose sat quietly for a moment, deep in thought. It made perfect sense that Ronnie would try to protect others around her. She looked down at her broken legs and nodded. *Always the caretaker*, she thought to herself. "Maria, has Ronnie ever done something like this before?" She motioned at herself. "I mean, has she ever taken anyone in who had nowhere else to go?"

"Never," the housekeeper replied. Rose sensed hesitation on Maria's part and waited patiently for her to continue. "I was surprised when she brought Tabitha here and even more so when she called to say that you would be staying. Ronnie is a very private woman." She looked like she wanted to say more but decided against it. "I have a house to clean, and you have some lunch to finish up. She'll be calling again soon." Maria stood and retrieved the glass from the desk. "By the way, remind her that Tabitha's appointment is tomorrow, they called today."

"Oh, that's right, I forgot." Rose looked to make sure the feline wasn't around. "How long is she supposed to be there?"

"She goes in early in the morning and comes home after five in the evening," the housekeeper replied.

"Poor thing." The young woman's face took on a sympathetic look. "She won't even know what's going on. But I suppose it's better than letting her suffer through that heat again."

"Oh, don't remind me." Maria shook her head. "I was ready to throw her out in the snow with all that yowling."

"You weren't the only one. I thought for sure that Ronnie was going to do it the one night she wouldn't stop crying." Just then the subject of conversation sauntered in and jumped on the bed to claim her nap space.

"Enjoy it while you can, missy," the housekeeper said to Tabitha, who responded by licking her paws and rubbing her ear.

"She's so cute," Rose said, reaching over to pet the cat.

"Cute, sure," Maria scoffed. "You try making dinner with her underfoot and tell me how cute she is." She leaned over and scratched Tabitha's head. "If you're a good kitty and stay in here while I get the mopping done, I'll give you an extra cat treat before I go, how's that sound?"

"Oh, she likes that idea," the young woman said when Tabitha began to purr. "I'll keep an eye on her."

Once Maria left, Rose set the cordless phone on her lap and waited for Ronnie's usual after lunch phone call.

"There goes our bonuses," Susan sighed before tossing the report back on Ronnie's desk. "I don't think I've ever seen a lower earnings quarter. Do you realize what a banner year it would have been without that?"

Ronnie opened the folder again, the numbers still incomprehensible. The losses in the real estate division were enough to make the entire year mediocre in terms of profit. Although the entire board of directors was made up of family members and knew exactly what was going on, the rest of the business world didn't, and Cartwright Corporation had some serious explaining to do. "The whole year. Everything we've done has been wiped out by him." Ronnie ran her fingers through her hair and looked at her sister. "You realize that this is just the tip of the iceberg. What do you think those auditors are going to turn up when they go back to when he first took over?"

"You think he's been stealing the whole time?"

"No, the annual audits would have picked something like that up. When did he start missing deadlines and taking lots of time off?"

"I don't know...February, March maybe?"

Ronnie nodded. "Sounds right. He took that loan out the end of April." She picked up her mechanical pencil and rested the tip against her lips. The action had a calming effect on her, reminding her of the fair-haired beauty waiting for her at home. "I think whatever drug he's into, he started doing back then. Probably crack or heroin."

"Crack? Ronnie, only junkies do crack."

"How do you think they became junkies, Sis? I don't think crack cares if the person is rich or poor so long as they have enough for the next bag, or hit, or whatever it is they do with it." Ronnie sighed and tapped the pencil rhythmically against her chin. "He needs help, Susan. Probably rehab."

"That's pretty, when'd you get that?" the redhead asked, changing the subject.

"Rose gave it to me for Christmas." Ronnie stopped tapping it and held it out to look at the marbled swirls of blue and green accented by a thin gold band. "It has a matching pen." Unbidden, a smile came to her lips, one that was not missed by her younger sister.

"So how's she doing?"

Ronnie looked up at Susan in response to the softer tone of her voice. It was a subject they hadn't spoken of since the party. "She's um...fine. Sees the doctor next week to have her casts changed. I think they're going to give her a short one for her right leg."

"Oh, that's good." A silence fell between them. Ronnie usually could tell when her sister was just being solicitous, but this time, there seemed to be no hidden meaning, no secret agenda in her words.

"Yeah. She says it doesn't hurt her much at all, although the itching is driving her batty."

"I bet. Remember when you broke your arm? I don't know how many times Mother caught you trying to stick a hanger or a ruler down there to scratch." The redhead kicked her shoes off and sat down on the couch. "So what did you get her? And come over here for a while. I'm tired of talking across the room."

Dark eyebrows raised in surprise. "Since when have you wanted to talk about Rose?"

"I didn't say I wanted to talk about her, I just asked what you got her for Christmas, that's all." Susan looked down at her fingernails, obviously avoiding her sister's gaze. Ronnie was hesitant to open up, uncertain about the sudden change of attitude.

"Some clothes and a couple of computer programs," she offered, making no effort to rise from her chair. "I didn't go overboard." Truth was that she had spent far more than originally planned, but the smiles that Rose gave her were worth every penny.

"I didn't say you did, Ronnie." Seeing that her sister wasn't going to join her on the couch, Susan stretched her legs out and let her feet rest on the far cushion. "Did she like them?"

"Yes, she liked them." Ronnie looked down at her pencil and smiled, turning the writing implement over in her hands.

"So things are going well between you two?"

"Susan, she's just a friend. I've told you that." She stared at the pencil for a few seconds before speaking again, this time in a lower voice. "It really is beautiful, isn't it?"

"It's very nice," the redhead agreed. "I guess it didn't take her long to figure out your habit for eating every pencil in sight."

"I don't eat them." A slight blush colored the executive's features. "I bite them. There's a difference. I can't help it. I've done it since I was a kid, and I'll probably continue to do it until I'm an old lady."

"Well, Sis, I'm willing to bet that you won't be biting that one." She pointed at the mechanical pencil.

"No, it's too beautiful. Besides, I'd probably chip my teeth on it."

"You said it has a matching pen?"

"Yeah, right here." Ronnie reached behind her for the blazer resting across the back of her chair and fished the pen out of the inside breast pocket. "She even made sure it had blue ink instead of black."

"You know, I never saw anyone so particular about what color they write with." Susan rose and crossed over to the desk to get a better look. Ronnie reluctantly handed it over. "Oh, that is nice." There was silence for a moment before Susan handed the pen back. "I was thinking that maybe Jack and I would come over some night for a visit. Nothing fancy, maybe one of those winter barbecues like you used to have."

"We haven't done one of those in what...two or three years now." Ronnie shook her head. "I can't believe it's been that long."

"Well then, we should do it. It'll be fun, and we'll get to meet Rose."

"You met her at the Christmas party, and as I recall, you weren't all that thrilled about it."

"Well...." A guilty look passed over the younger sibling's face. "Maybe I jumped to conclusions."

"Maybe you did," Ronnie agreed.

"So maybe I'd like a second chance," the redhead offered.

Silence fell between them for a minute before Ronnie reluctantly nodded. "We're right in the middle of the January thaw, so this would be the perfect time for a winter barbecue."

"Exactly. I'll even leave the boys with the nanny so you won't have to worry."

"No, you can bring them. They haven't been over in a while."

"I'll bring their PlayStation over so they have something to do." Susan reached over and squeezed her sister's shoulder. "You know they love beating you up in that wrestling game of theirs."

"They still have that? I thought that was for that little black game system they had."

"Oh, they still have that one somewhere. They only use the PlayStation now. I just got them a new wrestling game. I don't know the name of it, of course."

"Doesn't matter. They'll have my guy on the mat in three seconds flat just like they always do, except Ricky. He likes to throw my guy out of the ring a dozen times and put him into a coma before counting me out." The sisters laughed, breaking the tension of the past few weeks.

"How about Saturday?"

"Sounds good, excuse me." Ronnie pressed the button on the buzzing phone.

"Your mother on line two, says it's urgent," Laura's voice said.

"Thank you." She looked at Susan. "Now what?"

Rose held the phone against her chest, debating for the fourth time in an hour whether she should call Ronnie or not. The executive always called her by two, and it was now going on four. When the phone did ring, it startled Rose enough that she almost dropped it. "Cartwright residence."

"Rose?"

A smile instantly crossed the young woman's face. The background sound of someone being paged for radiology was enough to wipe the smile away. "Where are you?"

"I'm down at Albany Med. I'm fine, Tommy was in a car accident."

"Oh, no." Rose's legs throbbed with the memory. "Is he hurt badly?"

"I don't know yet. The doctors are still with him, and they haven't told us much. Apparently, he lost control going around a curve and ran into a telephone pole. Hey, I've got to go. The police are talking to Mother."

"Okay, let me know what's going on, all right?"

"I'll call you later."

Ronnie hung up the phone and stood next to her mother, impatiently listening to the officer's words. "...excessive speed."

"Everyone speeds in that area," Beatrice snapped. "Perhaps if the state would take better care of the roads, something like this wouldn't have happened," she said indignantly.

"The best roads in the world aren't going to help when the driver is intoxicated, ma'am." The policeman pulled a notepad from his chest pocket and flipped to a page covered with writing. "They found a dozen empty beer cans on the floor of the front seat. A Breathalyzer taken at the accident scene showed his blood-alcohol level twice the legal limit. You still want to blame the roads?"

Unable to protest and at a loss for words, Beatrice turned to her oldest daughter. The silent request was understood. It was time for the family caretaker. "Sergeant Mitchell," Ronnie said, stepping between the officer and her mother. "What happens to Tommy now?"

"After they get done stitching him up, he'll be taken over to the county jail and booked. If he gets there early enough, Judge Turner will set bail today, otherwise it'll be tomorrow." He shook his head. "I'll tell you this, Miss. If you don't get that fellow some help soon, you'd better plan on spending lots of time here." He put the pad away and took a step back. "He was lucky this time. There's something to be said for automatic seat belts and air bags. We could be looking at something far worse here than a few cuts and bruises."

"Yes, very lucky." From the corner of her eye, Ronnie saw Susan wrapping an arm around their mother, who looked torn between berating the officer and breaking down in tears. The family caretaker understood her mother's struggle. This was a problem that the Cartwright name and money couldn't fix. "Oh," she turned to the officer. "What about his car?"

"It's been impounded. We'll let you know when you can have it picked up. It's totaled, though."

"I want to see my son," Beatrice announced.

"Once they finish with him, he's going up to the jail. You can see him there once he's booked."

"Sergeant," Ronnie gave him a soft smile, hoping to defuse the tension in the air. "Would it hurt anything if she saw him for just a minute?" She saw him waver and moved in, lowering her voice so her mother wouldn't overhear. "I think she needs to see him now, not after they've cleaned him up, don't you?" He looked down at the floor for a second before giving a small nod.

"He's a mess, Miss. You need to get him help."

"I will," she promised.

"Just for a minute and I have to stay with you."

"Thank you." She turned to face her mother and Susan. "He's going to let us see him for a minute." As they moved to follow the policeman, Ronnie felt her sister's hand on her arm.

"Are you sure this is a good idea?"

"No," Ronnie admitted. "But I don't think hiding the truth from her is the best thing either. Maybe she does need to see him now to see what he's doing to himself."

In thirty-three years, Ronnie could only remember a handful of times when her mother cried. No matter how much something upset Beatrice, she kept it inside, a trait that she passed on to her oldest child. Yet the sight of Tommy in a hospital bed, his face bloodied and bruised, was enough to bring tears to the matriarch's eyes. He opened his eyes at the gasp and looked at his mother, his eyes taking a moment to focus before he let his head drop back down onto the pillow. "What'd they tell you?" he asked.

"That you had an accident, sweetie." Beatrice walked over to the bed and took his hand in hers.

"I don't know what happened, Mother...." He licked his lips as if parched. "I was up working late last night, and I guess I must have been tired. I went out to get some breakfast, and I must have fallen asleep at the wheel." He looked up through blackened eyes and gave his mother an apologetic look. "I'm sorry you had to come all the way out here."

Beatrice patted his hand and used her free hand to wipe her tears. "It's all right, honey. I'm here now. We'll call Richard Jenkins and have him meet us at the jail. I'm sure he can take care of everything."

"I guess I shouldn't drive tired, huh?" he joked, his face twisting with pain as he tried to sit up. "Oh, it hurts." His sisters exchanged dubious looks at the exaggerated groan. Sergeant Mitchell politely coughed and looked at his watch.

"Mother, I think it's time for us to leave," Ronnie said, putting her hands on the smaller woman's shoulders. "Why don't you and Susan wait for me out in the waiting room? I want to talk to Tommy for a minute."

Beatrice nodded and headed toward her younger daughter, who quickly led her out of the room. Ronnie listened to her mother's voice trail off as they disappeared down the hallway. "...and he's such a handsome boy, Susan. I hope he doesn't end up with any scars."

"So what's up, Sis?" Tommy grinned at her, his trademark Cheshire cat look not working too well with a broken nose and bloodied lip. His grin faded when Ronnie moved closer, her face not showing anger, but concern.

"Tommy, you need help. Things are only going to get worse." Despite all that had happened between them during the last couple of months, this was still her brother. "If you get treatment, maybe they'll drop the charges."

"Treatment?" he scoffed. "You make me sound like one of those bums who live in the gutter."

"Lots of people with money and status go into treatment, Tommy. You could go to the Betty Ford Clinic if you wanted to. I understand that's a great place."

"If it's so fucking wonderful, then you go there."

"This time it was a pole, next time it could be another car—or worse. This has to stop." She ran her fingers through her hair, frustration making itself known with a long release of breath. "You obviously have a drinking problem and probably a drug problem, too."

"One look and you can tell that, right, Dr. Cartwright?" he sneered.

"You stole Rose's pills from my house, Tommy! You tried to break into the safe in the office, and you've forged my name on bank loans. If it's not drugs, then what is it? You tell me because I can't understand why else you'd be doing these things."

"Is that what this is about? Your friend can't find her stupid pills, and of course since I was in your house once in the last three years, you decide it has to be me."

"Twice," she corrected, her jaw clenched with anger. "Or don't you remember the night you flipped my coffee table?"

"Get out of here, Ronnie," he growled. "I fell asleep at the wheel, nothing more. You're just trying to poison everyone against me."

"I'm trying to help you, Tommy. You need rehab before you kill yourself or someone else."

"What I need is a fair shake, something I don't get with you around, oh, mighty Veronica, queen of the Cartwrights."

"Tommy...."

"Fuck you, Ronnie!"

"Miss Cartwright...." She was surprised to find the sergeant still in the room, having forgotten all about him. "You can't do anything more here. Why don't you go see to your mother and I'll deal with him?"

"That's right, Ronnie, go see Mother and show her what a good daughter you are," Tommy sneered. "Maybe she'll even forget that her pride and joy is a dyke."

Dead silence descended on the room. Ronnie's brain tried desperately to rewrite what it had heard to no avail. Her head hung down, the long black tresses hiding her face from the officer's view. Her emotions swirled, and it was several breaths before she found her voice. "I really hope you get help, Tommy." She walked out of the room and went in the opposite direction of the waiting area, unable to face her family yet.

Once outside, Ronnie leaned against the cold brick of the building. With her jacket still upstairs in the waiting room, the silk blouse was little defense against the cold wind. Still she stayed where she was, hoping that the bitter chill would freeze some of her pain. Ronnie was torn between being angry at her brother and worrying that he was on a self-destructive course with only two possible endings—jail or death. His hurtful words replayed in her mind, and she wanted nothing more than to be home, curled up against Rose. Rose...blue eyes closed, and she let her mind fill with the vision of the honey-haired woman. Ronnie lost herself momentarily in the imaginary comfort of Rose's arms when she felt a very real hand on her shoulder.

"It's cold out here, come inside," Susan said, holding out her sister's jacket.

"Thanks." Ronnie took the jacket and hugged it to her chest. "I'll be up in a little bit. I just need some air." The warmth of the leather permeated through the silk, letting her know just how cold it really was.

"I know what he said," Susan admitted, taking the jacket and holding it out for Ronnie to slip her arms in. "Sergeant Mitchell pulled me aside and told me."

"Terrific. Maybe he'll put it in his report, too." Ronnie stood up long enough to get the jacket on, then leaned back against the wall.

"He promised me he wouldn't say anything. He was just worried that you were upset." Susan put her hand on her sister's shoulder. "Why don't you take off? Go home to Rose. I'll stay here with Mother and wait for Mr. Jenkins."

Ronnie's first thought was to accept her sister's offer and escape to the one person who made her feel comfortable. To get away from this mess that she didn't want to deal with and return to her sanctuary. But while being the oldest meant being in charge, it also carried with it a great deal of responsibility. She sighed. "No, you know I can't leave until it's over."

"I know, I just thought I'd at least offer." Susan looked at the falling snow and shivered. "You know I'm freezing out here."

"Why don't you go home to Jack and the kids? I can handle Mother."

"No, if you have to be there, then I should be there, too. Come on, misery loves company." Susan and Ronnie walked back inside and headed for the waiting room. "I um...I told Mother that I agreed with you about the drug thing."

"You did?" Surprise showed on the older sibling's face. The redhead nodded.

"I thought maybe she'd believe it more if I told her that I thought he was doing drugs, too."

"What'd she say?" Ronnie saw her answer on the younger woman's downtrodden face.

"She doesn't believe that it's as bad as I told her, and I even mentioned what you told me about those pills missing from your house and the bank loan." Susan looked up at her sister, and they shared a quiet but sad understanding—nothing they said would change their mother's opinion. They reached the outer doors of the emergency room.

"Well...one thing, I guess..." Ronnie began. At the expectant look, she smiled. "It's nice to know you're on my side in this. It makes it easier."

"Hey, we may not be best friends kind of sisters, but we're still sisters," Susan said. "Besides, I'm holding you to the winter barbecue this weekend."

"Deal." Together they walked back into the waiting area to face the long evening of waiting around as the wheels and paperwork of justice turned slowly.

Chapter Fifteen

The sound of a car door shutting woke Rose from her sleep. She yawned and rubbed her eyes, noting by the red numbers of the clock that it was well past midnight. "Ronnie? I'm awake," she called when she heard the sliding glass door close.

A moment later, the tall figure appeared in the doorway. "I'm sorry, did I wake you?"

"No," the young woman lied while turning on the lamp. "I wanted to be awake when you came home anyway." She patted the empty space on the bed next to her. "So what happened?"

Ronnie sighed and flopped down on the bed, her head gratefully sinking into the thick pillows. Both shoes hit the hardwood floor, and pantyhose-covered toes wiggled in relief. "Ah, much better." Her watch followed her bracelet to the small side table. "Tommy was drunk and loaded with heroin and ran his car into a telephone pole."

"Was anyone else hurt?"

"Thank God, no. He walked away with a busted nose and a few bruises. They found some cocaine on him when they searched him at the jail."

"Cocaine? Oh, Ronnie, that's awful."

"You should have seen Mother's face when they added possession to the list of charges. I still can't believe they gave him bail." She rubbed her face vigorously with both hands. "I don't know, Rose," she sighed. "That stuff's going to kill him, and he doesn't even care. I tried to talk to him about going to rehab, but he wouldn't listen." A brief look of hurt crossed Ronnie's face at the memory of her brother's hateful words. "I guess whatever I say doesn't matter."

Rose heard the sadness in her friend's voice and knew there was more to what happened than she was letting on. She shifted on the bed, turning so her upper body was facing Ronnie. "Has he always had this animosity toward you?"

"No." Ronnie sighed and stared at the ceiling. "When we were younger, Tommy was my shadow. Anything I did, he wanted to do. If I was interested in something, he was interested in it."

"What happened?"

Ronnie shrugged. "I don't really know. We got older and things changed. I think he always assumed that since he was the only son that he would be the one to take over when our father stepped down. I think he resented me because of that."

"Yet you still try to help him."

"He's my brother. What else can I do?" She laced her fingers behind her head. "He had such potential, Rose. I hate seeing what these drugs are doing to him."

"Maybe there's still hope that he'll seek treatment on his own."

"Maybe," Ronnie conceded. "I suppose anything's possible. God, he just gets me so angry sometimes. I could have had him arrested for embezzling, and I didn't. You think he cares? No, I try to help him, and he turns around and calls me a d—" She stopped the word before it left her throat. "...a damn bitch," she amended. "Ah, doesn't matter, I guess."

"It matters." Rose reached over and placed her hand on Ronnie's shoulder. "Maybe your family doesn't care, but I do. He had no right to hurt you like that. You don't deserve it. You, Veronica Cartwright, are one of the most loving, gentle people I've ever met, and anyone who doesn't see how special you are is blind."

Ronnie reached over and tousled the younger woman's hair. "That goes both ways, my friend." There was more, so much more she wanted to say, but fear held her back. Part of her wanted to pull Rose into her arms and keep her there for eternity, and the other part screamed the truth that would keep them forever separated. Her playful mood disappeared as the latter part won out. "Hey, I think we'd better get to sleep."

"Oh...okay." Rose was surprised by the sudden change but realized that perhaps it was better to wait than to push the issue. There were still parts of Ronnie that were closed to her, and she didn't want to do anything to make her friend uncomfortable. She settled back on her own side and waited for her companion to join her under the covers.

Ronnie looked at the woman waiting for her, and Tommy's words echoed through her mind. "Maybe I should go to my own room. You're sleeping through the night without pain and you'd probably like to have the bed all to yourself again."

"I guess...if that's what you want," Rose said quietly, biting her lower lip. "I suppose you'd probably be more comfortable in your bed anyway."

"Yeah, I suppose so." Ronnie noted that her companion's voice held the same tone of regret yet she still sat up and collected her shoes. "I'll see you in the morning." She stood up and walked to the door. Her hand was on the door handle when she heard a quiet sniffle. She turned to see sad pools of green looking at her. "Hey, what's wrong?" she asked softly.

"N-nothing, I'm sorry. I'll see you tomorrow, Ronnie." Rose turned her head away but not before Ronnie saw a tear roll free. A second later, the bed shifted as she added her weight. Long fingers cupped Rose's chin, forcing her to turn and meet the concerned gaze.

"What's wrong?" Without thinking, her thumb began stroking the soft skin beneath it. "Tell me, Rose."

"Are you still happy having me here? I know it's been an inconvenience and–" She was stopped by Ronnie's finger on her lips.

"You listen to me. You are not an inconvenience to me. And yes, I'm still happy with you here. What brought this on?" She could have kicked herself as she immediately realized the answer to her own question. "I thought you'd be more comfortable without me in your bed. It's not that I don't want you here, I swear."

"Are you sure?"

"I'm sure."

"I guess I'm just being silly. Getting all upset just because you want to sleep in your own bed." Rose wiped her eyes with the back of her hand. "I can just imagine what your family would say if they found out you were sleeping with me. They'd probably think I was turning you into a lesbian or something. We can't have that now, can we?"

Ronnie let out a deep breath and shook her head. "No, we can't have that." She stood up and gathered her pillows. *No, can't have them thinking that Veronica Cartwright is a lesbian, can we? Wouldn't want to mess up the family's perfect image. It's okay that Tommy is out wrapping cars around poles and breaking into places, but heaven forbid I take a woman into my bed.* "I'll see you tomorrow, Rose."

"Leave the door open so Tabitha can get in, please."

"Sure. Good night."

"Night, Ronnie. Pleasant dreams."

"You too." She shut the light off and left the room, a heavy blanket of loneliness settling over her.

Opening the door to her room, Ronnie was struck by just how foreign it seemed to her to sleep without Rose. The silk blouse and skirt landed in a pile at the foot of the bed, followed quickly by her bra and pantyhose. She pulled the blanket back and sat down on the cool sheets. Seconds ticked by as loneliness gave way to anger. Anger that grew until sleep was no longer an option. A few minutes later, her sweats were on and she was heading for the basement to work out some aggression.

Thwap! Thwap! Over and over, the punching bag took the fury and rage that was a woman torn between what she needed and what was expected of her. "Damn it! Why can't they understand?" Ronnie cried out to the empty gym. "I'm not hurting anyone!" Her gloved fists struck the bag over and over. Thwap, thwap, thwap. "Why is it so wrong? Why?" Her only answer was the creaking of the punching bag on its hinge as her blows caused it to sway.

On the floor above, Rose lay in the dark, listening to the muffled sounds coming from the basement. *Oh, Ronnie, what did he say to hurt you so much?* She hugged the pillow tightly against herself, wishing it was her friend she was holding. Suddenly, the sounds from below stopped, followed a few minutes later by the sound of the basement door opening. "Ronnie?" she called out.

"You okay?" The tall figure appeared in the doorway, her silhouette invisible against the darkness of the night.

"I um...I...would you mind spending one more night with me?"

"Is everything all right?" Ronnie crossed the room and put her knee on the edge of the bed.

"I just...I had a bad dream and can't get back to sleep," she lied. There was silence while the executive struggled with her inner demons. Finally, Rose felt the blanket being pulled back and the soft warmth of Ronnie's body nestling against hers.

"Better?" the throaty voice asked.

"Mmm," Rose snuggled closer, resting the back of her head against the soft crook of the offered shoulder. "You comfortable?"

"Very" came the sleepy murmur. "Night, Rose."

"Night, Ronnie." She closed her eyes and smiled as Ronnie's breathing became deep and even. "Everything will be fine. Rest well," she whispered before allowing sleep to claim her, as well.

"Ronnie, may I speak with you for a minute?" Laura asked, poking her head around the door.

"Sure, come in." Ronnie set her pen down and looked up, noting the smile on the young secretary's face.

"I wanted to tell you the good news myself before everyone in the office hears it."

"You're pregnant," the executive guessed. The young woman nodded happily. "Congratulations. I know you and Mike were trying. How far along?"

"Thanks, I'm three months now. I have a feeling that Mike's made himself that quarterback he always wanted. I'm certainly gaining enough weight." She looked at the couch, then at her employer.

"Please, take a seat. So you're going to be going out on maternity leave just in time for summer."

"That's what I wanted to talk to you about. Mike doesn't want me to work once the baby's born. He just got a promotion and thinks that we can make it on one income."

"So you're going to resign when it gets close to the time?"

"Actually...Mike doesn't want me to wait that long. He doesn't want me to have any undue stress." Laura rubbed her belly absently. "I'm going to leave just before my third trimester starts."

Ronnie realized that only gave her three months to find a new secretary. The idea of wading through the endless résumés and interviews threatened to give her a headache. "Well...I appreciate that you're going to stay on for a while. It would be nice to have a smooth transition between you and your replacement."

"I'll put a notice in the paper and notify the employment agencies," Laura offered. "I'll make sure to be clear on your requirements." She stood up.

"Okay, Laura. Have a draft of the ad prepared for me by morning, will you? I'd like to get someone in here and settled before you leave."

Once alone, the executive picked up the phone and dialed the familiar number. Two rings later, the sweetest voice she'd ever heard answered. "Cartwright residence."

"Why do you always answer the phone like that? You know it's me," she teased.

"Just habit, I guess," Rose answered. "How's it going?"

"Actually, today is flying. I might come home early. What's for dinner?" She leaned back, kicking her shoes off and sticking her feet up on the edge of her walnut desk.

"I'm not sure. Maria usually doesn't start dinner until around four or so."

"Why don't you tell her not to bother tonight? I'll pick up some Chinese for us."

"That sounds great."

"Is there something good on TV, or do you want me to stop and pick up a movie?"

"Sure, sounds good. Hey, my speed is up to fifty words a minute now."

"Oh, yeah?" A tiny thought formed in the back of her mind. "Have you been studying those business letters and forms?"

"Of course. I even retyped some old letters you had lying on the desk just to get the practice."

"Good." Ronnie smiled broadly at the extra effort on Rose's part. "Hey, Laura told me today that she's pregnant."

"Oh, yeah? That's great."

"Great for her, lousy for me. Now I have to find another secretary. I hate looking for a secretary. I'm worse than Murphy Brown when it comes to them."

"Oh, please," Rose laughed. "I've been watching that in the mornings. She had one who talked to the devil."

"I had one who believed that Satan was going to swoop down and take over any minute. Needless to say, she didn't last long. I have terrible luck with them. Laura's the best I've had, and it took me six months of wading through the flotsam of the secretarial world to get her." A buzz on the phone brought Ronnie's attention to the flashing light of line two. "Hon, I've got to go. Tell Maria not to bother with dinner, and I'll be home in a little while."

"Okay, Ronnie, I'll see you soon."

"Bye."

"Bye."

"Hon?" Ronnie whispered, amazed at how easily the word slipped out when talking to Rose. She gazed at her beloved mechanical pencil for a few seconds before reluctantly pressing the button on the phone. "This is Veronica Cartwright."

Chapter Sixteen

"Prepare to meet the Crusher, arg arg arg," Susan's oldest son Ricky said. "He's gonna pulverize you."

"Worse than the Undertaker?" Rose queried.

"Oh, he's nothing compared to Crusher." He caught his aunt walking past. "Hey, Aunt Ronnie, come see me pulverize Rose."

"Can't you find something nicer to play? Whatever happened to Pac-Man?" she said as she entered the living room.

"Pac-Man?" The twelve-year-old laughed and pressed several buttons in rapid succession, throwing Rose's man out of the ring and onto the mat. "I've seen that game in the arcades. Boring. You've got to get with the times, Aunt Ronnie. It's *Virtual Fighter* and *Super Wrestlemania* now." He lowered his voice so only Rose could hear him. "Next thing you know, she'll bring out those old records she has from the eighties."

"Hey, I like the music from the eighties," she protested.

"That's 'cause you're old like Aunt Ronnie and Mom."

"Old? I hate to tell you, Ricky, but twenty-six is not old."

"Twenty-six? Oh, man, that's way old. Come on, get your man back into the ring before he gets counted out."

"Why? Every time I get back in, you throw him out again."

"That's the point," the boy replied, moving his character into position. Rose looked at Ronnie and rolled her eyes, causing her to laugh before she left the room.

Ronnie found Susan out on the sun porch, monitoring the steaks and burgers cooking on the grill. The late January thaw had the temperature in the lower fifties, downright balmy for Albany. Susan's other sons, Timmy and John, were enjoying the bright sunshine, riding bikes they found in the garage. "Ricky sure enjoys those video games, doesn't he?" she said as she walked over and sniffed the cooking meat.

"I can't get him away from them," Susan replied. "Do you think we should start frying up the mushrooms yet?"

"No, not for another couple of minutes or so." They were interrupted by six-year-old John riding up on the purple bike, tears streaming from his eyes.

"What's wrong, honey? Did you fall?" Susan went into mother mode, lifting her son's arms to look for any scrapes. He shook his head, still blubbering.

"Timmy won't stop teasing me 'cause I'm riding a girl's bike," he wailed, pointing at the flowered basket on the front.

"I'll take care of this," Ronnie said, holding her hand out to take the smaller one in her own. "Come on, John. There's some tools in the garage. We'll take that basket off, will that be better?" She received a shaky nod in reply. With her nephew in tow, Ronnie headed for the garage.

Satisfied that the meat would be okay without supervision, Susan stepped inside to warm up for a little while and to check on her oldest son. She found him still playing the wrestling game with Rose, who only made token efforts to fight back as her character was beaten time and again. "Having fun?"

"Oh, yeah, Mom. Rose is more of a challenge than Aunt Ronnie," he replied, his eyes never leaving the screen.

"Ricky, why don't you go play pool with your father? I want to talk to Rose for a few minutes."

"But I'm having fun," he whined.

"Richard..." she said in that age-old "mother" tone. The game controller landed on the floor, and a pouting boy headed for the game room. Rose set her controller on the couch next to her, nervousness setting in as it did when Susan ran into her at the Christmas party.

"Where's Ronnie?" she asked.

"Out helping John with the bicycle," the redhead said as she sat down on the cushion previously occupied by her son. "So your legs are getting better?"

"Dr. Barnes says my right leg is healing beautifully." She looked down at the bright white of her new casts, the left leg still encased up to the hip, but the other one stopping just below the knee.

"What about the left one?"

Rose sighed, remembering the x-ray of her ankle that resembled a road map. "That one will take longer. I broke it pretty good."

"That's too bad." There was a brief silence before Susan spoke again. "That pen and pencil set you gave Ronnie is very nice."

"Thank you," Rose replied. "She had been complaining that she could never find a pen when she needed one, and I thought she'd like it."

"She loves it. I never see her use anything else now. And I never thought I'd see her stop biting her pencils." Susan looked at the graphics flashing on the television, begging them to press the start button and enter another round of video wrestling. "You know, I love my sister very much. I don't like to see her hurt."

"She's a very special person," Rose agreed, uncertain where the conversation was going.

"I hope you understand just how much she's putting on the line having you here." Susan's voice held no reproach, just concern for her sister. She turned sideways on the couch, looking carefully at the young woman across from her. "She was hurt very badly by Chris. I just hope that doesn't happen again."

"What did he do?" Rose asked. Susan's eyebrow raised, and her face took on a confused look. Remembering her sister's repeated denials of a relationship, she now questioned her previous assumptions.

"Um...oh...well, I think maybe you should ask Ronnie about that. I need to check on the steaks. Excuse me." She stood up quickly and left, leaving a confused Rose to watch her retreating form.

With no boy to keep occupied with video games, she decided to venture out and look for Ronnie. With one leg in a short cast, it was much easier for her to maneuver herself in and out of her wheelchair. She found Ronnie on the sun porch, talking to her sister. "Hi there," Ronnie said with a smile when she saw Rose wheel her way out. "You want a jacket? It's warm but not that warm."

"No, this sweater is plenty warm," the young woman assured. "Ricky is playing pool with his father, and I thought I'd come out and see how everything was going." She sniffed the air appreciatively. "Smells great."

"Mmm, yes it does." Ronnie lifted the cover and gazed hungrily at the steaks.

"Don't even think about it," Susan admonished. "I thought you were going to do the mushrooms and peppers."

Ronnie laughed and nodded. "All right. Come on, Rose. You can help me cut up the peppers." She opened the sliding glass door and motioned for the younger woman to go first. "Susan, remember we want ours done medium, not burnt."

"Keep it up and you'll get hockey pucks," Susan said, reaching for the flame control in a mock threat.

"Well then, I would know you were the one who cooked it," Ronnie replied with a teasing grin, feeling far more relaxed around her sister than she had in weeks. There was a familiarity about having her family around that was nice, but it was made that much more so by the presence of Rose.

After dinner, the two older boys joined Ronnie and Jack in the game room for pool while Rose volunteered to play a video game with John. To her surprise, he had no interest in the wrestling game, instead putting in a race car game where they competed against each other. Unlike his aggressive oldest brother, John was content to stay in his own lane and not try to run Rose off the road, despite the bonus points allowed for doing so. Of course she let him win, letting up on the speed button at the last minute to allow him to take the lead. As Susan puttered about, she glanced in at them from time to time, surprised when she saw John sitting on Rose's lap as they engaged in another race. She watched for several minutes unobserved, noting how gentle the young woman was with her son, showing him how to make his car go faster and not crash while moving around the corners. She never heard her older sister slip up behind her. "Is there anything else that has to go in the dishwasher?"

"Oh, God, Ronnie, I didn't know you were there," Susan said. "I was just checking to see what John was doing." Together they watched the young woman and boy for a few minutes. "She seems like a nice person, Ronnie."

"She is a nice person," Ronnie corrected. "I don't think Rose has a mean bone in her body."

"Well, they're fine. Let's go see what Jack and the boys are doing."

"They're still playing pool. I just came out to make sure everything was picked up and in the dishwasher." She followed her younger sister into the game room, turning at the last moment to take one more look at Rose.

It was just after six when Susan's car pulled out of the driveway. Ronnie set the dishwasher, then joined Rose in the living room. "So movies or television tonight?" she asked as she sank into the couch cushion.

"Oh, either one is fine with me, but haven't we seen all your movies already?"

"Well, there's always HBO or pay per view. I think that new Whoopi Goldberg movie is on tonight." Ronnie looked around but didn't see what she was looking for. "Where's the *TV Guide*?"

"Oh, over here." Rose picked it up off the end table and passed it over. As she did, she noticed the light beige polish on Ronnie's perfectly manicured nails. "That's a pretty color." She took the larger hand in her own to get a better look.

"You know, I bet this color would look nice on you, too." She looked at Rose's nails, and an idea came to her. "Looks like you could use an emery board."

Rose withdrew her hand and smiled. "Yeah, I guess I haven't paid much attention to them lately."

"Why don't we do them tonight?" Ronnie asked. "I've got tons of polish in almost any shade you can imagine." At Rose's hesitation, she added, "Come on, it'll be fun, just like a slumber party." Ronnie gave a little pout coupled with puppy dog eyes, pleased immeasurably when the young woman smiled and nodded. "Great. I'll get everything, and you can head into the bedroom. The light's better in there anyway."

A short while later found them on the bed, Rose propped up against the headboard and her companion sitting cross-legged next to her. Surrounding them were cotton balls, a bottle of remover, and several bottles of quick-drying nail polish. Ronnie took the smaller hand in hers and began to shape the flat ends of Rose's nails. "Okay, so let's do some girl talk."

"Okay," Rose said with a smile. "Let's see, what haven't we talked about yet?" She used her free hand to tap her finger against her chin. "We haven't talked about sex."

"Something you don't know?" Ronnie queried with a grin. "I understand there are books out there...."

"Oh, you...." Rose playfully swatted her friend. "That's not what I meant and you know it." They exchanged friendly smiles while the file moved on to another nail. "I mean, why does someone like you not have a husband and kids running around? You can't tell me you don't have offers."

"Oh, I get offers all the time, I just ignore them. Other hand please." She turned the emery board over and resumed her task. "Most of them are just opportunists looking for a boost up with my money."

"And the others?"

"The others are just not what I'm interested in. Maybe I'll settle down someday but not right now." She released the hand she was holding and waved at the pile of bottles. "So which color?" She reached in and picked out a light pink. "I think this would look good. Bright red would be too dark with your skin tone."

"Sure, go ahead." Rose held her hand out dutifully. Ronnie scooted closer and handed her the open bottle to hold.

"So what about you?" Ronnie asked while drawing the small brush along the length of the nail.

"I haven't dated much. Nowadays most men expect the woman to help pay when they go out, and you know I couldn't afford that." She looked down at the half-finished nail. "Oh, that is pretty."

"Told you you'd like it," Ronnie said as she moved on to the next finger. "And not all men expect the woman to help pay."

"The ones I know do, or else they expect something else. I've had to wrestle my way out of cars more than once."

Ronnie chuckled. "I think that's a rite of passage now. You're not a woman unless you've had to beat off Horny Harry at least once. It's really amazing how many of them think with the wrong head." She turned Rose's hand to get to the thumb. "It's not worth my time to deal with it."

"Did you ever get caught?"

"Caught what? Doing it?" Ronnie shook her head. "Other hand. You?" The answering blush piqued her curiosity. "What happened?" She capped the polish and leaned forward expectantly.

"God, this is embarrassing. How did we get on this topic anyway?"

"You suggested it," Ronnie replied, wiggling her eyebrows.

"Oh, yeah." Still smiling, Rose looked down at her lap. "I was sixteen and living with Delores. I went out on a date with this guy from school. He was dropping me off, and we were in his car parked in her driveway. I never heard her come out."

"You were otherwise occupied?" Ronnie couldn't help smiling at her friend's increased blushing. "That must have been awful."

Rose nodded. "We weren't exactly doing 'that,' but we were pretty close. She grounded me for the rest of the school year, and I had extra chores from then out."

"Jeez, I hope your next date went better than that." Ronnie opened the bottle of polish and resumed her task.

"He wouldn't go out with me again after the way she yelled at him. Called his parents, too. I was humiliated. He wouldn't even talk to me at school because he got in trouble."

"We all have our embarrassing moments," Ronnie said gently, giving the hand within hers a squeeze.

"Your turn, tell me about Chris." The brush stopped mid-nail, and Ronnie's face looked like she swallowed the wrong way.

"Chris?" Her voice squeaked, and she had to clear it. "Who told you about Chris?"

"Susan said Chris hurt you very badly. What did he do?"

Ronnie felt her heart pick up speed and licked her lips nervously. "What did Susan tell you?"

"Just that Chris hurt you badly. She didn't say anything more. I'm sorry, if you don't want to–"

"No, it's all right." Ronnie returned her attention to the hand she was holding. *How much do I tell her?* She looked up at the gentle face, trying to gauge her reaction. "Um...I met Chris while I was at Stanford."

"How long did you two go out?"

"We were together for about three-and-a-half months. I was young and in love, and I guess...Chris wasn't."

"What did he do?"

"Betrayed me." There was a touch of the long ago hurt in her voice. "After I broke it off, Chris called my parents and asked for money." She mentally cursed herself for letting Rose believe that her ex-lover was a man but still found she couldn't bring herself to utter the hidden truth. "Threatened to take our relationship public."

"That's terrible!" Rose gasped. "No wonder you don't date much."

"Much?" Ronnie gave a short laugh. "I haven't seriously dated anyone in years. I have an escort service I use when I have to have a date for a formal affair."

"Not worth the hassle, eh?"

"Absolutely not worth it," Ronnie said emphatically. "Okay, you're done." She released the smaller hand, deliberately drawing her forefinger along the length of Rose's as they separated. "So I got to pick your color, you pick mine."

Green eyes perused the various shades before deciding on one. "Now you are someone who can wear the deep reds. I think this would look nice on you." She held up a dark shade called Heart. "You know that red blouse you wore last week? This shade would be perfect with that." She focused on the strong hands resting in Ronnie's lap. "You have strong hands, you know that? Must be all that working out." Deciding that her nails were dry enough, Rose took Ronnie's hand in hers.

Gotta have some way to release my tension, Ronnie thought to herself. Sharing a bed didn't allow her the privacy she usually had late at night to relieve herself in another way. She tried hard not to think about how nice it felt to hold hands with Rose, even if they were both being careful not to smudge the freshly painted nails. The warmth, the softness...with a start, she realized that the young woman was speaking to her. "I'm sorry, what?"

"Nothing, I was just teasing."

"What did you say?"

"I asked if you worked out so much because you were frustrated." Rose blushed at her attempt at a bold joke. "Because you're down in that gym so often."

Ronnie chuckled. "If that was the case, I'd be down there all the time. Of course there are other ways to take care of that problem," she said, deciding that she liked the pretty color rising to the young woman's cheeks.

"Uh, yes, there are," Rose agreed, looking down. She finished the nail she was working on in silence. It wasn't common for her to discuss sex with anyone, and she felt like a teenager, curious and embarrassed at the same time. "Do you do that?" she practically whispered as she brought the brush to the next fingernail.

"Everyone does that, Rose."

"Yeah, I'm sure they do, I just didn't think...I mean, I can't imagine...." The image of Ronnie touching herself formed in her mind for an instant before she forced it away. "I don't mean that I imagine you...well...you know...I mean...." She stammered to a stop, having now fully embarrassed herself. "Oh, God, this topic was my idea?" She laughed and shook her head. "I guess I should have picked something I had a little more experience in."

"You're cute when you blush, you know." Ronnie gave a smile full of teeth and jerked her head back at the mock pass at her nose with the polish brush. "Obviously, we've both had bad luck when it came to romance."

"You know that doesn't mean you won't ever find love again." Rose began working on the last nail. "You're a very special woman, Ronnie. Any man would be lucky to have you...oops." She reached over and grabbed a cotton ball to wipe away the errant swipe of polish.

"Yeah, well, maybe someday I'll find someone, but I'm not worried about it." She held her hand up and smiled. "You did a good job, Rose. They look great."

"Thanks, you did, too." She held up her own hand for comparison. "Look how much smaller my hand is than yours." She pressed their palms together and chuckled at the difference.

"What do you want to do now?" Ronnie asked, not making any move to withdraw her hand. She didn't want it to end, not yet. "The night is still early. I know, how about we braid each other's hair?"

"Oh, that sounds like fun," Rose happily agreed. "I love your hair. I bet you'd look great in one of those French braids."

"Whatever you want to do. I trust you not to make me look like Pippi Longstocking."

"Ohh…." Rose gave a fake pout. "But you'd look so cute."

"And just what do you think I'd make you look like if you did that?" Ronnie chuckled. "Do you want me to do your hair first?"

"No, I wanna do yours first. You have nice hair. Besides, you have to give those nails another minute or two to dry." The older woman obliged, turning around so her back was to Rose. Blue eyes fluttered shut at the feel of gentle fingers sinking into her hair. The soft, melodic voice drifted in. "So thick and long. I don't know how you manage not to spend hours brushing it."

"I have many skills," Ronnie said with a grin. "And a damn good hair dryer," she added.

"It's very pretty," Rose whispered, pulling her fingers through the sable strands. "When the light shines on it, some parts seem almost jet black while others seem lighter, like a chestnut."

"It does get a little lighter in the summer. I figure it's from all the chlorine in the pool."

"Mmm." Rose began to twist the hair into a braid. "I bet you were happy to have the pool last summer. Albany was absolutely scorching."

"Does yours get lighter? I bet it does."

"Yeah, it becomes almost blonde." Small fingers continued to twist the dark hair, careful to keep the braid straight. They kept up the chitchat, but Rose's concentration was on what her hands were doing, not what they were talking about. When she reached the end and tied it off, her fingers automatically landed on the broad shoulders before her. She experimented by squeezing gently and was rewarded with a deep groan. "Sounds like you could use a massage."

"I'd love one," Ronnie replied, leaning into the pressure. "You've got a great touch."

"Thank you." She slipped her fingers and thumbs under the neck of the T-shirt and began kneading the muscles hidden under warm flesh. Rose moved as far as the opening would let her, giving a gentle tug on the shirt.

"You don't have to do that."

"I know, I want to." She gave another tug. "It's not like there's anyone else here to do it, and besides, if I can't give my best friend a backrub, who can?" She moved her hands out of the way as the light gray shirt was removed.

"That's nice," Ronnie said.

"What's nice?" Rose's fingers went back to work.

"Best friend." She turned to meet soft green eyes. "That goes both ways, you know. I've never had anyone I could talk to like you." On impulse, she pulled the younger woman to her for a hug.

At first, Rose was startled, but then she relaxed against the warmth of the bare skin. With her face buried in the crook of Ronnie's neck, she inhaled the mixture of perfume, soap, and the other woman's own scent. As the embrace continued, she became cognizant of where her forearm rested against the swell of bared breasts. She had never touched another woman's breasts before and found herself curiously focused on the new sensation. They were soft, warm...for a brief instant, she had the urge to cup one in her hand to feel its weight, but Ronnie's body shook with a chuckle, and the spell was broken. "What?"

"I said I know I'm soft, but you can't sleep there," she teased.

"Oh, I'm sorry, it's just...I um...." Rose's face colored and her mind refused to offer up any excuses.

"You felt like you were drifting off, and I figured your pillows were better than my boob." Ronnie turned away again and sighed as the backrub resumed.

"Oh, I don't know about that," Rose replied, moving her fingers down the length of her friend's spine. "Looks like you have plenty to make a pillow out of." She surprised herself with her boldness and quickly tried to laugh it off. "Not that I'm really lacking in that department myself." Her eyes fell upon a small triangle of skin darker than the rest just below Ronnie's shoulder blade. "Did you know you have a birthmark right here?" She poked the area in question.

"So I've heard. Never seen it myself." Rose continued to trace the mark with her fingertip, unaware of the effect her touch was having on Ronnie's senses. "It's um...not in a good position, even with mirrors."

"Hmm, it's very pretty. Just a little thing, no more than my fingertip. It's just below your shoulder blade." Her eyes studied the landscape of her friend's back, noting every freckle and beauty mark. Where her eyes went, her hands followed, splaying out and running up and down. "You have a strong back, Ronnie." *In fact, everything about you is strong*, she silently mused. *Strong shoulders, strong arms, even your jawline is strong.* She never realized that her hand had moved and was now gently stroking up and down the length of Ronnie's left bicep.

"Um...I think that's good, Rose."

"Hmm? Oh." She pulled her hands back and watched as Ronnie put her T-shirt back on.

"Okay, your turn. Scoot forward."

Long, dexterous fingers moved through her hair, against her scalp, massaging while braiding. Rose didn't know when her eyes closed or when Ronnie started humming. She gave up trying to figure out what she was feeling and lost herself in it. She pressed back against her friend's fingers, sighing audibly when Ronnie took the hint and began pressing her thumbs against the base of the skull. "That feels so good," she murmured, a lazy smile coming to her face.

"Talk about needing a massage," Ronnie replied. "That's it, relax against me." Rose did as the rich voice told her, letting her upper body rest upon Ronnie's. The Dartmouth nightshirt was big on her, the larger neck allowing the large hands to reach her shoulders without hindrance. Rose sighed again as the strong fingers forced her muscles to relax. She sank deeper against the larger frame behind her. Her shoulders were completely limp, but Rose discovered another part of her was far from that state. She didn't need to look down to realize that her nipples were tightening up. As Ronnie's hands moved beneath the nightshirt, the cloth rubbed against the pink puckered skin. Eyes closed, Rose imagined those strong hands moving down. Her eyes flew open with the realization of what she was feeling...arousal. "Hey...um...why don't we turn on the television? I'm sure there's something on there that we can watch." She reached for the remote, hoping her voice didn't sound as nervous to Ronnie as it did to her own ears.

Broken out of her own musings by Rose's sudden move, Ronnie could only mumble an approval. The noise of the television filled the air. It took a moment for her to realize that Rose wasn't going to lean back against her anymore. Disappointed that the massage was over, Ronnie returned to the earlier task of braiding the honey-colored hair. Five minutes before, she was content, cozy, and comfortable. Now her body felt cool without the warmth of Rose's against her. She let out a silent sigh and resigned herself to be content with just touching the soft tresses.

Rose was also feeling the loss of their body contact. It took effort on her part not to lean into Ronnie's fingers and start the massage over again. *Why am I feeling like this? What's gotten into me? It's just Ronnie.* She tried to imagine how it would feel if someone else was touching her, but an accidental brushing of the other woman's hand against her collarbone blew that thought away. She began to lean into Ronnie's touch again and had to stop herself. *This is crazy. It's just that no one has ever touched me like this before, that's all. It's just Ronnie.* She repeated the words over and over in her head until the braiding was done. When Ronnie moved out from behind her and she settled back against the pillows, Rose felt anything but relaxed. Her body was wide awake and burning with a fire that she hadn't felt in years. In fact, the room seemed quite warm to her at the moment. Her only hope was that sleep would come quickly. "I'm tired," she said over a fake yawn.

"Really?" Ronnie looked at the clock. "It's still early."

"Yeah, I don't know, I think your neck rub is putting me to sleep. You can stay up if you want to, the TV won't bother me." She closed her eyes and nuzzled deeper into her pillow.

"I don't want to keep you up. I'll go downstairs and work out for a while. I'm sure that'll tire me out."

"Oh, you don't have to leave," Rose protested, although an idea was forming in her mind.

"No, it's no problem, really. I could use a workout," she reassured, climbing out of bed and shutting off the television. "I'll be back in about a half hour, forty-five minutes, or so."

"Okay." *Perfect.*

Rose waited until she heard the music wafting through the floorboards before bending her right knee and drawing her legs apart. Self-pleasuring was not something she did often, but her fingers had no trouble slipping between her slick lips and locating her excited clit. "Ah...." Her fingers felt cool surrounded by the liquid warmth, and the sensation was heightened when she drew the length of her finger across her clit. She filled her mind with erotic images while her passion grew. Her left hand pushed its way under the nightshirt and latched on to....

...her nipple became hard under the rhythmic pumping. Lying on the thick blue workout mat, Ronnie let her free hand travel into her sweatpants to cup her mound through her panties. "Ohh...." Long fingers pushed the cotton against her wet curls, then farther until the crotch was saturated with her juices. Shifting for leverage, Ronnie caused some slack to form in the panties, and she used it to her full advantage, curling her fingers under the elastic edge and between her nether lips. Eyes closed, her fingers became Rose's fingers. Imagining the honey-haired woman touching her so intimately caused Ronnie's hips to buck against the mat and her breath to quicken. It was a fantasy she hadn't allowed herself to entertain until now, and she was surprised by its power. It was too much to deny anymore. She was in love with Rose Grayson; nothing could change that. Reality could never be, but here, now, on a mat in her private gym, the fantasy could live. Here there was no accident, no broken bones, no shattered lives. Here was just her and Rose, loving each other. Ronnie's fingers moved through the black curls and pink lips with old familiarity, but the touches were somehow different, more intense. She was more than ready when two long fingers found her entrance and slid....

...inside to her first knuckle. Rose brought her other hand down and rubbed herself furiously. The full-length cast was the only thing keeping her hips even remotely on the bed. Her thigh muscles tensed, and she felt a twinge of pain in her left leg, but it paled in comparison to the pleasure her fingers were bringing. Her fingers pumped in, back, then in deeper still as her fantasy lover brought her to the edge. Rose pushed in as far as she could, but there was more...more that she couldn't quite reach. That special place was so close and yet so far away. Teeth gritted, face contorted, she strained to reach orgasm. Pumping so deep that it hurt the webbing between her fingers while her left hand never ceased in its frantic efforts against her clit, Rose felt herself teetering on the brink but unable to fall over the edge. Then the familiar voice came to her. "Yes, that's it, Rose. Let it go, that's right." Ronnie's low tones rumbled through her, setting off electric charges that moved from her breasts to her clit where the final explosion came with shattering force. "Oh...."

"...Rose!" Ronnie cried out as the pulsing waves crashed through her. Sure, deliberate movements drew out the pleasure, allowing her a few more seconds with her fantasy lover before falling limply back to the mat. Eyes closed, she lay there for several minutes, unwilling to let the fantasy go too soon. Eventually, her breathing slowed and reality returned. With it came profound sadness. No matter how much she did, it would never take away the truth about the accident. Nothing would take away Rose's pain. Ronnie sat up and wrapped her arms around her legs, hugging herself into a ball. *For so long, I haven't wanted anyone and now there's you.* She looked at the ceiling, then slowly buried her head against her knees. *What am I going to do? I need you in my life, Rose. I can't imagine what it was like before you came, and I dread the thought of you ever leaving.* At that moment, there was nothing Ronnie wanted to do more than to cuddle up against the smaller woman. She took a deep breath and sat up, knowing that the longer she stayed downstairs, the longer it would be before she could rest against Rose's warm....

....washcloth between her legs, removing any trace of her activities. Her task finished, Rose settled back under the covers and waited for Ronnie to return. In the darkness, she thought about what had happened. Never in her wildest dreams had she thought about having sex with another woman. Now her body still tingling from the intense orgasm, Rose tried to sort out her conflicting feelings. She cared very deeply for Ronnie, but that way? Still all it took was her thinking of Ronnie speaking low and sexy to her and Rose began to warm up again. She closed her eyes and she could see long, never-ending legs that led to a graceful swelling at the hip, then narrowed to a slim waist. Breasts that seemed neither too large nor too small for the tall frame. A slender neck led to a square jaw and high cheekbones, all accented by full lips and expressive blue eyes. But the mental review couldn't stay on the physical. The rich voice played in her ear while the sweet scent lingering on the nearby pillow filled her nostrils. Rose suddenly became aware of her own hand moving against her breast. The sudden silence as the stereo downstairs was shut off jolted the young woman out of her new fantasy. Her hands went straight to her sides, and she waited as the basement door closed and the one to her room opened.

"You awake?" Ronnie whispered as she entered the darkened room. She waited a couple of seconds before repeating her question. Satisfied that Rose was sleeping, she carefully slipped into bed. Their bodies were barely touching. She tried one more time. "Rose?" She waited for several breaths before settling down and wiggling in close. Her face buried in golden hair, her arm resting across the small waist, Ronnie gave a contented sigh and drifted off.

Long after Ronnie's breathing gave way to soft snores, Rose lay awake, her fingertips idly twirling across the back of the hand resting on her stomach. *It's too bad that Chris hurt you so much, using your love against you, threatening to tell everyone about....* Her eyes popped open as the question took shape. *Why would it be so terrible for you to be involved with a fellow student? It's not like you were sleeping with a professor or anything. Unless....* Her eyes grew wide.

Unless Chris is a Christine.

Chapter Seventeen

"Good morning, Maria." Rose wheeled her way into the kitchen, following the scent of fresh-baked cinnamon rolls.

"And a good morning to you, too, Rose. Would you like some coffee?"

"I'd love a cup, thank you."

"I'll take it to the table." The housekeeper reached into the cupboard and removed a mug without looking at it. By the time she realized which one she had grabbed, she'd already added the cream and sugar. "Well, I guess Ronnie will have to use another mug."

"You gave me her favorite again, didn't you?" Rose asked with a smile. It was another one of Ronnie's little quirks. Her morning coffee was always served in a black mug with the words "The Boss" across it.

"I'm afraid I did. I'll dump it out and give you another one."

"No, don't bother. Ronnie can live without her Boss mug for one day." It actually amused Rose that with the dozens of mugs that filled the cupboard, her friend was so attached to that particular one.

"Now you know she likes her coffee in that cup," Maria admonished.

"It's good for her to change her routine from time to time" came the playful reply as she took the mug from the older woman.

"And what are you two up to?" Ronnie asked as she entered the room. She picked the newspaper up and glanced at the headline before she noticed. "Stealing my favorite mug?" She crossed behind the young woman and sat down in the chair next to her.

"Don't worry, I know who really is the boss around here," Rose replied as she took a sip.

"Sometimes I wonder," Ronnie joked back. "Think you'll try to send me an email today?"

"Yeah, you wrote down what to do, didn't you?"

"It's next to the computer." She looked up to see Maria coming over with her coffee. She looked at the mug quizzically. "Where'd this one come from?" It was a Far Side cartoon mug with two deer on it. One had a bright red bull's eye on its chest. The caption underneath read, "Hell of a birthmark, Hal." Ronnie chuckled and drank from it.

"See, change is good," Rose said over the lip of her mug. Maria brought their breakfast over along with a carafe of coffee.

"If you ladies will excuse me, I'm going to get started on the laundry."

"Okay, thanks, Maria."

"Yeah, thanks."

Now alone, both women began to eat their breakfast. Ronnie had the fork in one hand and the newspaper in the other. Although she scanned the business section, the paper also had the added benefit of allowing her to peek over and study Rose unnoticed. The broken legs were hidden under the round table. With the reddish-blonde hair tucked behind the ears, Ronnie had an unobstructed view of the soft curve of Rose's cheek, the slight upturn at the end of her nose, the rust-colored eyebrows that rested above far-too-green eyes. Suddenly, those eyes turned and caught her. She ruffled the pages and looked down at the paper, hoping that the blush she felt wasn't too visible. "Um...I'm thinking about easing some of the workload off Laura. I have some letters that need to be updated. It's not that hard to do, but it is time consuming. You said you learned how to use the mail merge, didn't you?" Her eyes never left the newsprint, although she had no idea what the words on the paper were.

"Um hmm." Rose swallowed and set the cup down. "It was difficult at first, but once I got the hang of it, it's really pretty easy." Inside, she was excited. Ronnie was giving her real work to do, not just examples and tests in the computer programs. Real work that needed to be done and she was being trusted with it. "I'll make sure it's done right away, and I promise there'll be no mistakes."

Behind the paper, Ronnie smiled at the enthusiastic tone. "I'll email the files to you as soon as I get to work. I'm sure you'll have no problems with it." She set the business section of the paper down and poured herself another cup of coffee. "Well, let's see who the police picked up last night," Ronnie said as she picked up the local section. She flipped through the pages until she found the police blotter report listing all the people who were arrested or appeared in court. She spotted the name of an old high school friend under arrest for prostitution. "What?" She pulled the paper closer, knocking her coffee cup over in the process. "Damn." She stood up, the creamy yellow blouse now covered down the front with the wet beige of coffee. She undid the first few buttons, confirming that it had seeped onto her half slip, as well. "Maria!" She turned to see the housekeeper come out of the laundry room. "Coffee."

"On silk," the housekeeper tsked. "Veronica Louise, I go through more Woolite with you." She shook her head, causing Rose to smirk while sopping up the coffee on the table. "Well, get out of those wet things." Ronnie turned to head out of the room. "Now there's no need to be modest right now. You're not going to run upstairs with coffee dripping off your blouse. There's enough of a mess to clean right here."

"Fine." In one quick move, the blouse came off followed by the half slip. "It got the skirt, too." A tug of the zipper and that followed the other wet clothes into Maria's hands.

With Ronnie's back to her, Rose let her eyes travel up and down the tall body clad in only pantyhose and a lacy cream-colored bra. She concentrated but didn't feel the arousal that she had experienced the prior evening. All she did feel was guilty for staring at her friend's body. *This is silly. It's just Ronnie.* She averted her eyes when the half-clothed body turned around, looking up only when she heard Ronnie address her. "I'm going upstairs to change."

"Oh, you know what would look really nice on you? Those gray wool slacks and that pale blue blouse." Rose thought about the last time she had seen Ronnie wear that outfit and how it highlighted her eyes. "It looks great on you."

"The gray slacks, hmm?" Ronnie remembered how much Rose liked that particular combination. Goose bumps raised on her thighs. "I'd better go get changed before I freeze here."

Ronnie returned a few minutes later. She had to admit the wool pants were a much better idea than the skirt on this cold morning. "Okay, what do you think?" she asked, twirling around with the blazer folded over her arm.

"Looks great," Rose said. The slacks hugged in all the right places and the top outlined her soft curves nicely. "You look...nice."

"Thank you." Ronnie looked down into sparkling green eyes and smiled. "I'll email you those files once I get there." She fought the urge to give the young woman a peck on the cheek and settled instead for a squeeze of the shoulder. "I'd better get going before the traffic gets too bad."

"Oh, okay. I'll make sure to have that program up so I can get started as soon as it arrives."

"You don't have to rush, Rose. Whenever you get to them is fine." Privately, it pleased her to no end to hear the eagerness in her friend's voice. Ronnie had no doubts when it came to Rose's work ethic. "I'll try and be home early." The housekeeper exited the laundry room with the mop and bucket in hand. "I'd better get going before Maria finds a new use for that mop."

Ronnie winked at Maria as she closed the door. The bright blue Jeep disappeared from the driveway, leaving the two of them alone. The young woman decided it was time to get some answers.

"Maria, was it easy for you to learn to use email?"

"Lord no, child. When Ronnie first gave me that computer, I was afraid to turn it on. I didn't know what it would do."

"But now you like it?"

"I talk to my son in Arizona every night." She pushed the mop over the last drops of the spill. "You should have seen my phone bills before that."

"I bet when Ronnie was away at college, the phone bills were something." *Great segue, Einstein. Why not just come right out and say let's talk about Stanford,* she mentally berated herself. "I mean, she's just so close to her family and all."

"When the children were in college, it certainly was a trying time around here." The housekeeper picked up the breakfast dishes and headed for the dishwasher. "Every day one of them was calling for something or another." She picked up the carafe and poured some of the steaming liquid into a cup for herself. "I swear I was down at the post office almost every day mailing something to one of them."

"Let's sit and talk for a while," Rose said, pointing at the empty seat. "There's not much that has to be done today, and I have to wait for her to send me those files."

"Just for a little while. I do have vacuuming to do. Tabitha sheds more hair than any cat I've ever seen," Maria said as she refilled the young woman's cup. She sat down in the offered chair and took a sip of her own coffee. "They certainly were quite a handful then."

"I guess the independence that comes with being away from home must have been too much, huh?" She tucked a stray lock of hair behind her ear. "Ronnie sure had a rough time of it." She saw the flicker in the older woman's eyes and knew she had to tread carefully. "She told me about Chris." Instantly, Maria's eyes went to the table.

"That was a very sad thing and not something I care to talk about." The housekeeper took several swallows of coffee. "Some people are just trash, Rose. Plain and simple."

"Maria, may I ask you a question?" At the reluctant nod, she took a deep breath and continued. "Do you think I'm using Ronnie?"

"It doesn't matter what I think, Rose. What matters is what she thinks." The older woman drained her mug and gave a serious look. "I would hate to see her get hurt like that again."

"I don't know how anyone can know Ronnie for any length of time and want to use her," Rose said. "It must have been devastating for her to trust someone and have that trust shattered." She had no idea that the housekeeper's thoughts immediately went to the fully repaired Porsche tucked away in the garage. "To be at that age, to have something so private exposed to her parents...." Rose shook her head. "I just can't imagine why anyone would be so cruel to her. Did you ever meet Chris?"

"No, the gold digger never showed up here," Maria said. "I only spoke with her on the phone."

Bingo. The big question was answered.

The rusted-out station wagon chugged into the public parking garage and pulled into the first empty spot, not caring that it was reserved for the handicapped. If she got a ticket, so what, it would just go into the glove box with the rest of them. Tickets and insurance were not things that Delores Bickering wasted her money on. The empty cigarette pack hit the concrete ground as she lit the last one and walked away from her car. If things went well, by the time she returned, she would have plenty of money for cigarettes.

The Cartwrights have always liked things big. When the Wellington Hotel was erected in the late 1920s, it towered over the smaller Cartwright building next door. Ronnie's great-grandfather took it as a challenge, and the result was the erection of one of Albany's largest buildings, more than thirty stories high. Delores stood in front of it and sneered at the large logo carved into the reddish-brown granite above the doors. She pushed her way through the revolving door and into the spacious lobby. On the wall was a brass plaque welcoming her to the Cartwright Corporate Offices. Below it was a directory of departments along with the floors on which they were located.

Ronnie was just finishing off a fruit cup when the buzzer sounded. "Yes, Laura?"

"Um...there's someone here to see you," the hesitant voice said.

"Who?" A quick glance at her Day-Planner showed no appointments scheduled for that afternoon. She heard the secretary ask the visitor's name and clenched her jaw as soon as she recognized the voice. "Keep her out there for a minute." She hung up the phone and tapped the mechanical pencil against the desk. *Damn, what's that bitch doing here?* The answer came to her instantly. Now she had two options: be openly hostile toward the leech and throw her out or play along and let Rose see the truth. She swiveled in her seat and reached for the mouse. She clicked on the security icon, then on the camera one. A password and a few commands later, a small red light lit up on the security camera tucked discreetly in the upper corner of her office. It was time to expose Delores Bickering for what she really was. Ronnie pressed the button on the phone. "Send her in."

"Nice office," the large woman nodded approvingly as she looked around. "You hiring?"

"No." Ronnie couldn't believe she had the nerve to even ask such a question. "You're not here to ask me about a job."

"I came to talk to you about Rose. You know I'm the closest thing to a mother she's ever had."

"So you say." *Oops, watch it there, Ronnie. Wouldn't want Rose to see that.* "So what is it that you wished to see me about? Please, have a seat."

Delores flopped down on the couch and tossed her coat on the far cushion. "I would have thought someone like you would have a coffeepot in here for your visitors." Ronnie's eyes narrowed, but she kept her tongue. "Especially those who are relatives to your friends."

"You said you wanted to talk to me about Rose?"

"I've found a way to help her out."

"Help her out?"

"Yeah." The large woman sat up. "I've found her a job in Cobleskill. She can start on Monday. Pays six seventy-five an hour."

"Why would she want to work in Cobleskill? That's an hour away. Besides, didn't you notice that she has two broken legs? She's in no condition to work."

"It's in a telemarketing office. She won't have to stand up, just talk on the phone. Of course that means she'll have to move back with me."

"She already told you that she wants to live with me. Why would she change her mind now?" *What stunt are you trying to pull? Make Rose choose between us? I'll be damned if I'll let you take her away from me.*

"You don't understand. Rose and I have a deal. She owes me for taking care of her and promised to help out in any way she could."

"So you want her to move back with you and work at this telemarketing job so she can give you money?" Ronnie wanted to make sure there were no gray areas, no question about the leech's intentions.

"I think that's only fair. She lived under my roof and ate my food for years without paying anything, and now it's time for her to pay me back." Delores crossed her arms and leaned back.

"So everything you did for her when she lived with you she owes you for?" It sounded ridiculous, but no one was laughing.

"You could look at it that way. I look at it this way: I could have rented her room to someone who would have paid me. She owes me the money I lost by not being able to rent it. When she left, I had to start paying for a baby-sitter on bingo and bowling nights. My generosity can only go so far. I'm not rich, you know. I can't afford to be as charitable as you."

"So you've decided that Rose owes you all sorts of money because she lived with you when she was a teenager, is that right?" Ronnie felt the pieces falling into place.

"Exactly."

"And since she owes you all this money, you feel she should move in with you and work at this job so she can pay off what she owes you, right?"

"Right." The executive's lips pulled back into a smile much like a cobra just before it strikes.

"But since I'm her friend, you thought you'd come and see if there was something I could do, right?"

"Well, we're not talking about much to someone like you. If you're really her friend, I'd think you'd want to help her out," Delores said indignantly.

"And I could help Rose out by paying off her debt to you, is that the idea?" Ronnie was tired of the game and the dirty-looking woman who was trying to use Rose. "How much?"

"Well, you have to take into account how long she lived with me, then—"

"I said how much? Come on, I'm sure you had a figure in mind when you walked in here. How much do you think Rose owes you for taking care of her?" She pulled her checkbook out of the drawer and opened it up.

"Five...no, ten thousand."

"It will take ten thousand dollars for you to walk away and leave Rose alone?"

Dollar signs danced in front of Delores's eyes, and greed sang in her heart. She almost agreed when she realized that the rich woman was giving in much too easily. "Wait." She stood up and walked over to the desk, leaning her chubby hands on the polished wood. "What if I said I wanted fifteen thousand or even twenty?"

"Is that what it would take?"

"You're really willing to give me twenty thousand dollars?" Suspicion set in. "Why?"

"I have my reasons." She picked up the pen to write the check and stopped herself. Even if it was fake, she had no intention of using the pen that Rose got her. Reaching into the drawer, she pulled out another one and began writing.

"It's B-i-c-k-"

"I know how to spell it."

"You know," Delores laughed nervously. "I always knew she'd find someone to take her in." Her eyes widened as the zeros were added to the amount box. Feeling victory within her grasp, she relaxed and leaned against the desk, much to Ronnie's annoyance. "Twenty thousand dollars. Humph. May not seem like much to you, but I can get a new trailer for that."

Ronnie stood up and tore the check out of the book. "And for the cost of a trailer, you're willing to walk away, to get out of Rose's life and leave her alone forever, right?" Delores reached for it, but Ronnie held the check up in the air. "That's the deal. For twenty thousand dollars, you stay away, never call, never stop by. You'll forget that she exists."

"Give me that check, and I forget all about her." Her forefinger and thumb grasped the corner of the paper.

"Don't you even want to say goodbye to her?" Ronnie held the check tightly, refusing to give it up without an answer. She never expected the one she got.

"Why? Is it worth more money if I do?" Delores looked at her expectantly.

Ronnie forgot about the videotape in the shock of hearing the cold words. With an angry tug, she jerked the check back and stood up, her six-foot frame towering over the shorter woman. "You bitch." Blue eyes blazed with fury. "You never cared about her at all, did you?" Her hands balled into fists, crumpling the check. "You took her in just for the check each month and to have a built-in baby-sitter!" Knuckles turned white under the pressure, and the check suffered more damage.

"The check..." Delores pointed out. "We have a deal."

Ronnie lowered her head, long black tresses hiding her face. "The money. That's all you worry about, isn't it?" Her voice was quiet, low...the calm before the storm. "You used Rose for money. You used her as a child to get money from the state, and when she was struggling to survive, you took money from her." Her head jerked up, locking eyes with the woman she hated. "Now she's lying there with two broken legs, and instead of worrying about her, you're trying to get money from me."

"You want to get rid of me? Give me the check and I'm gone." Delores held her hand out.

"You want the check?" Ronnie flattened the rumpled check out, then held it out in front of her. She tore it neatly in two, then put the pieces together and tore it again. "I'm sure the state of New York paid you far more than you ever spent on Rose." Another tear. "There were weeks when she spent next to nothing on food for herself yet sent you a check because you managed to convince her that she owes you somehow." She threw the pile of confetti on the desk. Delores could only stand there and watch as her plan fell apart. "You've used Rose for the last time. Get out of my office before I have Security throw you out."

"You can't—"

"I can't what? Throw some lazy bum out of my own building?" Ronnie pressed her knuckles against the desk to keep from reaching across and striking the loathsome woman. The muscles in her forearms bunched and clenched in readiness. "You hurt Rose, and I won't allow you to do it again. You don't deserve to know someone as kind and gentle as she is. Come within sight of my home and I'll have you arrested. One phone call, one letter, any attempt to contact her and I'll make your life a living hell."

With all prospects of money gone, Delores had nothing left to lose. "You think you're so smart with all your fucking money. You don't know NOTHING!" She stormed over to the couch and snatched her cap and jacket. "You think Rose was the only foster kid I had?" The door opened and two beefy security officers entered, no doubt summoned by Laura after hearing the loud voices.

"Is there a problem, Miss Cartwright?"

"Escort this...." Bitch came to mind, but a sense of decorum had to be maintained at the office. "...woman outside and make sure she never comes in again."

"You keep your hands off me." Delores grabbed her bag and stormed out in front of the uniformed men. "You make sure Rose knows you're the one who made me stop talking to her. It's all your fault." The outer office door closed, leaving a confused Laura and a furious Ronnie standing there.

"Laura, take the rest of the day off. I'm going home early." She shut the door and walked over to her desk. The bits of check were tossed into the trash can, and her prized pen was put back in her desk drawer.

"Ronnie?" Susan opened the door and poked her head in. "What happened? I heard they called Security to your office."

"Nothing important, just some business that I had to take care of." She waved her hand dismissively. "Don't worry about it."

"You know I'm going to find out anyway, you may as well tell me." The redhead entered and shut the door.

"I am entitled to something of a private life." She sank into her chair, a bone-deep sigh escaping her lips. "Let this one go, Sis."

"Does it have to do with Rose?" The quick jerk of the head answered Susan's question. An awkward silence fell between them for several seconds before she spoke again. "Um...." The younger Cartwright looked down at her nails. "If um...well, I know you don't really have anyone close to you except Rose and well, I guess me. If...if you need someone to talk to...well, I'm here." She straightened up and took a step back. "The boys keep asking when they can come over again." Clearing her throat exaggeratedly, Susan continued, her gaze falling upon her older sister. "When I explained to John that Rose lives with you, he asked me if that made her his aunt, too."

"I told you–" Ronnie began only to be stopped by the redhead's upraised hand.

"I know. I told him that she wasn't, but if it was okay with her, he could call her that."

Blue eyes looked down at the desk. She understood the unspoken gesture behind the words. She stood up, and although never very affectionate to her sister, Ronnie reached over and wrapped her arm around the younger woman's shoulders. "How about tomorrow night? I'm sure Rose can't wait to have her wrestling guy trampled again." She released the casual embrace and returned to her seat. "But how about right now I take us out to lunch? Somewhere nice, how about Maurice's or Giovanni's?"

"Oh, that sounds nice, but how about trying that new Chinese place up on Western Avenue? I heard they have excellent food."

A small icon on the screen caught the corner of Ronnie's eye. With a start, she remembered the videotape. "Uh...yeah, that sounds good." She turned to the computer and shut off the camera. "Why don't you go get your coat and meet me down in the lobby? I have a couple of things here I need to finish up."

Ronnie took the video home and hid it in her bedroom, seeing no reason to show it to Rose right away. She knew the tape would hurt her precious friend, and that was the last thing she wanted to do again. Instead that evening and the ones that followed were spent lying next to each other on the adjustable bed watching television or on the couch watching movies. Sometimes they would forgo the electronic entertainment and just spend the time braiding each other's hair or doing their nails. It was a comfortable routine that she enjoyed tremendously. No mention was made about the continued sleeping arrangements, and Ronnie was fine with that. If she had her way, they'd always sleep together. She loved the way Rose's body fit against hers. They never talked about the increased hugs and affectionate touches, but Ronnie noted that they were instigated by both equally.

Rose kept her days busy working on projects for Ronnie. In addition to improving her skills, it also gave her an intense education in the way her friend's business was run. It gave them something else to talk about in the evenings other than themselves or what was on television. The late January thaw continued into February, promising an early spring. Already more grass was showing in the backyard than snow, and the sun coming through the windows was enough to heat up the room without turning up the thermostat. Of course at night, there was the added body heat of Ronnie to keep her warm. It was during those late-night hours that Rose thought about her relationship with her friend. With the exception of work, Ronnie was by her side constantly, not that Rose would ever complain. She relished the time they spent together. Often while watching television, her head would rest against Ronnie's shoulder or even in her lap. She enjoyed those times the best. Ronnie would absently stroke her hair or let a warm hand rest upon her shoulder. They were much more relaxed around each other now. Initial embraces in bed were no longer stiff, hesitant affairs. Now when it came time for sleep, Ronnie's arm would wrap around her waist, and warm breath would tickle her neck as they molded their bodies together.

Rose thought often about the growing affection between them. Hugs were a common occurrence, and she encouraged them as much as Ronnie did. When a tearjerker romance movie brought the need to be cuddled, there was no discussion or roundabout requests, they just snuggled up against each other. But while she enjoyed the attention and affection, Rose wasn't sure she was ready for anything more, or if Ronnie was even interested. There had been no kiss since they were under the mistletoe on Christmas, and their conversations stayed far away from matters of the heart or sex. Whether it was deliberate on Ronnie's part or not, Rose wasn't sure. She only knew that she was avoiding it, her feelings far too confusing to even think about giving them voice.

Like right now. They were lying in bed watching *Dateline NBC* and Ronnie's head was resting against her shoulder. Rose looked down at silky black hair mixing with her own. Her companion seemed so relaxed, so peaceful. Having her arm trapped between their bodies was no longer an acceptable position. "Lift your head up for a sec."

"Hmm? Sorry, am I hurting you?" The lazy drawl told Rose just how relaxed her friend was.

"Not at all. I just want to move my arm." She did so and quickly wrapped it around Ronnie's shoulder before the other woman could move away. "Now come back here." She tugged gently and was rewarded with her companion's head resting just above her right breast. "Comfy?"

"Mmm, very."

"Good." The commercial ended, and Ronnie's attention went back to the television. Rose's did not. Her fingers began plucking at the long dark tresses. "You have very soft hair."

"So you tell me. I think yours is softer, though. Mine's just thicker."

Rose's fingers sank into Ronnie's hair and began massaging her scalp. "Hmm, you might be right about that," she conceded. *But I like touching yours more.* Slowly, the small circles she was making with her fingers moved lower until they were stroking the smooth skin of Ronnie's neck. The television was completely forgotten by both women as the massage continued. *How far will you let me go?* A lone pinky ventured under the soft cotton shirt for a second, then pulled back. Again. "Did Chris ever rub you like this?"

Ronnie jerked upright, her eyes looking very much like those of a deer blinded by headlights. "Um, n-no...." She swallowed, her throat suddenly dry. "Why do you ask?"

"I just wondered." Rose now hesitated, the question not seeming like such a good idea anymore. "It's just...well, you like it so much. I would hope that someone did this for you before."

"Chris and I..." Ronnie searched for the right words. "We weren't...." It was a tossup between which was drier, her lips or throat. "We weren't physically close. There wasn't much cuddling." She sat up completely and shifted until she was facing Rose. "I thought it was true love then." A scornful laugh revealed the old pain. "Now I know better." She lowered her head and looked at her hands. Rose remained silent, sensing Ronnie struggling with some inner demon. Finally, the tall woman chose the easy way out. "At least the sex was good."

Jokes aren't going to work with me. I know you too well, Veronica Cartwright. "You know, I hate Chris for hurting you like that." She reached out and put her fingers under the strong chin, forcing blue eyes to meet hers. "And I don't hate many people in this world."

Ronnie pulled the hand away from her chin and held it within her own. "Funny." She looked down at their hands, her thumb idly brushing across the smaller woman's knuckles. "I feel the same way about people who hurt you." She paused for a moment, fear threatening to keep the words trapped inside. "You're very special to me." She lifted her head, and for several long seconds, they stared at each other.

Ohmygod, are you going to kiss me? Rose wasn't sure if she was excited or afraid as her heart began beating double time. Her lips moved, but no words came out.

"I think that's enough serious talk for tonight," Ronnie said, releasing the hold on the young woman's hand. The magical spell was broken, and both felt a keen sense of disappointment.

Rose was still thinking about that moment long after they settled down for the night. She turned her face to look at the sleeping woman beside her. *I wanted you to kiss me. Did you want it, too?* Careful not to disturb her companion, she propped herself on her right elbow and tucked her hair behind her ear. Hesitantly, she lowered her lips to Ronnie's cheek, planting the softest of kisses there. Her eyes adjusted to the dark, Rose saw as much as felt the small smile come to the sleeping face. "I love you," she whispered before lying back on her pillows. Intertwining her fingers with those resting on her belly, the young woman closed her eyes.

"Love you, too," Ronnie mumbled sleepily, unconsciously snuggling closer. The voice startled Rose for a minute before she realized that her friend was still sleeping. She turned her cheek to rest against the dark head and soon fell asleep herself.

Chapter Eighteen

Ronnie opened the *TV Guide* and began to read off the options. "*A Walk in the Clouds* is on. We saw that one already. *Sabrina*, that's boring." She turned the page. "Let's see what's on pay per view." A gentle tug on her wrist forced her to shift the guide so Rose could look on with her.

"There's that new Jim Carrey movie," the young woman offered.

"I'm not in the mood for Jim Carrey. Look, Bruce Willis blows up another building."

"I hate action movies. Let's watch a romantic one."

"Why a romance and not a comedy?"

"Well, it is Valentine's Day, silly."

"If two people are really in love, they don't need a day to celebrate it."

"You are such a cynic, Ronnie. Give me that." Rose took the *TV Guide* and began thumbing through the pages. "You know we could play a game or something if you wanted. I see you're two levels higher than me on *Rescuer of the Maiden*." She laughed at the sheepish grin on the older woman's face. "What do you do, play when I'm asleep?"

"It's addictive. Come on, find something for us to watch."

Fifteen minutes later, the television still offered up no suitable programs to watch. "There's what, a hundred, hundred and fifty channels on this and we can't find a thing to watch?"

"That's because you don't want to watch any love stories, and I don't want to watch any of those shoot-'em-up, blow-'em-up movies," Rose replied.

"So much for television." Ronnie pressed the off button and tossed the remote onto the coffee table. "This is a thrilling Valentine's Day."

"If you're bored, then let's do something different."

"Like what?"

Rose was also at a loss for what to do. Although she'd never believed it could happen, she was actually quite bored at the moment. In two months' time, they'd managed to watch every movie that Ronnie owned and played every game in the house several times. There really wasn't much else to do except.... "Talk."

"Hmm?"

"Let's make some hot chocolate, sit back, and talk. You know, one of our infamous girl chats." Rose's eyes held a twinkle of mischief.

"And what exactly would be the topic of conversation tonight? I'm not doing 'relive your most embarrassing moments' again."

"Oh, come on, you learned some pretty embarrassing things about me, too," the young woman chided.

"Well, that's true," Ronnie conceded. "And you do turn the cutest shade of red. Okay, I'm game, but let's go out in the kitchen and make dinner while we're talking."

Fifteen minutes later, Rose was sitting at the kitchen table cutting onions while Ronnie was standing at the island slicing mushrooms. "Answer me something," the young woman said while wiping at the endless stream of tears. "Why am I the one who always ends up cutting up the onion?"

"I can't stand them, makes me cry," Ronnie said cheekily.

"You're lucky you're not within my reach, Miss Cartwright," she playfully warned. Ronnie poured the steaming hot chocolate into two mugs, then added mini-marshmallows. She brought one over to the table and set it down for Rose.

"I'm within your reach now, what are you going to do about it?" Ronnie realized her mistake a second later when small fingers slipped around her waist and began to tickle unmercifully. "Hey now, heh heh, come on, Rose, I was only joking." She backed out of reach of the playful hands. "You just wait..." she said between breaths. "When you're out of this chair...I'll get even with you."

"Yeah, you and what army?" Rose was beaming at her, obviously quite proud of herself. "It seems to me that I only need my two hands to defeat you, oh, mighty warrior of the corporate world."

"That's because you know my weaknesses," Ronnie replied. *And I'm helpless when it comes to resisting you.* She walked behind the chair and put her hands on the smaller woman's shoulders. "And one weakness right now is that I'm starving. You want your steak broiled or sautéed?"

"Surprise me."

"Sautéed you said? Coming right up." She gave a gentle squeeze and went over to the refrigerator. "Oh, we've got éclairs for dessert."

"Sounds great. Maria always picks out the best food," Rose said. "You were practically drooling over the chicken last night."

"Another one of my weaknesses," she said while retrieving the steaks and butter.

"I'll have to tell your prospective suitors that the way to your heart is through your stomach."

And I'd have to tell them that my heart is already taken, Ronnie thought to herself. "And what about you? What secret things should I know to tell your prospective suitors?" She watched as Rose's attention turned to anything but her. "What's that? I didn't understand you."

"Um...." Her fingers traced the delicate pattern of her doily. "I dunno," she finally answered with a shrug. "I never really thought about what I would want in a lover."

Ah, now we're getting to something interesting. "Okay, so think about it now. Let's start with the basics: tall, dark, and handsome. Now what else?" She put the steaks on to cook, grabbed her mug, and headed for the table.

"Well, I guess I'd want someone who was intelligent, thoughtful, had a sense of humor but wasn't a practical joker, no problems with gambling or drugs or anything like that."

So far, I'm batting a thousand. "Would be attentive to your needs and wants...."

"But not at the expense of their own," Rose interjected.

"Right," she agreed. *Their own?* Her eyebrow rose slightly. "Okay, what else?"

"Hmm." The young woman tapped her finger on the tip of her chin. "Oh, well, there's honesty and trust. I'd have to know that they'd never lie to me. There has to be that trust."

No good on that one. What's with the gender neutrality? "Don't forget that he'd have to be able to fulfill your every desire."

Rose seemed to mull a thought over in her head for a moment before speaking. "I don't know how our parents did it. Waited until they were married to have sex."

Whoa, where'd that come from? "Um, I hate to burst your bubble, but I don't think they waited. I mean, would you buy a car without first taking it for a test drive?"

"Yeah, maybe that's why so many trade theirs in after a few years."

"I think they're just looking for a newer model."

"Maybe what they're really looking for isn't a car at all," Rose offered nervously.

"Perhaps." *Is this going where I think it's going?* Ronnie took a deep breath and plunged ahead into dangerous territory. "Not everyone is interested in cars." *Are you asking if I am?*

"And that's fine," the young woman blurted quickly. "If someone would rather have a truck than a car, more power to them."

"Whatever makes them happy, I guess." *You know I am and you're telling me it's okay, aren't you?* Another thought occurred to the dark-haired woman. *Or are you trying to tell me that you are?* "There are even those who like both." *There, cover all the angles, just in case.*

"Some people aren't sure what they like." Rose looked up for a split second, then back down at the table. "Maybe they thought they liked cars, but now they think they want a truck."

Ronnie let out a deep breath. *Oh, boy, how am I supposed to respond to that?* "Um, well...th-that's okay, too. But I think they should take their time and not rush into anything because of what they think someone else might like." She noted the nervous fingers tapping the ceramic handle. "Especially if they're not sure." *Let's see if I've got this right.* "Maybe they've only driven cars and now they have a friend who likes trucks. They may think they want a truck, too, but they really don't."

"So you're saying they shouldn't rush into anything, even if they really feel that they want a truck?" Green eyes rose to meet Ronnie's.

"Have they ever wanted a truck before?" As much as the metaphors were driving her nuts, Ronnie didn't want to do anything that might spook the obviously nervous Rose.

"No."

"I think the best thing is for the person to just spend time riding around with their friend and see if they really like trucks." *That's it, just leave everything the way it is, nice and safe.* The smell of sizzling meat gave her the perfect excuse. "Damn, I forgot about the steaks." Ronnie hopped up and went to the island. "Good, they're still fine. Now you see why Maria doesn't like me cooking."

"Oh, I thought it was because you used every pot and pan in the house."

"I see you two talk about me when I'm not around." Ronnie smiled inwardly at the thought. "I hope it's good things."

"Mostly good things," Rose teased. An uncomfortable silence followed broken only by the sizzling of the steaks as both women withdrew into their own thoughts. For Ronnie, the conversation revealed far more than she had hoped for. She looked over at Rose. *So you do feel something. I'm not imagining the increased touches and hugs.* But with that thought came fear. *I don't believe that you would ever use me like Christine did, but I can't put everything on the line again. I can't take that chance.* At that moment, Tabitha came bouncing into the kitchen, and Rose moved her chair to allow the cat to jump on her lap. *Then of course there's the minor detail of me being the one who hit you. I'm sure if that little piece of information got out, you wouldn't want to be my friend much less anything else.* Deep down, Ronnie knew she was right to keep things the way they were, no matter what her heart said. Rose had been hurt enough by her.

At the table, Rose was going through her own mental turmoil. She hugged the purring feline and blinked back emotions flowing too close to the surface. *So now you know I know.* She watched as Ronnie reached into the cupboard for the plates. *You know and you don't want me.* Rose wasn't sure if she should be relieved or disappointed. Her heart insisted on the latter.

Ronnie put the two plates on the table. "You need anything more to drink before I sit down?"

"No, this is fine, thank you." Rose never looked up from her plate, yet she knew those stunning blue eyes were staring at her. "It smells wonderful." She picked up her knife and fork and went through the motions of cutting her meat. Ronnie headed for the opposite side of the small round table, then stopped herself and sat next to Rose.

"There's more vegetables if you want them."

"No, this is good." Rose continued to push her meat around her plate.

Ronnie could only sit by helplessly and watch as Rose withdrew into herself. She hated the tension hanging in the air but wasn't certain what to do or say to break it. "Um, if you have any questions about trucks, maybe I can answer them for you." *Oh, that's brilliant,* she chastised herself. "I mean..." she stopped for a second when the blonde head lifted to meet her gaze. "I mean...I hate this awkwardness." They shared a small smile before Rose lowered her head again.

"I'm not especially thrilled with it myself."

"So talk." *Easier said than done.*

"I don't know what to say."

Ronnie's heart ached for the pain she heard. Without thought, she reached over and laid her hand on top of Rose's. The gentle return squeeze let her know the touch was welcome.

"Just say what's on your mind."

Several bites of steak disappeared before Rose spoke. "Have you had a lot of trucks?"

"Um...." It wasn't the question that Ronnie was expecting. "No, Christine was the only one." *There, I said her name. Let's get past this stupid car/truck thing.*

"Oh." Rose withdrew her hand and began to cut more meat.

"You can't look at me and talk about this, can you?"

"No." A slow blush crept up the young woman's neck. "I never was any good talking about that kind of stuff."

"More into action than words, eh?" Ronnie's joke did exactly what she hoped it would. Rose smiled at her and gave a playful swat.

"Actually, when it comes to that, I'm not really very good in either category." She relaxed slightly, maintaining the eye contact for several seconds before looking down again. "I don't have the experience."

"You mean...." *You're twenty-six years old. You can't be.* "B-but when you got caught in the driveway?" She watched the cute blush return to Rose's face.

"I told you, we weren't doing 'that.' We were working our way up to it when we got caught." The young woman pushed her plate away, giving up the pretense of eating. Ronnie did the same. "After that, well...it just never happened."

Ronnie fought to keep the smirk off her face. "So you've um...never...." The smirk refused to be hidden, and she had to look away. "...um, been taken for a test drive?"

"Stop laughing." Rose feigned anger, but the sparkle in her eyes gave her away. "No. No one's taken me for a test drive." She shot a devilish look at Ronnie. "That's not to say that no one's looked under the hood."

"We can't start this again." Ronnie drained her mug and stood up. "Since dinner obviously is over, let's go into the living room and relax on the couch." *I have a feeling this conversation is going to continue, and I'd rather talk under the soft lights instead of these fluorescents.* "I'll bring the éclairs."

"Don't bother for me." Rose watched her friend reach into the refrigerator and remove a beer. "Can I have one of those?"

Ronnie looked at her quizzically. "What about your Vicodin? I thought you weren't supposed to drink with that."

"I haven't had any today, and I won't take any tonight." Rose was by no means a drinker, but at that moment, her mouth was so dry that she was certain she could drain a six-pack with no problem.

"All right," Ronnie replied hesitantly. *Maybe I shouldn't drink. I need my wits about me when I'm with you, Rose.* She plucked two glasses from the rack and followed her friend into the living room.

She set the beers and glasses on the coffee table just as Rose was getting ready to transfer herself from the wheelchair to the couch. "Here, let me help."

"I can do it."

"It's easier if I help." She stepped forward and lowered her head. It had been too long since Rose let her help, and she missed the feeling of holding the young woman in her arms. One arm slipped behind the back, and she felt smaller arms wrapping around her neck. *Yesss, that's right, hold me.* She put her other arm under Rose's legs and lifted, nudging the wheelchair out of her way with her knee. But instead of putting her precious bundle down right away, Ronnie held Rose safely in her arms and gazed down at the face she loved. *If only things were different,* she thought as her eyes fell upon the soft pink lips so close to her own. In the back of her mind, she knew that a kiss would not be protested. As fate sometimes found the need to be cruel, Rose had to shift, causing the hard plaster of her cast to rub against Ronnie's forearm. It was an instant reminder to Ronnie of all the reasons not to act on her feelings. She set her friend down quickly but gently, turning away before she changed her mind. She walked around to the other side of the couch and sat sideways on the far cushion. A quick twist of her wrist and the beer was open. Ronnie didn't bother with the glass, taking several deep swallows straight from the bottle. "Do you want some background music?" *Oh, that's bright. It's Valentine's Day. All the stations will be playing love songs.*

"Sure." To Rose, anything was better than the deafening silence. Ronnie fiddled with the different remotes until she found the right one. She adjusted the volume to a point where they could barely hear it, then set the remote on the table. She opened the other beer and poured it into a glass without comment, then passed it to Rose.

"Thanks."

"You're welcome." Ronnie settled back against the arm of the couch and took another drink. They looked at each other, silently hoping the other would begin. A song started and ended without a sound from either woman. "Well, this is productive," Ronnie finally said.

"Maybe we should just drop it for tonight."

"No. We need to get this out in the open." Ronnie gave a deep sigh and reached for her beer. To her surprise, it was already empty. "Wow, haven't downed one like that in a long time." *Why am I so nervous? I know what I have to do.* "Rose, you mean a great deal to me, you know that." She forced herself to meet the young woman's gaze, hoping her words didn't sound as fake as they did to her own ears. "But I made a decision long ago that the business comes first." *Even over my own heart.* "I can't go back on that."

"Chris hurt you that badly?"

"Yes, she did. Not just me, she hurt my whole family. I promised my dad that it would never happen again." Ronnie had been looking down at her lap and picked her head up in surprise at the gentle touch on her outstretched ankle. "It's more complicated than that, but...."

"Your truck is parked in the garage and isn't going anywhere," Rose offered. Her words earned her a heart-warming smile.

"Something like that. I need another beer. How about you?"

"I'm doing fine with this one." She took another sip and watched Ronnie leave the room.

Now alone, Rose felt the nervousness she was trying to hold in check burst forth. Her sips became swallows, and her glass was half-empty by the time Ronnie returned. She watched the tall, lean body fold up onto the cushion and look expectantly at her. *I guess it's my turn now, huh?* She took another swallow, the alcohol bolstering her courage. She looked up at gentle blue eyes. "I don't know what I want," she whispered. "But I've never felt this way about anyone else, Ronnie." She looked away and finished her glass, her heart pounding painfully within her chest. Rose had no idea how they started on this conversation, but she knew they couldn't turn back from it now.

"So where do we go from here?" Ronnie's voice wavered, betraying the strong emotions fighting inside her. "I don't want to lose what we have." *I don't want to lose you.*

"I don't know." Rose looked longingly at her friend's beer. Ronnie smiled and handed it over.

"Thanks." Rose took several sips from the bottle before returning it. "I guess things can just stay the same. I mean, we're still friends, right?"

"Best friends," Ronnie corrected, passing the beer.

"Best friends." Rose smiled. "And best friends can sleep next to each other, and it doesn't mean anything."

"Right, and best friends can still hug."

"Absolutely." Rose was encouraged by the direction of the conversation. "And sometimes...." The pink blush began to rise on her cheeks. "...if it's a special occasion...they might even kiss." Her ears burned bright red, and she didn't dare look up. If she had, she would have seen the arched eyebrow and smirk directed at her.

"Yes, if there's a special occasion, I see no reason why best friends can't kiss." Ronnie's mind went back to the blissful kiss under the mistletoe. She cursed herself for taking it down after the holidays.

"I'll tell you a secret." Rose still couldn't look at her. "Earlier, when you picked me up, I thought...I mean, I hoped....you'd kiss me." She said the last words so low that Ronnie almost missed them. She upended the beer and handed the empty bottle back. "Sorry, I didn't realize I was that thirsty."

"Don't worry about it. There's plenty of beer. You want another one?"

"No...yes. Please."

Ronnie rose from the couch and knelt down next to Rose. With one hand, she reached out and turned the young woman's face to her. "I'll be right back." Her thumb brushed against a far-too-soft lip. "And I wanted to kiss you, too." She stood up and pressed her lips to the crown of golden hair. "You want that éclair now?"

With her fear dissipating, Rose found that her hunger had returned. She nodded and watched Ronnie leave the room. *You wanted to kiss me, too?* She reached up and touched the spot where her friend's lips had touched her hair. When Ronnie returned, Rose rewarded her with a beaming smile and fingers trailing over each other as the bottle was exchanged. "Thank you."

"You're welcome," Ronnie said while returning to her seat. She knew she was treading a dangerous line, but she couldn't stop herself. "Happy Valentine's Day, Rose." She held her bottle out.

"Happy Valentine's Day to you, too, Ronnie." The bottles clinked together, and they both took a healthy drink. "You remember in grade school when we used to give out valentines to everyone in class?"

"Yeah?"

"Well, back then, we'd ask our friends to be our valentines, right?"

"Right, I remember that." Ronnie smiled. "Rose Grayson, are you asking me to be your valentine?" She received a shy smile in reply. "I'll be your valentine on one condition." She set the beer down and moved closer. "You have to be mine, too." She was kneeling on the cushion next to Rose, their faces less than a foot apart.

"Ronnie?"

"Mmm?" Her focus was solely on the young woman's lips.

"Would Valentine's Day...be considered...a special occasion?" Caution deadened by the beer, Rose reached up and curled her left hand around the back of Ronnie's neck, the long dark strands sliding through her fingers. There was no answer, only a smile and the lowering of lips to hers.

Ronnie's memory of the Christmas kiss paled in comparison to reality. The soft, gentle brushing of lips together made her hungry for more, and she returned, nipping Rose's lower lip with her own several times before slipping her tongue out to taste the softness. She pulled back and received a soft whimper of protest. *Oh, yes, I could easily lose myself in you, Rose Grayson. Very easily.* "Happy Valentine's Day." Ronnie moved back to a "friendly" distance and retrieved her beer. To her immense pleasure, it was another second before green eyes fluttered open and focused.

To Rose, all the stories about fireworks and bells going off were true. She felt absolutely dizzy and couldn't figure out if it was from Ronnie's kisses or the amount of alcohol she had consumed. The tingling sensation on her lips screamed its choice, and her heart pounded in agreement. "H-happy Valentine's Day to you, too." She looked over and saw the Cheshire cat grin on Ronnie's face. "What?"

"I've never had my kisses leave someone breathless before." She reached out and took the younger woman's hand in her own. *Look at the way you look at me. If you knew the truth....* Ronnie glanced at the clock, noting that it was far too early to feign being tired. "You want to watch a movie?" Without waiting for an answer, she reached for the remotes. A second later, the music stopped, replaced by Chevy Chase bumbling through a *Vacation* movie. "There we go."

Rose glanced at the television, then back at the woman who had just kissed her senseless. Ronnie refused to look her way. *You're not fooling me. That movie just isn't that interesting. What are you afraid of? I won't hurt you like Chris did, I swear.* She understood that her friend needed some space, and Rose was willing to give it. The evening had answered many questions. She now knew that her feelings were reciprocated, at least partially. The kiss had proven that. Her fear of going further had been assuaged by Ronnie's declaration that she didn't want to take their relationship to that stage. But right now Rose needed...something. "Ronnie? Can I lie down on your lap?"

"I'd like that." They settled into the familiar position, Rose's head on her lap and Ronnie's hand lightly stroking the golden hair beneath it. But now the touch carried with it a new meaning in light of the recent revelations. The gentleness was still there but wrapped in a layer of love that moved from one to the other. Ronnie's fingers strayed to trace the outline of the small ear hidden by Rose's hair. The hand resting on her knee began to move, as well, tracing lazy circles through the thick cotton of her sweats. Ronnie wished she'd worn shorts so she could feel those fingers moving across her skin. *Oh, God, how am I going to do this?* She looked down at Rose. *If you only knew how much I want to make love to you right now. I don't know if I can do this, being so close to you and not being able to touch you the way I want to.* Her index finger traced down to the pointed chin. *I love you so much, Rose.*

Much later, it was time for another test. The house was locked up, and the lights were all turned off for the night save the small lamp next to the bed. Rose was getting ready to get into bed when she felt Ronnie's strong arms wrap around her and lift her up. "I figured I'd help again."

"Uh-huh," She noted that the tall woman made no effort to release her, not that she was complaining. "I suppose I owe you some sort of reward for helping me?" A smile tugged at the corner of Ronnie's mouth.

"Well, you don't 'owe' me one, but if you'd like to give me a reward, I certainly won't mind." She lowered them to the bed, her mouth scant inches away from Rose's. Both women were fully aware of the way their upper bodies were pressing together.

"I don't mind." She smiled as their lips met, amazed at how perfect it felt. When Ronnie pulled back, Rose pushed forward, prolonging the contact for another second. Too soon for her comfort, the weight above her moved, replaced by the warm blanket.

"Good night, Rose." Ronnie settled in next to her, the long arm wrapping around her waist as usual. Rose smiled in the darkness. As nerve-wracking as it was, the day had turned out far better than she had thought it would. In their own way, they spoke of their fears and feelings, and now they were lying together like they did every night. Although she knew that some things had changed between them, there was so much more that stayed the same. She brought her hand down to intertwine her fingers with the larger ones. "Night," Ronnie's sleepy voice murmured as she squeezed their fingers together.

"Night."

Chapter Nineteen

In the weeks that followed, both women adjusted to the new facet of their relationship and all that it entailed. The revelation and acknowledgment of feelings allowed them more freedom when it came to showing their affection for each other. There was far more touching, and both were quite creative when it came to defining the term "affectionate friends." For Ronnie, there was nothing more enjoyable than an evening spent exchanging soft touches and gentle kisses with Rose curled up in her arms. She continued to tell herself that she wasn't breaking her promise to her father since she and her golden-haired goddess weren't lovers. Yet with every look, every touch, Ronnie knew that she was lying to herself. She was bewitched by the young woman with the gentle smile and soft laugh.

"Penny."

"Hmm?" Ronnie looked down to see smiling green eyes looking up at her. They were in her favorite position, sitting on the couch with Rose curled up in her lap. It had been almost a week and a half since the right cast was removed and the left one shortened down to just below the knee. The weight difference was a blessing on Ronnie's thighs, and the softness of her companion's body was also quite welcome.

"I said penny for your thoughts. You seemed to go away there for a while."

Ronnie brought her hand up to cup the younger woman's cheek. "Nothing, just thinking."

"About? Or should I guess?"

"You," Ronnie said simply, drawing a beaming smile from Rose. "I care about you so much. You...." Her thumb traced over the razor-thin scar on her companion's cheek, a grim reminder of the hidden truth. "I'm glad you stayed with me. I'm very lucky."

Rose smiled and nuzzled her cheek against the large hand. "I'm the one who's lucky." Locking blue eyes with her own, she continued. "I'll never understand why you took me in, a complete stranger, and did everything you could to help me." She snuggled closer, resting her head on Ronnie's chest. "I'll always be grateful to you for that. And this." She waved her hand to indicate their intimate position. "You don't push me or make me feel uncomfortable."

"Never," Ronnie said vehemently. "I never want to do anything to make you feel that way."

"And you wouldn't. I know that." Rose's face turned serious, and she sat back slightly. "I bet you wish I'd hurry up and make up my mind about whether I liked trucks or not." It was a thought that played itself constantly in the back of her mind, especially after some rather heated kissing exchanges.

"Hey," Ronnie whispered, "That's something that only you can decide." *Screw the euphemisms.* "I know we don't talk about it much but...." She hesitated, not at all certain she wanted to broach the subject with the object of her desires sitting on her lap. "It's more than just caring about another woman." She held up a finger to silence Rose's protest. "Put your feelings about me aside for a minute. Think about what it means to be a...lesbian." After so many years of being ashamed of what she was, Ronnie found it hard to actually speak the word out loud.

"It is more accepted these days," Rose said softly.

"Not in my world." Ronnie said the words harsher than she intended, bitterness coloring her tone. In a lower voice, she added, "Not in my family." Her mind flashed back to that fateful day in her father's study when she was forced to accept the lifelong punishment. Looking down at her beloved, Ronnie decided that if that was the only thing holding her back, she'd walk away for a chance to be with her Rose. But the thin white line and the remaining plaster turned the deadbolt on that door.

"Nothing has to change," the gentle voice said quietly. "We're both happy, and no one is being hurt." Ronnie felt soft arms wrap around her and squeeze gently. She happily returned the embrace. "Come on," Rose said. "Your sister is going to be here soon, and I'm sure you don't want her to see us like this." She tried to move off but found herself held in place by Ronnie's strong hands.

"I don't want to let you go." The words held far more meaning than just that moment, and Rose knew it. She leaned forward and kissed Ronnie.

"I'm not going anywhere." Their lips brushed together again, and fear was lost in the face of love. As it always liked to do, the grandfather clock chimed the hour and broke the moment. With

Ronnie's help, Rose stood on her right leg and slipped the crutches under her arms. "Where did you put the markers? You know the boys are going to want to decorate the new cast."

"I think they're in a drawer out in the kitchen. Speaking of which, we should probably make some cookies for the boys."

They entered the kitchen just as Susan's minivan pulled into the driveway.

Ronnie opened the sliding glass door and waved them in. "Outta the way, me first," twelve-year-old Ricky said as he stormed past with the PlayStation in hand. Ten-year-old Timmy and six-year-old John quickly followed, both making the same amount of pre-teen boy noise. Rose quickly backed herself up against the island to avoid being run over by the trio.

"No running in my house," Ronnie called out uselessly.

"I don't know about them, they never listen," Susan said as she stepped inside, followed by Jack. She spotted Rose and smiled. "Rose, dear, you're up on crutches." She walked over and held her hand out. The young woman balanced herself on her right foot and returned the gesture. "So you're doing better?"

"Yes, everything is going well, according to Dr. Barnes."

"Well, good, I'm glad you're doing better. You shouldn't stand up for so long, though." She shot her older sister a look and pulled out a chair. "You just sit down right there. If you want anything, I'm sure Ronnie will get it for you." Rose started to protest but decided it was easier to give in. To her surprise, Susan sat down in the adjoining chair. "Jack, go see what the boys are up to. I don't want to replace any of Sis's things." Once he left the room, the redhead motioned at the empty chair. "Come sit down, I don't want the boys to overhear this." Rose and Ronnie exchanged confused looks as Ronnie sat down.

"What's going on? Everything all right with you and Jack?"

"Of course everything's fine with us. We've been happily married for thirteen years," Susan replied.

"So what's the problem?"

"You know that diamond brooch that Daddy gave Mother on their twenty-fifth anniversary?" The oldest Cartwright nodded. Her father had spent an extravagant amount, even for a family as rich as they were. It was one of Beatrice's most prized possessions. Susan looked down at the lace tablecloth. "It's gone."

"Gone? What do you mean gone?" Ronnie's eyes were wide with disbelief. "She keeps it in her safe when she's not wearing it, doesn't she?"

"She said she put it in there. Only four people know the combination. Mother, you, me...." The sisters looked at each other, then slowly nodded in agreement.

"Tommy." Ronnie's hands bunched into fists. Rose had never heard a name said with so much loathing, as if it were a curse. Without thinking, she reached over and placed her hand over the larger one. She realized her mistake when she felt the flinch and withdrew. They exchanged looks before Ronnie spoke again. "When did she discover this?"

"Yesterday. You won't like this," Susan began. "She said she had gone to her friend's house for bridge Tuesday night, and when she got back, she noticed the picture frame wasn't flush against the wall, but she didn't think anything of it."

"Is the safe behind the picture?" Rose asked.

"When was the last time Tommy was there?" Ronnie asked, nodding at the same time to reply to her beloved's question.

"Saturday night." The redhead sighed. "I think he took it, and I told Mother that, too."

"You told her?" The eldest Cartwright didn't bother hiding her surprise. "You told her that precious Tommy might have stolen from her? What did she say?"

"Just what you'd think she'd say," Susan replied. "She accused me of teaming up with you against him and that we didn't understand how difficult things were for him. But I think she believes me." She turned to Rose. "Our mother doesn't always see things as clearly as she should."

"That's one way to look at it," Ronnie said, secretly pleased that her sister had invited Rose in on what was obviously a family discussion. "More accurately is that she sees only what she wants to see, and anything that disturbs that vision is wrong." She sighed and scratched her head in frustration. "Nothing we can do about what she thinks. What about the brooch?"

"We'll pay on the claim, of course. That's not the problem."

"No, the problem is a boy who thinks that drugs make him a man. Why didn't you call me about this?"

"I only found out about it yesterday, and I didn't want to disturb your weekend." She looked at Rose pointedly. "Besides, I knew I'd see you today."

Ronnie ignored her sister's blatant implication. "So what are we going to do about him? Now he's stealing from his own mother."

"I had the locksmith come by and change the combination on her safe. Cartwright Insurance will pay the claim. There really isn't anything else we can do."

"Is that all he took, just her brooch?"

"Yes," Susan nodded. "All the other jewelry was still there. But only we'd know that Daddy's brooch was the most expensive piece in there. She's got that necklace that looks like it's worth more than it is, and that was left alone."

"Tommy knows what everything is worth. Mother only takes it out on special occasions. He probably figured she wouldn't notice right away." Ronnie looked over at Rose, silently wishing they were alone. A deep anger welled within her, and only the young woman's embrace could ease it. *The hell with it, you already think we're lovers.* She took a deep breath, reached out, and wrapped her hand around Rose's smaller one. Susan gave what was clearly an uncomfortable smile. *You started it.* Ronnie squeezed her friend's hand once, then withdrew. She glanced sideways to see Rose's surprised and questioning look. She smiled and hoped that Rose would understand. *Sometimes I just need to touch you.*

"So...um...let's talk about other things. Did you get the recipe from Maria for the stuffed chicken?"

"I did, but I'm not in the mood to fuss around with that tonight. You'll have to come over during the week and have her make it."

"Do you mean that one with the broccoli and that sauce?" Rose asked. "That's delicious. Maria said you always liked that."

"Well, Ronnie liked it, too." The young woman's disarming smile caused Susan to return one in kind. "Maria makes the absolute best stuffing."

"Yes, she does," the eldest Cartwright agreed. Rose smiled to herself remembering the red box that read, "Stove Top," sitting on the counter one evening. She decided to keep the housekeeper's secret. Besides, she'd tried making Stove Top before when she lived alone, and it never turned out as well as Maria's.

With the subject off the physical gesture and on to a more familiar topic, Susan relaxed visibly. "That's why Ronnie got to keep Maria. She cooks so well that if she worked for me, I'd be as big as a house."

"Sometimes I feel that way, too," Rose said, patting her stomach.

Raised voices drifted into the kitchen, and Susan flinched. "I'd better go see what they're up to before one of them kills the other."

"We'll be there in a minute," Ronnie said, standing close to Rose's chair. Once they were alone, she leaned down for a kiss. "I think Susan's warming up to you."

"I don't know. When you touched me, she looked like she swallowed a bug."

"You don't know her like I do. Believe me, if she was really upset, you'd have known it."

"If you say so." Rose allowed Ronnie one more kiss before reaching for her crutches. "Did you call for the pizzas yet?"

"Damn, knew I forgot something. What should we get?"

"How about a large cheese, two supreme, and a pepperoni and mushroom?" Susan's shrill voice came from the living room. Apparently, there was a battle of wills going on between her and Ricky.

"Can you call it in for me? It's three on the speed dial."

"Sure." Rose picked up the phone and pressed the button while Ronnie went to prevent World War III. She got through on the first try and placed the order. She hung up and positioned her crutches under her arms when the phone rang. Thinking it was the pizza place calling back, Rose picked it up. "Hello?"

"R-Ronnie?" She didn't recognize the voice, but she certainly understood the tone. The woman on the other end of the phone was crying.

"No, this is Rose."

"Would you please tell Ronnie that her mother is on the phone? I-it's very important," Beatrice sniffed.

"Hold on just a second." Realizing that she couldn't hold the phone in one hand and use her crutches, Rose set it on the counter and worked her way into the living room.

Susan had hold of Timmy and Jack was holding Ricky as the two boys hurled insults at each other.

"You cheated."

"Did not!"

"Did so!"

"Did not!"

"Enough!" Ronnie's voice boomed over the squawking. "I don't care who cheated or whose turn it was. If you two can't play nice, I'm going to shut it off."

"But he started it."

"Timothy!" Both his parents yelled.

"Ronnie." Rose leaned on her crutches. "Your mother is on the phone." As the tall woman passed her, she spoke in a lower voice. "She sounds like she's been crying." That caused Ronnie to hesitate for a second before picking up the phone. A crying parent never meant anything good.

"Mother? Mo–...Mother...Mother, stop crying. I can't understand you." She silently motioned for Rose to get Susan. "Okay, tell me again, slowly." The redhead entered the kitchen just as Ronnie was piecing together what her hysterical mother was trying to tell her. "Are they sure? Okay, okay, Mother, slow down...what did he say?" She turned her back to the other woman and leaned against the island. "Mother, listen carefully to me. Did he say for sure that it was Tommy?" At the mention of her brother's name, Susan's hand went to her mouth.

"Did something happen?"

"Who called you?" Ronnie waved her sister away. She had enough to do trying to understand what Beatrice was telling her. "No, Susan's here. We'll stop by and pick you up. Yes, Mother, we'll be there in fifteen minutes. No. Don't call anyone else. If they need to be called, I'll do it later. No, don't call a cab. We'll be right there. Yes, I promise...bye." She pressed the off button and set the phone down on the counter.

"Ronnie?" Susan took a step forward. "Did something happen to Tommy?" No response. "Ronnie?"

"Tommy...." Her back to them, she gripped the edge of the island. "He was going eastbound in the westbound lane of the Thruway."

"Oh, my God," Rose whispered. Ronnie pushed herself to a standing position and faced them.

"Rose, I need you to watch the boys until we get back. I'm sure they'll just eat pizza and play video games."

"Of course," the young woman replied. "Anything, you know that."

"I'll get Jack and our coats," Susan said, her voice shaky. She left the room to get her husband. Rose hobbled over to her tall companion. For several seconds, neither spoke. Finally, Ronnie broke the silence.

"I don't know how long we'll be gone. Try to put them to bed by ten. There are plenty of rooms for them to choose from."

"I'll take care of it," Rose promised. She reached up and cupped Ronnie's cheek. "I love you."

Ronnie gave a shiny-eyed smile. "How do you know just what to say?" She pulled her love close and kissed the top of her head. "I love you, too, Rose. Don't kill the kids or play any game that involves tying you up, okay?"

"I think I can handle them. You have more important things to worry about." She felt Ronnie step back and realized that Jack and Susan had entered the room. "I'll call you as soon as I know anything."

"They can't have any caffeine or sugar after seven. John has to be in bed by eight, and the other boys can stay up until ten." Susan rifled through her pocketbook. "I can't find the keys. Jack, where are the keys?"

"I'm driving," Ronnie said firmly. The change in her tone caused Rose to look at her. The change was startling. Gone was the soft, sensitive woman she was privy to. In her stead was a stoic, commanding presence. The young woman realized that this was the executive, the leader of a multi-million-dollar company. Although she understood the need for the two identities, Rose still wished desperately that Ronnie didn't have to be the caretaker all the time. She watched them leave and prayed that everything would be okay.

It was four in the morning when a drowsy Rose hobbled into the kitchen to make a pot of coffee. She passed the time by drinking coffee at the kitchen table and rereading the daily paper. Tabitha popped in from time to time, demanded attention, then left. Three days worth of newsprint and half the pot of coffee slipped by before Ronnie's Jeep pulled into the driveway. She went to the door, opening it in time to see Jack helping his wife and mother-in-law out of the vehicle. "Oh, Lord," she whispered, knowing that the worst had happened.

Ronnie took over for her brother-in-law and helped Beatrice inside. "What rooms did you put the boys in?" she asked as she passed.

"The rooms on either side of yours and the one at the end of the hall," Rose said, choking back a lump in her own throat. Until she saw the crushed look on their faces, she had been holding on to the hope that Tommy had somehow survived the accident. Ronnie nodded and looked at Jack.

"The room across from mine is empty. You two stay there. I'll put Mother in my room." She took her mother's pocketbook and set it on the counter. "Mother? Come on, I think you need to lie down for a little while."

"But I have to call–"

"I'll take care of letting everyone know. You need to lie down." She saw Jack leading his wife out of the room. "Come on, we're going upstairs now."

"Horrible...it's just so horrible..." Beatrice cried.

"I know, Mother. Come on now." Ronnie led the grieving woman away.

"Rose, do you think you can make a pot of coffee?" Ronnie asked when she returned to the kitchen fifteen minutes later.

"I already did. Your cup is on the table." Ronnie looked at the familiar mug, then at her companion. "I figured you'd need some coffee," Rose said with a shrug. "I've had a bit myself." They both looked over at the nearly empty pot.

"That was good thinking." She rubbed her eyes. "What time is it anyway?"

"Almost five thirty."

"I guess I should wait before I start calling everyone." Ronnie wrapped her hands around her mug and stared at the beige liquid. Uncertain what to say, Rose remained silent, giving her companion the time she needed. Blue eyes shined with unshed tears but remained focused on the coffee. After an extended silence, Ronnie began to speak. "The witnesses said he turned into the off-ramp instead of the on-ramp." Her lower lip quivered, and she blinked rapidly. "He was picking up speed and hit a dump truck just before the entrance to the highway."

"Ronnie, I'm so sorry." She put her hand on the strong forearm.

"They um...." The blinking increased as she battled to keep the tears in. "They have to do an autopsy." Her voice hitched. "They think he...the drugs...." A sob escaped her lips, and Ronnie found herself being pulled into Rose's arms.

"I've got you," Rose cooed. The chairs scraped across the kitchen floor as they moved closer, neither wanting to break the contact. The caretaker needed comfort, and Rose was the only one who could provide it.

"I-it isn't fair. He's too young," Ronnie choked. "The drugs...."

"I know." She kissed the dark forehead. "I know." She began rocking as hot tears soaked her shirt. Sobs wracked the tall frame, but Rose held on, murmuring comforting words and gently rubbing Ronnie's back. "I've got you...that's right, let it go."

"It's those damn drugs," she cried.

"I know." Rose continued rocking and holding her beloved until finally the tears subsided and the sobs reduced to sniffles. She felt Ronnie pull back and released her embrace. "Better?" She received a shaky nod. "Come here." She took a linen napkin off the table and wiped the wet face. "Blow...that's better."

"Thanks, I just needed...well, that." She wearily sank back into her chair and shook her head. "This is just so hard to believe." There was nothing that Rose could say to that, so she scooted her chair over until their knees were touching. Ronnie laid her hand atop the smaller one and squeezed. "The next few days are going to be rough."

"You don't have to go through this alone." The young woman brought her free hand up and cupped her love's cheek. "I'll be right here with you, I promise." She looked at the clock. "It's still too early to call everyone, and you really need some rest. You've been up all night."

"What about you?" For the first time, Ronnie noticed the dark circles under the beautiful green eyes. "Did you sleep at all?"

"I dropped off sometime around two, but I was up by four."

"We both need some sleep." She stood up, then frowned. "I have to take the couch. If someone wakes up...." There was no need to finish the sentence.

"Why don't I take the couch? You need the comfortable bed more than I do."

"I'm too tired to argue with you."

"Then don't," Rose said firmly. Ronnie looked at her and wondered if anyone else was able to speak to her in that manner and get away with it. She suspected not, except perhaps Maria. Her eyes saddened at the thought of breaking the news to the housekeeper who had known Tommy all his life.

"There's so much to do. I have to call the cousins...."

"You can do all that after you've had a couple of hours' rest." Rose forced herself up on her crutches. "Come on now, I'll lie with you until you fall asleep." Ronnie nodded wearily. She needed to rest, and there was no doubt that with Rose by her side that she would be able to do just that.

After going to the bathroom and changing into her sweats, Ronnie crawled into bed. "You sure you won't fall asleep?" she mumbled groggily while arranging her pillows.

"No, I've had so much coffee that I don't think I'll be able to sleep." She held her arm out. "Come here, let me hold you." Soon a dark head was nestled against her chest. "That's right," she began stroking the long black hair. "You rest and let me worry about you for a change."

Rose was humming softly and gently rubbing her sleeping companion's back when she heard the car pull into the driveway. Her eyes closed slowly with the realization that it was now Monday and that in less than a minute, Maria was going to walk through the door, completely unaware of the previous evening's events. She looked over at Ronnie and knew she couldn't wake her for this. "I'll take care of it," she whispered before placing a gentle kiss on the sleeping woman's shoulder.

She entered the kitchen just as Maria was closing the sliding glass door. "Oooh, that wind," the housekeeper said as she removed her coat. She turned and realized that she wasn't alone. "Oh, good morning, Rose. Is that Susan's car in the driveway?" At that same moment, she noticed the half-empty coffeepot and the newspapers strewn about the table.

"Yes."

"Rose, what's going on? Where's Ronnie?"

"She's sleeping. Maria, please come sit down." Rose leaned her crutches against the island and pulled out a chair.

"Why is Susan here? Are the boys all right? Did something happen to Jack? Is–"

"No, they're fine. Please sit down." Rose let out a breath and waited for the housekeeper to take a seat before sitting down herself.

"You're scaring me. What happened?" Maria's voice was full of worry. Rose felt her throat tighten even before she spoke. "I wish there was an easy way to tell you this." Realizing that her words were only making the older woman more upset, she took a deep breath and continued. "Tommy was killed in a car accident last night."

Like a mirror shattering, Maria's face lost all composure, and she broke down into tears. As she did with Ronnie, Rose took the grieving woman in her arms and comforted her. The housekeeper recovered after a few minutes and stood up. "Well then, I believe that there are things I should be doing." She walked over to the coffeemaker. "I'm sure that a fresh pot would be in order."

"Maria, you don't have to do that. Not today."

The older woman turned and looked at her. "Rose, I'm not a Cartwright. I remember when her father passed away. I worked for that man for twenty-five years, and on the day of his funeral, I was here making sure there was enough food for the people who were going to be arriving after the graveside service."

"That's awful," Rose gasped. "Ronnie wouldn't give you the day off?"

"Ronnie wasn't in charge then, her mother was." Maria poured the coffee into the sink and turned on the faucet. "She said she needed me here to take care of everything for her. What was I supposed to do?"

"I'm sure Ronnie won't expect you to work." She hobbled forward another step and spoke in a lower voice. "Beatrice is here, too."

"Well then, she'll be expecting hot tea when she comes down." Maria opened the cupboard and fished out the teapot. "What time are you going to wake Ronnie up?"

"I figured I'd give her another half hour or so. She was up all night."

"Hmm, Beatrice usually wakes up by eight. You probably should wake Ronnie once the coffee is ready." Rose nodded in agreement.

Maria followed Rose into the room and set the steaming cup of coffee on the nightstand. "I'll start breakfast for the boys. I'm sure they'll be up soon."

"Thank you, we'll be out in a few minutes," Rose said, her eyes never leaving the sleeping woman. Once she heard the click of the door closing, she leaned her crutches against the wall and lay down next to her companion. She propped herself up on one elbow and looked down, silently wishing she didn't have to wake Ronnie. Even in sleep, her face showed the signs of grief. Closed eyes still showed the puffiness of crying, and there was no peacefulness in the chiseled features. "Ronnie? Time to wake up, hon."

"Hmm?" Eyes that didn't get enough sleep opened with momentary confusion. "What time is it?"

"About quarter of eight," the young woman replied. Ronnie groaned and sat up.

"I guess I'd better get up then. I have a busy day ahead of me." Her eyes widened at the sight of her coffee being handed to her. "Oh, thanks." She took a sip and smiled appreciatively. "I needed this." She took another sip, then looked at Rose quizzically. "Did you make this?"

"Maria did."

"Oh, God, Maria." Ronnie put her hand to her mouth. "I have to–"

"I took care of it for you," Rose said in a low tone, her eyes betraying just how difficult it was for her to be the bearer of bad news.

"Come here." The tall woman leaned her back against the headrest and held her right arm out.

"But you have things to do," she said, although there was nothing more in the world she wanted to do at the moment than curl up in Ronnie's arms.

"I can spare a minute." Sad blue eyes looked at Rose. "I really need to hold you." They snuggled up together, the reddish-blonde head resting against Ronnie's. "Thank you."

"If there's anything I can do...."

"You're doing it right now," Ronnie said, pressing her lips against Rose's head. "I just need a few minutes of peace with you before I go out there and face anyone." She took another sip of coffee and began idly stroking the honey hair. "There's going to be hundreds of people coming in and out for the next few days. Tabitha will be spending a lot of time in the laundry room." She nuzzled her cheek against the soft hair, then took another drink. "If Jack and Susan stay, would you help keep the boys occupied? They like playing video games with you."

"Of course, Ronnie. Anything you need." As much as she didn't want to, Rose pulled away from the embrace. "I'd better go back out there and see if Maria needs any help making breakfast. Besides, I'm sure you want to get dressed before everyone wakes up."

"Maria shouldn't have to work today." Ronnie was surprised to receive a quick hug. "What was that for?"

"I knew you wouldn't make her work."

"Of course not. How could I expect her to work after this? She practically raised Tommy."

"Your mother did when your father died." She watched Ronnie's jaw tense.

"I'm not like my mother," she said tersely. She flung the covers back and stood up. "Rose, would you mind telling Maria?"

"No, I don't mind at all," the young woman said just before Ronnie closed the bathroom door. She picked up the empty mug. "I'll have fresh coffee waiting for you when you come out." It was easier said than done as Rose tried to figure out how to maneuver with her crutches. The solution was to hold the handle by her teeth, which earned her a disapproving look from Maria once she entered the kitchen.

"You're as stubborn as she is, aren't you?" the housekeeper chastised as she took the mug. "You know I would have come and picked it up. You didn't need to carry it all the way out here."

"Maria, Ronnie said you didn't have to stay today. I'm sure we can handle everything."

"Was that her idea or yours?"

"Hers."

"I see." The housekeeper nodded. "I would expect that from someone as generous as Ronnie. However, I think I should stay."

"Why? You're just as upset as everyone else, why should you stay and work?"

"Maria? Maria, are you down there?" Beatrice called from the top of the stairs.

"That's why," the older woman said. She walked out to the living room and looked up at the matriarch. "There's tea waiting for you, Mrs. Cartwright."

"Oh, good, you are here." Beatrice walked down the stairs, her face showing the signs of a grieving mother. "It's terrible, isn't it? Just simply terrible."

"Tragic," the housekeeper agreed.

"Where's my daughter?" She finally noticed Rose leaning on her crutches. "Hello, dear. Aren't you Ronnie's little friend? The one who was in the wheelchair?"

"Yes, ma'am. My name is Rose."

"Rose, where's Ronnie?"

"She's getting dressed. She'll be out in a minute."

"Has she started to call anyone yet?"

"I'll be doing it in a minute," Ronnie said as she exited Rose's room. She appeared composed, but Rose knew it was an act. The puffy eyes told of new tears of grief waiting to pour out. "Good morning, Mother."

"There's nothing good about this day, Veronica. You'd better get started. Call your Aunt Elaine first." The matriarch strode into the kitchen, effectively dismissing her daughter.

"I guess I'd better start making some phone calls." Ronnie looked in the direction of the kitchen and shook her head. "I'm going to use the phone in the office. Excuse me."

Rose waited until the door to the room closed before speaking to Maria in hushed tones. "Why was she so mean to Ronnie?"

"She's not trying to be mean," the housekeeper explained. "Beatrice has a certain way of handling things. This is her way."

"I know she's hurting, but so is Ronnie. Can't she see that?"

"Some people can't see past their own pain, Rose." Maria looked at the kitchen. "I have to get in there."

Rose stood there for a moment, her first instinct to keep Ronnie company. But then she realized that there was a better way to help her friend. Steeling herself, she followed Maria into the kitchen.

Beatrice was sitting at the table with a cup of tea in one hand and a handkerchief in the other. "Mrs. Cartwright, would you mind if I sat down here?" Rose asked sweetly. "I still can't stand for any length of time yet."

"Well, yes, sit down. Maria, some more tea."

"Thank you," the young woman said as she took a seat. The housekeeper approached with the teapot and a cup of coffee for Rose. They exchanged glances but said nothing. Beatrice looked at her watch.

"I would think Ricky would be up by now. He's always an early riser."

"He was up late. I had trouble getting him to sleep."

"That's right, you watched them, didn't you?" Rose nodded. The matriarch sipped her tea. "That Ricky. He's a lot like Tommy, you know."

"I'm afraid I didn't get to know your son. Why don't you tell me about him?"

Ronnie stepped into the kitchen an hour later looking for her coffee. Her throat was becoming dry after making so many calls. An eyebrow arched at the sight of her mother, Rose, and Susan sitting at the table chatting. Since Beatrice's back was to her, Ronnie hoped she could sneak in, get her coffee, and get out. The sound of her sister's voice, however, dashed that hope. "Ronnie."

"Morning, Susan." She turned and faced the table. "Mother, Frank and the kids will be here in a little while. Most of the others will be here this afternoon."

"Did you make the arrangements? I want you to make sure that he gets the best, the very best."

"I'll take care of it," Ronnie said. "I have a few more calls to make. Laura can handle the business associates and the press releases." Maria handed her the mug. "I'll be back out later."

"Did you reach your Aunt Elaine?"

"I got her answering service. She'll call back."

"But you're on the phone." The matriarch's voice raised a notch. "She won't be able to get through. Veronica, I don't want her to hear about this on the news."

"I have call waiting, Mother. She won't get a busy signal."

"She can't hear about this on the news. Thomas was her favorite nephew."

"I left a message with her service." *What do you want me to do? I can't make her call me.* She gulped her coffee, wincing at the burning heat going down her throat.

"Mrs. Cartwright, would you like some more tea?" Rose asked.

"Not right now, dear. I should go spend some time with my grandsons." She looked at her younger daughter. "Susan, I assume if you and Jack have another child that you will name him Thomas."

"Mother, we've decided that three–"

"Nonsense. You're certainly young enough, and it's not like your figure could be ruined by another child. Your sister continues to show no interest in having children." The matriarch rose to her feet. "I'm going to go visit with the boys, then you can take me home, Ronnie. I'll let you know when I'm ready."

The tall woman's knuckles turned white as she gripped the handle of her mug and glared at her mother's retreating form. Susan stood next to her sister. "She doesn't know what she's saying. She's just hurting over Tommy."

"She knows exactly what she's saying, Sis. The problem is, we keep putting up with it." She turned to Rose. "People are going to start arriving soon. You might want to go into your room before it happens."

"No." She picked up her crutches. "I can help. I'll keep an eye on the kids so the adults can be together. I don't mind."

"Thank you," Ronnie said softly.

Rose smiled, and Ronnie found herself helplessly lost in it.

ACCIDENTAL LOVE

"Ahem." Susan's polite cough broke the moment.

"Ronnie, I'll make sure Mom gets home. You worry about getting in touch with everyone," the redhead said.

Chapter Twenty

It was almost nightfall by the time Susan and her family took Beatrice home. Ronnie made it a point to stay hidden in the office as much as possible, but unbeknownst to her, Rose was doing her best to keep the matriarch away from her. When the minivan backed out of her driveway, Ronnie breathed a sigh of relief and stepped into the living room. *Damn.* In her hiding, she hadn't noticed that the number of relatives arriving was outpacing those leaving and now close to thirty Cartwrights were floating around. She spotted Rose immediately and made a beeline for her. "Hi."

"Hi. Your mother left."

"I see that." Ronnie looked around, her tall frame allowing her to see past the mass of people. "Do you think they could be a little louder?"

Hidden from the sight of others, a hand worked its way to the small of Ronnie's back and began rubbing in gentle circles.

"They'll be leaving soon, won't they?"

"Well, there's no reason for them to stay. They all said their condolences to Mother. They're just hanging out here because they have no place better to be." A loud crash from the game room drew her attention. "I'll be right back."

The crash turned out to be a bar stool complete with its occupant. "Hey, Cuz," the drunken man slurred. Two of the half-dozen men standing around moved in to help him up. A Breathalyzer wasn't needed to know that they were all quite drunk.

"Frank, what are you doing?"

"The boys and I were just raising a few to Tommy." He wobbled back onto his now upright stool. She walked past him and stepped behind the bar.

"A bottle of scotch and half a bottle of vodka. You guys have been toasting him quite well, I believe." She capped the vodka and shut the light off behind the bar. "I think it's time for your wives to take you home." She walked around shutting off lights and hanging up the cue sticks. One by one, the men grumbled and left the room, not all unassisted. It took her slightly longer to break up the bunches of women gathered together talking about every imaginable subject. Only when the last relative was gone did Maria appear with the vacuum. "Don't bother tonight," Ronnie said.

"Look at this room," the housekeeper said incredulously.

"It'll be here in the morning, Maria. It's been a long day, and I'm exhausted. Please, just leave it until tomorrow, okay?"

"If you wish. I'll be here first thing as usual. Should I pick up anything special at the market?"

"No, there's nothing–"

"A roll of chocolate chip cookie dough," Rose interjected. "Um, you know how kids love cookies. Maybe it'll keep them occupied." She caught the slight upturn of a smile on Ronnie's lips and knew her idea was well received. "Better make that two," she amended, her eyes never leaving those of her friend.

An hour later, two bodies were curled up around each other, both fighting yawns. "You are an incredibly thoughtful woman," Ronnie mumbled into the young woman's ear.

"Mmm?"

"The cookies. And I know you put up with my mother to keep her away from me." She squeezed the shoulder beneath her hand. "You don't know how much I appreciate that."

"You had enough to worry about." She squirmed back into the warm body behind her. The biggest advantage of having her cast shortened was that she could snuggle up as close as she wanted to Ronnie. "She's not that bad."

"That's because she's not your mother."

"True."

"It's a good thing, too." The hand that had been squeezing Rose's shoulder moved down to her waist.

"Why's that?"

"Because," Ronnie flipped the smaller woman onto her back and put her hands on either side of the golden head of hair. She relaxed her shoulders, bringing their lips so close that their breath mingled. "That would make you my sister, and I guarantee there are times when my thoughts of you are far from sisterly." Even in the dim moonlight, Rose could see the roguish grin before it was replaced with a more serious face. "You don't know how much you've helped me today. You made me feel...well...very special."

"With everything you mean to me, how could I do anything less?" She reached up and caressed the chiseled face above her. "And you are special. I know it's going to be hard dealing with your family for the next few days, but I'll be right there to help you through it. Come on now, you're tired, I'm tired, and tomorrow is going to be another long day. Enough talk for tonight." Rose put her hand on Ronnie's shoulder and pulled, forcing the taller woman to lie down against her. "That's better."

"Rose?"

"Mmm?"

"Can I stay like this...in your arms?" The woman who usually took charge sounded almost like a scared child in her request. As hard as it was for Rose to hear Ronnie in such pain, it filled her heart to know that it was she who Ronnie turned to for comfort.

"Always," she whispered, tightening her hold.

"I can't believe he's gone." There was a long silence. "I know things have been hard between us lately, but that's not what I see when I think of him."

"What do you see, Ronnie?" she whispered, her hand moving to stroke the long dark hair. "Tell me about the Tommy you grew up with, the one you loved."

"He was the cutest little boy." Rose felt the body against hers relax as happy memories surfaced. "We were close when he was little. Whatever I was doing, he wanted to do. He was my shadow." A tear fell, and Ronnie swallowed hard.

"Hey, will you do something for me?"

A nod. "Anything."

"Think back to a happy time, just you and Tommy. Close your eyes and picture it in your head." She waited a few seconds. "Are you seeing it? Now tell me about it. Is it summer or winter?"

"Summer."

"Inside or out?"

"Out. We're at the family camp."

"What are you two doing?"

"Fishing." Rose felt Ronnie smile against her chest. "It was a perfect day. We were on the dock, just the two of us." Her brow furrowed. "I don't know where everyone else was."

"Don't worry about them," the young woman cooed, continuing her gentle stroking of the dark tresses. "You were fishing with Tommy. Did you catch a fish?"

"I didn't, but he did." She relaxed against Rose again. "Nice foot-long bass. Fought like the devil, too."

"Close your eyes. Now think about that day and how much fun you and Tommy had together. That's right...." Rose closed her own eyes and let the deep and even breathing near her ear lull her into the same peaceful sleep.

Rose was a constant source of support for Ronnie. The autopsy report had come back with unpleasant news. A variety of illegal drugs were found in Tommy's system. While the Cartwrights had hoped to keep that information private, they were a name in Albany, and although the morning news reported that one of the Cartwrights had died in a freak accident, the evening news was not as kind. One station, finding the perfect excuse to reuse old footage, hooked the news of Tommy's autopsy with a report on drugs in Corporate America. It produced, much to the family's dismay, a gaggle of news reporters around Ronnie's home, not accepting her short statement that the family was in mourning and had no comment on the findings. Before the day was out, they received word that the driver of the dump truck had filed a suit against Tommy's estate. Beatrice declared the autopsy nothing less than an "exaggerated fabrication" and the truck driver "a greedy opportunist" trying to take advantage of an unfortunate accident. Rose listened to the remarks and nodded often, doing her part to make things easier on Ronnie.

But by the day of the funeral, Ronnie's patience and tolerance were both in short supply. The past few days had piled frustration upon frustration, and the family seemed blissfully ignorant of the strain they were putting on her. Not only did they gather at her house to mourn, they gathered to visit with one another, allowing Ronnie no privacy or peace. Despite Rose's best efforts, Beatrice still managed to slip past and grill her daughter about every detail of the service. There was bickering from the littlest thing like who rode in which limousine to who would be the pallbearers to which lot in the family section Tommy should be buried. Ronnie kept her anger inside, releasing only after everyone had gone. Then her punching bag would be the recipient. Only when she was both physically and emotionally exhausted would she curl into bed and seek the comfort of Rose's arms. The role reversal felt odd yet at the same time comforting to Ronnie. In the small woman's embrace, she was able to let the stress go and find peace. It reinforced her inner strength, allowing her to face the challenges of the recent events.

"Maria will be here in a few minutes to pick you up." Ronnie zipped up her skirt and pulled on the blazer. "There, I believe I'm ready now." She put a small black hat on over her pinned hair.

"I wish I could be there with you," Rose said earnestly.

"I know, hon." She cupped the younger woman's chin. "I don't know what I would have done without you these past few days."

"I don't know what I would have done without you these last few months," Rose countered.

"You know if I had my way, you'd be right up there next to me."

"It's better if I stay in the back with Maria. It'll be easier to get in and out with my crutches."

"Oh, let me help you with your sneaker before I go."

"I can get it, Ronnie. You'll wrinkle your skirt."

"Sit." Her long fingers made quick work of loosening the laces. She knelt down and put one hand on the back of Rose's calf. Using her knee as a footrest, she put the sneaker on her companion's foot and began tying it. "Remember, the church is going to be packed. Make sure you get a seat. I don't want to find you leaning up against the back wall, got it?"

"Got it." Rose leaned over and adjusted the bow on Ronnie's blouse. "Got your handkerchief?"

"And a spare."

"All right then, I guess you're ready." Rose paused for a second, then put her hands on the taller woman's shoulders. "Ronnie, I know you think you have to be this big, strong superwoman, but you don't. Even though you had problems, he was still your brother, and I know you loved him. If you have to cry, do it." Her words earned her a gentle kiss on the forehead as Ronnie stood up.

"I'll see you after the service." Ronnie remained stooped long enough to tuck an errant strand of red-gold hair behind Rose's ear. *If only there was a way to have you with me today.* She knew it was going to be hard without her beloved companion by her side.

As expected, the church was packed with friends, family, and business associates of the Cartwrights. Despite Ronnie's words, Rose was content to stand against the back wall, but a man sitting in the last pew stood and offered his seat. Remaining at the wall, Maria took possession of the crutches so no one would trip over them. From their position at the rear of the large church, it was impossible to see

Beatrice and her daughters in the front pew. Rose listened to the monotone words as the priest went through the standard phrases of comfort and prayers of solace. When the end drew near, she motioned to Maria for her crutches, deciding it was easier to get out now than wait and get caught in the throngs of people.

Just as she was getting into Maria's car, the doors of the church opened. From her vantage point, she could see the six men carrying out the casket and watched as Beatrice exited, flanked by her daughters. Rose squinted but was too far away to really see Ronnie's eyes. Her friend's head was hung and her arm was around her distraught mother. She saw that Susan was also providing support to the grieving woman as they walked down the steps and into the waiting limousine. Realizing that Maria was waiting for her, Rose put her crutches in the backseat and got into the car.

Just as Ronnie had predicted, friends and family members began pouring into the house less than a half hour after the funeral had ended. Long tables lined one wall of the living room, stacked high with breads, meats, and cheeses. Leaning against one wall out of the main flow of traffic, Rose noticed that it was the first place people went to as they arrived.

The floodgates were open, and close to fifty people were there by the time Ronnie arrived with her mother and sister. Rose spotted the mane of dark hair above the rest of the crowd and began to work her way over. The trip was made easier as she had been spotted, and the determined executive met her halfway. "Hi."

"Hi yourself," Ronnie said. "Quite the crowd." She scanned the area, quickly noting those who would be problems as time went on and the drinks continued to flow.

"Ronnie, can you come into my room for a minute?"

"Sure," she replied, grateful for any chance to get away.

The first thing Ronnie noticed when she entered the room was one of her outfits neatly laid out on the bed. "I thought you'd be more comfortable in your slacks," Rose said with a shrug. To Ronnie's pointed look at the shoes on the floor, she added, "I know how much your feet hurt after being in heels all day. Flats are perfectly acceptable with those slacks. I've seen you wear them before."

"So you had Maria pick these out for me?"

"No," Rose replied with a proud smile. "I picked them out myself and brought them down here. Maria was busy."

The thoughtfulness almost brought Ronnie to tears. Blinking rapidly, she reached out and let one finger trace Rose's jaw. "Thank you." She took a step back and kicked off her shoes. "I'd better get changed and back out there. I'm sure someone is looking for me. Probably my mother." She added the last part under her breath. The skirt hit the floor followed by her half slip.

Ronnie dressed quickly and turned back to Rose. "Ah, I feel better already."

"Is there anything I can do for you?" Rose asked. "Other than trying to keep your mother busy? She's getting tired of me hanging around her, you know."

"I heard. Susan will run interference for the most part. You can either stay in here, which I recommend highly by the way, or you can just go out there and listen to my cousins and second cousins and God knows who else ramble on about nothing of importance."

"Well, when you put it that way." Smiling green eyes accompanied the sarcastic remark. "How can I resist?"

To Rose, the sound was nothing but a general din. Ronnie, on the other hand, spent years learning how to work a crowd and was able to pick out the individual conversations easily. As she moved through the room, she carefully listened to the different snippets. By the time she reached Frank, she knew more about the new boat her cousin was buying than he did. The knowledge allowed her to slip effortlessly into the conversation. Moving from person to person, Ronnie canvassed the room. When she thought she'd said hello to everyone, she tried slipping out to the kitchen where she had seen Rose go a few minutes before.

"Ronnie." Blue eyes rolled at the sound of her mother's voice.

"Yes, Mother?" She turned to see Beatrice standing behind her. For that instant, the agitation she'd had at her parent dissipated in the face of the grieving woman. Ronnie instantly softened her tone. "Is there something you need?"

"Where's your sister?"

"I don't know." She craned her neck to see over the crowd, but there was no sign of the distinctive red hair. "Maybe Jack took her home."

"Now, Veronica," the wrinkled hands went to her hips. "You know Susan wouldn't leave without saying goodbye to me," she admonished. "Honestly, sometimes I wonder what you're thinking."

"I'm sorry, Mother. I wasn't thinking." Ronnie resisted the urge to rub her temples. It was a useless defense against a mother headache anyway.

"Well, Tommy's death has affected us all." Beatrice dabbed at her eyes with her handkerchief. "Your father had such high hopes for him. A tragic shame, that's what it is." A gnarled finger raised itself into the air, and the matriarch's eyes grew wide. "I have it."

"Have what?" Ronnie asked hesitantly, certain she wouldn't like the answer.

"The perfect way to pass on Tommy's legacy. He always did enjoy his time in college. You can set up a scholarship in his name." A self-satisfied smile formed on the older woman's face. "Yes, that would be the perfect way to honor him."

"We can talk about that some other time, Mother."

"There's nothing to talk about," Beatrice said firmly.

"I think I'd better go see if everything's all right in the kitchen." Ronnie took a half-step back in preparation of a quick escape.

"Nonsense. I'm sure Maria can handle anything that comes up," Beatrice said dismissively. "Why don't you go find your sister?"

"That sounds like a good idea, Mother. Be right back." Ronnie turned and moved through the crowd as quickly as she could.

"...Bullshit, John. I told you to sell when they were at forty-eight and an eighth. It's not my fault you didn't do it." People quickly moved away from the two angry men, forming a circle.

"You're my broker. You're supposed to take care of these things for me. Do you have any idea how much money I lost?"

"You knew they were talking merger." Ronnie broke through the circle at that moment. "If you don't act fast, you lose out."

"Like Sally Ryan?" The executive took a deep breath. Old girlfriend's names were never a good sign.

"You knew she didn't have a date for the dance. It's not my fault I asked her out before you."

"You knew I wanted to go out with her. She was all I talked about all year."

Ronnie knew this was going to quickly escalate into a classic Cartwright scuffle. She stepped between the fighting brothers. "ENOUGH! You're supposed to be mourning Tommy's death, not fighting over some girl you lost fifteen years ago." An intense throbbing began behind her eyes, the sign of a relative headache. "John, you're not in high school anymore. Build a bridge and get over it." The men exchanged foul looks and stormed off in different directions. A murmur of words, then everyone else returned to their previous conversations. Ronnie ran her fingers through her hair forcefully.

"You okay?" a soft voice from behind her asked.

"Yeah." She turned to see familiar green eyes looking up at her with concern. "Really, Rose. I'm fine."

"Just making sure. I heard you yell."

"Just a typical Cartwright get-together," Ronnie sputtered. She caught a flash of orange-red out of the corner of her eye. "Uh-oh." Susan and her mother were approaching fast. "I see Mother found you," she said once her sister was within earshot.

"I told you she hadn't left yet," Beatrice said. The look in Susan's eyes made it clear she wished she hadn't been found. *Oh boy, this is gonna be a good one,* Ronnie thought to herself. "I was just telling your sister that I want to go through Tommy's things. I assume you still have boxes up in the attic."

"What, from when he lived here? He took what he wanted, and I threw out the rest."

"But there were trophies and ribbons and awards...."

"If he didn't take them, they're gone."

"And it never occurred to you that I might want those things?" Beatrice stood directly in front of her eldest child. "How could you be so inconsiderate?"

"Mother!" Susan exclaimed. Rose stood there quietly, her attention focused on the twitching of muscle in Ronnie's jaw.

"Tomorrow I'll go over to his apartment and see if he kept anything."

"Don't bother. Your sister will take me over and I'll look for myself." The sisters exchanged glances. Susan shrugged her shoulders. This was the first she was hearing of it, as well.

"I think you should wait a few days, Mother. His belongings aren't going anywhere." Ronnie was worried about what they would find there.

"Nonsense. Tomorrow will be fine."

"I don't think tomorrow–"

"Veronica Louise!" The twitching became a solid clench. Rose moved closer to her friend and discreetly placed her fingertips against Ronnie's back. The muscles were bunched and tight, another indication of Ronnie's tension. She pressed slightly and began rubbing in small circles.

"Fine, Mother. Susan and I will take you there tomorrow." *Great, now I have to go over there tonight and check things out.* She leaned almost imperceptibly into the gentle touch of Rose's fingers.

"Honestly, I don't know why you make things so difficult, Ronnie. On this day of all days, you have to be stubborn." Beatrice dabbed at dry eyes with her handkerchief. "I ask a simple thing. I just want something to remember my son by, and you have to be difficult."

"Mother...."

"No, Susan. I asked one simple thing of her. Just because she couldn't get along with her brother is no excuse for upsetting me."

Ronnie's back was now a solid band of tension, and it took her a moment before she could relax her jaw enough to speak. The gentle circling motion on her back increased in pressure. *You think I'm about to lose it, don't you?* She cast a sideways glance at her companion. Seeing the look of understanding and support in those green eyes was enough to keep the sharp remark from passing through her lips. Instead she looked at her mother and nodded. "I didn't mean to upset you. I guess we're all still in shock." Ronnie knew she was caving in, but today was not the day to make a stand with her mother. "I'd better go check on things. Excuse me."

Ronnie entered the kitchen, pleased to see that the only person there was Maria. She walked to the refrigerator and pulled out a bottle of water. She took a long swallow before speaking to her housekeeper. "Do you have any aspirin? I have a pounding headache, and I really don't want to go out there again."

"Been talking to your mother again, haven't you?" Maria opened a drawer and pulled out her purse. "I'm sure there's some Tylenol or Motrin in here."

"Sorry," Susan said as she entered. "She's in rare form today." The two sisters stood near the end of the island. Maria found something to do in the laundry room, allowing the two women their privacy.

"When was the last time you were at his place?" Ronnie asked before tossing three pills into her mouth and taking several gulps of water.

"This one? I've never been there. Why would I go to his apartment?"

"We're going to have to go there, you know. Who knows what it looks like or what things he may have lying out." She put the bottle back into the fridge. "Can Jack keep an eye on the kids?"

"I'm sure he can." Susan looked at her watch. "We're going to be leaving in a few minutes. You want to meet at Tommy's place around six or seven?"

"Seven would be better. Who knows how long everyone's going to stay?" Ronnie looked out the glass door at the cars that littered her driveway. "At least another hour or two."

"And then there's Mother."

"Oh, no." Ronnie shook her head. "You are not going to leave her here with me. When you go, she goes." She cast a glance at the living room. "Speaking of which, what's she up to?"

"I don't know. After you walked away, she kept going on and on until Rose asked her something about Tommy and his trophies. I saw that as my escape and took it." The redhead leaned in and spoke in a conspiratorial tone. "Personally, I don't think Rose is really interested in his trophies."

Ronnie smiled. "She isn't. She's trying to keep me from committing matricide."

"Did you want to bring her along tonight?" Susan offered.

"No. Hopefully, we won't be there long." She paused for a moment, then added, "It was nice of you to ask." She sighed and rapped her knuckles on the countertop. "I suppose I can't hide out here forever."

"I'll take Mother with us when we leave. You won't have to suffer much longer."

"How did I ever survive eighteen years with her?" Ronnie asked, shaking her head in bewilderment. "I can't get through one day without wanting to tell her off or wring her neck."

"Oh, that's easy," the redhead smiled. "I was there most of the time."

"That's right, you were." Ronnie tapped an elegant finger on her chin. "I remember you." She dodged a playful shove. "Weren't you the one who ran into Dad's car with your bike and blamed me?"

"Um...well, that was a long time ago, Ronnie. Weren't you the one who forgot to unlock your window one night and had to sneak back in through mine?"

"Ah, true." She wrapped her arm around her sister's shoulders. "But weren't you the one..." she began as they walked back into the living room.

Ronnie put the key in the lock. "What's that smell?" she asked, wrinkling her nose. Susan shrugged and pulled a scarf out of her pocketbook. The door opened, and Ronnie flipped the switch. "Son of a bitch," she breathed. Clothes were tossed everywhere, the couch cushions were on the floor, the coffee table and every other horizontal surface was covered with beer cans and trash. Stale beer and unwashed clothes mixed with another unidentifiable smell.

"Oh, my God," Susan said as she took in the scene. "This is disgusting."

"Sad is more like it," Ronnie muttered, picking up a small square mirror she found lying on the counter. The telltale razor blade was resting next to it. "It's a good thing we came here first." She showed her sister the mirror clouded with a fine white powder. "There's no way we can have Mother see this place looking the way it does." Susan nodded in agreement. Ronnie tossed the offensive mirror onto the counter and unzipped her jacket. "I guess we'd better look around for some boxes and trash bags for all this shit." To her surprise, the redhead who was averse to any kind of domestic work didn't argue.

"I'll put some music on," Susan said, kicking a path to the stereo. "Let's see, how does this one work?" She hit the power button and was immediately blasted with an insanely high decibel of noise.

"SHUT THAT THING OFF!" Ronnie yelled while covering her ears. A second later, there was peaceful quiet again.

"How could he stand listening to it that loud?"

"Damned if I know. Maybe the drugs affected his hearing. Come on, let's get to work. I want to get home at a decent hour." The kitchen shared a half-wall with the living room, allowing the two sisters to talk while packing up the garbage. Ronnie lifted the lid to the trash can in the corner. "Oh, God." She covered it up quickly. "I think I found out where that smell is coming from," she choked, taking a few steps back.

"I can't smell that anymore," Susan called from the far side of the living room. "All I smell is beer." She moved a cushion to find a half-eaten pizza glued to the carpet. "Oh, Ronnie, I don't want to touch this."

"I'll tell you what. I'll clean up whatever it is you're looking at if you get these dishes out of this...I guess you'd call it water." She reached closer with the tips of her fingers but just couldn't get herself to touch the slimy liquid. "I know I'm not touching it."

"We should have brought gloves." The redhead picked up an empty beer case and started throwing bottles into it. "So things are good between you and Rose?" she asked casually.

"We get along fine, yes." Ronnie arched an eyebrow. "Susan, I told you–"

"I know, I know. You're not lovers, you're just friends." The younger sister waved her hand dismissively. "I give up trying to figure it out." She put the case down and walked over to the counter that separated the living room and kitchen. "She gives me the same story you do, but you don't act like friends."

"We have a lot of work to do here, Susan."

"Ronnie, look at me." When she spoke again, her voice was softer. "I don't care. I've watched the way the two of you act around each other."

"And what do you see?"

"What do I see?" Susan gave a small smile. "I see you happy in a way that I never thought you would be." She laughed at her sister's blush. "Come on, you asked the question. Really, Ronnie, it's obvious to me that you're hooked on her. As for how Rose feels about you...she's not Chris."

"No, she's not. Rose has never asked me for anything. Whatever I've given her, it's because I wanted to."

"I see that," Susan replied. "You don't think I've been watching? You take more days off than you ever have and you don't go anywhere. I don't see any new cars, although I haven't seen your Porsche around. Did you sell it?"

"Yes." The truth was that as soon as it was repaired, she signed it over to Hans to sell at whatever price he could. "Rose doesn't want any cars or expensive things. She doesn't even have a driver's license. She's not trying to get anything from me."

"You don't have to defend her, Ronnie. I was just saying that I didn't see any of the things that would tell me that she was using you. I don't think she is. I like her."

"You like her?" Surprise showed on Ronnie's face. That was a rare admission from her younger sister. "Sooo...it's okay with you if we were...a couple?"

"I'm not going to pretend that I understand why you want to be with a woman. It doesn't make any sense to me." She raised her hand to keep her sister from speaking. "But it's your life. If Rose makes you happy, that's all that matters. So, yes, it's okay with me if you're a couple." She watched Ronnie come from behind the counter and happily accepted the hug. "It's your life, Sis. If Rose is the one for you, don't let anyone keep you apart," she whispered into the dark hair.

Ronnie pulled back until they were arm's length apart. "What made you change your mind? I remember you calling her everything but a reincarnation of Christine."

"I was wrong," Susan shrugged. "Hey, it happens." She brushed her hands together. "Enough of this sensitive chat. We have work to do here. You wanna try and get the stereo to a volume that doesn't shatter glass?"

"Sure." Ronnie worked her way across the room, the smile never leaving her face.

Chapter Twenty-one

"She said that?"

"Yup...oof."

"Oops, sorry about that." Rose moved her elbows from Ronnie's chest and lay down, her arms crossed over the older woman's left breast. She rested her chin atop her interlaced fingers. "So she really said she likes me?"

"She said she likes you." Ronnie smiled in the dark, letting her hand gently rub the smaller woman's back. She continued to stare at the ceiling. "See? You've won over the Cartwright women."

"Not all of them."

"Honey, even I haven't won over my mother yet. I think you'll just have to accept that two out of three ain't bad."

"Well...." Rose crept up until their faces were even, gold and black hair mixing about their shoulders. "There's really only one Cartwright's opinion that matters to me." Ronnie's eyes closed as soft lips pressed against her own. "And right now that Cartwright needs to get some sleep." Despite her words, Rose couldn't resist dropping down for a longer kiss. "Mmm, sometimes I wonder if I'm really Cinderella and you're holding the glass slipper."

"If I was, that would make me a very lucky woman," Ronnie replied.

"I'll never understand what made someone like you take a chance on someone like me." Rose shifted most of her weight onto the bed and claimed Ronnie's shoulder as her pillow. "Sometimes I'm afraid that this is all some wonderful dream and I'm going to wake up and find you gone." She felt Ronnie's arms tighten protectively around her.

"I'll never let that happen, Rose. I won't ever let you go back to the way you used to live."

"That doesn't scare me." She nuzzled deeper into Ronnie's shoulder.

"Then what does?" Ronnie asked softly.

"Losing you," she quietly admitted. "All the money and possessions in the world don't mean a thing to me without you."

"I love you, too," Ronnie whispered, lifting her head up long enough to place a kiss on the top of Rose's head. They snuggled together, bumping legs until they found a comfortable position. Ronnie continued to stroke the reddish-blonde hair until sleep finally overtook them.

The clock read just past six when the call of nature pulled Rose from her slumber. Sleepy green eyes opened and focused on the woman sleeping beneath her. It took a few minutes to extricate herself from the human puzzle they had formed during the night. After a quick trip to the bathroom, Rose went to the kitchen and started a pot of coffee. She was pouring the steaming liquid into two mugs by the time Ronnie padded into the room. "Good morning. I thought you'd like some coffee."

"Mmm, yes, thanks." The tall woman walked over and wrapped her arms around Rose from behind. "Good morning, hon." She pressed her lips to the top of the young woman's head. "I've got to pick up Mother in a couple of hours."

"Then you definitely need your coffee," Rose said, handing over the two mugs. "And if you're going to kiss me good morning, do it right."

"Mmm, morning breath. No kisses until after I brush my teeth."

"I'll take my chances."

"Really?" An eyebrow raised slightly as she set the mugs down. Turning around, she took first one crutch, then the other and put them to the side before gathering Rose in her arms. "So you want a good morning kiss, hmm?" She lowered her head and poured all of her love into a series of soft kisses. Her lips nipped and coaxed until she felt the young woman's mouth open for her. Ronnie swallowed soft moans as her tongue explored the inside of Rose's mouth. *Oh, yeah, you like that, don't you?* To her utter surprise, she felt a very insistent tongue pushing into her own mouth. Now it was the executive's turn to moan. When they broke apart, both women had to take a few seconds to get their breathing under control. "How's that?" she asked in a husky voice. "Does that meet with your approval for a morning kiss, hmm?"

"Very nice." Rose leaned up for another quick brushing of lips before reaching for her crutches. *Kiss me like that every morning, and I'll be happy forever.* She reluctantly pulled back, her whole body screaming for more contact with the tall woman. "You'd better drink your coffee before it gets cold."

Ronnie looked at the clock. "I'd much rather spend the day with you, you know." The phone ringing drew a frown from the executive. "I'll get it. With my luck, it's probably Susan trying to duck out of dealing with Mother today. Cartwright residence...Yeah, good morning to you, too, Sis. What's up?" Rose watched as dark eyebrows furrowed in puzzlement. "Mmm hmm, she's awake...no, we just got up and were having coffee." Now the eyebrows shot up and blue eyes locked with green. "Well...sure, that sounds fine to me. Let me ask her, hold on." Ronnie held the phone to her chest. "Susan wants to know if you'd like to go out for breakfast."

"Uh, sure." It would be the first time that she'd gone out of the house with the exception of doctor's appointments and the funeral. She watched as a beaming smile came over Ronnie's face.

"Sure, sounds good, Susan." They finalized arrangements while Rose sipped her coffee. By the time Ronnie hung up the phone, her own coffee had cooled enough to drink in four long gulps. "We should get going here. We're supposed to meet in forty-five minutes. I'll run upstairs and get ready." She picked up Rose's now empty cup and set it with hers in the sink. "Do me a favor?"

"Anything."

"Wear that rust-colored shirt." A shy smile came to Ronnie's lips. "I think you look really nice in it."

"I don't think any of the skirts go with it."

"The khaki pants do. I think the leg is wide enough to get over the cast."

Rose smiled. When she had opened those clothes on Christmas, she had thought then that they'd go well together. She also knew that Ronnie had a weakness for that particular shirt. "Sure, but it'll cost you."

"Cost me?" Puzzlement turned to amusement when she saw the calculating grin on the young woman's face.

"You have to wear that red cotton shirt and those black jeans."

"The baggy ones or the tight ones?"

"The tight ones." Rose realized how it could be taken and blushed. "I just think they look good on you," she mumbled, looking away as her ears turned an even brighter shade of red.

"Uh-huh," Ronnie smirked. "You're cute when you blush, you know."

"You've told me that before."

"It's still true." She walked over to the table and knelt down until she was eye level with Rose. "Actually, the truth is, you're beautiful anytime—with or without a blush." She leaned in and gave Rose a peck on the cheek. "Come on, I'm starving."

"Can I get you ladies something to drink to start off?" the waitress asked. The three women were sitting in a booth, Susan by herself on one side. Rose opened her mouth, but before she could utter a sound, Ronnie spoke. "Coffees on this side, and she'll have tea...lemon, no cream. We'll be ready to order when you return."

"I'll be right back with your drinks."

"Do you know what you want?" Ronnie asked without looking up from her menu. It took a gentle nudge under the table for Rose to figure out that the question was directed at her.

"Um...." Green eyes scanned the menu, noting with great alarm the prices that ran down the right side. *Seven fifty for two eggs and toast? Two ninety-five for coffee?* Her appetite shrank in direct proportion to the prices. "I'm not really all that hungry. Maybe just a muffin and coffee."

"Oh, no, Rose," Susan said. "You have got to try their eggs Benedict. They're the best in Albany, I swear."

"No, I'll be fine with the muffin, I'm sure." She knew without looking that she was the recipient of a questioning gaze from Ronnie. *Maybe she'll forget that my stomach grumbled earlier.* The waitress returned with their drinks and looked expectantly at Ronnie.

With a nod of her head, she indicated Rose. "She'll have two eggs over medium with toast, bacon, and home fries. I'll have the same except I want my eggs over hard. Susan?"

"I'll have the eggs Benedict."

"All right, I'll have your food brought out to you shortly."

Rose looked at Ronnie dumbfounded. "I said I was fine with a muffin."

"Susan, would you excuse us for a moment, please?"

"Sure, Ronnie. Actually, I think I need to make a trip to the ladies' room." She picked up her purse and left the table.

"Why did you do that?" There was no accusation in the young woman's tone, just curiosity.

"Why did you lie about not being hungry?" Ronnie countered. "Look at me. Tell me you only wanted a muffin and that the cost had nothing to do with it." Her right hand slipped under the table and began stroking Rose's left thigh. "I understand that you think about how much everything costs. I wish you didn't, but I know you do. I also know that I wasn't going to sit here and let you watch us eat a nice breakfast when I know you're hungry." A smaller hand gripped hers under the table and squeezed.

"Okay, thank you." Rose leaned closer. "Bacon and eggs sounds wonderful."

A short time later, Rose was wiping up her plate with the last bit of toast while the two sisters talked.

Ronnie looked at her watch. "We'd better get going here."

"Wait." Susan laid her hand across the table, urging her sister to remain where she was. The redhead looked at Rose with such seriousness that it made the young woman's pulse quicken with nervousness. "I just wanted to say something to you before we leave." She licked her lips and cast a quick glance at her older sister before continuing. "Rose, I love my sister very much. With Tommy gone, well...it just helped make me realize that I was being selfish to her. I've never seen her happier than when she's with you."

"Susan, don't embarrass me," Ronnie warned playfully, although the heat was rising to her ears.

"You be quiet or I'll tell her about the time you took Dad's car for a joyride and got picked up by the police," the redhead warned. "Now as I was saying before I was so rudely interrupted, she's happy, and that's what's important." She picked up the bill and glanced at it before passing it across the table to her sister. "Your turn. Seven ninety-eight for the tip."

"Thanks, you know I hate figuring that out."

A few minutes later, the bill was paid, and they were standing next to their vehicles, which were parked next to each other.

"I have to drop Rose off, then I'll meet you at Mother's," Ronnie said as she shut off the alarm and unlocked the passenger door.

"Okay, don't be too long." The redhead turned toward Rose. "It was nice of you to join us for breakfast."

"Thank you for inviting me," the young woman replied. "And thank you for what you said in there...about her deserving to be happy."

"Yeah, yeah, everybody's happy," Ronnie said with a fake growl. "Except Mother, who's going to have a fit if we don't get over there."

"I was being serious," Rose said, batting the tall woman's arm.

"So was I." She looked at her younger sister. "Susan, I do appreciate what you said in there...as well as last night."

"Think they'll say anything if two sisters hugged in public?"

"Do you really care if they did?" Ronnie countered. They embraced, then to Rose's surprise, Susan gave her a quick one-armed hug. They said their goodbyes and were soon on the road.

After being dropped off at the house, Rose found herself with nothing to do. Ronnie was certain not to be back until mid-afternoon. She puttered about, wandering in and out of every room on the first floor. Then her eyes followed the stairs. Curiosity got the better of her, and she positioned her crutches on the bottom stair.

Although she had been in Ronnie's bedroom before, this was the first time she really looked around. *This is big enough for an entire apartment.* A padded bench seat sat below an impressive bay window. An open door off to the side led to the private bathroom, and the young woman made a mental note to check it out later. Rose saw that her friend had not one but two dressers, as well as the incredible walk-in closet. A full-length mirror trimmed in matching wood stood in one corner. The king-size bed was complemented by a headrest, complete with lights and shelves, as well as nightstands on either side. On the wall opposite the bed was a smaller version of the entertainment center downstairs. Rose opened the doors to reveal a twenty-seven-inch television, as well as Ronnie's DVD collection. Her eyes skimmed over familiar titles, looking for something interesting to watch. One row caught her eye, and she picked one up and looked at the title. *Oh, Ronnie, I didn't know you had these kinds of movies.* She grinned and put one in the DVD player. *Well, this should be interesting.* She positioned the pillows on the bed and sat down to watch her first adult movie.

To her surprise, there actually was a plot. Rose didn't pay attention to the title but figured out quickly that it was about two female lovers in prison who are separated into different cells by a mean warden. The first sex scene appeared quickly, and green eyes widened at the sight of the two naked women kissing each other. It was the same slow, gentle kisses that she shared with Ronnie. Then their kisses changed, becoming more passionate, and one woman began to moan as the other pinched her nipple. Suddenly, Rose's dreams had another dimension added to them as she tried to imagine Ronnie making the same sound. "Mmm...." She watched the two women begin their acts of pleasure, and each one she imagined doing with her companion. The arousal was immediate, but more than that was another feeling, one far more important. The women on the screen made Rose realize that it was more than a physical act. Even though they were actresses playing a role, every touch was tender, loving. Between the moans and cries were repeated declarations of love for each other. *That's why they call it making love,* she realized for perhaps the first time. Now she understood what she was denying Ronnie...and what Ronnie was denying herself by honoring her promise to her father. Rose shut the DVD player off and stared at the blue screen for several long minutes while the final pieces of the puzzle fell into place.

"Did you try the spare ribs?" Ronnie asked, smacking her lips in satisfaction. "I tell you, there's nothing like good Chinese takeout."

"No, I haven't tried them yet," Rose replied quietly, her eyes never leaving her plate, the contents of which were being pushed around aimlessly by her fork.

"You should. The egg rolls are pretty good, too. Not greasy at all."

"Um hmm." The broccoli and pork suffered more rearranging.

"Rose, is something wrong? You've been quiet ever since I arrived home."

"Ronnie, can I ask you something?"

"Anything, you know that."

"If you never made that promise to your father...if nothing was standing in your way...would you want...." Rose shook her head and looked up with fear and uncertainty in her eyes. "Would we be lovers?"

Ronnie stood up. "I think we're done eating. Let's go into the other room and talk. I'll take care of the dishes later."

"Yes, that would be better," Rose agreed, pushing herself up on her good foot. *Yes, you and I curled up together....* "Ronnie? Would it be all right if we just went into the bedroom? I mean, we can always watch television in there, right?"

The warning bells and whistles went off in Ronnie's head, and she swallowed reflexively. "Uh...are you sure?" Considering the topic of discussion, she wasn't entirely certain that lying on the bed together was a wise idea.

"Yes." And with that word spoken aloud, Rose realized that yes, she really was sure...about everything.

"You want to change first?" Ronnie asked while turning down the covers.

"No, we're fine just the way we are." She leaned her crutches against the wall and patiently balanced herself on one foot. Once the bedcovers were ready, she slipped between them and rolled onto her side to face the woman who had captured her heart. Ronnie started to join her. "Wait." Rose reached over and turned on the lamp. "Would you shut off the light?" Soon the brightness was replaced by a warm, soft glow.

"So we're in bed and you wanted to talk," Ronnie offered when she was settled.

"So we are," Rose agreed. Leaning up on one elbow, she looked down at endless blue eyes. "Are you going to answer my question? If you hadn't made that promise to your father, would we be lovers?"

"I thought you weren't sure...."

"Forget about that for a minute." Rose reached out and ran her fingertip lightly down the older woman's jaw. "If it were just you and me, nothing else." Ronnie was still wearing her red shirt, and with three buttons undone, the vision was entirely too tempting. Her fingertip moved down the chiseled jaw to the long throat and beyond, stopping only when it encountered the lacy edge of a bra. She did note with some pleasure that Ronnie's breathing had increased.

"Rose, I love you. You know that." Ronnie reached out and cupped her cheek. "If there were no obstacles, if it really was just you and me, yes. I would be very honored to be your lover." She was rewarded with a quick kiss. The curious fingertips were driving her crazy, but she couldn't find the strength to stop them.

"Ronnie...." The distracting digits slowly undid the next button on the red shirt. "It's just you and me. There are no obstacles."

"Rose...." Her body responded immediately to her shirt being unbuttoned. Nipples hardened under the white bra, and her whole body tingled with excitement. She opened her mouth to protest and found a warm, soft tongue pressing against hers. "Mmm." Under the gentle insistence, Ronnie relaxed and let the young woman take control. Rose felt the surrender and eased up the pressure of her lips. Her free hand traveled on its own volition, gliding under the cotton shirt and against warm skin. In a move that shocked both of them, the wandering hand closed over the soft lace cup and squeezed gently.

"Mmm."

"You like that," Rose observed, giving the firm mound another squeeze and enjoying the immediate reaction. Leaving her hand where it was, she lowered her head until her lips were against her lover's ear. "Ronnie," she husked. "I love you, and I want to make love with you." She accented her statement by suckling a willing earlobe, then working her way up to Ronnie's mouth, sliding her left leg between the longer ones.

"Rose...." She reached out with every intention of stopping this before it went too far, but instead of her body obeying her mind, her hand closed around Rose's, encouraging further exploration. Ronnie was on fire, and she struggled to find a reason to resist. "W-we shouldn't."

"Why?" Rose pulled her hand out from under the cotton shirt and looked at Ronnie with all seriousness. "Tell me why we should keep denying this to ourselves."

"I promised–" Fingers pressed against the full lips.

"No." There was a quiet anger in Rose's voice. "No, Ronnie. You can promise many things, but giving up your happiness forever is not one of them." She gently traced one defined black eyebrow. "You can't promise to give up my happiness either." Green eyes fluttered down to study full lips before traveling back up to become lost in endless pools of blue. Ronnie didn't move, still struggling with her inner demons. Propped on her right elbow, Rose used her left hand to undo her blouse, gravity causing it to expose more and more flesh as each button was undone. She smiled at the intense look in Ronnie's eyes. Once the rust-colored shirt was hanging loose, Rose took the larger hand in her own and brought it to the area covered by her beige silk. "No, don't fight it," she whispered when she felt Ronnie's resistance. She pressed her breast against the warm hand and groaned when she felt the tentative squeeze.

Rose's limited experience hadn't prepared her for the jolt that Ronnie's touch brought her. Another squeeze and now she was sure that she would simply die without Ronnie's caress. She felt herself being pushed back onto the bed and didn't resist. Dark tresses tickled her face, and the tongue seeking entrance to her mouth was insistent. *Nothing can feel better than this,* she thought to herself wistfully as she returned the kiss with equal gusto.

"I love you," Ronnie breathed as the kiss finally ended. She was propped up on her elbow, her body half on top of the smaller woman. She felt Rose trying to tug her shirt out of the jeans. "Wait." Rolling up to her knees, she unbuttoned and unzipped her pants. She undid the last button on her shirt and slowly pulled the tails out. It now hung loosely on her body, open enough to show a glimpse of her bra beneath. With a slowness that was torture to the young woman's nervous system, Ronnie slid the shirt off her shoulders, letting it pool on the bed behind her. "This too?" she asked, fingering the front catch of her bra.

"Please," Rose begged. Her lover smiled at the urgency in her voice. A quick twist and the cups fell apart. The bra landed on top of the shirt, and for several seconds, neither woman spoke. Rose's eyes were taking in the most beautiful sight she'd ever seen, and she said so with the look on her face. "Kiss me again."

Oh, yes, this is so much better, Rose thought to herself as her hands traveled over the bare skin of Ronnie's back. She was acutely aware of the places where her shirt was open and their skin touched. They shared a series of lazy kisses until she felt a restless hand trying to push her shirt off. "Yes," she agreed, trying to take it off while still lying on her back.

"Please...let me." Rose nodded and let herself be pulled into a sitting position. Her shirt was tossed against the leather chair in Ronnie's quest to get it out of her way. The beige bra ended up on the floor. She lowered herself back to the bed, but her lover remained where she was. Hearts pounded and bodies pulsed as they stared at each other's breasts openly. Where her own areola was a light pink, Ronnie's was darker, almost brown. Rose looked down and was surprised to see her nipples standing out like little erasers, the skin around starting to pucker. *Even the coldest day doesn't make them stand up like that,* she mused as she looked back to see her lover's nipples doing the same thing.

"You...are...beautiful," Ronnie husked. She lowered herself down, and slowly—far too slowly—bare skin touched bare skin. Both groaned softly and smiled in recognition of the mutual pleasure. Long fingers sank into golden hair while smaller ones wrapped around a muscled back. Their mouths played a game of give and take, tongues dancing back and forth as they floated in each other's love.

Rose gasped when Ronnie's lips moved down to her throat. "Oh...oh, yes, that's nice." Her hands came up and clasped Ronnie's head. She felt the lips part and the soft tongue lick her skin. "Yes, Ronnie...mmm, that feels so good."

"Yesss." The older woman's body was pressing against hers, betraying the rising passion. Rose let her right hand drift down Ronnie's back until she reached the waistband of the black jeans. Since they were still undone, there was plenty of room for her to slip inside. As she gripped the firm cheek, her lover whimpered against her skin and began sucking her neck in earnest. "Rose...."

"Yes, Ronnie...that feels so good." She squeezed harder and was rewarded with renewed squirming.

"You're going to drive me crazy, you know that?" Ronnie said breathlessly as she reclaimed Rose's lips with her own. Nostrils flared with ragged breaths as they kissed passionately. "I can't concentrate when you do that," Ronnie admitted as she shifted her ass away from the distracting caresses. She nudged the smaller legs apart with one of her own, settling so her lips were even with the young woman's breasts. Long black hair formed a soft canopy that tickled as it moved over the fair skin.

"But...." Whatever Rose was going to say was lost when she felt a kiss on the underside of her breast. Ronnie answered with a muffled moan and continued to lick and nibble the soft flesh. "Feels so good...." *Oh, this is heaven. Nothing can feel better than this.* Rose felt warm breath on her nipple an instant before a wet tongue rolled over it. "Oh, Ronnie, yesss...."

Fumbling attempts with teenage boys never prepared Rose for the sensation of being lovingly suckled. The pulling sensation was answered with a pulsing deep between her legs, and her hips moved of their own volition. Her hands were buried deep in the dark hair, and Rose was torn between holding Ronnie where she was and begging her to give the other one the same attention. Before she could decide, the loving tongue and lips released their treasure. "Oh, don't stop...."

"I'm not stopping." Using her arms on either side of the young woman's body to brace herself, she leaned down for a kiss. "I love you, Rose."

"I love you." As their mouths continued to give and take, small hands worked their way between warm bodies and cupped two willing mounds of flesh. Ronnie's moan vibrated through their lips, and Rose answered with one of her own. Her fingers became more focused, moving in smaller circles until they were stroking the hardened tips.

"Oh, honey," Ronnie gasped. "Y-you can't...unggh...do that." She rocked back out of reach and shook her head. "I told you I can't concentrate when you do that."

"It feels so nice." Rose reached out only to have her hands stopped by larger, more powerful ones.

"Yes, it does," the older woman agreed. She kissed each knuckle, then the palms before releasing the small hands.

"I want...." *How do I say this without sounding crude?* "I want...." She wrapped her arms around Ronnie's torso and pulled herself up, ducking her head in time to bring her mouth to its goal.

"Oh, God, Rose!" Strong hands held her in place, and the young woman happily ran her tongue over the darkened areola.

"Oh, that's nice," Rose purred, licking the puckered skin again. Strong but gentle hands pushed her back onto the bed. Ronnie quickly covered her and began planting a series of kisses down her neck.

"Let...me...show...you...how nice...my Rose."

Rose couldn't stop moaning. Ronnie's mouth and hands were in constant motion on her breasts. Her hands clasped and unclasped the dark hair, and her hips were thrusting against the other woman's torso. "Ronnieeee...." She looked down to see the mouth loving her breast. "You feel...oh, God, keep doing that...." Her breathing quickened, and her hips pressed up hard against Ronnie. Her lover answered with a downward thrust against her thigh, making both acutely aware of their own wetness. "Please...I need...." Rose tried to reach between their bodies for the button to her pants.

"Yesss...." Ronnie took over the task, releasing the breast she was suckling and rising up to give herself room. Long fingers made quick work of the button and zipper, but instead of removing them, Ronnie settled back down, lying sideways over Rose to allow her right hand to slip between khakis and white cotton panties.

"Oh, yes, yes!" Rose cried as two fingers pressed against her most sensitive area. She cupped Ronnie's face and pulled her up for a heated kiss. Her rocking hips caused slack in the material, giving more room for fingers to explore. They moved under the elastic, then retreated, alternating soft brushes with firm rubs. Rose was rising fast, faster than she had ever known, and it scared her. She buried her head in the dark hair and clung tightly. "Ronnie...." The fingers changed direction, rubbing the cotton in a circular motion against her clit. Rose whimpered and jerked her hips frantically. "I can't...oh, Ronnie...please...I...."

"Shh...I've got you...."

"Ronnie...oooh...." Her hands clutched desperately at her lover's shoulders. "Please...harder...oh...yes, Ronnie, yes...." Warm breath caressed her ear.

"Rose, I love you."

"Yesss." A pounding started deep within and gained momentum as it spread outward.

"My precious Rose, you're close, I can feel it." The pressure and rhythm increased.

"Yes...harder...ooh...." Teeth clenched, Rose teetered on the edge for an agonizing length of time. Then one long finger snaked under the soaked panties and slipped between her swollen folds. Once, twice, three times across her clit, and the world exploded. "Ronnieeeee....ah," Rose cried out as the orgasm crashed over her, robbing all reason and sense. A husky voice murmured words that she didn't understand into her ear, and she was vaguely aware of being rocked gently, but reality was a plane far, far away from her at that moment. She felt her body go limp and trusted the strong arms around it to protect her as she drifted off in the afterglow.

Long minutes later, Rose found the strength to raise her head and look into loving eyes of blue. "I love you."

"Mmm, I love you, too," Ronnie said, sealing her words with a kiss.

Rose nuzzled deeper into her lover's embrace. "I could just stay like this forever."

Ronnie was deliriously happy and content to spend the rest of the evening cuddling despite not having found her own release yet. All that mattered to her was the gentle woman in her arms. Minutes ticked by before the reddish-blonde head lifted again. "You okay?"

"Terrific," Rose replied, kissing the bare flesh near her lips. "You are wonderful."

"I aim to please."

"Mmm, good aim."

"Did I tell you that I love you?"

"Once or twice, tell me again." Rose flashed a brilliant smile that Ronnie felt the need to reward with a series of kisses.

"I...love...you...with...all...my...heart." Unable to resist, Ronnie deepened the kiss, rolling them over so she was on top. But when she began to kiss a line down the smaller woman's throat, she was stopped by insistent hands. She lifted up, and the hands moved to claim her breasts. Understanding the unspoken request, Ronnie locked her elbows to hold herself above her lover's body. She had forgotten how sensitive her nipples were until she felt Rose's palms rub across them. She moaned and arched into the touch.

"You like this," the young woman observed.

"Very...." The hands moved, and Ronnie now found her nipples being brushed by inquisitive thumbs. "Very much." She felt Rose's forefingers join and begin squeezing in a pumping motion. She tried to watch, but it felt too good, and her eyes refused to stay open. "Yes, Rose, that's it...nice and gentle...mmm."

"Ronnie...." The small hands left her breasts and gently urged her forward. Taking the hint when she saw the pink tongue dart out and wet lips in anticipation, Ronnie straddled Rose's body and leaned forward until her breasts were swaying just above the waiting mouth. This time, she forced herself to watch. Her eyes moved from golden hair and fair skin to russet eyebrows framing green eyes. The path continued, past the soft cheekbones and upturned nose to the soft lips and loving tongue providing relief to her aching nipple. As if what her eyes were showing her wasn't enough, Ronnie's ears were treated to the pleasure of constant mmms from Rose, and hands that had been casually touching her body now slipped under the waistband of her jeans.

"Let me...ooh...take them off. I need to take them off." She regretted her request when she felt the warm mouth leave her sensitive flesh.

"Yes," Rose agreed, trying to push the black material down.

"I'll get it." Rolling off her lover, Ronnie quickly shucked her jeans and panties. Before she could return to her previous position, she found herself pinned down by her small but insistent lover. Soft lips and an even softer tongue reclaimed her breast while a khaki-covered thigh slipped between her legs. The coarse material rubbed against an already swollen clit, and Ronnie cried out at the contact.

"Did I hurt you?" Rose asked, her eyes fearful.

"No." She reached out and stroked the young woman's cheek, gently urging her to resume her task. "No, honey, you didn't hurt me. Please...just keep doing..." Ronnie sighed as the warm tongue caressed her breast again, "...what you're doing." She spread her legs wider, and the shift caused her thigh to press up between Rose's legs. The mmms were interrupted by what Ronnie considered to be a very cute squeak, and she repeated the motion, earning a deep groan and a return thrust. Ronnie's long fingers easily slid under the khakis and panties to grip soft round flesh.

"Oh, Ronnie...."

"Take these off, Rose." Her fingers crept lower until they brushed over wet curls. "Let me touch you." An emphatic nod was all Ronnie needed to roll them over. As she worked the material over the cast, a flicker of guilt tried to slip in, but love quickly shut it out. Her eyes traveled upward, her pulse quickening at the wet spot visible in the crotch of Rose's panties. Reddish curls peeked out, teasing with a hint of what was hidden. Wresting away from the temptation, Ronnie gazed upon the firm abdomen, perfect breasts, the look of desire and passion on her beloved's face. "You are so beautiful," she whispered reverently. Hooking her fingers under the waistband, she removed the last barrier before gathering Rose up in her arms.

For long minutes, they cuddled together, exchanging kisses and gentle touches while becoming used to touching and being touched. It was Ronnie who took the first step, moving her hand down and running her fingers through reddish tufts. "You like that?" she murmured, her lips a hairsbreadth away from Rose's ear.

"Mmm, that's nice. I want to touch you, too."

"I'd like that," Ronnie admitted, shifting them until they were lying side by side. She had to scoot up slightly to accommodate Rose's shorter reach, but soon fingers were playing in both light and dark curls. "You're soft, like a kitten," Ronnie said. Her middle finger moved lower, wetting itself on slick folds. Bringing it up to her mouth, Ronnie licked the sweet essence. "Mmm....oh!" She was taken by surprise when Rose's finger not only touched her nether lips, but dipped between them, brushing against her clitoris. Her hand shot down and gripped the small wrist. "Please...." Using her longer fingers to guide, she took two of Rose's fingers and pressed them against her center. "Ah...oh, yes." Ronnie raised her knee and opened herself up to her lover. "Rose, please...." She pressed the smaller fingers against her in a circular motion. She felt the slickness on her inner thighs and dimly noted that her own self-pleasuring never produced such a copious amount of fluid.

"I've got it," Rose said, leaning over and gently nudging the taller woman onto her back. With her head resting on Ronnie's breast, she noted the different textures under her fingertips. Soft and hard, wrinkled and smooth...and there was more just beyond the limits of her reach—a dark cavern that beckoned her to come explore its depths. "Ronnie...do you want me to...go inside?" The last words were spoken hesitantly, uncertain what her lover's limits were. The answering groan and hip rise spoke louder than words. Using her stomach as a pivot, Rose turned herself so her head was resting on Ronnie's stomach, giving her left hand plenty of room to move. Slowly, hesitantly, Rose pushed one finger in. She was amazed at the feeling of hot, wet muscle surrounding her finger. Ronnie's reaction was immediate, crying out and rising her hips off the bed.

"Yes, Rose, more...please, Rose...yesss." She put a second finger in, then a third. The transformation was amazing. The head of a major corporation was incapable of forming a complete sentence. Rose's name became a mantra on Ronnie's lips, combined with words such as "harder," "faster," "deeper," and the occasional "oh, fuck" just to round it out. Ronnie bucked beneath her, but she refused to let go of her prize. The feel of inner muscles squeezing her fingers excited Rose, and there was no doubt in her mind that her lover's voice was a good two octaves higher than normal. The metal bed frame squeaked with each thrust, and Ronnie's cries became more urgent. "Rose...."

"I'm right here." She turned her head and kissed the soft skin.

"I...Rose...." Ronnie's thighs trembled.

"Yes, Ronnie, yes." She felt the muscles surrounding her fingers tightening and began pumping as hard and fast as she could. Suddenly, she was caught in a grip too powerful to break as her lover's hips arched off the bed. "Yes...I love you, Ronnie."

"I...." Dark bangs stuck to the sweat-soaked forehead, and every word was torn from gritted teeth. "Love...you...oh, Rose...Rose, I, I...ohhh."

"Yes, Ronnie...yes." They rode it out together, Rose buried deep inside her lover. Only when the last spasm passed did she remove her fingers and snuggle up in Ronnie's arms.

"That's a pretty big smile you have on your face," Ronnie said when speech returned.

"I'm happy."

"Mmm." She kissed Rose's forehead. "I'm glad to hear it."

Cuddling up as close as she could, Rose rested her head on a broad shoulder. "Was it...what you expected?" *Did I really please you?*

"It was everything I wanted and more." Using her forefinger and thumb, she raised green eyes to meet hers. "How about you? This is your first time. How are you doing with this?"

Rose brought their lips together. "I feel very...very loved." She put her head back on Ronnie's shoulder. "Mmm, nice."

"Just nice?"

"More than nice." Rose scooted down and rested her head on her lover's abdomen. "I think I'll make this my new pillow." With the warmth of Ronnie against her, she let her eyes close.

Some moments in life are just simply perfect. For the new lovers, this was one of them. Relaxed...sated...simply enjoying the feel of each other's bodies. Ronnie's hand played over her lover's back, alternating between lazy figure eights and long sweeping passes from shoulders to hips. Rose returned the loving touch with one of her own, letting her fingers glide over a supple thigh. The tender caresses were nice, but arms could stay empty for only so long before the need grew too great. "Come here," Ronnie whispered, holding her arms out. Soon they were cuddled together, sharing soft kisses and gentle words of love. Eventually, the lamp was shut off, and sleep never claimed two happier women.

Chapter Twenty-two

Sleepy blue eyes opened to a curtain of gold. Ronnie smiled, enjoying the feel of the golden hair upon her face. She stretched in place, reveling in the feel of skin against skin. It was a wonderful feeling and one she had no wish to end soon. She glanced at the clock and groaned. She was torn between studying the sleeping woman and waking her up before Maria arrived. *I have the rest of our lives to watch you sleep.* "Rose...honey, time to wake up." A gentle shoulder shake...nothing. "Rose...Rose...." The sleeping lump groaned and burrowed under the covers. "No, no, no," Ronnie chuckled. Hooking her fingers on the edge of the blanket, she pulled it away to expose their naked bodies to the cool morning air. Rose's hand automatically reached out for the missing warmth only to be caught by Ronnie's larger one. "Good morning." She pulled the hand up to her lips and began kissing each knuckle. "I...love...you...Rose."

"Mmm, love you, too," the young woman replied, turning bleary green eyes up to look at her lover. "How about we sleep in today, hmm?"

"I'd love to, but Maria's going to be here soon." She ran her finger down the length of Rose's cheek. "I didn't wake up in time to call and tell her not to come," she apologized.

"It's okay. You didn't know that we would...." She blushed. "You know...."

"Make love?" Ronnie offered, rolling them over until she was lying on top of her lover. Her hair hung down, brushing against Rose's cheek. Unable to resist, she lowered her lips for a kiss. "I love you." She reluctantly pulled back. "But right now I have to pee...bad."

"Better make it quick 'cause I'll be right behind you," the young woman said, reaching out for her crutches.

When Rose returned from the bathroom, she discovered Ronnie half-dressed. Feeling a bit awkward with her own nakedness, she crossed over to her dresser and began pulling out clothes to wear. She sat down on the edge of the bed and reached for her panties. The next thing she knew, she was flat on her back with six feet of raw woman lying on top of her. "Do you have any idea how much I love you?" Ronnie husked, blue eyes darkened with emotion. Lips lowered and were met halfway by an equally eager pair. Soft moans of pleasure filled the air as the kiss deepened and tongues danced together. Rose's hands were happily playing across the broad expanse of back and had just slipped down to cup Ronnie's ass through her clothes when they heard the sound of Maria's car pull into the driveway. New lovers being what they were, the kiss didn't end until they heard the sound of the car door shutting. "I suppose we have to stop." Ronnie's tone made it clear that stopping was not what she truly wished to do.

"If we must," Rose replied, leaning up for one more quick kiss before her tall lover stood.

"Unless you want to give Maria an eyeful." Ronnie pulled a gray cotton T-shirt over her head and tucked it into the waistband of her sweats. "I'll go keep her company while you get dressed." Unable to resist, she stole one more sweet kiss before leaving the room.

"Good morning, Ronnie," the housekeeper said as she stepped inside and closed the sliding glass door. "It's cold out there this morning. I thought we'd seen the last of the snow this season."

"Oh, there'll probably be one more good storm to annoy us before spring arrives," Ronnie said, taking the daily paper from Maria's hands. At that moment, Tabitha ambled into the kitchen, looking for her morning meal. "Mrrow? Mrrow?"

"And where do you think you're going?" Ronnie asked as she scooped the feline up in her arms. "Hmm? What's that? You want sliced turkey for breakfast, did you say?" The answering purr and finger lick caused both women to laugh.

"That cat is so spoiled," Maria said as she headed for the laundry room to hang her coat up. "I know both of you slip pieces of meat under the table for her when you're eating. That's why it's so hard to keep her out of the kitchen."

"Oh, it has nothing to do with the scraps you 'accidentally' drop on the floor while you're cooking, right?"

"Good morning," Rose said as she entered the room. "Oh, Maria, I hope you're planning on making a hearty breakfast because I'm simply starving this morning. Morning, Tabitha." She stood directly in front of Ronnie and began stroking her cat, although her eyes never left the smile on her lover's face. "I hope you slept well," she whispered.

"The best. How about you?" Ronnie's voice carried the same soft tone that had soothed Rose after their lovemaking, and she reacted to it without thought, pressing her head against the taller woman's chest, drawing a startled squawk from Tabitha.

"Wonderful." She pulled back and petted the cat, turning the purr motor back on. "Wonderful and hungry."

"I'll have breakfast ready in about twenty minutes," Maria said without looking up from the eggs she was whisking. When she turned her back to begin making coffee, Ronnie took advantage to lean down and give Rose a gentle kiss. Tired of being squished between the lovers, Tabitha wormed her way free and padded to the living room. With the coffee now brewing, Maria turned to ask Ronnie a question but found herself speechless at the sight of the two women kissing. She looked away and resumed her cooking. After taking their seats, Ronnie pulled out the business section of the paper to read while Rose took the local.

When the coffee was ready, Maria filled two mugs and brought them to the table. "Here you go, Rose," she said sweetly.

"Thank you."

She set a yellow mug down in front of. A sable eyebrow raised at the unfamiliar cup, but before she could comment, Maria had already returned to the island to turn the eggs over. She exchanged a quizzical look with Rose before shrugging and returning to the stock market report.

A short while later, Maria returned to the table with two plates. Ronnie's plate contained a small cheese omelet and toast while Rose's was laden down with a stuffed omelet, a slice of fresh melon, and toast with grape jelly.

"Thank you, Maria. You know exactly how I like it." The young woman beamed, earning a smile from the housekeeper.

"Yes, I do. Now if you ladies will excuse me, I do have to get going on the laundry." She took an empty basket from the laundry room and went to collect the dirty clothes. The lovers returned to their breakfast before a thought went through Rose's mind.

"Ronnie, she's gonna see the clothes tossed all over the room." Her face colored with embarrassment.

"I hope she checks under the bed. I think that's where your underwear ended up."

"Ronnie!" She swatted the muscled arm. "It's not funny."

"I know it's not," Ronnie said. "Come here." She moved her chair slightly and pulled Rose against her. "Honey, she's going to find out sooner or later."

"Think she'll be okay with it?"

"Of course. I've known Maria since I was a little kid. She knows how much you mean to me. I'm sure she'll be happy," Ronnie said confidently.

But the housekeeper was anything but happy. She returned with a basketful of dirty laundry just as the women were finishing their meal. "Ronnie, I need to speak with you," she said testily before going into the laundry room. The washer lid opened, then closed with a bang.

"What's going on?" Rose asked worriedly.

"I don't know, but I'll go find out." Ronnie threw her napkin down and entered the laundry room, shutting the door behind her.

"What's going on, Maria?"

"You know it would be a lot easier for me if I didn't have to look all over the place for your clothes."

"You wanted to talk to me about leaving my clothes on the floor? I've left them lying around before and you never got this upset." She stepped closer. "You were upset before breakfast. That mug isn't dirty, you gave me that ugly yellow thing on purpose. Why?"

"I'm not a fool, Veronica. I have eyes." Wrinkled hands held sweat socks in a death grip. "How could you do this?"

"I assume this has nothing to do with clothes. You're talking about Rose and me." The housekeeper didn't respond, merely continuing to torture the socks. "What's the problem, Maria? It's okay to be a lesbian as long as I don't act like one?" Her jaw tensed in anger. "Rose has been living here for over three months. You had to know that we were sleeping together."

"Sleeping, Ronnie, sleeping." Maria jerked the sheets out of the basket and stuffed them into the washer. "You certainly weren't 'sleeping' with Rose last night." She haphazardly tossed some detergent in and slammed the lid shut. "It's wrong, Veronica. Just plain wrong what you're doing to her."

"Why is it wrong to love her? Why is today any different than yesterday? Help me understand why you're so upset because right now I don't understand!" Ronnie slammed her hand on the dryer, the noise reverberating through the small room. "She isn't like Christine, Maria. This is Rose we're talking about."

"I know she's not like Christine, Ronnie. I never said she was. Rose is a sweet, kind, gentle woman who deserves all the best that life can give." She huffed over to the counter and began sorting clothes. "And this isn't about what sex you choose to sleep with. I just don't want to see her get hurt."

"Hurt?" She put her hands on the housekeeper's shoulders and turned the older woman to face her. "Maria, I love Rose. I would never hurt her."

"You don't think keeping the truth from her is going to hurt her?"

"And just what truth am I keeping from her?"

"I know about the accident...I saw the Porsche before Hans fixed it."

Ronnie leaned against the dryer, hoping her legs would keep her upright. "Oh, God," she whispered. She looked at her lifelong friend and housekeeper with panicked blue eyes. "Maria, you can't say anything. You can't tell her."

"Tell her?" The older woman ran her fingers through her short salt and pepper hair. "No, Ronnie, I won't tell her. I know my position well." She turned back to the pile of clothes. "Besides, it's not my place to say anything, it's yours." She paused for a moment. "Or are you going to just let her continue thinking you're her knight in shining armor?"

"I...I can't tell her. I can't lose her, Maria. I can't." Her voice hitched, and she had to look away. "I would give up everything to be with her, but I can't do that."

"Better she should go on believing that some drunk hit her and you came to her rescue than to admit that you were responsible." She paused, debating whether she really wanted to ask the next question or not. "Were you drunk?" At the lack of response, she turned, reading her answer in the tall woman's face. "Dear God, Veronica...you were."

Long dark hair formed a curtain as Ronnie lowered her head and nodded ashamedly. "It was snowing...I...I never saw her until it was too late." She took several breaths before speaking again. "I would give anything to change what happened that night." She looked up, blue eyes shining. "But I can't. Please, you can't say anything to her."

"I won't tell her, Ronnie. I'm not going to be the one to ruin that child's happiness, even if it is a lie. She's had too many ugly truths already."

"I love her, Maria. I love her more than I've loved anyone in my life, and I can't lose her." She stood next to the older woman and leaned her elbows on the counter. "If I can..." she stared at the wall, "...I'll spend the rest of my life making her happy. Give me that chance."

"The longer you keep the truth from her, the worse it's going to be when she does find out. You owe her the truth."

"I know," she acknowledged. "But I can't. Not yet."

"You go see to her. I have things here I need to do." At Ronnie's questioning look, she said, "Go on, I'll be fine once I'm done in here. I just need a few minutes."

"What was that all about?" Rose asked when Ronnie exited the room, shutting the door behind her.

"She's just having a bad day, that's all. I think Tommy's death still has her upset."

"Are you sure it's nothing I've done?"

"I'm sure it's nothing you've done, hon." Ronnie leaned over and gave Rose a quick kiss on the head. She lowered her lips until they were level with a shapely ear. "I'd love to cuddle up on the couch with you."

"I thought you didn't want to give Maria a show," Rose said.

"What?" She put her hand to her chest as if to say "who me?" "You don't think I can keep my hands to myself?"

"No." Rose smiled and balancing on one foot, set the crutches aside and wrapped her arms around Ronnie's waist. "I'm not sure I can keep my hands to myself." She reached down and grabbed a handful of soft rear. "See what I mean?"

"Have I turned you into a sex addict overnight?"

"No, of course not." Rose blushed and leaned her head against Ronnie's chest. "I just enjoy touching you so much. I know you like it, too."

"Very much so."

"You know...." Green eyes looked up and became helplessly lost in blue. "I don't care what we watch as long as I can be in your arms." Lips brushed together just as Maria came out of the laundry room. There was no mistaking the love passing between the two women. It mollified the housekeeper somewhat, and she was able to put a smile on her face when Rose turned to look at her. "Maria, I'm sorry about the clothes. I'll make sure to put them in the hamper from now on," she said, thinking that the messy clothes were the reason the housekeeper was so upset.

"I'm sorry, Rose. I didn't mean to snap like that. I don't know what's come over me. Why don't you sit down and let me get you some more coffee?" She picked up the empty cups and bustled past them. "Ronnie, you shouldn't let her stand like that for so long." Ronnie complied, helping Rose into her chair.

"I think I just got yelled at," she whispered.

"I think you did, too" came the like reply. "You'd better sit down."

"Good idea." A quick peck to the cheek and Ronnie took her seat. Maria returned with the coffees and smiled pleasantly at Rose, dispelling the young woman's worries. "Here you go, dear."

"Thank you."

"Well, I think we'll take these out to the living room and leave Maria alone," Ronnie said as she rose to her feet.

"I'll meet you in there in a minute," Rose said as she tucked her crutches under her arms. "I need to pee."

Ronnie took their cups into the living room and had just sat down to wait when she heard Rose call out for her. She walked to the bathroom door and answered. "I'm right here, Rose. What do you need?"

"Could you bring me a pair of undies?" the clearly embarrassed voice on the other side of the door asked.

"Why? What's...oh." *Damn.* "Okay, wait right there. I'll get them." Ronnie tried to keep the disappointment from her voice as she walked over to the dresser. *Of all the times for her to get her period,* she mused, pulling out a pair of sensible white cotton briefs from the drawer. She entered the bathroom to find a clearly embarrassed Rose sitting on the toilet, the soiled panties in the sink waiting to be rinsed out.

"Of all the times to be a woman," Rose said as she took the clean pair. She did her best to smile. "I guess the timing's lousy, huh?"

"It happens," Ronnie replied. "How are the pants?"

"I don't think I got them." A quick check confirmed her statement. "I'll be out in a few minutes."

"Take your time." Ronnie leaned down and kissed her lover's forehead. "Don't worry about it, Rose. It's what...four, five days tops? We'll survive."

"Four or five days." The young woman repeated the words as if they were a death sentence. Her eyes flickered at her lover, and an idea formed in her mind. "You know, just because I have it doesn't mean–"

"Yes, it does. I want it to be mutual," Ronnie said firmly, despite what her body was telling her.

"But–"

"No buts. We can wait until then." Seeing the look on Rose's face, she knelt down and hooked the small chin with her fingers. "Hey, look at me. I've waited years for you. A few more days isn't going to kill me." She let her finger travel down the delicate throat and to the vee formed by Rose's shirt. "I love you." She stood up and retrieved the soiled panties. "I'll run these out to Maria so they can be washed right away while you finish up in here."

When bedtime came, Rose dressed in her usual Dartmouth shirt while Ronnie donned her sweats and T-shirt. They slipped under the covers and snuggled up together for a moment before the young woman let out a soft chuckle.

"What?" Ronnie asked.

"Sorry, it just seems strange to be dressed after last night," she admitted, her fingers sliding up under the short sleeve of Ronnie's shirt and caressing the soft skin found there.

"There's nothing that says we have to be dressed," Ronnie pointed out. Without warning, she sat up and peeled off her shirt, the light from the lamp revealing her ample breasts to Rose's gaze. "Why don't you take yours off, too?"

"Well...I suppose it won't hurt anything."

"Of course not." Hungry eyes took in the sight of mouth-watering nipples as the Dartmouth shirt was removed. "God, Rose..." Ronnie swallowed, "...you are so beautiful." She covered the smaller body with her own and let their mouths find something better to do than talk. Rose's lips parted willingly as the kiss deepened, and her hands went around her lover's back in an attempt to pull their bodies even closer. Passions flared and hips were unable to remain still. "Rose...." Ronnie's lips moved to the delicate skin of the young woman's neck and began to kiss their way down only to be stopped inches from the pink puckered skin of her goal.

"Ronnie...I have my period, remember?" She laughed at the dejected look on her lover's face. "It's only for a few days." Her fingers grazed the sides of Ronnie's breasts. "Of course...." One thumb brushed over a darkened nipple. "...you don't." The other thumb duplicated the motion. "Ronnie...let me make love to you."

"I can't." Ronnie traced the outline of the younger woman's lips with her finger. "I want to give you the same pleasure you give me." She paused. "You know...there are some couples who have sex even with their periods."

"I don't know, Ronnie...that seems icky to me. I just can't do it." Rose rolled onto her side and propped her head up with her hand. "I love you, but I can't let you touch me there right now." She reached out with her free hand only to have it stopped.

"No, you don't. No teasing me." Ronnie reached over and shut the light off. "I love you, Rose. Go to sleep."

"You're sure I can't do anything for you?" Her hand went wandering again, this time reaching its goal.

"Rose...." Ronnie reluctantly removed her lover's hand from her breast. "Only if it's mutual." She leaned over and her lips found Rose's. "Now go to sleep."

The alarm went off, signaling the start of a new day. Ronnie woke and headed downstairs for her morning workout, figuring Rose would sleep until she returned. She was surprised, therefore, when she came back to find the young woman sitting at the table, completely dressed and drinking coffee. "I thought you'd still be sleeping."

"Oh, no. Did you forget what day this is?"

Ronnie poured coffee into her mug. "Hmm?"

"You said we could go to the office today. Laura's leaving at the end of the week."

"Was that today?" She tried to look serious, but the tug at the corner of her mouth gave her away. "I remember, hon. I just figured you'd take your time getting up." She took a sip of coffee. "You won't have to do any work today anyway, just get used to the way the office operates and learn how to work the phone."

"If there's anything for me to do, I'll do it, I don't mind," Rose said as she handed over the paper to Ronnie.

"How did I get so lucky?" Ronnie reached out and caressed the young woman's cheek.

"I think the luck is on my side."

"I believe my heart would argue with you on that one." Ronnie leaned over for a kiss and was met halfway. "I love you, Rose."

"Love you, too."

It was the most enjoyable ride to the office Ronnie ever had. It was almost a sightseeing tour as they traveled through the various streets of Albany. In an attempt to avoid going anywhere near Washington Park, the sight of the ill-fated accident, Ronnie took a long, roundabout route through the downtown area until she reached State Street and the Cartwright Building. She dropped Rose off in front of the mammoth building before continuing on to the parking garage. A few minutes later, she returned and held the door so the young woman could enter.

Having never been inside the palatial structure, Rose was awestruck by the high arch ceilings and wide open space of the lobby. A large brass plaque welcomed them to the building. "Our elevators are over here," Ronnie said, smiling to herself at the look on Rose's face. "I take it you like my building."

"It's beautiful. And so big."

"A lot of people work here."

"Do they all work for you?"

"No." Ronnie pressed the up button, frowning when she looked up and saw how many floors away the elevator was. "Most of the lobby and first five floors are rented out to other companies and businesses. The rest of them work for me."

"I know it's a big company and all, but just how many people work for Cartwright Corp.?"

"Ask Susan, she knows. I think between all the different divisions, there's somewhere close to four thousand working for us across the region, but I'm not totally sure. Ah, here we go." The elevator opened and several people exited. Rose noted the immediate change in her companion's stance. Gone was the relaxed, comfortable Ronnie. The woman before her was now the powerful and awe-inspiring Veronica. They entered, and the button was pressed before the doors could close. "You might as well lean back against the wall, Rose. It's going to be a long ride to the top."

Ronnie held the door open as Rose came through on her crutches. "Laura, I'd like you to meet your replacement, Rose Grayson. Rose, this is Laura." The women exchanged pleasantries while Ronnie flipped through her messages. "All set? Rose, Laura will show you around and get you situated. I'll be in my office if you need anything." She exchanged a wink with Rose before closing the door.

The executive's desk was piled high with paperwork, and lunch was the last thing on her mind when Rose knocked and poked her head around the door. "Hungry?"

"Is it that time already?" Ronnie looked at her watch and raised an eyebrow with surprise at the amount of time that had passed. "There's a deli downstairs if you want to call and have them deliver something." She looked up and found herself lost in green eyes. She stood and nodded at the door. "Come inside and close it." Rose did as she bade and sat down on the couch, letting her left leg rest on the cushions. Ronnie knelt next to her, nuzzling soft lips against the shell of the young woman's ear. "You know how much I love you?" she whispered.

"You know I could sue for sexual harassment," Rose teased. "The big bad boss coming on to her innocent young secretary...ohh...." Her eyes fluttered shut when Ronnie's mouth moved down to nip her throat. "Mmm, lucky secretary."

"Lucky boss," Ronnie murmured in reply as her lips traveled along Rose's neck. "Let's forget about lunch." Her long fingers reached to undo Rose's top but found themselves stopped.

"Ronnie, we can't do this. How is either of us supposed to get any work done if you keep me trapped on your couch?" She released the older woman's fingers and put her hands on broad shoulders in an attempt to keep Ronnie's mouth from traveling any lower. "What do you want for lunch?" She saw the wicked glint in blue eyes before she felt warm breath caressing her ear. Her eyes widened at the erotic words whispered in an incredibly sensual tone. "Um...oh, God...you can't talk to me like that."

"You like it, do you?" Ronnie's eyebrow quirked at the thought. "Hmm...." She brushed golden hair out of her way and lowered her lips to the young woman's ear. "I have every intention of making love to you right here on this couch." Her voice was pure seduction, and her hands moved to deliver on her promise, cupping Rose's breast.

"Ronnie, we can't do this now." She shifted away from the all-too-erotic touch. "I have my period, remember?"

"You know, a brave warrior would be willing to enter a bloody battlefield."

"Veronica!" she squeaked, playfully slapping the older woman's shoulder. "I can't believe you said that." She gently pushed Ronnie away and sat up. "You need to get your mind out of the gutter and think about lunch."

"I already told you I'm not hungry...for food." Her mouth claimed Rose's as she moved onto the couch, covering the smaller body with her own.

The door opened quickly. "Hey, Ronnie, I thought maybe we could catch some lunch at...." Susan's voice trailed off as she watched her sister bolt up off couch and turn away. The redhead smirked as a rather embarrassed Rose sat up and hastily refastened the buttons that skillful fingers had undone. "Oh, I guess you already have plans for lunch. Hello, Rose."

"Hi, Susan." The young woman looked down guiltily.

Unable to resist, the younger Cartwright looked at her sister. "You really need to remember to lock your door when you don't want to be interrupted, or do you still want to keep telling me that nothing's going on?"

"Most people know better than to walk into my office unannounced. You said something about lunch?" Ronnie growled, her body thrumming with desire for what she couldn't have...yet.

"Well, I don't want to interrupt your plans."

"We didn't have plans yet," Rose said, regaining most of her composure. "I had just come in to ask Ronnie what she wanted when...." The feeling of her lover's hands on her body was still fresh, causing her to take a deep breath. "Um, what did you have in mind?" She forced herself not to look at Ronnie.

Susan smirked before continuing. "They just opened a new Chinese place on North Pearl Street. I heard their buffet is fabulous."

"You know what Mother would say if she knew you ate from a buffet in public?" Ronnie teased. "Sure, sounds good to me." She saw Rose reach for her crutches. "Oh...there's absolutely no parking near it." The raven-haired woman thought for a moment. "I know, I'll meet you downstairs, drive you over, then bring the car back to the garage. It's only a five-minute walk from here."

"You don't have to do that," Rose said. "That's not far at all. I can make it."

"I don't know, Rose...crossing State Street with all that traffic at noontime." Ronnie shook her head. "Susan, why don't we just have them deliver something here?"

"That's fine with me."

"Are you sure?" Rose asked. "You seemed like you wanted to get out for a while."

"No, just wanted something other than the soaps to keep me company for lunch today." The redhead looked at her watch, the phone, then her sister. "But I really am hungry." Another thought occurred to her. "Where are we going to eat?"

"Why not the conference room?" Ronnie replied.

"Can't. Brooker has a meeting in there."

"Isn't there a lunchroom?" Rose asked innocently. The sisters looked at each other and chuckled.

"There's a deli in the lobby and a break room down the hall but not really any lunchroom," Susan said. "Most people go out for lunch or eat at their desks. Lunchrooms tend to make people take longer breaks, and that reduces productivity."

"Oh, don't get her started on that again," Ronnie warned. "First it'll be the slackers, then the smokers, then the gossipers." She walked over and put her hands on her younger sibling's shoulders. "Before you know it, she'll issue all sorts of memos, and I'll have the clerical union screaming at me again."

Lunch and the rest of the workday flew by. As Ronnie expected, everyone who met Rose liked her immediately, and the young woman settled into her new position. Ronnie quickly learned the fringe benefit of having her lover be her secretary. She couldn't get enough of the honey-haired woman's kisses and would call her into the office just to taste the sweetness of Rose's mouth one more time. Fantasies played through the executive's mind. Fantasies that included her, the overstuffed leather couch in her office, and Rose naked and waiting. Alas, she knew they would remain only that. As much as they loved each other, there was a time and place for everything, and in her office during working hours was not it. Opening her date book, blue eyes fell on the upcoming Saturday. She was certain Rose would be over her period by then. The marbled blue-green pen twiddled in her fingers before she absently drew a heart in the memo section of the page. Soon the heart found letters doodled within it. *R.G. + V.C.* Pitiful renditions of roses began filling the margins, but when Rose spotted them later, they caused the young woman to burst into happy tears. While Ronnie was surprised by the reaction, she was more than willing to offer comfort, taking her lover into her arms and resting her chin on top of the golden hair. It was one of the times she enjoyed most, holding Rose in her arms, being the proud warrior protecting her delicate companion. It was at those moments that Ronnie felt whole, complete. She knew that she could never live without the dancing green eyes and laughing smile of her precious Rose.

Chapter Twenty-three

When Saturday came, Ronnie was awake with the sun, visions of making love to Rose over and over dancing in her mind. It was a particularly lively image that she focused on as she slipped out of bed and sauntered off to the bathroom.

"Oh, son of a bitch!" The shouted exclamation woke Rose from her sleep.

"What's wrong?"

"Nothing." Another muffled curse, then the sound of water running.

"Ronnie?" Rose picked up her crutches and made her way to the bathroom. "You okay?"

"Yeah," Ronnie answered from the other side of the door. Her underwear ended up in the sink with water running over them. She cleaned herself up, then opened the door. "Guess what I got?" she said as she walked past, treating Rose to the sight of firm cheeks wiggling below the gray T-shirt.

"You're kidding."

"Nope." She jerked a clean pair of panties out of the drawer and pulled them on. "Talk about lousy timing." She leaned over and gave Rose a quick kiss. "But you should be done," she whispered in a husky voice, her hands slipping under the hem of the Dartmouth shirt in search of twin mounds. The young woman backed out of reach.

"Wait a minute there, missy...I couldn't touch you when I had mine."

"B-but...." The executive pouted, realizing where the conversation was headed...and she wasn't happy. "Rose...you know that just because you can't touch me, that doesn't mean–"

"Don't even think about trying that. It didn't work when I tried it, remember?" The young woman's eyes took in the athletic body before her and sighed. "I was looking forward to it, too, you know."

"But...but...." Ronnie was silenced by Rose's fingers against her lips.

"I hope you get over it quickly, darling," the young woman cooed. "Maybe next month you'll reconsider when I want to touch you."

Rose wished Ronnie could be in the room with her when Dr. Barnes removed the cast, but an important meeting forced the executive to stay at work while Maria drove the young woman to the appointment. The small reciprocating saw sliced through the plaster, ticking her in the process. "Just a little more," the doctor said. The saw was set down, and a pair of scissors cut through the cotton and released the cast's hold on Rose's leg. The first thing she saw when she looked down at her leg was the long strands of blonde hair sticking out past dried, flaky skin. She wiggled her toes, frowning at the tinge of pain that went through her ankle. She had been doing it for several weeks, and the response had always been the same yet Rose somehow believed that when the cast came off the pain would go away. After all, it didn't take that long for her right leg to heal up and take her weight. "When can I start walking on it?" She flexed her foot, hissing at the agony it caused.

"I'm afraid walking isn't something that's going to happen for a while yet, Miss Grayson."

"But...." She looked at the physician fearfully. "You said no more casts."

"That's right, no more casts," Dr. Barnes reassured. "But your ankle suffered a great deal of trauma. It can't be left unsupported. You'll need a brace." She crossed the room and retrieved one from the drawer. Dark blue canvas covered flat metal rods, and Velcro straps held everything together. Rose looked at the object with disdain. It represented the crushing of her hope and yet another reminder of the accident. She listened quietly as the doctor explained the need for physical therapy and stressed that the ankle was too weak to support any weight yet and a dozen other things that Rose didn't want to hear. Her only consolation was that she could remove it to take baths. As much as she had been looking forward to soaking in a hot tub of water, it seemed insignificant now.

Maria's attempts to get the subdued woman to talk on the way home were met with mumbled answers or silence. Once inside, Rose announced she was tired and retreated to her room. Hoping against hope that the doctor was wrong, she set her crutches against the wall and let her left foot rest against the ground. There was a twinge of pain but nothing she couldn't live with. She leaned forward, putting more weight on the tender ankle. Blinding pain shot through her, and she collapsed onto the floor. Her tear ducts opened, and her breath came out in wracking sobs. Maria came in and helped her into the bed where Rose quickly cried herself to sleep.

Ronnie entered a short time later, having been called home by the worried housekeeper. It took only a brief explanation of what happened at the doctor's office for her to realize why her lover was so upset. Rose had been excited at breakfast about the prospect of having the cast gone completely. Drawn into the young woman's good mood, Ronnie never gave any thought to the possibility that they might replace the cast with a brace. In fact, she had been more focused on the knowledge that her period was finally over, and after a week and a half, she'd finally be able to make love to Rose again. Now looking at puffy eyes and the telltale wet spot on the pillow, she felt a sliver of guilt. All amorous thoughts far from her mind, Ronnie kicked her shoes off and climbed into bed beside her lover.

Rose felt a gentle rubbing on her shoulders as consciousness returned. She inhaled the scent of Ronnie's perfume and smiled, knowing her beloved was there with her. She rolled over and winced at the pain in her ankle. "Hi."

"Hi yourself," Ronnie replied, her brow furrowed with concern. "Did they give you anything for the pain?"

"More Vicodin," she shrugged, her tone low. "I can take a bath now but nothing else." She let herself be drawn against the taller woman and buried her face into the silk blouse. "I still have to use the damn crutches." She snuggled closer, her fingertips tracing the outline of Ronnie's bra. "I tried to put weight on it," she admitted. "But it hurt too much." Her legs shifted against each other. "And now it itches." Ronnie nodded, remembering when Rose's right cast was removed. "Anyway," Rose continued. "How was Laura's final day?"

"Good. She loved her going-away slash baby shower party."

"Good, I'm glad she enjoyed it. Sorry I wasn't up to coming."

"She understood. She loved the baby outfits and blankets, by the way." Ronnie's knuckles brushed against the softness of Rose's cheek. "But right now I don't want to talk about her. You've had a pretty rough day of it. Look, your cast is off and the doctor said you could take baths now, right?"

"Right...."

"So how about we let Maria go home early today and you and I take advantage of that obscenely large tub I have upstairs, hmm?" Sensing Rose's hesitation, she added, "There's jets, and I have a full bottle of bubble bath just waiting for you. If you're a good girl, I might even be convinced to join you."

"Are you done with...?" Ronnie's eyes twinkled with mischief as she nodded. Rose gulped. "Oh." The finger that had been tracing the bra line now ran back and forth against the back catch. "That means I can touch you now," the young woman murmured, her voice a sensual whisper. "I missed that, you know. Touching you." She lifted her head, her lips finding Ronnie's. "Don't punish me like that again."

"I won't," the executive vowed, knowing full well what the younger woman was feeling. "How does your ankle feel right now? Think you're up for that bath?"

"Are you going to join me?" Rose asked brazenly, the vision of a wet, naked Ronnie causing her heart to beat faster.

"I'd love to."

Ronnie turned the dimmer, causing the bright light to mellow to a soft yellow before her lover entered her bedroom. "Sit on the bed, I'll help you undress," she offered. Saving time, she began to strip, getting the skirt and blouse off before realizing that Rose was standing there watching her. She turned to face her, slowly removing the rest of her clothing. She stood there naked, her dark curls standing out in contrast to her skin. Rose swallowed several times as her eyes wandered up and down Ronnie's body.

"So beautiful," she whispered.

"My turn to see your beauty," Ronnie countered, leading Rose to the edge of the bed. The crutches were placed out of the way, and one by one, buttons opened to reveal creamy white flesh. At last, all the clothes were removed, leaving only the dark blue brace to mar the image. Careful not to jar the tender ankle, Ronnie opened the Velcro straps and removed the brace. "I think a shower first to scrub off all this dead skin would be a good idea."

"You're going to hold me up in the shower?"

"No, there's a bench built in to the wall, and the showerhead is attached to a hose. It's one of those massager kinda ones."

"You really do have–"

"All the toys?" Ronnie interjected. "Yup." She grinned broadly as her eyes landed on her nightstand drawer and her mind filled with images of what was hidden inside. "You know Rose..." her voice took on a husky quality. "I have some toys that you haven't seen yet."

"What kind of...oh." Green eyes widened in surprise, then narrowed with the thought of the possible uses. "Those kind of toys."

"Mmm hmm." As they kissed, Ronnie pressed her body against Rose's, moaning when she felt the younger woman's thigh press against her swollen center. She returned the favor, grinding her muscled thigh against Rose's wet folds. "Keep this up and we'll never get into that bath," she husked. With great self-control, Ronnie lifted herself off the smaller woman's body and scooped her into her arms. She smiled when she felt Rose's arms wrap around her neck.

"I like it when you hold me like this," the young woman said, planting gentle kisses all over Ronnie's shoulder and collarbone. Far too soon, they were in the bathroom and Rose had to release her embrace. Balancing on one foot and leaning against the wall for support, she waited while Ronnie turned on the water and adjusted the temperature. Once it was ready, she helped Rose into the shower and knelt down next to her. "If I'm too rough on you, let me know, okay?"

But she was anything but rough. She gave the washcloth a generous lather and began gently scrubbing Rose's skin. Bit by bit, the dead skin sloughed off, leaving fresh pink behind. When that task was completed, Ronnie used her shaving gel to work up a good lather before her razor removed the itchy hair from Rose's leg. She left long enough to turn on the hot tub and add bubble bath before returning to the shower. "That's a big tub. It's going to take about ten to fifteen minutes to fill up. Do you want to wait or get in while it's filling?"

"I'd rather wait and sink into it all at once. It's been so long since I've had a bath."

"Deal. Let's get you dried off. You can sit on that padded bench over there until it's ready." She walked over to the linen closet to get more towels.

Rose leaned back and eyed the swaying hips and firm derriere appreciatively. The stack of towels blocked her view of Ronnie's breasts when the woman returned, but she knew she'd see them up close and personal very soon. Her wish was granted a minute later when strong arms picked her up and held her tight against the soft mounds. Rose took advantage of her position to nibble her lover's neck while being carried to the tub. Rose reached out for the sides of the tub as Ronnie knelt and lowered her in.

"Careful of your ankle, you don't have anything protecting it in here."

"Ohhhh....this is nice," the young woman purred as the hot water swirled around her. A molded seat beckoned her to sit down, and she did, surprised to find tiny jets massaging her back. She twisted to see that there were in fact several rows of tiny holes shooting out streams of water beneath the surface. "This is heaven." She settled back, smiling as she watched Ronnie join her.

"So you like this, hmm?" Ronnie sat in the seat next to Rose, the height difference causing her nipples to stand out above the water while the young woman's hid below the suds.

"I see definite benefits to this tub." A gentle but determined hand moved underwater. Without thought, Rose spread her legs, giving Ronnie the access she needed. "Some...definite benefits...uh-huh." Rose turned her head and found her lips claimed by her dark-haired lover. The kiss quickly turned heated, and when Ronnie's hand moved up to cup her breast, Rose was certain she was going to orgasm right then and there.

"It's been a long eight days," Ronnie rasped, her eyes teased mercilessly by the bubbles that refused to let her see the treasures hidden beneath. She pivoted and straddled Rose's thighs, intending to kiss her lover senseless. Before Ronnie could reposition herself, Rose's mouth had accepted the obvious invitation and claimed her nipple. "Oh, Rose...." Blue eyes closed as she let the young woman have her fill of first one, then the other breast. She finally pulled back to look down into beautiful green eyes. "You keep that up and we won't be in here for long." She sank back into her seat.

"I couldn't help myself," Rose said as a cute blush worked its way up her cheeks. "You moved and suddenly they were there."

"I haven't turned you into a sex maniac with only one night of passion, have I?" Ronnie teased.

"Only when it comes to you." The young woman's hand moved beneath the water to rest on her lover's thigh. "I love you, and I love touching you."

"That goes both ways, you know," Ronnie said, resting her hand on Rose's cheek. "I'd better move to the other side or you'll never get a chance to soak."

"No, I'll be good. I'd rather have you next to me."

Good turned out to be a relative term as both took advantage of the intimacy the hot tub offered. Lips found a reason to meet often, and breasts were never so clean. Soapy hands roamed freely, sometimes teasing, sometimes caressing, always promising an appropriate reward for such a long wait. Ronnie's patience had been tested to the limit. Her fingers roamed over silky skin yet she couldn't touch the way she wanted. "Rose...." Her voice sounded raw, deeply sensual in its roughness. "I think it's time to get out of the tub."

Rose's mind closed to everything except the large palms caressing her aching nipples. "Oh...you know just how to do that...." The touch was sweet yet torturous at the same time, just the right amount of friction as Ronnie drew small circles with her palms. Rose threaded her fingers through the silky black hair, only the ends actually having gotten wet, and pulled her lover in for a kiss. Ronnie's hands became sandwiched between twin pairs of heaving bosoms, and it only served to make both women want more. The kisses were passionate, driven by days of aching need, both silently choosing to not pleasure themselves but rather wait until now, until this moment. Ronnie backed up long enough to free her hands from their soft prisons and scoop the smaller woman into her arms. She climbed out of the tub and paused long enough for Rose to grab some towels off the shelf before continuing into the softly lit bedroom. She set the young woman down on the coverlet, not worrying about it getting wet. They took turns toweling each other dry, both knowing that there was one spot that had no intention of drying off anytime soon. Rose was only partially dry when Ronnie pressed her back onto the bed.

"I think, my little Rose, that I am hopelessly in love with you." Ronnie punctuated her statement by giving Rose's nose a peck. "Actually, I know I am," she corrected. "You're the best thing that ever happened to me. I know that sounds corny and all, but it's true." She ran one finger down Rose's cheek. "I love you."

Rose's wait was over when she felt Ronnie's lips upon hers. "Yesss...." Dexterous fingers found her nipple and squeezed gently. She returned Ronnie's kiss with fervor, her hands coming up to return the pleasure. Tongues darted and danced, giving and taking as they moved from one woman's mouth to the other. When the kiss finally broke, Rose dropped her head back on the bed, fully intent on taking a moment to recover. Ronnie shifted down, letting her damp curls brush against Rose's thigh. "Ronnie, where are you...unggh...." Her nipple was surrounded by wet warmth, a skilled tongue working in concert with straight white teeth to pull the most wonderful sensations out of her body. "Yes, Ronnie." She buried her fingers deep into the silky hair, urging her lover on. Her hips began bucking upward in search of relief, finding it in the supple skin of Ronnie's thigh. "Oh!" She rose up again, digging her heels into the bed. "Ow, ow, ow...wait...."

Ronnie was off in a flash and reaching for the lamp. "What's wrong? Did I hurt you? Was I too hard? What?" The words came out in a worried flurry.

"No, no, it wasn't you," she groaned, reaching for her unprotected ankle. "I wasn't thinking." The bed lifted slightly as Ronnie rolled off, returning a moment later with the brace.

"I'm not taking any chances on you hurting yourself again." The brace was secured, the fit was checked, then Ronnie smiled at her lover. "Now where was I?"

"I believe you were right here," Rose added helpfully, using her hands on either side of Ronnie's face to guide the woman back to her erect nipples. "Ahh...." She lay back and let lover suckle her breasts, losing herself in the feeling. But soon those loving lips moved down, planting soft kisses on her torso before brushing over her rust-colored curls. Rose realized what was about to happen the instant she felt her legs being separated. She sighed, and her hands locked on Ronnie's head, refusing to break the connection. Long fingers separated her folds, but before she could react to the warm breath caressing her most intimate location, Rose felt Ronnie's tongue touch her.

"Mmm," Ronnie moaned with approval.

"Ohh...Ronnie...unnggh...." It was exquisite and indescribable, a rising higher than any she had ever known yet there was no fear. Rose bucked against the invading muscle, her fingers talons against the dark head. Despite the death grip, Ronnie moved upward, claiming Rose's lips with her own as eager fingers found a wellspring of desire waiting for them.

Rose arched her hips, groaning loudly when she felt the long digit slip into her. Ronnie's cheek pressed against hers, hot breath caressing her ear. "Oh, Rose...that's so nice..."

"N-n-n-nice..." the young woman repeated, her focus tunneling to the spot where they were joined. Ronnie's finger filled her deeply, deeper than any before yet Rose needed "More...ooh...." It was exquisite. She felt a sense of loss as Ronnie retreated back to the edge of her opening, then cried out with pleasure when two fingers stretched her fully. Rose desperately sought her lover's lips. They kissed hungrily, passionately as a rocking motion was established. Unable to use her left leg for support, Rose brought her right heel up and arched into Ronnie's thrusts. "Yesss...."

"Oh, Rose...you feel so good, I love you." The rhythm increased steadily. Ronnie's thumb found an erect clitoris and brushed against it.

"Oh, God!" Rose's head pressed back against the bed, her lower body thrusting of its own accord.

"Yesss," Ronnie growled back, her lips moving to Rose's throat. She straddled the young woman's right thigh and began rocking against it. The body writhing beneath her drew Ronnie's passion to new heights. The gasps and cries in her ear urged her on, her fingers searching out new places deep within Rose. The need to please her lover was all consuming. Turning her head, Ronnie sought out another pleasure spot, an erect nipple begging for attention.

It was too much for Rose. The wetness against her leg, the fingers nestled inside her, the warm mouth loving her breast...a fire started deep within, pulsing outward until her legs stiffened, her breath caught in her throat, and her muscles clamped down, refusing to let Ronnie's fingers go. "Oh, Ronnieeee...I...I'm...."

"Yes, hon." Trapped fingers wiggled as much as they were able. "I've got you, let it go...."

"I...." The inner muscles convulsed, the orgasm crashing through with more force than any Rose had ever known before. Loving words were whispered in her ear, guiding her back to earth gently. Rose's eyelids refused to open, her body pulsing with aftershocks. It was several seconds before she realized that her grip around Ronnie's body was probably keeping her lover from breathing. She relaxed her arms, letting them fall limply back to the bed. "Oh, Ronnie," she husked, her mouth dry and her body feeling completely boneless.

"I've got you, hon." Rose slowly opened her eyes, the gentle light allowing her to see the loving smile on Ronnie's face. "I'm going to pull my fingers out now, okay?" Rose nodded and shuddered slightly as Ronnie pulled out.

"You're wonderful," Rose whispered, snuggling into her lover's arms. As Ronnie's hand caressed her cheek, Rose inhaled the scent of herself, and her body twitched with the recent memory of where those fingers had been. Her left hand worked its way between their bodies and grazed wiry dark curls. Ronnie groaned, and her hips jerked forward in response. "Lie back," Rose whispered.

Rose shifted until her lips found a crinkly point to draw into her mouth. The firm hand on the back of her head spoke just as loudly as the moan that came from Ronnie's lips. Her fingers found hot wetness waiting for them. Lifting her head up from its task for a second, Rose brought her fingers to her lips and tasted them, her tongue snaking out to draw off every drop. "Rose...God, that's sexy." Inspired by her lover's words, the young woman proceeded to make a show of cleaning her fingers, rewarded by the anxious squirming beneath her. With desire, curiosity, and a good dose of nervousness, Rose pushed herself downward until her lips were near the dark triangle of hair. The hand on the back of her head remained, gently urging her on. Ronnie's legs parted wide in invitation. Rose settled into position, her lips scant inches away from their goal. Coarse dark hairs tickled her lips before her tongue parted the way and sank in to taste the sweet liquid. Ronnie's breaths came quickly as Rose's mouth learned its way around. "Oh, Rose, right there...no...yes, right there, yesss."

Long legs wrapped around her shoulders, pinning Rose in place. Not that she minded, the feeling of Ronnie reacting to her tongue was enough to keep the young woman in that position forever. She alternated between licking Ronnie's clit to dipping lower and drinking in more of the liquid evidence of her effect on the woman she loved. Gasps and moans fueled her on, her goal to send Ronnie over the same wondrous pinnacle that she had been sent over just a few minutes before. When she wrapped her lips around the small shaft and began sucking, Ronnie cried out and drove her hips upward, grinding herself against Rose's face. Going on instinct, the young woman began sucking harder, her tongue firmly moving back and forth. Soon Ronnie's legs trembled and Rose wrapped her arms around them to keep her position. The muscles in her neck strained against Ronnie's upward thrust as a loud cry was torn from the other woman's throat. Rose sucked as hard as she could, her tongue moving rapidly over the engorged clitoris. Her joy at Ronnie's moment of release rivaled the feeling of her own orgasm, and her own sex throbbed in response. Staying away from the hypersensitive clit, Rose let her tongue travel along the folds, not wanting to end the intimate moment. Only when she felt Ronnie's hands urging her up did she relinquish her prized location and give the lips covered with dark curls a final kiss. Strong arms pulled her up to rest against a broad shoulder. For long minutes, neither spoke, content to simply rest in the afterglow. Hands traveled lazily over bared skin, silently communicating their love for each other. "I love you," Ronnie finally whispered, giving Rose a kiss on her forehead.

"Mmm, love you, too." Rose lifted her head and looked down into contented blue eyes. "Don't ever make us wait like this again."

"I promised you before I wouldn't," Ronnie said softly.

"I know, I just wanted to remind you." Rose put her head back down and sighed contentedly. "Can we sleep up here tonight? I'm comfortable."

"We can sleep anywhere you like." Ronnie looked over at the clock. "It's too early to go to sleep. Want to make love again?"

"Hmm, let's see." Rose picked her head up and smiled devilishly. "Hmm, sleep or make love to the most wonderful woman in the world." She put her finger against her chin. "Boy, what a tough decision."

"Well, let's see what I can do to sway you," Ronnie said, rolling the smaller woman onto her back. "Shall I start at the top and work my way down or from the bottom up?"

Watching from her spot on the floor, Tabitha yawned and began cleaning herself, certain her mistresses wouldn't let her on the bed anytime soon.

At Rose's insistence that she could navigate the stairs with her crutches, Ronnie had the adjustable bed moved into one of the guest rooms and the young woman's belongings moved into her room. Tabitha discovered the window seat to be much more comfortable than her cat bed, much to Maria's dismay every time she went in to vacuum. While Ronnie showed off her muscles moving the furniture around to accommodate the extra dresser, Rose stood next to the entertainment center and went through the videotapes in search of something for them to relax and watch. An unlabeled tape on top of the cabinet drew her attention. Wondering if it was another one of Ronnie's adult tapes, Rose put it in the VCR and turned on the television. To her utter surprise, it was a video of Ronnie's office, and Delores was standing there. The volume was muted, and her former foster mother looked like she was screaming. Rose hit the stop button and rewound the tape. "Honey, why didn't you tell me that Delores stopped by your office?"

Ronnie dropped the dresser where it was and turned to face her lover. "I didn't want to hurt you."

"Was this before or after she had been here?"

"After."

"What happened?" She glanced at the VCR when it clicked off, announcing the tape was rewound. "Did she ask for money?" she asked quietly.

"Rose...." Ronnie walked up behind her lover and wrapped her arms around the smaller woman, crutches and all. "You are everything to me. I didn't want to see you hurt with this."

"I want to see what happened." She moved out of Ronnie's embrace and worked her way to the bed. "Sit next to me," she urged. By the time Ronnie joined her on the bed, Rose hit the play button.

The tape started with Delores entering the room and looking around. "Nice office. You hiring?" Rose immediately colored with embarrassment. Ronnie noticed and put her arm around the smaller woman, pulling her close. She knew the rest of the tape would be hard to watch. The scene played itself out, culminating with Delores being escorted out of the office.

"That's it," Ronnie said, reaching for the remote just as she watched herself tell Laura to take the rest of the day off. To her surprise, Rose held the controller out of reach.

"No, wait, there's more." On the screen, Susan entered the office. "Ronnie? What happened? I heard they called Security to your office." The dialogue continued, drawing Rose in as she studied her lover's reactions. She shut the VCR off and looked at Ronnie. "I love you, you know."

"I know. I was just trying to protect you, that's all."

"I saw that," Rose replied. She leaned her head against the older woman's shoulders. "I noticed you didn't use the pen I gave you to write that check."

"No, I couldn't. Even though I knew I would tear it up, I couldn't use your pen to do it," Ronnie admitted. "Rose...has she tried to contact you at all?"

"No, not since that day she was here and took my check." She squeezed her tall lover against her. "It was all a lie with her," she said quietly, staring at the blank screen. "You're the one who taught me what love means." Green eyes looked into endless blue. "Love is about giving, not taking." She snuggled closer. "Like what you and I have. It's not just about the sex. It's about honesty and caring and all the little things." She gave Ronnie a gentle kiss. "What we have is...." Rose fought for the words. "...is...." Nothing came. No one word could describe how she felt about being with Ronnie. Finally, she shook her head in defeat. "All I know is that when I'm with you I feel complete."

"Funny, I feel the same way about you." She returned the kiss, using her tongue to part Rose's lips and slip inside for a quick taste. "I love you forever, Rose."

"No more secrets, Ronnie." The young woman's lips moved along the executive's jaw. "Nothing hidden between us."

Ronnie stiffened at the words. *You don't know what you're asking, Rose. You can't know* all *my secrets. I can't risk losing you.* Ronnie decided that distraction would work and began nibbling the earlobe framed by golden tresses. "Speaking of hidden." She opened first one, then two buttons on Rose's shirt. "Why don't you and I jump in the shower and play?" She let her tongue trace the outline of Rose's ear and lowered her voice to a throaty husk. "Hmm? I promise to make it worth your while." Another button surrendered to dexterous fingers. "What do you say, Rose? I know you've been wondering about that shower massager."

"It really will...?"

"Um hmm....I'd be happy to show you." She scooped Rose up in her arms and headed for the bathroom, determined to put all thoughts of the past out of her mind.

Chapter Twenty-four

As the flowers bloomed and the days grew longer, Rose worked hard on her physical therapy. She took every opportunity to strengthen and build endurance in her ankle. While Ronnie made sure she stayed off it at home, her lover was unable to keep such a tight eye on her at the office. Rose had progressed from no weight bearing to toe-touching, and the footrest under her desk provided the perfect resistance object to practice with during the day. When she would overdo it, as was common, Rose found that Ronnie was always willing to provide a foot massage that made all the aches and pains go away. Of course it often led to the new lovers finding other things to touch and rub, but that was fine with Rose. The professional decorum they kept during the day at work was gone the instant they entered the house. Whether at the kitchen or dining room table, the two women sat next to each other, sharing from one another's plates and passing kisses along with the salt. Dessert required only one bowl with two spoons, and the warmer evenings were spent on the bench swing cuddled up together looking at the stars. It was heaven on earth and Rose couldn't imagine being any happier, except to be rid of the crutches.

When the day came in early June that the crutches could be left behind at Dr. Barnes' office, Ronnie insisted that they celebrate by going out to dinner. It was followed by a movie, then a late-night stop at one of the small drive-ins that opened during the warm weather for soft ice cream and a few more minutes out. They arrived home after eleven, but neither showed any signs of being tired. On the contrary, an offered overture was accepted, and their lovemaking went on long into the night.

The night hadn't even given way to the dim gray of morning when a horn blared in the driveway, waking Ronnie from her sound sleep. "What the hell...?" Grabbing her robe from the end of the bed, she donned it and padded over to the window. "Tabitha, get down. I swear you leave enough hair here to make another cat." She leaned her knee against the white cushions of the window seat and looked out, her eyes widening in surprise at the truck and boat sitting in her driveway. "Oh, damn." She mentally thought about the date. She opened the window and stuck her head out. "Frank!" The man standing next to the truck smiled and waved up.

"Hey, Cuz, hurry up, the fish are biting."

"I forgot all about opening day. I can't go."

"Go where?" a sleepy Rose mumbled from the bed before sinking her head back into the pillow and promptly falling back to sleep.

"What do you mean you can't go? You're awake, aren't you? You have a lifetime license and today's opening day. You have to go. We always go, and I want to try out my boat on the Mohawk." He looked at his watch. "Come on, Ronnie. I want to get there in time to catch something."

Opening day for bass season was a long-standing date between Ronnie and her oldest cousin, a tradition that dated back to when they were kids. She looked over at the naked woman on the bed, then stuck her head back out the window. "Frank, can Rose come?"

"Blondie? Sure, just hurry it up, will ya?" He looked at his watch again.

"Be down in five minutes." She shut the window and walked over to the bed. "Rose...Rose, get up, hon."

"Did I hear you telling someone we were going fishing?" She picked her head up and looked at Ronnie, who tossed her robe on the bed and started opening various drawers.

"Yup. It's opening season for bass today, and Frank's here to take us fishing."

"I don't remember you mentioning anything about us going fishing today...or anytime for that matter." Rose sat up and stretched lazily, drawing an appreciative look from Ronnie. "And why go so early? It's not like they're going to pack up and leave the water if we wait a couple more hours."

"If we wait any longer, they won't be biting. Come on, lazybones. It'll be fun."

Rose sat in the jump seat behind the passenger seat, affording her a good view of the maniac that Ronnie entrusted their lives to. Frank firmly believed that his state-of-the-art radar detector would warn him of any approaching speed traps, and the eight-cylinder Ford flew up the highway at stomach-churning speeds. "So, Blondie, you been fishing before?" he called over the blaring sound of country western music.

"Um...no, not in a boat."

"You're baiting her hook, Cuz," he said to the passenger. "I hope she doesn't get seasick."

"Of course not." Ronnie turned in her seat. "You don't get seasick, do you?"

"I don't know, but I might get carsick if he keeps driving like this," Rose said low enough for only Ronnie to hear.

"He's trying to make up for lost time."

"We'll make up a lot of time if we're all in the hospital."

"I'll slow him down," Ronnie assured, turning back in her seat. "Hey, Frank, you know the troopers have those laser detectors now. You can't avoid them. Look, the trooper station is a mile up the road. You don't want to get caught again this year, do you?"

The speedometer slowed to a reasonable rate just as they did indeed pass a waiting trooper hiding in the tree-covered median. "Damn, they've got more of them out this year," he said, keeping a better eye on his speed. Rose dared a glance at the dashboard, pleased to see only two digits near the end of the orange needle. Snaking her right hand around the seat, she gave Ronnie's arm a gentle squeeze of thanks.

Frank backed up to the dock, stopping the boat a few feet from the waterline. "We'd better get her in before I put the boat in the water." They exited the truck, and Frank climbed into the boat, a twenty-two-foot-long, top-of-the-line Ranger Bass Boat. Ronnie picked Rose up and after dropping the cane off in the truck, lifted the young woman into Frank's beefy arms. A few seconds later, Rose was seated on one of the cushioned benches. "Here. You'd better put on a jacket. Ronnie would kill me if you became bait."

"I thought there weren't any dangerous fish in this river," Rose said as Ronnie started the truck up and backed the boat into the water.

"There aren't, although the bullheads can give you quite a sting."

"Don't you go scaring her," Ronnie called from the truck. She gathered the various poles and tackle boxes from the back and passed them to Frank before untying the boat and moving the truck to the parking area. He had the motor running and ready to go by the time she returned.

"Okay, ladies, hang on now. It's time to go fishing." He backed away from the dock and pointed up the river. "Let's just see what four hundred horses can do on the open water." The water behind them churned, and the bow rose up as he gunned the engines. Rose looked nervously at Ronnie.

"Please tell me he doesn't drive a boat like he drives that truck."

They stopped several miles upstream, the main motor pulled up in favor of the trolling motor. Ronnie baited Rose's line first, then her own. Frank set up a couple of lines for himself and took position at the bow of the boat, settling himself into one of the upraised swivel chairs. Ronnie helped Rose into one at the stern and took the one next to it for herself. The early morning sun was beginning to lighten the sky, and as expected, the fish were jumping. Frank quickly made the first catch, a small-mouthed bass that barely made it over the limit. It landed in the holding tank with the hopes of being culled later.

"Having fun?" Frank asked.

"Just dandy," Ronnie replied, sending her line out once again.

"Hey!" Rose held her pole in a death grip. "I think I've got something." The tip of her pole dipped once, then twice, then a high whining sound filled the air as the fish took off, taking Rose's line with it. Ronnie's pole hit the deck and her arms went around the smaller woman, helping her steady the pole.

"Start bringing back your line, don't let him get any slack or he'll wiggle off." Her hands covered Rose's, and together they worked the spirited bass.

"Got a lunker there, eh?"

"Feels like it, Frank. Sure is bigger than that minnow you tossed in there a few minutes ago," Ronnie said, enjoying the feel of Rose in her arms. "Come on, honey, reel this baby in and show him who's boss here." Eventually, she felt the presence of her cousin behind her. "Grab the net for this one, Frank."

"Oh, Ronnie, it's too strong. You take the pole." Rose tried to hand the rod over, but Ronnie refused it.

"No, you can do this, Rose." She released her grip and stepped back. "That's it, keep the line taut, wear him down."

"Oh, my, he feels so big," the young woman exclaimed, the line still tugging hard with the fish's attempts to escape. Suddenly, the fish jumped straight out of the water, showing them all what she was up against.

"Holy shit," Frank exclaimed. "Hang on, I've gotta get the big net."

"You've got a monster there, Rose," Ronnie said, standing at her lover's side. Thinking that her cousin wasn't looking, she reached over and put her hand on the younger woman's shoulder, stroking it lovingly. The bass finally tired and allowed itself to be brought alongside the boat where Frank scooped it up in the net.

"Son of a bitch, what a big fucking fish," he said happily, sticking his hand into the gill to hold it up so they could see it.

"Nice language, Frank," Ronnie admonished, looking from her cousin to Rose pointedly.

"Oh, she's heard it before," he said, drawing a glare from Ronnie. "Hey, Blondie, you sure caught one hell of a large-mouth here. I should have brought a camera."

"Look how big he is," Rose said. "Can he go back now?"

"Back?" Frank laughed. "Honey, this isn't the kind of fish you throw back. This is the kind you take to the taxidermist and have mounted."

"Mounted?" She turned to Ronnie, who was busily removing the hook. "I don't want to keep it."

"I can't believe how big he is," Ronnie said, taking the prized catch from Frank. "Rose, are you sure you don't want to make him into a trophy? He's a beaut."

"I'm sure."

"Don't you want to even touch him before I throw him back?"

"No."

Ronnie and Frank exchanged looks before she dropped the fish back into the water. She baited Rose's hook again, and they returned to fishing. "He's not mad because I threw the fish back, is he?" Rose asked once Frank was out of earshot.

"Mad? No, not mad. Shocked, but not mad." Ronnie turned to face soft green eyes. "You are so gentle that it's amazing." She reached out and cupped Rose's chin with her hand. "I can't believe you let a prize-winning catch like that go back, though. You're definitely not the fishing type."

"No, I guess I'm not. I am having fun, even if I do like to let the fish go."

Ronnie smiled and sat back in her seat. "Just as long as you're having a good time."

"Any time I'm around you I'm having a good time," Rose replied, drawing a warm smile from her lover. Frank yelped with another bite, but the bass paled in comparison to the whopper that Rose had caught. Ronnie went to the bow to help him. "Gee, Frank, catch another dozen or so of these and there might be enough for a sandwich," she teased, holding up the small fish.

"Hardy har har, Cuz." He frowned when Ronnie measured the fish, too short to keep. "Maybe Blondie will catch us another one."

"Her name is Rose."

"Oh, yeah?" Frank turned toward the woman in question. "Hey, Blondie, having a good time?"

"Yes," she called back, happily watching both her and Ronnie's poles. "This is fun."

"Dunno how you managed it, Cuz," he said, looking at Rose pointedly. "Nice girl. If I believe the rumors floating around, I should expect to see her at all the family functions from now on."

"What rumors?" Ronnie deliberately lowered her voice, not wanting Rose to overhear. "What have you been hearing about her?"

"Come on, Ronnie. We're Cartwrights. You know there are no secrets in our family. Everyone knows you two are sharing the sheets," Frank replied. "Gotta admit after all the shit that happened when you were in college, I didn't think you'd go for another woman again." He looked at Rose. "But she seems very nice."

"I don't think who I do or do not sleep with is anyone's concern."

"Relax, Cuz. It's not a big deal. Hey, at least you nailed yourself a nice one. Not like you'll have to go elsewhere looking for it when you have something like that waiting for you at home."

"Hey, Ronnie, I think you've got something," Rose yelled out while watching the tip of the pole jerk.

"Yeah, you got something all right," Frank teased low enough for only his cousin to hear. "Quite the catch if you ask me."

Sure is, Ronnie thought to herself as she worked her way to the stern.

It was around ten o'clock when they finally made their way back to the dock. Rose's fish had been the biggest of the day, although Ronnie did pull in two impressive-looking ones. Frank used every lure in his tackle box and had nothing worthwhile to show for his efforts. Male pride made him throw back the puny catches he did make. They went to an out-of-the-way diner for a bite to eat before returning home. While Rose made a beeline for the bathroom, Frank helped Ronnie take the poles and tackle inside. "Good day of fishing, Frank."

"For you and Blondie, maybe," he snorted. "I would have had better luck catching a cold."

"The season's just started, Frank. You'll get a trophy catch next time, I'm sure."

"Yeah, but no matter how big it is, it won't compare to your catch, Cuz." He looked at his watch. "Speaking of catches, if I don't show up home soon, the boss is gonna think I found myself a cutie like yours."

"There's no one like Rose," Ronnie said emphatically.

"I don't doubt that. Must be something pretty special to stay with you after the accident."

"Um, Frank...." She led him outside, away from anywhere Rose could hear them. "You have to watch what you say. She doesn't know about the accident."

"What do you mean she doesn't know? Isn't she the one who has been on crutches and all? I mean, she is the reason your Porsche got damaged, isn't it? I was at the emergency room with you that night, then after that, she shows up. It doesn't take a college degree to figure that one out."

"She doesn't know about the Porsche," the executive clarified. "Look, Frank, that kind of thing can't get back to Rose."

"You've never told her?" He rubbed the short stubble on his face and looked at the house. "Oh, man, Ronnie. You're walking a thin line with that kind of secret. Damn, the worst things I've kept from Agnes were a few insignificant affairs."

"And I'm sure the mother of your children appreciates that," Ronnie said dryly.

"Mother of most of my children, you mean."

"Does she know about the boy?"

"No. I know enough to cover my tracks." He opened the door of his truck and pulled himself up onto the bench seat. "She's a nice girl, Ronnie. Bring her fishing anytime." He turned the key, the Ford roaring to life. "See ya Monday at work."

"Bye, Frank." Ronnie waited until he was out of the driveway before turning and heading back into the house.

Chapter Twenty-five

Rose was typing a memo when the phone rang. "Veronica Cartwright's office. Miss Grayson speaking."

"Hi, Rose, it's Wendy from accounting. Is Ronnie around?"

"I'm sorry. She's in a meeting right now. Is there something I can help you with?"

"I'm right in the middle of Ronnie's quarterly tax estimates, and I can't find the paperwork for her Porsche."

"Porsche?" *Ronnie never said anything to me about having a sports car other than the Mustang.* "Wendy, are you sure? I know she has the Cherokee and the Mustang, but I don't know anything about a Porsche."

"Hmm, she did unless she got rid of it. Anyway, I need the paperwork on it or I can't finish this up. You think you can find it and have it sent down to me?"

"Sure. I'll look for it right now."

"Thanks, Rose. I'll be waiting for it."

"Okay, bye."

"Bye."

Rose put the receiver back in the cradle and reached for her cane. If there was such a car, Ronnie would have that paperwork in her private files. Reaching into her desk drawer, she retrieved a small key and headed into Ronnie's office.

Sure enough, behind the files for the Cherokee and Mustang was a folder marked Porsche. Rose pulled it out of the cabinet and returned to her desk. She set the folder down and called Susan's secretary to cover for her while she took the file to Wendy. When she picked the folder up again, a Polaroid fell out. She looked at the red car, thinking it too speedy for Ronnie's tastes. Opening the folder to put the picture back, her eyes fell on a receipt sitting prominently on top of the other papers. It was a repair bill from Hans's Import Cars. Her eyes widened at the total at the bottom. *I can't imagine paying a repair bill like that.* Calculations of hours and materials filled up the receipt, but it was a hand-scribbled note just above the total that caught Rose's attention. "Repairs started 12-5, completed 12-23."

The young woman slumped into her chair, feeling very much like a sledgehammer had struck her in the chest. *Repairs started 12-5.* Right after the accident. If that wasn't enough, another receipt showed the Porsche had passed inspection only a week before. "Oh, God...." A sick feeling churned in her stomach, and she had to swallow several times to keep her coffee down. *There was no mysterious stranger driving drunk. It was Ronnie.* Tears started to fall, smearing mascara down Rose's cheeks. *That's why you wanted to help me so much. It was all a lie to protect yourself.* Dabbing her eyes with a tissue, Rose reached out with shaky hands and opened the Rolodex. Her lower lip quivered and her vision blurred as she tried to find the number to the cab company that Ronnie used to pick clients up from the airport. *It was all a lie.* Her hands shook so hard that she misdialed twice before finally reaching the right number. Rose's voice wavered as she spoke with the dispatcher. She was informed that one was only a block away and would meet her in front of the building. Without waiting for Susan's secretary to arrive, Rose gathered her purse and cane and left the office. *It's okay, Ronnie. You don't have to worry about me anymore.* She choked back a sob. *I understand.*

Maria was surprised to see a cab pull into the driveway and even more so to see Rose step out. She opened the sliding glass door. "What are you doing home in the middle of the day? Rose? Child, have you been crying?"

"It's nothing, Maria. Where's Tabitha?"

"She's lying down somewhere, why?" Rose didn't answer, instead walking past the housekeeper and heading for the stairs. "Rose? What's going on? Where's Ronnie?"

"At work" came the sad reply. To Maria's dismay, the cab seemed to be waiting for Rose. A few minutes later, the young woman came down the stairs, one of Ronnie's suitcases in her hand.

"What is going on? Where are you going?" To her surprise, green eyes were rimmed with red.

"Would you please tell the man that this is the only bag? I have to get Tabitha." She set the suitcase at the bottom of the stairs and went back to retrieve her cat.

"Rose, wait." Maria followed her up, stopping the young woman with a firm hand on her shoulder. "What's going on? Did you and Ronnie have a fight?"

"Did you know that she was the one who hit me?" The look in the housekeeper's eyes answered the question. Rose nodded. She had suspected as much. "I wish you had told me. I wish she had told me." She swallowed hard, not wanting to start crying again. "I need to get Tabitha."

"Where are you going? Does Ronnie know you're leaving?"

"Maria, I can't talk about this. Please, I just want to get my cat and get out of here." At that moment, the orange and white feline appeared at the top of the stairs. "Tabitha, come here, honey." She scooped the cat into her arms. "Come on, sweetie. We have to go now."

"Rose, have you talked to Ronnie? You need to talk to her before you go and make any rash decisions."

"There's nothing left to say," the young woman sniffed, angrily wiping away an errant tear. "I'll return her suitcase as soon as I can."

"Where will you go?"

"I don't know," she admitted. "I just have to get away." The cab horn beeped, drawing her attention. "I need to go now. Please take care of yourself, Maria."

"Rose, please don't leave. I'm sure if you just talk to Ronnie—"

"No." Her ankle was beginning to throb from the overuse. "Let her know that I'm not going to sue her or anything so she doesn't have to worry." She walked out to the kitchen, then through the screen door. The driver helped her and Tabitha into the car, then came to the doorway to get the suitcase. Maria handed him a bag containing a box and several cans of cat food, her other hand busily pressing the speed dial on the phone.

"Two percent growth is not what I expected when I hired you for this position," Ronnie said, her eyes darting from the report in front of her to the nervous manager. The shrill sound of the phone drew a glare from her. *It had better be damn important to ruin a perfectly good chewing out.* "Excuse me." She reached for the phone before the annoying ring could be heard again. "Veronica Cartwright...who?...well, where's Rose? Why are you answering my phone? Fine...put her through." She looked at the man seated across from her. "That's all for now. I'd better see higher numbers next quarter." She turned her attention back to the phone. "Maria? What's wrong?"

Susan was walking down the hall toward Ronnie's office in search of her secretary when she saw her sister tear down the hall and head for the stairway. "Ronnie, what's going on?"

"I can't talk now. Gotta go." The door opened, and the dark-haired woman disappeared, footsteps pounding down the metal stairs. The redhead entered her sister's office. "Margaret, what happened here?"

"I don't know, Ms. Cartwright. Rose called me to come cover for her for a few minutes while she ran something down to accounting, but when I got here, she was gone. I assumed she couldn't wait and went down, but I haven't seen her since." She pointed at the folders strewn about Rose's desk. "Funny thing is, Wendy called up a few minutes ago looking for her."

"You mean Rose never showed up?"

"No. I was going to go look for her, but then Miss Cartwright's housekeeper called and sounded really upset. I put her through to the conference room. Then Miss Cartwright came racing in here and grabbed her purse and left. Didn't say a word to me. Do you want me to stay here?"

"No, that's all right. You can go back to your desk now. I'll close up in here. I don't think either of them will be back today." Once her secretary left the room, Susan looked through the papers on Rose's desk. Seeing the folder for the Porsche, she opened it. The receipt on top still showed watermarks where tears had apparently fallen. *Funny, I don't remember her saying anything to me about being in an....* "Oh, my God," she whispered. "No." Sitting in the chair, she turned the computer on and logged in under her ID. She opened the personnel file and compared the dates to the receipt. "Oh, Ronnie." The pieces clicked into place, and she had no doubt that they clicked for Rose, as well. She thought about calling Ronnie's house but decided instead to drive over. If what she thought had happened, her sister would need her.

When Susan arrived, Ronnie was on the phone. "What do you mean you don't know where she was dropped off? How many women with cats do you drive around every day? Well, can you at least tell me if it was a hotel or a bus station? You think it was a hotel? Any idea which one? You're a lot of help, thanks," she said sarcastically, slamming the phone down. "They don't know or they're not saying. Damn useless cab companies." She looked up to see her sister standing there. "What are you doing here?"

"I thought you might need help." She pulled out the adjacent chair and nodded at Maria's motion toward the coffeemaker. "I saw the paperwork for the Porsche on Rose's desk. Ronnie, I have to ask. The accident...."

"It was me," Ronnie answered sadly.

"And you never told her?"

"No."

"So now she's found out on her own and decided to leave you?"

"Looks that way," Ronnie sighed, staring at the phone. "Came here, packed a few clothes, took Tabitha, and left."

"Maybe she just needs some time to think about it."

"I'd say she's already thought about it." She combed her fingers through her hair. "She's gone, Susan. She...she left me."

"Ronnie, she'll come back. You two love each other."

"She thinks I lied to her."

"You did lie to her," the younger Cartwright pointed out. "Ronnie, you have to expect that she'll be upset about this. You hit her and lied about it. I can't believe you kept that a secret. How did you think she'd react to finding out? Especially after the two of you have...you know...become lovers."

"I can't be without her, Susan." Her eyes fell on the empty chair that only hours before had been filled by Rose eating her breakfast. "I need her." She looked at the phone again. "How many hotels can there be in Albany? Maria, get me the phone book."

"I'll help. Where's the phone for the other line?"

"In the office. Ask them first if they take pets. That should eliminate most of them."

Forty-five minutes worth of calling hotels turned up no sign of her beloved Rose. Ronnie was beginning to become upset and frustrated when Susan came out, a piece of paper in her hand and a triumphant smile on her face. "I tried to think like she would. You know how she's worried about money. I started calling the cheaper motels and voilà, I found her."

Ronnie took the scrap of paper and looked at it. "The Arcadia? That roach motel on Central?"

"It must be the cheapest motel in Albany that allows pets." Ronnie shut the phone book and stood up. "I've got to go see her."

"Ronnie, wait." Susan put her hand on her sister's shoulder. "Maybe you should call and talk to her on the phone first. You're upset, she's upset. Maybe a face-to-face confrontation isn't such a good idea. What if you get there and she doesn't want to talk to you?"

"She'll talk to me," Ronnie said. "Why wouldn't she? Rose is a reasonable woman. I'm sure once I explain what happened that she'll forgive me and come home where she belongs."

"I hope so," Susan replied, not entirely convinced that her sister was right.

Ronnie pulled her car into the pothole-ridden parking lot. She was certain that she'd be able to get Rose to come home with her. Surely, she wouldn't choose to stay in such a disgusting place once she heard what Ronnie wanted to say. She was about to go into the office to ask which room was Rose's when she saw the familiar orange and white cat jump into one of the upper-level windows.

Rose stomped on the roach she saw scurry out from behind the toilet. Tomorrow she would call around for another place to stay. *Knock knock.* "Rose?" Ronnie's voice startled her. She hadn't expected to deal with Ronnie so quickly. She walked across the stained carpet and stood behind the door, pressing her forehead against the cool metal.

"Go away, Ronnie," she said softly.

"Rose, please let me in. We need to talk."

"Please, Ronnie. Go home. I'm fine."

"You're not fine. If you were fine, you'd be home with me." The doorknob jiggled, showing her frustration with talking through the steel door. "Rose, please just let me in so we can talk."

"There's nothing to say, Ronnie. Go home. You don't have to worry. I won't sue you or anything."

"Sue?" The doorknob jiggled again. "Rose, let me in. I'm not worried about you suing me. Come on, honey. We need to talk."

"So talk. I can hear you." Rose knew she couldn't open the door. She was on the verge of tears as it was and to see Ronnie would be more than enough to push her over the edge. "What did you want to say?"

A long silence. "I wanted to say that I love you. That I want you to come home with me and talk about this. Please, Rose, I'm sorry I lied to you."

"Sorry you lied or sorry I found out?" She closed her eyes. "Ronnie...please just go home."

"I can't leave without you."

"You...you were my knight in shining armor, you know. I really thought you had come down and rescued me like a real-life Cinderella." She didn't bother wiping the tears that ran down her face. "And all this time you were just trying to protect yourself. What a fool I was."

"No, Rose, you don't understand."

"What don't I understand? You hit me, lied about it, made me think that everything you were doing was out of the goodness of your heart, then you let me fall in love with you," she lashed out, slamming the side of her fist against the door, startling the woman standing on the other side. "Damn you, Ronnie. Damn you. Why did you let me fall in love with you?" The sobs refused to be held back, and Rose collapsed to the floor. "Please go away. There's nothing left to say." She hugged her knees against her chest and cried.

"Rose, please." The young woman refused to answer, even when the request was repeated several times. Eventually, Ronnie walked away, her footsteps against the creaking wood drawing even more pain from the young woman's heart. Rose threw herself on the threadbare blankets that covered the bed and cried herself into a restless sleep.

"Come to my house for dinner tonight, Ronnie," Susan urged. "You know Jack and the kids would love to see you."

"No. I have things to attend to here."

"No word from Rose yet?"

"She left the Arcadia a week ago and checked into the Lawrence. Trades in one dive for another." Ronnie rubbed her face with her hands. "She left instructions with the front desk not to let any calls through. They keep taking messages, but she won't return my calls."

"Have you been over to try and talk to her again?"

"What's the point? I did that twice, and she wouldn't even open the door for me." The strain had taken its toll on the beautiful woman. Dark circles under her eyes were a testament to the lack of sleep. Her cheeks were drawn, her hair given only the barest of care. "She just keeps telling me to go away."

"Ronnie, I hate to say this, but maybe you should consider moving on."

"I can't, Susan. Don't you understand that she's everything to me?" She looked at her younger sister. "I need her like I need air or water. I feel so empty without her." She turned her head away, angrily wiping away the tears that seemed to form so easily during the past week. "What's all this worth?"

"Hmm?" Susan didn't understand the question.

"What's all this worth? What are gains and ratios and profits worth if there's nothing to show for it? What's the precious Cartwright reputation and status worth if the one woman I need most in my life won't even speak to me?"

"Ronnie, you're talking crazy now. You know as well as I do that this business has to survive and make money."

"For what? So we can have a few more zeros in our bank accounts?" Ronnie stood up and looked out the window. "It doesn't mean anything without her."

"Veronica?" Both women turned to see Beatrice standing in the doorway. "I was downtown doing some shopping, and I was hoping you girls would join me for lunch." She stepped inside and shut the door. "What happened to your friend? I thought she replaced Laura."

"She left," Ronnie said without elaboration. "I'm too busy for lunch today, Mother. Maybe Susan can go with you."

"Well, it's nothing important I guess." She sat down on the leather sofa. "So your little reformation project left? I could have told you it wouldn't work. Those people don't understand what hard work is all about. They just want to sit around and collect a check. I suppose she's filed for unemployment to pick your pocket some more."

"Rose isn't like that, Mother. She didn't quit because she didn't like to work. There were other reasons."

"There's no excuse for leaving a good-paying job, Veronica, except pure laziness. It's in their blood."

"In whose blood, Mother? The poor white trash you love to talk about?" Ronnie's hands gripped the back of her chair, knuckles white with the strain. "I'm sure there are people like that, but Rose isn't one of them. She's good and honest and would give her last dime to help another person out, and I won't have you talking like that about her again, do you understand me?"

"Veronica...." Beatrice's tone was low, warning.

"No. I've had it. You badmouth everyone who isn't a blueblood like us. Rose has never ever done anything to earn your dislike, yet you treat her like a bastard at a family reunion. Well, like it or not,

Mother, I love Rose, and that's all there is to it." Susan took a step back, certain that her mother and sister were about to have a battle royal with words. Never had any of them stood up to their mother, and now Ronnie had just announced her defiance on the most taboo of subjects.

"I thought that issue was settled years ago, or have you forgotten your promise to your poor deceased father?" Beatrice now stood in front of Ronnie's desk, her hands resting on the mahogany top. "You swore to him that you were through with those perverted ideas."

The strain of losing Rose sapped any tact or restraint Ronnie had left. Blue eyes burned with anger. "You two forced me to promise that no matter how I felt. You think telling me not to love women would make those feelings go away? It didn't. What is so wrong with loving another woman? Why is it so hard for you to accept?"

"Veronica, think about your position for a minute."

"Fuck my position, Mother!" Ronnie shoved away from her chair and took a step toward Beatrice, noting that Susan quickly stepped between them. "Face it, Mother. Your oldest daughter is a lesbian. You can't change that, so you'd better learn to accept it. Rose is my lover, and I'll give up everything I have to keep her." She lowered her voice, the tone deadly serious. "Including my family."

"Ronnie, maybe this isn't the best time to talk about this," Susan said, trying to guide her sister away from their mother.

"No, Susan," Beatrice bristled. "It's obvious that your sister has decided to throw away everything her father and I worked for all these years."

"Mother, there's no reason why she can't be that way and still do a good job running the company."

"Whose side are you on, anyway?" The matriarch turned on her younger daughter. "Don't tell me that you accept this, that Jack accepts it."

"It isn't for us to decide who Ronnie loves, Mother." She looked at her older sibling and gave her a small smile. "And yes, Jack and I do accept Rose."

"I can't believe this." She walked over to the couch and retrieved her bag. "I would have thought after poor Tommy's death that you would have realized what can happen from hanging out with the wrong element. And just how do you think the shareholders will feel about this?"

"It's none of the damn shareholders' business who I'm sleeping with," Ronnie snapped. "It's not like they can vote me out of office."

"You don't own controlling interest, Veronica. Don't forget that."

"Actually, Mother," Susan interjected. "With Tommy's shares between us, we hold fifty percent of the stock. All we need is Frank, Michael, or John to vote with us, and we have controlling interest."

"So that's it?" Beatrice's lips were pursed, her frustration obvious. "Fine. If Veronica wants to throw her life away and you're willing to help her, so be it. I'll call a cab from downstairs." She stormed out of the office, leaving the sisters alone again.

"Well, that was productive," Ronnie sighed, sinking back into her chair. "I stood up to her finally, and it doesn't even matter because Rose is gone."

"You know I'm never going to hear the end of this, don't you? I'll guarantee there'll be a message on my machine when I get home."

"I know, Sis. I'm sorry you had to get in the middle of that." She picked up her pen, the present making her heart ache even more for her beloved Rose.

"Ronnie...do you want me to try and talk to Rose?"

"Do you think it would make any difference? She won't talk to me."

"I don't think it could hurt," Susan said.

"I'd make a deal with the devil if I thought it would get her to talk to me again." She looked up at her sister. "Please. If you think there's anything you can do or say to make her understand how I feel, do it."

"Which motel is she at?"

"The Lawrence on Central. About eight miles west of the Arcadia."

"That's almost on the city line of Schenectady, isn't it? The one that puts out all those gaudy Christmas decorations each year?"

"That's the place."

"I'll go talk to her, but you need to tell me what really happened that night. She deserves to know the complete truth, not just whatever those papers she found told her."

Ronnie hesitated, then nodded in agreement. "I was out at Sam's...."

Chapter Twenty-six

"There you go, sweetie," Rose said as she put the plate of canned food down for Tabitha. She threw the empty can in the trash just as there was a knock on the door. "Who is it?"

"Susan Cartwright."

"Um...." Rose looked out the peephole, verifying that the redhead was alone. "I'm not really in the mood for company right now."

"Rose, it really is rude to leave someone standing outside the door."

"But...." Reluctantly, she undid the chain and bolt and opened the door. "Susan, if it's about Ronnie...."

"Of course it's about Ronnie," the redhead said as she breezed past Rose and entered the room. "My sister is heartbroken, and you won't even give her the chance to explain. Hello, Tabitha."

"Mrrow."

"There's nothing really left to say, is there?"

"You tell me." Susan sat down on one bed and motioned for the young woman to sit on the other.

"She lied to me."

"Yes, she did...about the accident. Not about how she feels for you. There's a difference."

"How can anything built on a lie be real?" Rose stood up and limped over to the tiny cube refrigerator to get some bottled water.

"Again, she lied about the accident. Everything else was real, Rose. Her feelings for you are real, and you have to know that."

"I know she feels something—"

"If you could see her, you'd know that it's more than that." She reached out and took Rose's hand. "Listen to me. We're talking about my sister here. I know her. She's not one to take people's feelings lightly, especially her own. Rose, this is killing her. She's not eating, she's not sleeping, nothing matters to her now."

"It hasn't been a picnic for me either."

"Then why not go and talk to her? Come on. Think about it for a minute. If all she wanted to do was cover her tracks, then why did she stick around at the hospital? Why didn't she just drop you off and let them worry about taking care of you?"

"I don't know...maybe she felt guilty."

"Tell me something, Rose, when the two of you, you know...did it feel like guilt to you?"

"No, of course not."

"Then why do you assume that everything she did came from guilt?" Susan smiled inwardly at the confused look on Rose's face. "If she was just guilty, she wouldn't have opened up her home to you. She wouldn't have gone to the lengths she did to take care of you. She could have put you up in a nice place somewhere and paid someone to take care of you. You know she has the money to do that. She took you in because she cares. Look, I know you're hurting, too, but you have to look at the whole picture. Ronnie loves you."

"How am I supposed to forgive her?" Rose said, her voice cracking. "It's been six months, and I still can't walk without pain. I have scars."

"You see this?" Susan rolled her sleeve up to reveal a small white scar near her elbow. "Ronnie and I were fooling around on our bicycles, and she wiped out, causing me to fall. I broke my elbow and had to spend the summer in a cast. I still can't extend that arm completely, and I know whenever it's going to rain now. Do you think I shouldn't have forgiven her for that?"

"Of course not. It was an accident."

"Exactly. It was an accident when she caused me to fall off my bike, and it was an accident when she hit you with her car."

"It's not the same, Susan."

"Isn't it? Tell me something. Do you think she meant to hit you with her car?"

"No."

"Then it was an accident, right? Even if it was partially her fault, it was still an accident." She shifted her rear on the bed, trying to find a spot where the springs weren't trying to poke through the thin blanket. "What do you remember about that night?"

"Not much," Rose admitted. "I was trying to get home and some men started chasing me. I remember running frantically through the park, then onto Madison Avenue. The next thing I remember is waking up in the hospital."

Susan nodded, the events fitting with her sister's description. "Did you run out from the corner or the middle of the street?"

"I think it was the middle. It was snowing, I don't know."

"Ronnie says she was going up Madison when you darted out from between some parked cars. She said there was no way for her stop in time."

"Then why make up the story about coming up after the accident?"

"She had some wine at dinner and worried that she'd be arrested for drunk driving. Yes, she lied to cover her tail, but she made sure you were taken care of. She tried to do the responsible thing, Rose. You have to give her credit for that."

"It was an accident," the young woman whispered. "If she hadn't been drinking–"

"She still would have been unable to avoid you. If you're looking for someone to blame, blame the men who were chasing you."

"But why didn't she tell me the truth later?"

"What happened when you did find out the truth?"

The young woman looked at her lap. "I left her."

"You never gave her a chance to explain, did you?" She reached out for the woman she considered a sister-in-law. "Rose, the accident wasn't her fault. She may be guilty of bad judgment but not anything else. Do you love Ronnie?"

Lifting her head to show eyes glittering with unshed tears, Rose replied, "Yes."

"Do you think she would willingly hurt you?"

"No."

"Then why are you punishing her for what was clearly an accident? Let me take you home, Rose."

Ronnie was sitting on the couch, the pendant she had given Rose for Christmas in her hands. There had been no word from Susan, and Ronnie feared that her sister's intervention would have no effect on Rose. The sound of the sliding glass door opening drew her attention toward the kitchen. When she saw Susan enter the living room alone, Ronnie's heart sank. She opened her mouth to speak, but there was nothing to say. Rose was gone and wasn't coming back. Tears started down her cheeks.

"Ronnie?"

"It's all right, Susan. I know you tried your best." Blue eyes stared at the pendant. "Did she...say anything?"

"She said a lot of things, but maybe it would be better if you just asked her yourself." It was then that the sliding glass door closed, alerting Ronnie that Susan was not alone.

"She's here?" She stood up and quickly wiped at the tear streaks on her face. She sprinted past her sister and into the kitchen without waiting for an answer.

Rose barely had time to set Tabitha on the floor before she found herself caught in Ronnie's powerful arms. The cane clattered to the floor as the tall woman spun her round and round, hugging her tightly.

"You're...crushing...me."

"Oh, I'm sorry." Ronnie quickly set her lover down and retrieved the cane. "It's just...well...."

"It's all right," Rose said, reaching out to take the larger hand in her own. She was surprised to see such a haggard expression on Ronnie's face. She realized that the separation was just as hard on her lover as it was on her. "I missed you, too."

"Please don't leave again," Ronnie blurted. She hadn't meant to sound so desperate, but the thought of not having Rose in her life was too much to bear. "I'll do anything...just don't leave."

"I can't promise that," Rose said sadly, turning away and leaning her hand against the counter. "I have questions, Ronnie. We need to talk."

"I think that's my cue to leave," Susan piped in from her position in the archway between the kitchen and living room. "Sis, get Rose's suitcase from my car."

Ronnie's eyes never left her lover. "Sure...I'll be right back, okay?"

"I'll be here," the young woman replied softly, giving a wan smile. Ronnie reluctantly opened the sliding glass door and stepped outside. Susan walked over and put her hand on Rose's shoulder. "Are you going to be all right?"

"Yeah," she nodded, turning to face the redhead. "Thanks."

"Rose, I know Ronnie hurt you, but don't forget how easily you can hurt her, too. Be gentle with my sister. She loves you very much."

Once Susan was gone, an awkward silence fell over them. They stood in the kitchen, both lost in their own thoughts and fears. Tabitha padded into the room and spotted the unmarred black of Ronnie's slacks. "Mrrow?" She rubbed up against her tall mistress and began purring.

"Hey there." She bent down and picked up the happy cat. "How you been? Have you been taking good care of Mommy?"

"She missed you, you know," Rose said, moving a couple of steps closer. "She kept crying for you and looking at the door." She looked down at the floor. "I kept crying, too," she added quietly. Ronnie set Tabitha down and closed the remaining distance between them just as Rose's lip started to quiver. "It just felt like some kind of horrible nightmare that I couldn't wake up from." Ronnie's arms went around her just as the young woman collapsed into tears.

She held Rose tight, fearing that she would disappear like a butterfly if she let go. "Do you want to go sit on the couch and talk?"

"Sure," the young woman sniffled. "If you want to."

"Whatever you want to do, Rose. If you'd rather sit at the table...."

"No, the couch would be nice." The motel room didn't have a couch...well, not one that she felt safe sitting on. Hands resting on each other's backs, the couple walked into the living room. Rose took her usual cushion at the end while Ronnie hesitated, then sat down at the opposite end instead of the middle. To her surprise, the young woman scooted over to occupy the empty cushion. Ronnie took it as a good sign and rested her hand on Rose's knee.

"I love you, Rose."

"I know." She took a deep breath and looked into the blue eyes that haunted her dreams. "And I love you, too. I wouldn't have come back if I didn't."

"I'm sorry about lying to you. I wish there was some way I could make it up."

"Do something now."

"Anything."

"Tell me what really happened."

"Rose, it's in the past. Why can't–"

"Because I need to know what happened," she interrupted. "Please, Ronnie. You owe me the truth."

Ronnie nodded and swallowed. "It happened so fast." She shook her head, the dark tresses waving with the movement. "It was just so quick." Looking into gentle green eyes, she continued. "I never saw you, Rose. I was driving and thinking about how I wasted the evening with a jerk, and all of the sudden, there you were. I hit the brakes, but with the snow on the ground...." Her eyes closed briefly at the memory of the total silence that preceded the horrifying thud. "There was nothing else I could do." She looked away again, focusing on the grandfather clock. "There was so much blood. I thought I killed you. When I realized I hadn't, I put you in my car and drove you to the hospital as fast as I could."

"Why did you stay around?" Ronnie felt a small but insistent hand on her chin, forcing her to meet Rose's gaze. "You did your job, you got me to the hospital. You could have left and no one would ever have known. Why didn't you leave?"

"I needed to make sure you were all right. When they didn't think you had insurance, they wanted to ship you off to the county hospital. I wanted to make sure you got the best care and that's at Albany Med, so I lied about the insurance."

"And you were stuck after that?"

"No. Maybe until I had you sign the papers," Ronnie admitted. "But not after that."

"Then why did you keep coming back?"

Ronnie gave the only answer she could, the honest one. "I wanted to see you. To get to know you better."

"You know what I remember about those first few days?" Rose looked toward the ceiling. "It's mostly fuzzy glimpses here and there, just snatches really. They must have been giving me some powerful drugs then."

"They were," Ronnie agreed.

"I remember looking up and seeing you." She smiled warmly and looked at her lover. "There you were, this wonderful woman telling me that everything would be all right."

"You asked me if I was an angel."

"You were to me, you know. My own personal guardian angel looking out for me every step of the way. You were my knight in shining armor, my hero." She lifted Ronnie's arm and rested her head against her chest. "I didn't know why you took such an interest in me, but I was grateful." Her voice grew sad. "Now I know."

"No." Ronnie rested her palm against Rose's cheek. "That first night, I acted out of self-preservation and fear, but don't you ever think that I pretended to care after that." Blue eyes searched green, begging them to understand. "I can't explain it, but there was something about you, Rose Grayson. I couldn't stop thinking about you, and the only time I was happy was when I was with you. I think I fell in love with you from that first day you woke up in the hospital."

"What happened to the Porsche?"

"I had it fixed, then sold it. I couldn't bring myself to drive it again." She reached down and began stroking the golden hair cascading over Rose's shoulder.

"Ronnie?"

"Mmm?"

"When you realized that I was falling for you, why didn't you tell me then?"

Ronnie pulled the young woman closer, holding her secure in her arms. "By then, I'd already fallen for you...hard." Taking a chance, she leaned down and placed a gentle kiss atop the golden head, pleased when she felt Rose lean into it. Turning her head so her cheek rested where her lips had just been, Ronnie continued. "I tried so hard to pretend it wasn't happening, but every day I fell in love more and more. I was scared that if I told you the truth that you'd leave me. I couldn't lose you, Rose, I just couldn't." The gentle squeeze encouraged her. "When you left...when Maria called me...." Words failed her.

"I didn't know what else to do, what to think. It hurt so much." Rose's fingers idly stroked Ronnie's hair. "But as much as that hurt, it was worse not being with you."

"I love you, Rose." She cupped the young woman's chin, and their eyes met. "I can't change what happened in the past, but I can give you my word that I'll never lie to you again." Her thumb brushed against Rose's lower lip. "I know you can probably never forgive me for lying, but I love you, and I know you love me."

"I do," the young woman said earnestly. "I've never loved anyone the way I do you."

"You don't know how much I wish that accident never happened, that you never had to suffer through all that pain."

"But Ronnie...." She kissed the thumb resting against her lip. "If it never happened, then we wouldn't have met. Sometimes things happen for a reason."

"Then can we move on from here?"

"I'd like that." She leaned her head against Ronnie's chest. "Honey?"

Ronnie smiled at the endearment and gave Rose a quick kiss on the forehead. "Yeah?"

"Can we just stay like this forever?"

Ronnie smiled broadly and squeezed her lover against her. "Sure."

"You almost done in there, birthday girl?" Ronnie called from the other side of the door.

"Almost." Rose fastened the top and looked at her reflection in the mirror. "Honey, don't you think this bikini is a bit...revealing?"

"It's meant to be that way."

"You're a pervert, Veronica Cartwright, you know that?"

"Only with you, my dear." Tired of waiting, Ronnie opened the bathroom door and was treated to the sight of Rose standing there with only the skimpy bikini top on. "Very nice," she drawled.

"Nice for you maybe," the young woman countered, pulling the yellow bottoms on. Reddish gold tufts of hair peeked out from the side. "Great." She pulled them off again and headed for the toiletries.

"Why don't you go on ahead, honey. I have to take care of something first."

"Sure you don't want any help? I'd be happy to help you."

Rose picked up the razor and smiled at her lover. "If you 'helped' me, we wouldn't get anywhere near the pool today." Ronnie stepped up from behind and wrapped her arms around the smaller woman.

"So? Would that be such a bad thing?"

"You are incorrigible. I'm certain this bikini is more of a present for you than for me." She looked from the shaver to her pubic hair and back at the shaver again. "I'm not sure if I need a razor or a weed whacker."

"Yeah? Try having black hair. The slightest stubble shows." Her hand began running circles on Rose's abdomen, steadily heading south. "You sure you don't want help?" she queried while nuzzling the smaller woman's ear.

"Isn't this why we didn't get to go swimming yesterday?" She stopped the wandering hand and stepped out of Ronnie's embrace. "You go bring the iced tea out and I'll be down in a few minutes."

The late August sun beat down on the white concrete, causing the barefooted executive to stick to the shady areas while taking the pitcher of iced tea to the table. The pool was crystal clear and ready for swimming. All that was missing was Rose. Ronnie set the tray down and walked to the diving board.

Rose arrived just in time to see her tall lover walk down the length of the board. The two-piece black thong bikini Ronnie wore hid nothing, much to the young woman's enjoyment. Her own pale yellow outfit was a bit more reserved but not by much. Instead of being a thong, it had a small strip that covered the crack of her rear and half of each cheek. The top, however, barely covered her nipples, and she was certain that once again Ronnie had purchased a smaller size to make her show more cleavage.

The tall, athletic form sprung off the board and dived into the water with barely a splash. Rose walked over to the shallow end and lowered herself into the pool. Soon Ronnie joined her and the two splashed and played about for a while before retiring to the padded lounge chairs.

"God, it's hot out here today," Rose said before draining half her glass.

"The humidity is up," Ronnie replied, wringing the excess water from her hair. "Five minutes and I guarantee you we'll be wanting to go back into the water." She wiped her brow. "I think I'm perspiring already." She took her glass and lay down on the lounge chair, grateful that the umbrella provided shade for them against the burning sun. She didn't see Rose fish an ice cube out of the pitcher and gasped in surprise when it landed on her chest. "Whooo, that's cold!" she yelped.

"I thought you said you were hot," Rose grinned. The predatory look in her lover's eyes quickly apprised her that she had made a mistake. "Uh-oh. Um...Ronnie, honey, you know I love you, right? You wouldn't think of seeking revenge, right?"

"Me?" The tall woman feigned innocence, her fingers digging cubes out of her glass. Before Rose could move out of the way, Ronnie pinned her to the lounge chair and shoved several cubes between the yellow bikini top and creamy white skin.

"Oooh, Ronnie, get them out of there. Oh, that's cold." She pulled the top up, baring her breasts and freeing the ice, which bounced harmlessly to the concrete ground.

"Well, that was worth the effort," Ronnie quirked, her mouth only inches away from nipples made erect by the cubes. "Would you like me to help warm you up, birthday girl?"

"Ronnie, we're outside." Rose looked around even though she knew no one was around.

"Well then," Ronnie said, "I'd better make sure you're covered." Her left hand covered one breast while her lips converged on the other. She tasted the chlorine of the water on Rose's skin but didn't care. She was on a mission, and only her lover's cry of passion would satisfy her. Things were heating up quickly, and Ronnie was certain her fantasy of making love poolside was about to come true when the sound of a car pulling in the driveway caught her ear. "Damn," she muttered, moving off her lover. "Someone's here."

Rose barely got her top back into position when Susan's sons came running around the side of the house. "Aunt Ronnie, Aunt Rose!" the younger boy shouted.

"Mommy said we could come over here and go swimming today, isn't that great?" Ricky had his arms full with the PlayStation and obviously was planning on taking over the television for a few hours if the amount of games he brought with him were any indication.

John jumped onto Rose's lap and wrapped his arms around her neck. "Aunt Rose, would you go swimming with me?"

"Sure, hon, but only in the shallow end."

"Okay." His little face beamed. "Can Tabitha go swimming with us, too?"

Rose laughed at the thought. "No, John. Tabitha is a cat. Cats don't like water."

"Speak of the devil," Ronnie said, nodding her head in the direction of the house. The sliding glass door had been left open, and the curious feline wandered out in search of new worlds to conquer. She looked at the boys. "Why don't you boys go get changed? The pool house is right over there. Grab yourselves each a couple of towels." She turned to Rose. "You think you can handle things out here?"

"Sure." She scooted the boy off her lap. "John, I think there's a ball in the pool house that we can play with. See if you can find it, okay?"

"Okay, Aunt Rose." He followed his brother away from the pool. Ronnie watched them leave. "Looks like we're going to have company for a while."

"Seems that way," the young woman agreed. "Why aren't they using their own pool?"

"Susan said something about her pump breaking. Sorry, hon, I know it's your birthday and all, but–"

"No, it's fine that they're here," Rose said. "I just wish I was wearing something else. I feel really naked in this." She tugged at the thin strap of her bikini top.

"I'll get you a T-shirt."

"Make it one of yours or else bring a pair of shorts with you, too."

Ronnie returned a few minutes later carrying one of her T-shirts. She had changed from her two-piece bikini to a more appropriate black one-piece that covered most of her rear and provided very little cleavage. She called it her "family get-together" suit.

An hour later, Jack was busy tending the grill while the women and boys played in the water. Timmy and Ronnie raced each other across the length of the pool while Rose and John splashed around in the shallow end, occasionally playing with the brightly colored beach ball. When the young woman asked Ronnie where Susan was, she received a vague answer about the redhead not being a swimmer. John's fair skin showed signs of turning pink, and when Rose offered to take him inside, Ronnie stepped up and said she had to go get something anyway. A few minutes later, Jack came over to the pool and whispered something in Timmy's ear, causing the boy to exit the water and head inside, leaving Rose alone in the pool.

Feeling awkward, she climbed out of the water and wrapped herself in a towel, thinking to herself that Ronnie had been gone too long. She headed for the house when Jack stopped her. "Rose, come take a look at these steaks and tell me what you think."

"Sure, Jack." She moved over to the grill and looked at the various pieces of meat sizzling over the gas fire. "I hope everyone's hungry. You made quite a bunch here. They look fine, though. Maybe a few more minutes."

"Could you keep an eye on them for me? I have to visit the men's room." He handed her the turning fork and walked away.

A few minutes later, the steaks were done, and there was no sign of Ronnie or anyone else. Rose carefully piled the food on a plate and shut the grill off. "Where is everybody? I thought we were having a cookout," she said to the empty air.

"Mrrow?"

"Hi, Tabitha," she said to the purring fluff pile that appeared at her feet. "Should we go in and see what's going on?"

"Mrrow?"

"Let's go." She picked up the plate and headed for the house.

"Up a little," Susan said. "No, that's too high. Bring it down a bit." Ronnie stood on one of the upper rungs of the ladder, thinking that her sister was a pain in the ass when it came to decorating. The banner was perfect where it was before, but the redhead insisted that it would better if it was up just a foot. John, Ricky, and Timmy were busy running multi-colored rolls of streamers around the living room.

"We have to hurry up or she'll see it," Ronnie grumped. She spared a glance at her watch. "Where's Maria, anyway? She was supposed to be here with the cake a half hour ago."

"She'll be here, and if you'd just make it level, we'll be done," Susan said. They turned at the sound of the door sliding open. Ronnie shoved the thumbtack through the banner and stuck it to the wall. She had just hopped off the ladder when Rose stepped through the archway.

"HAPPY BIRTHDAY, ROSE!" they shouted, echoing the words printed on the banner. The young woman stood there speechless, her eyes wide with surprise. While she had thought it odd that no one except Ronnie had wished her a happy birthday, she chalked it up to them not knowing. She had never guessed that Ronnie would throw her a party. John tugged on her wet shirt. "Aunt Rose, does this mean I can give you your present now?"

"In a little while, John," Susan said, shooing her son away. "We have to eat first." Rose continued to stand there, totally shocked. "Rose?"

"Um...uh...oh, my." She looked at her lover. "You planned this?"

"Maria's on her way with your cake, and Frank and Agnes are stopping by later," Ronnie replied, crossing the room to stand in front of the overwhelmed woman. "Happy birthday, honey."

"It's been so long since anyone gave me a party for my birthday," the young woman whispered. "I can't believe this."

"Believe it. You can count on this being an annual occurrence from now on." She looked at the boys. "You guys go help your father make up the plates." Once they left the room, she turned her attention back to Rose. "I love you. You didn't think I'd let your birthday go by without throwing you a party, did you?"

"You didn't say anything except about the bikini so I thought...." The young woman shook her head and smiled. "I should have known. Cartwrights love parties."

"Well, that may be true, but this particular Cartwright had more of a reason to throw you a party than just your birthday." At Rose's quizzical look, Ronnie merely gave a sly smile. "You'll see later. Come on, go get changed into something dry so we can dig into dinner before it gets cold."

Maria arrived a short time later, the backseat of her car taken up with a large sheet cake. Ricky and Timmy got fingers full of frosting before Ronnie could get it placed out of reach. John insisted on sitting on Rose's lap during dinner, and the sight made Ronnie smile. The people who meant a great deal to her were there to help celebrate the birthday of the person who meant the most to her. Not a word was said when Maria joined them for dinner, and the atmosphere was relaxed and comfortable. Little side conversations took place all around her, but Ronnie paid them no attention. Her focus was on the green-eyed beauty and the thought of the present hidden in the office.

Frank and Agnes arrived just as dinner was ending. Rose had to laugh at the sight of the big burly man carrying a fishing pole wrapped in dainty paper. "Gee, Frank, I have no idea what you got her," Ronnie said with a smirk.

"You know, fishing poles aren't the easiest things in the world to wrap," he replied. "Took Agnes forever to get it wrapped." He walked over to Rose and gave her a kiss on the cheek while handing her the present. "Happy birthday, Blondie."

"I guess it's time to open presents," Ronnie announced.

It wasn't just any fishing pole but a top-of-the-line with sensitive tip and left-handed reel. "It's beautiful," she said as the final wrapping was removed.

"Maybe next time you go fishing you won't toss the lunkers back in," Frank said with a smile.

"Oh, I probably will," Rose admitted. "But it sure is fun to catch them."

"I wouldn't know. I've got more sunfish than bass this season," he grumbled good-naturedly.

"Aunt Rose, will you open my present now?" John asked, holding the gift in his hands.

"Of course I will, sweetie," she said, taking the present from him. It was a bottle of her favorite perfume, and she gave the young boy a kiss on the cheek. "Thank you, John. It's very nice." She looked up at Susan and indicated her silent thanks with her eyes. Timmy and Ricky gave her presents, as well, followed by a joint present from Susan and Jack. Maria gave her a brooch that was simply breathtaking.

Ronnie excused herself and went into the office. Rose watched her leave, wondering what her lover was up to. She returned a few moments later carrying a big, bulky-looking box covered in green wrapping paper. Jack and Ricky moved everything off the coffee table to make room for the box. Rose stood and smiled. "Thank you," she said. "I wonder what on earth it could possibly be. Looks kinda big." The box was easily as long as her outstretched arms and half as high.

"Looks can be deceiving," Ronnie replied, sharing a knowing grin with her sister as Rose began unwrapping the large box. While the box itself proclaimed that a twenty-seven-inch color television was waiting inside, the young woman knew from the weight that it wasn't the case. Besides, there were already a half-dozen televisions floating around the house as it was. Surely, Ronnie wouldn't have bothered to buy another one. Her curiosity was piqued when she opened the box to reveal another box inside, this one wrapped in red holiday paper. "I ran out of birthday wrap so I used Christmas paper. I hope you don't mind."

"Ronnie, you could have wrapped it in newspaper and I wouldn't have minded," Rose assured, pulling the smaller box out. Ricky moved the first box out of the way. The red box was unwrapped and opened only to discover another box inside. "Oh, blue paper this time."

"Wouldn't want you to be bored with the same old paper," Ronnie joked. Two more boxes with different colored papers had the boys in fits of laughter and the adults chuckling.

"I can't watch this," Frank said with a huge grin on his face. Tabitha was having a grand time playing with the paper as it fell to the floor.

"How many boxes did you wrap?" Rose asked after the sixth box opened only to find another one waiting inside.

"Oh, a few more." The devilish grin and wiggling eyebrows sent Susan's sons into renewed giggles. Finally, a coat box wrapped in silver paper with gold ribbons was revealed. "That's got to be it," Frank said. Jack and Susan nodded in agreement. With all the excitement of a child, Rose opened the box to reveal a bright green and black ski jacket. "Oh, that's very nice," the young woman said, pulling it out of the box and holding it up for all to see.

"That is nice, even if it is a bit early for snow," Susan said. Rose was already standing up to try it on. It fit perfectly.

"Sharp," Ricky said. John added a request for one in the same colors. Ronnie merely stood back and smiled at the image before her.

"It may be early for snow here but not everywhere." The corner of her lip curled up with a smile. "Rose, what's in the inside pocket?"

"The inside...?" Rose unzipped the jacket and pulled out a stack of papers. The bright stripes on the outer paper left no doubt as to its contents.

"I hear the Alps are just lovely this time of year," Ronnie drawled. "I do believe we both have some vacation time stored up."

"Oh. my God, tickets to Switzerland?" Rose's fingers trembled as she pulled not two but ten tickets out of the sleeve. "Ronnie...."

Her voice stilled as the names of several far-away countries appeared before her eyes.

"I believe Germany, Austria, and Greece are in there too, aren't they?" Ronnie teased just before an overjoyed Rose flew into her arms.

"Ronnie, you are something else," her sister said.

"I can't believe you," Rose whispered into Ronnie's neck. "This is too much."

"Nothing is too much for you, honey," she whispered back. "We'll take the laptop and write it off as a business expense." That made the woman in her arms chuckle. "Seriously, I would love to take you on a tour of Europe, and this is the perfect time of year to go."

"I love you."

"Love you, too. You're not crying on me again, are you?" Ronnie stepped back to see that indeed Rose was weeping with joy. Susan came up alongside them and handed the teary-eyed woman a handkerchief.

"Thank you." Rose took a few seconds to compose herself before turning to face the rest of the guests.

Maria came up to give the young woman a hug. "What a beautiful gift," the housekeeper said.

"It is very nice," Agnes said, shooting her husband a look. "It seems some people would rather spend time with the ones they love instead of running off to some lake in the middle of nowhere for two weeks."

"Umm...." Frank looked at his cousin for support and found none as she was too busy beaming at the happiness on Rose's face. Now that there was no more need for a cane or frequent visits to the physical therapist, it would be a good time for them to take a nice long vacation where Ronnie could show her lover all the beauties of the world. Although she had been to many of the countries already, she knew the memory would pale to the new ones that would be created with Rose by her side. When the jacket was placed back in the box, Ronnie smirked to herself. Not every present had been opened yet.

After the last of their guests left, they retired to the living room. Rose kicked her shoes off and tucked her feet up under her legs. "I can't believe you planned a vacation without me knowing. How did you do that?"

"Easy. My travel agent did the work. All I did was tell her what countries I wanted to visit. One phone call, a couple of emails, and voilà."

"You are amazing." Rose wrapped her arms around Ronnie. "I've only dreamed of going to places like that."

"Well, now your dreams will soon be a reality." Ronnie leaned down for a quick kiss. "I'm glad you like your presents."

"I love them, and I love you," Rose replied. "You didn't have to do this."

"It makes me happy to make you happy. You know that."

"You are wonderful."

"You think so, hmm?" Ronnie's heart began beating faster. "We may not have started out in the best of ways, but I can't imagine my life without you."

"I feel the same way," Rose said.

"I'm glad to hear you say that." Her face became as serious as it had ever been. "I think you missed something in your jacket pockets."

"What? After all this?" The young woman held her hands out to indicate the stack of presents and the airline tickets. She picked the jacket up and laid it on her lap. As her hand fell over the pocket, she felt the hard object hidden within. "Ronnie?" Her fingers traveled over it, her eyes widening. "Is this what I think it is?"

"I don't know," Ronnie replied. "Maybe you should open it up and find out." As the zipper was opened, she added, "I hope you like it."

Rose's hand trembled as she pulled out the small velvet box. Tears were already beginning to well up in her eyes. "Oh, God...." Her hands shook even more, and Ronnie had to steady them with her own.

"Open it, Rose."

The jewelry box opened to reveal a gold band adorned with a triple row of diamonds across the top. "Oh...." Ronnie's equally shaky fingers removed the ring, turning it around for her to see the inscription.

To my Rose, love forever, Ronnie

"Rose, would...." Ronnie's voice cracked, and she had to swallow and start over. "W-would you be mine...forever?" The young woman couldn't find her voice and had to give a shaky nod, tears of happiness streaming down her face. "I love you, Rose." Holding the ring between her fingers, she took the smaller hand in her own. Tears fell from her own eyes as the gold band slid over Rose's ring finger. As it passed over the last knuckle, their fingers intertwined, and both tried to bring the joined hands to their lips. Ronnie used her strength to gently press her lover back down on the cushions while their fingers separated. Rose's hands went to the hem of Ronnie's shirt and slipped beneath.

"I love you, Veronica Cartwright."

"And I love you, Rose Grayson."

Lying on the floor, Tabitha looked up at her mistresses. With a healthy stretch and a yawn, the orange and white feline stood up and headed for the stairs. It looked like she would have the bed to herself for the night.

THE END

About the author

BL Miller was raised in New York but now lives in central Maine with her two cats. A self-described romantic mushball, she spends her free time writing lesbian fiction and painting garden gnomes. Her other works include "Josie and Rebecca The Western Chronicles," with by Vada Foster, as well as "Graceful Waters" and "Crystal's Heart," co-authored with Verda Foster.

Other Titles Available from Intaglio Publications

Code Blue
KatLyn
1-933113-09-X
$18.50

Crystal's Heart
B. L. Miller & Verda Foster
1-933113-24-3
$18.50

Gloria's Inn
Robin Alexander
1-933113-01-4
$17.50

Graceful Waters
B. L. Miller & Verda Foster
1-933113-08-1
$18.50

I Already Know The Silence Of
The Storms
N. M. Hill
1-933113-07-3
$17.50

Incommunicado
N. M. Hill & J. P. Mercer
1-933113-10-3
$17.50

Infinite Pleasures
Stacia Seaman & Nann Dunne
(Editors)
1-933113-00-6
$18.99

Southern Hearts
Katie P Moore
1-933113-28-6
$16.95

Storm Surge
KatLyn
1-933113-06-5
$18.50

These Dreams
Verda Foster
1-933113-12-X
$17.50

The Cost Of Commitment
Lynn Ames
1-933113-02-2
$18.99

The Last Train Home
Blayne Cooper
1-933113-26-X
$17.99

The Price Of Fame
Lynn Ames
1-933113-04-9
$17.99

The War Between The Hearts
Nann Dunne
1-933113-27-8
$17.95

The Gift
Verda Foster
1-933113-03-0
$17.50

The Western Chronicles
B L Miller & Vada Foster
1-933113-38-3
$18.99

Counterfeit World
Judith K. Parker
1-933113-32-4
$17.95

Misplaced People
C G Devize
1-933113-30-8
$17.99

Forthcoming Titles Available from Intaglio Publications

The Chosen
Verda Foster

Assignment Sunrise
I Christie

With Every Breath
Alex L. Alexander

The Illusionist
Fran Heckrotte

Lilith: Book Two in the Illusionist Series
Fran Heckrotte

Bloodlust: Book Three in the Illusionist Series
Fran Heckrotte

Printed in the United States
39968LVS00007B/108